The Dark Monk

ALSO AVAILABLE IN THIS SERIES

The Hangman's Daughter

The Beggar King: A Hangman's Daughter Tale
(forthcoming)

The Warlock: A Hangman's Daughter Tale
(forthcoming)

OLIVER PÖTZSCH

The Dark Monk

A Hangman's Daughter Tale

Translated by
LEE CHADEAYNE

MARINER BOOKS
HOUGHTON MIFFLIN HARCOURT
BOSTON NEW YORK

First Mariner Books edition 2012

The Dark Monk: A Hangman's Daughter Tale was first published in 2009 by Ullstein Buchverlag GmbH as *Die Henkerstochter und der schwarze Mönch*. Translated from German by Lee Chadeayne. First published in English by AmazonCrossing in 2012.

www.hmhbooks.com

Library of Congress Cataloging-in-Publication Data is available.
ISBN 978-0-547-80768-3

Printed in the United States of America
DOC 10 9 8 7 6 5 4 3 2 1

For my grandmother, the matriarch of our family,

and for my mother, who still tells the best stories

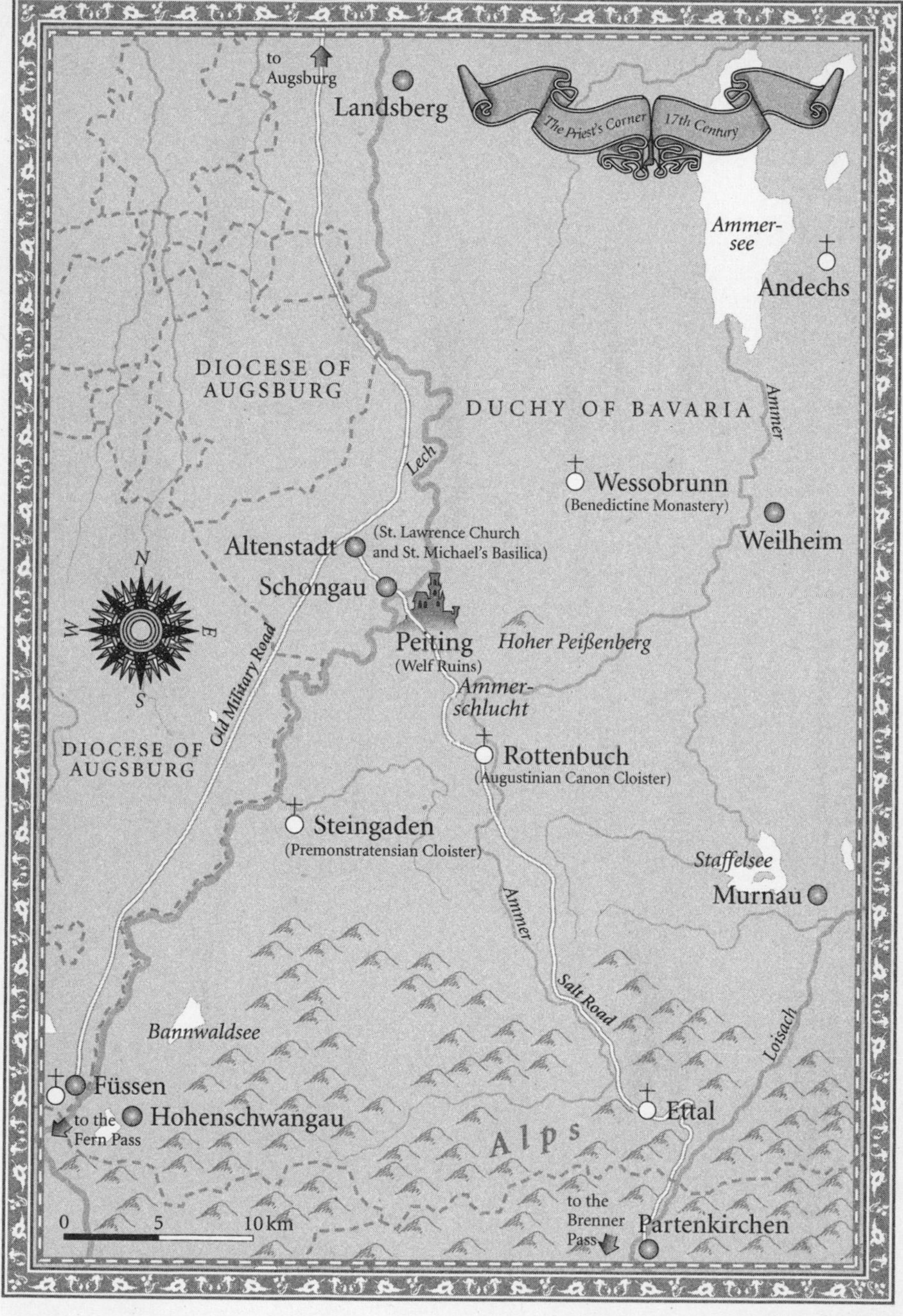

The Priest's Corner
17th Century
to Augsburg
Landsberg
Ammersee
Andechs
DIOCESE OF AUGSBURG
DUCHY OF BAVARIA
Ammer
Lech
Wessobrunn
(Benedictine Monastery)
Weilheim
Altenstadt
(St. Lawrence Church and St. Michael's Basilica)
Schongau
N
E
S
W
Peiting
(Welf Ruins)
Hoher Peißenberg
Old Military Road
Ammerschlucht
DIOCESE OF AUGSBURG
Rottenbuch
(Augustinian Canon Cloister)
Steingaden
(Premonstratensian Cloister)
Staffelsee
Murnau
Ammer
Salt Road
Loisach
Bannwaldsee
Füssen
to the Fern Pass
Hohenschwangau
Ettal
Alps
to the Brenner Pass
Partenkirchen
0
5
10 km

DRAMATIS PERSONAE

PRINCIPAL CHARACTERS

JAKOB KUISL, hangman of Schongau
SIMON FRONWIESER, son of the town doctor
MAGDALENA KUISL, the hangman's daughter
ANNA MARIA KUISL, the hangman's wife
GEORG AND BARBARA, the hangman's twin children

CITIZENS

BONIFAZ FRONWIESER, Schongau town doctor
BENEDIKTA KOPPMEYER, merchant woman from Landsberg am Lech
MARTHA STECHLIN, midwife
MAGDA, housekeeper of the St. Lawrence Church in Altenstadt
ABRAHAM GEDLER, sexton of the St. Lawrence Church in Altenstadt
MARIA SCHREEVOGL, wife of a town alderman
FRANZ STRASSER, innkeeper in Altenstadt
BALTHASAR HEMERLE, carpenter in Altenstadt
HANS BERCHTHOLDT, son of the Schongau master baker
SEBASTIAN SEMER, son of the presiding burgomaster

ALDERMEN

JOHANN LECHNER, court clerk
KARL SEMER, presiding burgomaster and innkeeper of the Goldener Stern Inn
MATTHIAS HOLZHOFER, second presiding burgomaster

JAKOB SCHREEVOGL, stove maker and alderman

MICHAEL BERCHTHOLDT, master baker and alderman

AUGSBURG CITIZENS

PHILIPP HARTMANN, hangman of Augsburg

NEPOMUK BIERMANN, owner of St. Mary's Pharmacy in Augsburg

OSWALD HAINMILLER, merchant from Augsburg

LEONHARD WEYER, merchant from Augsburg

THE CHURCH

ANDREAS KOPPMEYER, priest of the St. Lawrence Church in Altenstadt

ELIAS ZIEGLER, priest of St. Michael's Basilica in Altenstadt

AUGUSTIN BONENMAYR, abbot of the Premonstratensian Monastery in Steingaden

MICHAEL PISCATOR, superintendent of the Augustinian Monastery in Rottenbuch

BERNHARD GERING, abbot of the Wessobrunn Benedictine Monastery

MONKS

BROTHER JAKOBUS

BROTHER AVENARIUS

BROTHER NATHANAEL

"We delight in marvelous things. One proof of that is that everyone embellishes somewhat when telling a story in the assumption he is pleasing his listener."

—ARISTOTLE, *Poetics*, XXIV

PROLOGUE

ALTENSTADT NEAR SCHONGAU
ON THE NIGHT OF JANUARY 18, 1660, AD

WHEN THE PARISH PRIEST ANDREAS KOPPMEYER pressed the last stone into place and sealed the opening with lime and mortar, he had just four hours to live.

With the back of his large hand, he wiped the sweat from his brow and leaned back against the cool, damp wall behind him. Then he looked nervously up the narrow, winding staircase. Was something moving up there? Again, he heard the floorboards creaking as if someone were moving stealthily across the floor above him in the church. But it could have just been his imagination. Wood warps, and the St. Lawrence Church was old and crumbling. It was not for nothing that workmen had been there for the last few weeks repairing the building so that it wouldn't someday come crashing down during mass.

A January storm was whistling around the weathered walls and shaking the wooden shutters. But it wasn't just due to the cold down here in the crypt that the priest was trembling. Pulling his worn cassock tightly around him, he scrutinized the bricked-up wall once more and then started the climb back up the stairway to the church. His steps echoed on the worn, frost-covered stairs. Suddenly, the howling of the storm got louder so that he could no longer hear the soft creaking in the balcony above him. He must have been mistaken. Who would still be here in the church at this hour, for heaven's sake? It was way past midnight. His housekeeper Magda had gone to bed hours ago in the little rectory next door and the old sexton would not return until it was time to ring the bells at six in the morning.

Pastor Andreas Koppmeyer climbed the final steps out of the crypt. His broad figure completely filled the opening in the church floor. He was more than six feet tall, a bear of a man who, with his long, broad beard and bushy black eyebrows, looked like the personification of an Old Testament God. When Koppmeyer stood before the altar in his black robe and delivered his homilies in a deep, gruff voice, his appearance alone caused his flock to tremble and instilled in them the fear of purgatory.

With both hands, the pastor gripped the slab covering the crypt. It weighed several hundred pounds, and he panted as he pushed it back over the opening. It made a crunching sound as he set it down, but it covered the crypt perfectly, as if it had never been opened. Koppmeyer examined his work with satisfaction and then made his way back through the storm.

As he started to open the church door, he noticed that snow was already gathering in high drifts in front of the portal. With a groan, he pressed his shoulder against the heavy oaken door until it opened a crack and he was just able to squeeze through. Snowflakes lashed his face like little thorns and he had to close his eyes as he trudged back to the rectory.

It was only about thirty paces back to the little house, but it seemed like an eternity to the pastor. The wind tugged hard at his cassock and it fluttered around him like a tattered flag. The snow was almost up to his hips and even Koppmeyer, with his massive body, had to struggle to move forward. As he fought his way step by step through the storm and the darkness, he kept thinking of the events of the last two weeks. Pastor Koppmeyer was a simple man of God, but even he had noticed that his discovery was something extraordinary, something a little too sensitive for him to deal with and that would best be left to others. He did the right thing in hiding it behind the wall and letting more powerful, knowledgeable people decide whether it should ever be opened again. Perhaps he should not have written the letter to Benedikta, but he had always trusted his younger sister. She was amazingly bright and well read for a woman and he had often asked her for advice. Surely she would know what to do this time as well.

Andreas Koppmeyer was suddenly wakened from his reveries. Out of the corner of his eye, he thought he saw something moving to the right, behind the woodpile near the house. He squinted and held his hand over his eyes to protect them from the snowflakes, but he couldn't make out anything. It was too dark and the falling snow made it even harder. Shrugging, he turned aside. Probably just a fox trying to sneak up on the chicken coop, he thought. Or a bird looking for a place to hide from the storm.

Finally, Koppmeyer reached the door to the rectory. Here, on the south side, the drifts weren't as high. He opened the door, squeezed his massive frame into the hallway, and bolted the door. At once he was enveloped in silence. The storm seemed far, far away. On the open hearth in the main room, a small fire was still burning, spreading warmth and comfort, and behind it a stairway led up to the housekeeper's room. The priest turned to the right and walked through the main room on his way to his private quarters.

On opening the door he was met by a sweet, rich fragrance. His mouth watered when he saw where it was coming from. On the table in the middle of his room was a clay bowl filled to the top with delicious doughnuts. Koppmeyer moved closer and touched them gently. They were still warm.

The priest grinned. His dear housekeeper Magda had once again thought of everything. He had told her he would be in the church longer today to lend a hand with the renovations. He had taken a loaf of bread and a jug of wine along with him just in case, but the housekeeper knew that a man like Koppmeyer needed more to live on than that, so she had made the pastries for him and they were here now waiting for someone to come and redeem them!

Andreas Koppmeyer lit a candle from the fire on the hearth and sat down at the table. He was delighted to see that the doughnuts were heavily coated with honey. He pulled the bowl over to him with both his huge hands, took one that was still warm, and bit into it, smacking his lips with pleasure.

They were delicious.

Chewing silently, the priest felt the warmth flowing back into his body. Soon he was done and reached for the next doughnut. He picked apart the softest one and pushed the steaming pieces into his mouth faster and faster. For a moment he thought he noticed an unpleasant taste, but it was at once covered by the sweet taste of the honey.

After the sixth one, Koppmeyer finally had to give up. He peered down into the bowl one last time and saw just two doughnuts at the bottom. Sighing deeply, he rubbed his stomach, then more than satisfied, headed for the adjacent room, where he at once fell into a deep sleep.

The pains, accompanied by a slightly nauseous feeling, announced themselves just before the first cock crow. Silently, Koppmeyer cursed his indulgence and sent a brief prayer to heaven, knowing that gluttony was one of the seven deadly sins. Most likely Magda had intended the contents of the bowl to last a few days, but the doughnuts had simply been too delicious! Now God was punishing him right away with nausea and bodily aches and pains. Why did he have to start stuffing himself in the middle of the night? It served him right!

As he was getting out of bed to relieve himself in the chamber pot that was placed at the ready for such occasions, the stomach pains intensified. Flashes of such pain coursed through his body that Father Koppmeyer had to grab the edge of the bed, moaning. He sat up and hobbled into the main room, where a pitcher of water stood on a little table. He sat down and drank the cool liquid in one long gulp in the hope of relieving the pain.

On the way back to his room, a stabbing pain worse than anything he had ever experienced shot from his throat down to his stomach. Koppmeyer tried to shout, but the cry stuck in his throat. His tongue was like a stopper made of flesh plugging his airway. He sank to his knees while tongues of fire crept up his throat. He vomited mushy clumps, but the pain did not subside. On the contrary, it worsened until all Koppmeyer could do was to crawl around on all fours like a whipped dog. His legs suddenly gave out altogether. He tried to shout for the housekeeper, but the fire had long since consumed his throat.

Slowly the priest began to realize that these were no normal stomach pains and it wasn't just that Magda had simply let the milk go bad. He could tell he was going to die. He lay there in abject misery.

After some minutes of fear and despair, the priest reached a decision. With his last bit of strength, he leaned against the front door and pushed it open. Once again, the storm lashed his face, a wall of cold and icy thorns. The howling of the wind seemed to be mocking him.

Following the tracks he had made some hours before that were still partially visible, he crept back to the church on all fours. Again and again, he had to stop and lie down when the pain got the better of him. Snow and ice crept under his cassock, his hands froze into shapeless clumps, and he lost all sense of time. One thing was uppermost in this mind: He had to reach the church!

Finally, his head bumped against a wall, and after a few seconds he realized he had reached the portal of the St. Lawrence Church. With his last bit of strength, he forced the frozen stumps that had once been his hands into the crack in the door and pulled it open. Once inside, he was no longer even able to crawl on all fours. His legs kept collapsing under the weight of his heavy body, and it was only by crawling on his belly that he could manage the final short distance. He could feel how his inner organs were failing, little by little.

When the priest reached the slab over the crypt, he passed his hands briefly over the relief of the woman below him. He caressed the weathered figure like a lover and finally laid his cheek on her face. Paralysis was climbing up his body from his legs, but before it reached his hands, the priest scratched a circle with the jagged nail of his right index finger into the layer of frost atop the gravestone. Then the tension receded from the powerful body and he collapsed. Once more he tried to raise his head, but something was gripping him tightly.

The last thing Andreas Koppmeyer felt was how his beard, his right ear, and the skin on his face slowly froze to the gravestone. Cold and silence enveloped him.

The Dark Monk

I

SIMON FRONWIESER TRUDGED DOWN ALTENSTADT Street through the snow, cursing his vocation. In weather like this, farmers, servants, carpenters, even whores and beggars stayed out of the goddamned cold and inside where it was warm. Only he, the Schongau medicus, was required to visit the sick!

In spite of the heavy woolen coat he was wearing over his jacket and fur-lined leather gloves, he was miserably cold. Clumps of snow and ice had made their way under his collar and into his boots, melting there into a cold slush. When he looked down, he noticed a new hole at the tip of his left boot with his big, red, frozen toe peering out. Simon clenched his teeth. Why did his boots have to fail him now, of all times, in the dead of winter? He had already spent his savings on a pair of new petticoat breeches. But that was a necessity. He would rather a toe freeze off than do without the pleasure of the newest French fashion. It was important to observe the latest fashion, especially in a sleepy little Bavarian town like Schongau.

Simon turned his attention once more to the road. It had been snowing until just a few moments ago, and now, in the late-morning hours, a biting cold hung over the fallow fields and forests around town. The crust of snow on the narrow path through the middle of the road collapsed under his feet with every step. Icicles hung down from the branches, and trees groaned under the weight of the snow. Here and there the branches broke with loud cracking sounds and released their loads of snow. Simon's perfectly shaven Vandyke beard and black shoulder-length hair had by now frozen solid. He reached up and felt his eyebrows. Even they were caked with ice. Once again, he cursed loudly. It was the coldest damn day of the year and here he was having to trudge to Altenstadt on behalf of his father! And all that just because of a sick priest!

Simon could well imagine what was ailing the fat priest. He had gorged himself again, as he did so often. And now he lay in bed with a bellyache, asking for linden blossom tea—as if his housekeeper Magda couldn't make that for him! Probably old Koppmeyer had been out and about stuffing himself somewhere or had gotten involved with one of the whores in town, and now Magda had gone into a huff and Simon had to pay for it.

Abraham Gedler, the sexton of St. Lawrence's in Altenstadt, had shown up at the Fronwieser house early in the morning and pounded on the door. He had been strangely pale and uncommunicative and said only that the priest was sick and the doctor should come as fast as possible. Then, without another word, he had run through the snow back to Altenstadt.

Simon had been lying in bed, as usual at this hour, his head still aching from the Tokay he drank the previous night at the Goldener Stern Inn, but his father had yanked him out of bed, swearing vilely, and sent him on his way with nothing to eat.

Again Simon broke through the crust up to his hips and had to fight his way out of the drift. Despite the dry cold, sweat was pouring down his face. He grimaced as he pulled his right leg out of the snow, almost losing his boot in the process. If he didn't watch out, he'd soon have to doctor himself! He shook his head. It was crazy to tramp all the way to Altenstadt in this weather, but what could he do? His father, the city doctor Bonifaz Fronwieser, was busy caring for a fabulously wealthy alderman suffering from gout; the barber surgeon was bedridden with typhoid fever, and old Fronwieser would rather bite off his own finger than send the hangman to Altenstadt. So he sent his wayward son . . .

The scrawny sexton was waiting for Simon at the door to the little church located a little way out of town on a hill. Gedler's face was as white as the snow around him. He had rings under his eyes and was trembling all over. For a moment, Simon wondered if Gedler, and not the priest, needed treatment. The sexton looked as if he hadn't slept for several nights.

"Well, Gedler," Simon said cheerfully. "What's troubling the priest? Does he have intestinal obstruction? Constipation? An enema will do wonders for him. You should try one, too."

He was heading for the rectory, but the sexton held him back, pointing silently toward the church.

"He's in there?" Simon asked with surprise. "In this weather? He should be happy if he doesn't catch his death of cold."

He was heading into the church when he heard Gedler behind him, clearing his throat. Just in front of the entrance, Simon turned around.

"Yes, what is it, Gedler?"

"The priest . . . he's . . ."

The sexton lost his voice and looked down to the floor without saying a word.

Seized by a sudden presentiment, Simon opened the heavy door. He was met by an icy wind a few degrees colder than the air outside. Somewhere a window slammed shut.

The medicus looked around. Scaffolding towered above them along the interior walls on both sides, all the way up to the rotting balcony. A timber framework higher up under the ceiling suggested that a new wooden ceiling would be installed there soon. The window openings in the back of the church were chiseled out so that a steady, ice-cold draft swept through the nave. Simon felt his breath on his face like a fine mist.

The priest was in the rear third of the nave, only a few steps from the apse. He looked like a statue hewn from the ice, a fallen white giant struck down by the wrath of God. His entire body was covered in a thin layer of ice. Simon approached carefully and touched the white, glittering cassock. It was as hard as a board. Ice crystals had even formed over the eyes, which had been wide open in the throes of death, giving an ethereal look to the priest's face.

Simon wheeled around in horror. The sexton stood at the portal with a guilty look, turning his hat over in his hands.

"But . . . He's dead!" the medicus cried. "Why didn't you tell me that when you called for me?"

"We . . . we didn't want to make a big fuss, Your Honor," Gedler murmured. "We thought if we said anything in town, everybody in town would know about it at once, and there would be gossiping, and then maybe trouble with the remodeling here in the church."

"We?" Simon asked, confused.

At that very moment, Magda, the housekeeper in the rectory, appeared at the sexton's side, sobbing uncontrollably. She was the polar opposite of Abraham Gedler, round as a barrel, with fat, bloated legs. She blew her nose into a white lace handkerchief so large that Simon could see only part of her puffy, tear-stained face.

"What a shame," she lamented, "that any man must go that way, let alone the pastor. But I always told him not to gorge himself like that!"

The sexton nodded and kept kneading his hat. "He overdid

it with the doughnuts," he mumbled. "He left only two. And it finally caught up with him here while he was praying."

"The doughnuts . . ." Simon frowned. His fears had been confirmed—at least in part, except that the pastor was not sick, but dead.

"But why is he lying here and not in his bed?" he asked, more to himself than to the two of them standing there.

"As I said, he probably wanted to pray before he met his maker," Gedler mumbled.

"In this weather?" Simon shook his head skeptically. "Can I have a look around the rectory?"

The sexton shrugged and turned around to leave for the neighboring building with the maid, who was still sobbing. Magda had left the door open, so the snow had drifted into the main room and crunched under Simon's feet. On a table by the hearth stood a bowl with two greasy, glistening doughnuts. They looked delicious—brown, about the size of a palm, and coated with a thick layer of honey. Despite the recent encounter with the deceased, which was not exactly appetizing, Simon's mouth watered. He remembered that he had not yet had breakfast. For a moment he was tempted to try one, then thought better of it. This was a death vigil, not a funeral reception.

Standing at the pastor's bedside, the Schongau medicus retraced in his mind the pastor's last steps.

"He must have gotten up and gone over into the kitchen to get a drink of water. This is where he collapsed," he said, pointing to fragments of the mug and the sticky traces of vomit. The small room reeked of gastric acid and curdled milk.

"But why then, in God's name, did he go out to the church?" he mumbled. Suddenly, he had a hunch and turned to the sexton.

"What was the pastor doing last night?"

"He . . . he was in the church. Till late at night," Gedler added.

The housekeeper nodded. "He even took along a jug of wine and a loaf of bread. He thought he would be there a while. When I went to bed, he was still over there. I woke up again shortly before midnight, and I saw a light burning over there."

Simon interrupted: "Just before midnight? What is a pastor doing at that time of night in an ice-cold church?"

"He . . . he thought he had to have another look at the renovation of the choir vault," the sexton said. "It seemed in the last two weeks that the pastor was acting a bit strange. He was always over in the church, even in this cold!"

"The good man never left things for others to do," Magda interrupted. "A bear of a man. He knew his way around with a hammer and chisel like no one else."

Simon thought about that a while. The previous night had been the coldest in a long time. It was not for nothing that the workmen had stopped their work on the church now, in January. If anyone took up a hammer and chisel on such a night, there had to be a damned good reason to do so.

Without wasting any more time on the housekeeper or the sexton, Simon hurried back to the church. The pastor was still lying there on the ground, just as he had been when they had left. Only now did Simon notice that the corpse lay directly over a tombstone with a relief of a woman who looked like the Virgin Mary. The words of an inscription circled her head like a halo.

Sic transit gloria mundi.

"*Thus passes the glory of the world . . .*" Simon mumbled. "So true." He had often seen this inscription on gravestones. As far back as early Rome, it was the custom for a slave to whisper these words to a victorious general on his triumphal march through the city. Nothing of this world lasts forever . . .

It almost seemed as if the pastor, in a final gesture, had been pointing to the inscription with his right hand. Simon sighed. Had Andreas Koppmeyer really fallen victim here to the desires of the flesh? Or was the gesture a final admonition to those still living?

A sound made him jump. It was Magda, who approached him from behind. She stared wide-eyed at the frozen corpse, then looked at Simon. It seemed she wanted to say something, but she couldn't get the words out.

"What is it?" Simon asked impatiently.

"The . . . the two remaining doughnuts . . ." she started to say.

"What about them?"

"They are coated with honey."

Simon shrugged, then stood up and wiped the snow from his hands. There was nothing more for him to do here, and he was about to go.

"Well? They also put honey on them at the Stern—delicious, by the way. Is that where you got the recipe?"

"But . . . I didn't put any honey on them."

Simon felt for a moment as if the ground were slipping beneath his feet. Perhaps he had not heard her correctly. "You . . . you didn't put honey on them?"

The housekeeper shook her head. "Our honey pot was empty. I meant to buy more at the market next week, but this time I had to make the doughnuts without honey. Heaven knows who spread it on them, but it wasn't me."

Simon glanced at the frozen pastor and then looked carefully around the church. A cold draft passed through his hair, and he suddenly felt as if he were being observed. He left the church, Magda in tow, while the wind tugged at his coat as if trying to hold him back.

Once outside, he took the housekeeper by the shoulders and looked her straight in the eye. She was as white as a sheet.

"Listen to me! Send Gedler back to Schongau again," he said softly. "Tell him to get the hangman."

"The hangman?" Magda shrieked. Her face turned a shade whiter. "But why?"

"Believe me," Simon whispered. "If anyone can help us here, it's him. Now just stop asking questions and go—go!"

He gave the housekeeper a slap on her fat behind, then pushed the heavy doors, which closed with a loud squeal. The medicus quickly turned the bronze key in the lock and slipped it into his pocket. Only now did he feel a little more secure.

The devil was there in the church, and only the hangman could drive him away again.

A short time later, Simon was sitting in the drafty main room of the rectory chewing on an old crust of bread and sullenly slurping on some linden blossom tea that Magda had made for him. Actually, it was steeped from the dried blossoms that the medicus had brought for the pastor, who wouldn't need them now. The odor of the greenish-brown concoction reminded him of sickness and hangovers.

Simon sighed as he sipped on the hot brew. He was alone. The sexton was on his way to Schongau to get the hangman, and Magda had run to the village to spread the dreadful news. She could have kept it to herself if the priest had simply eaten himself to death, but not if he had been poisoned. Tongues were no doubt already wagging among the common folk in town about satanic rituals and who might have prepared the poison. The medicus shook his head. How he wished he had a cup of strong coffee now instead of this miserable tea, but the hard brown beans were carefully stored in a trunk at home, inside a leather pouch. Not many remained from his last shopping trip at the market in Augsburg, and he would have to be sparing with them because coffee was an expensive, exotic product. Only rarely did merchants bring it with them from their travels to Constantinople or even farther afield. Simon loved the bitter aroma that made it possible for him to think clearly. With coffee he could solve the toughest of problems and now, more than ever, he needed some.

Simon's musings were suddenly interrupted by a sound outside the window—a soft clicking or squeaking as if a rusty gate were slowly being opened. Carefully, he made his way to the door, opened it a crack, and looked outside. There was nothing there. He was about to step back inside when he looked down again and was shocked to see fresh tracks leading right to the front portal of the church.

The wide wooden door was open a crack.

Simon cursed. He reached into his coat pocket and could feel the cold steel of the church key. How in the world . . . ?

Nervously, the medicus searched the room for a suitable weapon. His gaze wandered from the hearth to a large cleaver. He reached for it; it felt cold and heavy. Then he went outside.

The tracks, clearly those of a large man, led from the walkway directly into the church. Simon made his way quietly through the snow, holding the knife like a sword in front of him until he reached the portal. From outside, nothing was visible inside the darkened church. Summoning all his courage, he stepped inside.

Farther back, the dead pastor was still lying on the floor. A bleeding Jesus on the cross stared wide-eyed and reproachfully at Simon from behind the apse, and along the sides wooden figurines of martyrs were standing in the niches, writhing in the throes of death, their bodies tortured, slain, and riddled with holes, like St. Sebastian on Simon's left, pierced by six arrows from a crossbow.

The scaffolding, which towered up into the gallery, glittered with hoarfrost. As Simon stepped inside, he heard a loud spitting sound. His knife in hand, the medicus turned around, frantically seeking the source of the sound and scrutinizing the shadows the martyrs cast on the walls.

"Put the knife down before you hurt yourself, you quack!" someone growled. "And stop prowling like a thief through the church. You wouldn't be the first one I've strung up for robbing the offertory box."

The voice seemed to be coming from high up in the balcony, and when Simon looked up, he saw a huge cloaked figure standing behind the rotting balustrade. The collar of his coat was turned up and a wide-brimmed hat hung down over his face so all that was visible was the end of a huge hooked nose. Little clouds of smoke rose from his long-stemmed clay pipe, and between his hat and disheveled black beard, two lively eyes flashed, mocking Simon.

"My God, Kuisl!" Simon cried with relief. "You scared the daylights out of me!"

"The next time you go sneaking through a place, remember to look up," the hangman scolded as he swung down the scaffolding. "Or the next time, your killer will lay you flat and that will be the end of the learned medicus."

Having reached the ground, Jakob Kuisl brushed mortar dust from his threadbare coat and snorted contemptuously, pointing the stem of his pipe at the pastor's corpse.

"A fat priest who ate himself to death . . . And that's the only reason you called me? As a hangman and butcher of worn-out horses, I'm responsible for dead critters, but dead priests don't concern me."

"I believe he's been poisoned," Simon said softly.

The hangman whistled through his teeth. "Poisoned? And now you think I can tell you what kind of poison it was?"

Simon nodded. The Schongau executioner was widely viewed as a master of his craft, not only with the sword, but also in the field of healing herbs and poisonous plants. When they fell ill, many simple folk preferred the hangman over the medicus for a concoction of ergot and rue for unwanted pregnancies, a few pills for constipation, or a sleeping potion made from poppies and valerian. It was cheaper and they didn't leave any sicker than when they'd arrived. Simon had often asked the hangman for advice about medicines and mysterious sicknesses, much to his father's chagrin.

"Couldn't you take a little closer look at him?" Simon asked, pointing at the stiff, frozen body of the priest. "Perhaps we'll find a clue to who the murderer is."

Jakob Kuisl shrugged. "I don't know what we'd learn from that, but I might as well, since I'm here. He took a deep draw on his pipe and eyed the corpse lying on the floor. Then he bent down and examined the body. "No blood, no sign of strangulation or a struggle," he mumbled, passing his hand over Koppmeyer's clothing, which was spattered with frozen bits of vomit. "Why do you think he was poisoned?"

Simon cleared his throat. "The doughnuts . . ." he started.

"The doughnuts?" The hangman raised his bushy eyebrows quizzically.

Simon shrugged and told Jakob Kuisl briefly what he had learned from the sexton and the housekeeper. "It would be best for you to come back to the rectory with me," he said finally, heading for the door. "Perhaps I've overlooked something."

As they exited the church, Simon cast a questioning sidelong glance at Jakob Kuisl. "How did you get into the church, by the way? I mean . . . I have the key here . . ."

The hangman grinned and held out a bent nail. "These church doors are like curtains. It's no wonder so many offertories are broken into around here. The priests might just as well leave the doors to their churches wide open."

When they arrived back in the rectory, Simon led the hangman into the main room and pointed to the two glazed doughnuts and the vomit on the floor.

"There must have been around a half-dozen of these doughnuts," the medicus said, "all coated with honey, though the housekeeper denies putting any on them."

Jakob Kuisl gingerly took a doughnut in his huge hands and smelled it, closing his eyes while his powerful nostrils flared up like those of a horse. It looked almost as if he wanted to inhale the doughnut. Finally he put it down, kneeled, and sniffed the pool of vomit. Simon felt himself gradually becoming nauseous. There was an odor of smoke, bitter stomach acid, and decay in the room — and something else that the medicus could not place.

"What . . . what are you doing there?" Simon asked.

The hangman stood up.

"I can always rely on this," he said, tapping his red-veined hooked nose. "I can detect any little illness, no matter how small, just by smelling a filthy chamber pot. And this filth here smells of death. Just as the doughnuts do."

He took a piece of dough in his hand and started to pull it apart. "The poison is in the honey," he mumbled after a while. "It smells like . . ." He lifted the piece to his nose again and grinned. "Mouse piss. Just as I thought."

"Mouse piss?" Simon asked with annoyance.

Jakob Kuisl nodded. "Hemlock smells like that, one of the most poisonous plants here in the Priests' Corner. The numbness creeps up your body from your feet right to your heart. You watch yourself die."

Simon shook his head in horror. "What monster would have thought up something like that? Do you think it could have been someone from the village? I could see a jealous worker in the church clubbing Koppmeyer from behind . . . But something like this?"

The hangman puffed on his cold pipe, lost in thought. Then he abruptly left the warm living room and headed for the door.

"Where are you going?" Simon called after him.

"I want to have a closer look at the dead priest," Jakob Kuisl grumbled from outside the house. "Something isn't right here."

Simon couldn't help smiling. The hangman had smelled

blood. Once he was onto something he was as precise as a Swiss watch.

Back at the church, Jakob Kuisl bent over the corpse and examined it closely. He walked around the body without touching it, as if he were studying its exact position. Just as it had early this morning, Andreas Koppmeyer's corpse lay on the slab of stone depicting the faded countenance of the mother of God surrounded by a halo. The priest's hair was white with ice crystals and he lay curled up on one side so that only his profile was visible. In the meantime, the skin on his face had taken on the color of a frozen carp. His left arm was crooked along his body and his right hand seemed to be pointing to the inscription over the Madonna.

"*Sic transit gloria mundi,*" the hangman mumbled. "*Thus passes the glory of the world . . .*"

"He even circled the words. See for yourself!" Simon said, pointing to a squiggle around the inscription. The line was shaky, as if Koppmeyer had drawn it in the ice with the last ounce of his strength.

"It was clear to him that his end was near," the medicus mused. "Old Koppmeyer always had a sense of humor; you've got to hand it to him."

The hangman bent down and passed his hand over the stone relief of Mary, whose head was surrounded by a radiant halo.

"One thing surprises me," he mumbled. "This is a gravestone, isn't it?"

Simon nodded. "The whole Saint Lawrence Church is full of them. Why do you ask?"

"Look around for yourself, you idiot." The hangman gestured broadly at the interior of the church. "On the other stones you always see images of the deceased—councilmen, judges, rich broads. But this one is no doubt the Virgin Mary. No woman would be so bold as to let herself be depicted with a halo."

"Perhaps it was a donation to the church?" Simon thought out loud.

"*Sic transit*—" the hangman mumbled again.

"*Thus passes the glory of the world,*" Simon interrupted him impatiently. "I know, but what does that have to do with the murder?"

"It's possible that it has nothing to do with the murder, but with the hiding place," Kuisl said suddenly.

"Hiding place?"

"Didn't you tell me the priest spent all last night working in the church?"

"Yes, but . . ."

"Look a little closer at the squiggle," the hangman mumbled. "Do you notice anything striking?"

Simon bent down and examined the circle a little more closely. Then it hit him.

"The circle isn't complete; it doesn't go around the entire inscription," he gasped, "but only around the first two words . . ."

"*Sic transit,*" Jakob repeated, grinning. "The learned doctor surely knows what that means."

"*This is the way* . . ." Simon murmured absentmindedly. Only then did he get it. "Through . . . the slab of stone?" he whispered incredulously.

"First we have to move it aside, of course." The hangman was already struggling to move Andreas Koppmeyer's huge frame aside. He grabbed him by the cassock and dragged him behind the altar, several yards away. "This will be his resting place for the time being," he said. "No point scaring any old woman to death who comes in to say her rosary." He spat into his hands. "Now let's get to work."

"But the slab . . . It weighs at least a couple of hundred pounds," Simon interjected.

"So what?" Jakob Kuisl had already wrestled the stone from its setting using a carpenter's nail as a lever. Now he grabbed it with both hands and raised it slowly, inch by inch. Tendons as thick as a man's fingers protruded from his neck.

"If a fat priest can lift it, it shouldn't be so heavy, should it?" he panted.

With a grinding sound, the massive stone slab crashed down right next to Simon's feet.

Magdalena Kuisl knelt in the bloody straw and pressed down on the swollen, bruised abdomen of Frau Hainmiller. The peasant woman screamed in her ear, making her wince. The expectant mother had been screaming for hours now, but it seemed like days to Magdalena. The night before, the hangman's daughter had come to the Hainmiller household along with the midwife, Martha Stechlin. At first everything seemed to point to a normal birth. The aunts, nieces, cousins, and neighbor women had already spread fresh straw and rushes, put water on the fire, and spread out linens. The air was redolent of smoked mugwort. Josefa Hainmiller, whose head was as red as beetroot, pushed calmly and regularly. It was the farm woman's sixth child, and up to then, she had always managed without difficulty.

But now Josefa was losing more and more blood. The bedsheets, pink-hued at first from the broken water, had now taken on the color of a butcher block. But the child simply wouldn't come. Josefa Hainmiller's initial whimpers gave way first to sobbing and then to loud screams so that her husband, horrified, kept knocking on the door and praying aloud to St. Margareta. He didn't dare enter—this was a woman's realm—but if his wife or the child didn't survive the birth, he already knew who was to blame: the goddamned midwife.

Martha Stechlin groped inside the mother for the child, who was lying crosswise in the uterus. Her arms reached up to her elbows inside the Hainmiller woman, whose dress had slipped up over her thighs, but still the midwife could not get a firm hold on the child. The face of the older midwife was spattered with blood, sweat streamed down her forehead, and she had to keep blinking as it dripped into her eyes.

Magdalena looked anxiously at the aunts and cousins. They whispered among themselves, murmured their rosaries, and kept pointing at the midwife. Just last year, Martha Stechlin had been accused of murdering a child and practicing witchcraft. Only quick action by Magdalena's father and the young medicus had saved her from the fire. Nevertheless, the midwife was viewed in town with suspicion, and it clung to her like a baby's first stool. People still called upon her when there was a birth or asked her for herbs to reduce a fever, but behind her back the good citizens crossed themselves to ward off her black magic.

Just as they do with me, Magdalena was thinking as she wiped strands of matted black hair out of her face. Her eyes, usually so cheerful, looked tired and strained, and sweat gathered in her thick, bushy eyebrows. She sighed as she continued to push down rhythmically on the mother's body.

Magdalena was grateful when Frau Stechlin had asked her about half a year ago if she would like to be her apprentice. As the daughter of a hangman, she didn't have many choices. The job of hangman was a dishonorable line of work, and people avoided her and her family. If she wanted a husband, her only real choice would be another hangman, and because that didn't interest her, she had to support herself. At twenty-one, she could no longer be a burden on her parents.

The vocation of midwife was just the right thing for her. After all, she had learned everything worth knowing about herbs from her father. She knew that mugwort was good for internal bleeding and parsley would ensure that unwanted children didn't come into the world. She knew how to prepare an ointment of goose fat, melissa, and mutton bones, and she knew how to prepare hemp seeds with a mortar and pestle to help a young girl get pregnant. But now, seeing all the blood, the whispering aunts and the screaming mother, she was suddenly no longer sure she really wanted to be a midwife. As she continued pressing and squeezing, her mind wandered. In another world, she could see herself standing at the altar with Simon, a wreath of flowers in her hair and an "I do" on her lips. They would have children, and he would make a modest income as the respected town medicus. They could—

"Stop dreaming, girl! We need fresh water!" Martha Stechlin's blood-spattered face turned toward Magdalena. She tried to speak in a calm voice, but her eyes said something else. Magdalena thought she could detect a few new wrinkles in the wizened face of the forty-year-old woman. In just the last year, her hair had turned almost completely gray.

"And moss to stop the bleeding!" the woman called after her. "She has already lost too much."

Magdalena, jolted from her reveries, nodded. As she went out into the hall, she glanced back into the overheated, dark room. The shutters were locked and the cracks filled with straw and clay. Out in the main room, women from the neighborhood were sitting on benches around the hearth and at the table, anxiously and skeptically watching the struggling midwife and her young helper.

"Ave Maria, the Lord be with you . . ." Some of the old women started saying the rosary aloud. Evidently, they assumed that Josefa Hainmiller would soon be with the good Lord.

Magdalena hurried down the hall, took a handful of moss from the midwife's bag, and filled a bowl of water from a copper basin on the hearth. When she returned to the main room, she slipped on the blood-soaked straw and fell flat on the floor. Water spattered the old women's skirts.

"Good heavens, can't you watch out?" One of the neighbor women looked at her angrily. "What is a young girl like you doing here, anyway? Damned hangman's girl."

A second neighbor woman chimed in. "It's true what they say. A hangman in the house brings misfortune."

"She is my apprentice," Martha Stechlin panted as she continued to grope around inside the screaming Frau Hainmiller. "Now leave her alone and bring me some fresh linen."

Magdalena clenched her teeth and got fresh water from outside. Tears of anger streamed down her face. When she returned, the women still hadn't calmed down. Disregarding the cries of pain, they started whispering and pointing at her again.

"What's the point of all this washing?" one of the older women asked. Her face was black with soot, and she had only three yellow teeth still left in her mouth. "Water has never helped during a difficult birth! You need Saint John's wort and wild marjoram to chase out the devil, and perhaps holy water, but in any case, not simple well water—ridiculous!"

For Magdalena, that was the last straw. "You foolish women," she shouted, slamming the bowl down on the table. "What do you know about healing? Dirt and foolish chatter—that's what makes people sick!" She felt as if she were going to suffocate. For much too long she had been breathing the sharp odor of mugwort, garlic, and smoke. Rushing to the window, she tore open the shutters. Light flooded the room as the smoke drifted out.

The neighbors and family members gasped. It was considered a tried-and-true rule that the windows shouldn't be opened when a woman was in labor. Fresh air and cold meant sure death to every newborn. For a while all that could be heard was the screaming of Frau Hainmiller, but it resounded now out into the street.

"I think it would be best for you to go now," Martha Stechlin whispered, looking around carefully. "In any case, you can't be of much help here anymore."

"But—" Magdalena started to say.

"Go," the midwife said, interrupting her. "It's best for all of us."

Under the withering gazes of the women, Magdalena

stomped out the door. As she closed it behind her, she heard whispering and the sound of shutters slamming. She gulped and struggled to hold back her tears. Why was she always so stubborn! This trait, which she'd inherited from her father, had often caused trouble for her. It was possible that this visit to the Hainmillers would be her last one as a midwife. Her behavior would soon enough be the talk of the town, and it would be best for her not to show her face around Frau Stechlin for a while, either.

She sighed. Wearily, she picked up her leather bag containing scissors, old linen rags, and a few ointments, threw it over her shoulder, and headed back to Schongau. Maybe she would at least see Simon today. When she thought of the young medicus, a warm longing and a pleasant tingling rose inside her and her anger subsided. It had been much too long since they had spent a few hours together. It was on Epiphany, when carolers wandered from house to house and young men frightened little children with wild-animal masks. Lost in the masked crowd, the couple had walked hand-in-hand, disappearing into one of the warehouses down by the Lech River.

The clatter of hoofbeats interrupted Magdalena's daydreams. A man on horseback was coming down the broad tree-lined road, which was blanketed knee-deep in snow. The hangman's daughter squinted to get a better look and only then realized it wasn't a man at all on the imposing stallion, but a woman. She appeared to be a stranger here; she looked all around as if she were searching for something.

Magdalena decided to stand by the side of the road and wait for the stranger. When the rider had approached to within a few yards, the hangman's daughter could see that the woman had to come from a wealthy family. She was wearing a finely woven, dark-blue cape and underneath it a starched white skirt with polished leather boots. She was holding the reins loosely in her fur gloves. But the most striking thing about her was the shock of reddish-blonde hair that protruded from under a velvet hood, framing a pale, finely chiseled, aristocratic face. The rider was perhaps in her mid-thirties, statuesque, and certainly not from around here. She looked like someone from a big city far away—perhaps from Munich—but how in the world did she ever wind up in here in Altenstadt?

"Can I assist you?" Magdalena inquired with a warm smile.

The stranger seemed to think this over, then smiled in return. "You can, girl. I'm looking for my brother, a pastor in this community. Andreas Koppmeyer by name."

She leaned over to Magdalena and extended her gloved hand. "My name is Benedikta Koppmeyer. And what is yours?"

"Magdalena Kuisl. I am the . . . midwife here." As always, it was hard for Magdalena to say she was the daughter of the town executioner. That often led to people making the sign of the cross or turning away, mumbling.

"Magdalena . . . a beautiful name," the lady continued, pointing to her bag. "I see you are just coming from delivering a child. Did everything go well?"

Magdalena nodded, looking at the ground. She hoped the lady didn't notice how she was blushing.

"I am happy to hear that," the lady said, smiling again. "But on another matter . . . Do you know where my brother's church is?"

Without saying a word, Magdalena turned around and headed back to the village. She was actually happy she had met the stranger—a little diversion would do her some good.

"Follow me, it's not far from here," she said, pointing to the west. "Behind the hills there, you can make out the Church of Saint Lawrence."

"I hope my brother is home," Benedikta Koppmeyer said, dismounting elegantly in order to give the reddish-brown sorrel a chance to rest. "He wrote me a letter. It seems important."

She followed Magdalena down the street in Altenstadt, holding her horse's reins in her hand. Suspicious villagers on both sides of the street watched the two women from behind closed shutters.

Simon stared into the black hole that opened up in front of them. A musty, damp odor rose out of the square opening, and a steep staircase, hewn into the rock, led down to the crypt. After just a few yards, the passage was enveloped in darkness.

"Shall we . . . ?" the medicus started to say, then stopped when he saw the hangman's grim nod. "We'll need a light," he said finally.

"We'll take those over there." Jakob Kuisl pointed toward two five-armed silver candelabras standing on the altar. "The dear Lord certainly won't hold it against us."

He seized the two candelabras and lit them with a votive candle burning in a niche in front of the statue of St. Sebastian, his body pierced by arrows.

"Come now."

He handed Simon the second candelabra and descended the stairway, Simon close behind. The steps were damp and slippery. As they continued downward, the medicus briefly thought he smelled something strange, but he couldn't place it and the odor soon vanished.

After only a few yards, they reached the bottom of the chamber. Jakob Kuisl held the candles up to illuminate the almost cubical area. Broken barrels and slats of wood lay around rotting. A splintered crucifix with a fading Jesus lay moldering in a corner, its paint flaking off. In another corner lay a bundle of rags. Simon leaned over and picked one up. Sacrificial lambs and crosses were embroidered onto the moldy linen, which crumbled in his hands.

Meanwhile, Jakob Kuisl had opened a trunk standing crosswise in the middle of the room and pulled out a rusted candelabra and a votive candle that had burned down to the base. Disgusted, he threw the objects back into the trunk. "Holy Saint

Anthony, thank you! We have found the church's storeroom," he grumbled. "Nothing but rubbish!"

Simon nodded in agreement. It looked as if they had found the junk room of the St. Lawrence Church. Evidently, for hundreds of years, everything for which there was no use up above had been brought down here. So was it just chance, after all, that the dead priest had come to rest right over the tombstone?

Simon's gaze wandered over the walls, where the candlelight caused outsized shadows to dance about. In the middle, exactly opposite where he stood, was a pile of rubbish—boards, splintered chairs, and a huge oaken table turned upside down against the wall. Behind the table something white was shimmering. Simon went over to it and moved his finger back and forth over the spot.

When he examined his finger in the light of the candle, it was white with lime.

And only then did he remember the odor he had noticed on the stairway. It smelled of lime. Lime and fresh mortar.

"Kuisl!" he cried out. "I think I've found something!"

When the hangman saw the fresh mortar, he heaved the huge oak table to one side in a single movement. Behind it a freshly walled-up, chest-high doorway came into view.

"Well, just look at that," Jakob Kuisl panted, pushing the rest of the clutter to one side with his foot. "The priest actually did lend a hand in the renovations. Just differently than we thought. It looks like he just recently walled up this entrance." He sunk his finger into the mortar, which was still wet.

"I wonder what's behind it," Simon said.

"I'll be damned if it's not something valuable," Jakob Kuisl said, scratching away at the fresh mortar with a nail until a brick wall became visible behind it. "And I'll bet the priest was killed for exactly that reason."

He kicked the walled-up doorway, and some bricks fell into an opening behind them, setting off a chain reaction. Cracking and then breaking into pieces, the whole wall collapsed. After a while the noise subsided, but a cloud of mortar dust hung in the air, blocking the view through the portal that was now open. Not until the dust had settled could Simon make out another room. In the middle of it stood something big and heavy, but it was too dark to see anything more.

The hangman climbed over the rubble and ducked through the low entrance. Simon heard him whistle through his teeth at what he saw.

"What is it?" Simon asked, trying in vain to see more than just a huge silhouette from his vantage point.

"It's best for you to come and see for yourself," Jakob Kuisl said.

With a sigh, Simon stooped down and followed the hangman through the narrow entranceway, shining his light into the second room.

The chamber was empty except for a huge stone sarcophagus resting on an even larger block of stone. The sarcophagus was simple and without ornamentation except for the relief of a long broadsword, a full five feet in length, depicted on its lid. At the head of the stone block, a Latin inscription was chiseled into the stone, and Simon drew in close to decipher it.

Non nobis, Domine, non nobis, sed nomini tuo da gloriam.

"*Not to us, o Lord, not to us, but to Thy name be the honor,*" the medicus read softly.

Somewhere he had seen these words, but he couldn't remember when or where. Bewildered, he looked at the hangman, who was kneeling now and also considering the inscription.

Finally, Kuisl shrugged. "You're the scholar," he grumbled. "Now show me your damned overpriced education was worth anything."

Simon couldn't help smiling to himself. Jakob Kuisl would

never forgive him for going off to the university while he, as a hangman, couldn't because of his dishonorable profession. Kuisl didn't think much of the learned quacks, and often Simon had to agree. But Simon would be better off now if he hadn't broken off his study of medicine after seven semesters in Ingolstadt for financial reasons and out of sheer laziness.

"I don't know where I've seen this saying," Simon cursed. "But I swear I'll figure it out. And when I . . ."

He stopped because he thought he'd heard a sound in the adjacent room, steps scraping along the floor and moving away quickly, something brushing against a wall. Or was he mistaken? Echoing underground crypts could play all kinds of tricks on your imagination. Perhaps the sound had come from the church above?

The hangman obviously had not heard anything. In the meantime, he had started running his hands over the walls but couldn't find any other exit.

"If I'm right, if the fat priest died because of this," he mumbled, "then there's got to be more down here than a stone grave. Or . . ." He turned again to the sarcophagus. "The secret is in the grave."

He went to the head end of the stone block and tried to push the cover aside. His face turned a bright red.

"Kuisl! You can't just . . ." Simon cried out. "That's disturbing the dead!"

"Oh, come now!" the hangman panted as he continued to struggle with the stone slab. "The dead don't care, and this one has been dead for so long that the living won't complain, either."

There was a grinding sound as the slab moved aside a half inch or so. Simon watched with fascination as Kuisl, all by himself, raised the slab that had probably been wrestled into place by a whole group of men long ago.

And no doubt they had used tools and ropes for that, too . . .

He was always astonished by the hangman's enormous strength. Once more the slab moved with a grinding sound, and a crack the width of a hand appeared.

"Don't just stand there gaping," Kuisl cursed between gasps. "Help me!"

Simon pushed, too, even though he was sure he couldn't be of much help. After a few minutes they had shoved the slab back a good half a yard, and panting, Kuisl shone his light around inside. A musty stench rose from the coffin and a skull grinned back at them. Faded white bones lay at the bottom of the coffin amid dust and rusting pieces of knight's armor. The hangman picked up a bone and held it to the light. Simon recognized from the few anatomy courses he had taken at the university in Ingolstadt that it was a man's upper arm bone. But what a huge one!

"My word," Kuisl whispered. "I have never in my life seen such a huge bone. He must have been a monster of a man . . ."

Simon gulped just thinking of a knight like this carrying a broadsword as big as the one on the relief.

"The sword," he whispered to the hangman. Suddenly, he was excited at the thought of rummaging through the grave of a mysterious warrior. He couldn't help but think of the ballads of King Arthur and the Knights of the Roundtable, which he had enjoyed reading at the university so much more than the same old nonsense about the four humors. "Check and see if the sword is in the coffin, too."

Jakob Kuisl nodded and continued rummaging about inside the sarcophagus, pulling out armament, rusty scraps of chain mail, some withered brown rags, and finally, a femur as large as a cudgel.

The only thing missing was the sword.

The hangman was about to give up when his hands suddenly felt something cold and smooth. It was a thin marble slab the size of a book and engraved with an inscription. He carefully removed it from the coffin. Each individual letter was decorated in gold leaf, and the inscription itself was in Latin, just like the one on the stone block.

After they had both studied it for a moment, Simon translated aloud, "*And I will tell my two witnesses to prophesy. And when they have ended their testimony, the beast that arises from the depths will fight, conquer, and kill them.*"

"What a confusing rant," Kuisl grumbled. "Can you make anything out of it?"

"I have to confess, it doesn't make any sense to me, either," Simon said, turning the marble slab over in his hands. "But it seems important, or it wouldn't have been placed here in the coffin. No sword, just this slab . . ."

His thoughts were suddenly interrupted by the sound of steps in the neighboring room. Someone was descending the stairway! Suddenly, seized with panic, Simon reached down for the femur on the ground and held it out like a club in front of him. The hangman stood alongside him gripping the silver candelabra even tighter in his right hand. Both waited for the steps to come nearer. Finally, a face appeared in the entrance—an exceptionally pretty face.

It was Magdalena, closely followed by another woman with red hair and a pale face. Each held a votive candle in one hand and seemed less frightened than surprised at seeing the two men before them.

"What in all the world are you doing down here, Simon?" Magdalena asked. "And what in God's name do you mean to do with the bone in your hand?"

Embarrassed, Simon placed the bone back in the coffin.

"That's a long story," he began. "It would be best for us to go upstairs."

Up above, outside the portal of the St. Lawrence Church, a dark figure crouched behind one of the snow-covered, lopsided gravestones, cursing softly. He had come too late! Obviously, the fat priest had already talked. There was no other way to explain how the quack doctor had been able to find the crypt so fast. And now two women knew the secret, too, as did this big, broad-shouldered fellow. Things were getting out of hand. He would have to ask around and find out who these people were and whether they were dangerous. Especially threatening was this grim-looking giant who was always smoking a pipe. The man could sense that. Something about the giant troubled about him. Pearls of sweat crept across his forehead like little bugs.

Hectically, he pulled a little glass phial from under his black cassock and dabbed a few drops on his neck and behind his ears. The enchanting fragrance of violets wafted through the cold air, and at once the stranger felt safe and unassailable again. He doubted that these simple people had found more down there than he and his allies had, but just to be sure, he would keep a close eye on them from now on. Maybe he would be able to learn more about this bear of a man who reeked of tobacco.

Like a dark shadow, the figure emerged from behind the gravestone and slinked away. Only the sweet fragrance hovered in the air for a while, and then it, too, was gone.

2

WITHOUT SAYING A WORD, THE HANGMAN, SIMON, and the two women climbed up the narrow stairway from the crypt. When they got to the main room of the rectory, Magdalena stared expectantly at Simon and only then did he begin to tell his story. But after just a few words, he hesitated. In all the excitement, he had forgotten to ask who the beautiful woman was sitting next to Magdalena. She was not someone from the village—that much was certain. Magdalena noticed his questioning gaze.

"I didn't introduce you yet," she said. "This is Benedikta Koppmeyer, the sister of Father Koppmeyer. She is looking for her brother."

Jakob Kuisl, who until now had been puffing glumly on his pipe, began to cough. His face was hard to make out behind thick clouds of smoke. Embarrassed, the medicus looked to one side. After a short while, Benedikta began to speak.

"What about my brother? There's something going on. I can see it in your faces."

Finally, Simon pulled himself together and began to speak hesitantly. "Well, your brother is . . . how shall I say—"

"He's dead," Kuisl interrupted. "Dead and gone. Pray for him. He will need it." Having said this, he stood and went outside. The creak of the door seemed to resound through the house for a long time as Simon struggled for words.

Benedikta Koppmeyer's face, already pale, seemed to become even more diaphanous as she stared at the medicus in disbelief. "Is it true?" she whispered. "Andreas is dead?"

"What does this mean?" Magdalena asked now, too. "Simon, explain yourself!"

Inwardly, Simon cursed the tactlessness of the dour, boneheaded hangman. He had seen him behave this way many times, yet Simon was always irritated by his coarse behavior, which was so unlike that of the Jacob Kuisl he knew who would spend hours poring over books or playing catch in the yard with his seven-year-old twins, Georg and Barbara.

After some hesitation, the medicus began to recount the morning's events. As he spoke, the priest's sister seemed to get a hold of herself again. She listened intently, with clenched fists and a look that showed Simon that this elegant woman had dealt with other tragedies in her life before this.

"I don't know what's going on here," she said finally. "But it at least explains the letter my brother sent me. He wrote of a strange discovery and that he didn't know whom to turn to. My brother and I"—she hesitated for a moment and closed her eyes briefly, her lips tightening into two narrow lines—"were very close, and this is not the first time he asked me for advice in an important matter. He always listened to his little sister," she said, forcing a smile.

"May I ask when exactly you received the letter?" Simon asked in a soft voice.

"Three days ago . . . And I left at once."

"Where are you from?" Simon replied.

Benedikta Koppmeyer looked at him in bewilderment.

"Haven't I mentioned that? I come from Landsberg, farther down the Lech River. My late husband had a wine business there, which I have been managing for several years."

And apparently not badly, Simon thought as he studied the elegant clothing of the merchant's widow. Once again, he was struck by her delicate features, which were beginning to show the first signs of age. Her mouth was slightly austere and hard—this woman was accustomed to giving orders—but at the same time, her eyes exuded an almost childlike charm. The cut of her clothes befit the latest French fashion and her whole appearance exuded noblesse, something that Simon all too often missed in Schongau.

He straightened up. "I assume you'd like to see your brother again," he said.

The merchant woman nodded, straightened up, and pulled her red hair into a bun. Finally, she followed the medicus outside. "*Évidemment,*" she whispered as she brushed past Simon in her flowing dress.

The medicus was thrilled. The distinguished lady from Landsberg not only dressed in the French fashion, but she also knew how to speak French! What a remarkable woman!

Magdalena hurried after them. If Simon had turned around, he would have noted the somber expression on her face. However, the medicus was still lost in thought about the elegant, urbane stranger.

After a good hour, the three set out on their way back to Schongau. They had laid out Koppmeyer's corpse in the charnel house next to the church, and Simon and Magdalena left his sister alone with her brother for a while. When Benedikta Koppmeyer returned, she still looked pale but had pulled herself together again.

Jakob Kuisl had left, which didn't surprise Simon very much. Many people had problems with the gruff, sometimes offensive nature of the executioner, but Simon knew him well enough by now to overlook that. He imagined that anyone who had hanged, beheaded, and quartered dozens of criminals in his lifetime just couldn't ever be a humanitarian, too. Simon still had a clear memory of the last execution a little less than a year ago. One of the mercenaries responsible for the brutal murders of children in Schongau had met his end on the wheel. Jakob Kuisl had broken every bone in his body and then waited two more days to garrote him. During the whole procedure, with all the shouting, screaming, and crying, Kuisl had not shown a bit of emotion. No flinching, no trembling, nothing.

They walked side by side in silence. Simon looked over at Benedikta Koppmeyer as she took her horse by the bridle and led it through the deep snow. She seemed lost in thought, obviously completely absorbed in grief over her dead brother. Simon did not dare to speak to her. Magdalena was silent, too, her eyes fixed straight ahead on the road. Simon tried to cheer her up once or twice, but her responses were surly and monosyllabic, and at last he gave up. What was wrong with her? Had he done something to offend her? He loved this girl, even if he knew that a marriage with the dishonorable hangman's daughter was out of the question. His father kept trying to convince him to pursue a rich burgher's daughter in Schongau. Simon was popular with the women in town. He dressed in the latest fashion, maintained a neat appearance, and always had a charming compliment on his lips. Women could overlook that he was a short man, only five feet tall, and he had had liaisons with a few of them in barns around town. Since he had met Magdalena, however, things were different. He was fascinated by this woman's temperament, but also by her education and knowledge of medicinal and poisonous herbs, even when Magdalena's stubbornness and occasional angry outbursts complicated their far-too-infrequent trysts.

On the other hand, what woman was simple?

After a short while, the forest gave way to open fields. Beyond that, the Lech River appeared like a green ribbon winding its way through the snow, and high on a hill, with the clear winter sky as a backdrop, stood the city of Schongau with its towers and walls. Simon felt relief as they passed through the city gate with its two sleepy guards. Benedikta, walking next to him, seemed more than exhausted. She had decided to seek quarters at the Goldener Stern Inn until the matter of her brother's death was cleared up. The medicus wanted to talk her out of it, but a glance from her silenced him. The merchant's widow did not look as if she would tolerate opposition.

Simon's thoughts returned to the crypt and the inscription on the coffin.

Non nobis, Domine, non nobis, sed nomini tuo da gloriam . . .

Where had he seen these words before? Was it at the university in Ingolstadt? No, it wasn't that long ago. In Schongau, then? In the city there were really only three places to find more books than just the Bible and a few farmers' almanacs. The first was Simon's bedroom, namely in a chest next to his bed, where he also liked to while away the hours during the day. The second was a small room in the executioner's house where Jakob Kuisl kept a cabinet of books on herbs and poisons, but also writings about the latest therapies. The third, finally, was the heated library of the patrician Jakob Schreevogl, a book lover who had become Simon's friend after the murders of the children last year, when the medicus had saved the life of the patrician's daughter.

Schreevogl . . . library . . .

Something clicked in Simon's mind.

Without waiting for the women, he ran through the city gate, startling the two constables who had dozed off.

"Where you going, Simon?" Magdalena called after him.

"Have to . . . take care of . . . something . . ." Simon blurted out as he ran. Then he disappeared around the next corner.

"Does he do that often?" Benedikta asked Magdalena as she walked along beside her.

The hangman's daughter shrugged. "You can ask him yourself. Sometimes I think I don't really know him."

Simon ran down the Münzgasse, past the town hall. In the square behind that were rows of elegant patrician homes, three-story buildings with ornate balconies, stucco work, and colorful murals attesting to their owners' prosperity. The city may have suffered during the Great War, but the city fathers had managed to keep themselves afloat in a new era. Payment of an exorbitant ransom had just barely managed to save Schongau from destruction by the Swedes. Enemy troops had burned down buildings on the outskirts of town, but the houses here in the market square still retained some of the splendor of past centuries when Schongau had been an important center of commerce. Only the crumbling plaster and peeling, faded paint gave evidence that the city on the river continued to waste away. Life continued elsewhere—in France, the Netherlands, perhaps even Munich and Augsburg—but certainly not in the Bavarian Priests' Corner at the edge of the Alps.

Although the sun hadn't set yet, the streets were practically empty. People had retired to their homes and were warming themselves by the hearth in the main room or by the kitchen stove. Here and there, behind the glass windows of middle-class homes, a candle or oil lamp flickered. Simon's goal was the three-story patrician house on the left belonging to the Schreevogls. As often as he could, he visited the alderman's house in order to browse his well-stocked library. By now he was pretty certain this was where he had first read the words they also saw in the crypt. It must have caught his attention some time or other while he was browsing through the library.

After he had rung twice, Agnes, the servant woman, appeared in the doorway and greeted him with a nod. Behind her, he could hear shrieks of joy. Clara Schreevogl came dashing toward him with outstretched arms. Ever since their adventure almost a year ago, Simon had become like an uncle to the ten-year-old orphan whom the Schreevogls had taken in and cared for like one of their own. She jumped into his arms, clinging to his jacket with her little hands.

"Uncle Simon, did you bring me something from the marketplace?" she asked. "Prunes or honey cakes? Please say you did!"

The medicus laughed and put the girl down. Whenever he went to browse through Jakob Schreevogl's library, he paid a visit to Clara as well. Usually, he had a little present for her: a top, a carved wooden doll, or a candied fruit with honey.

"You're like a leech, do you know that? And one with a sweet tooth, too!" He stroked her hair gently. "This time I haven't come with anything. Look in the kitchen and see if the cook has a few dried apples for you."

Clara walked away, pouting. Footsteps now could be heard on the wide spiral staircase that led to the upper floors. Jakob Schreevogl approached Simon in his bathrobe and slippers. The alderman had wrapped a scarf around his neck. He was pale and had a light cough, but his face brightened when he caught sight of Simon.

"Simon! What a pleasure to see you!" he called from the stairway, spreading his arms out. "In this beastly cold, anyone who will pay a visit inside these four walls and help to pass the time is welcome."

"It looks like what you need is rest and a good doctor," Simon replied with some concern. "As luck would have it, there happens to be one present. Shall I perhaps . . ." He reached for his doctor's bag, which he had been dragging around with him since the morning, but Schreevogl waved him off.

"Oh, come now! It's just a simple cold. Half the town is sicker than I am. Let's hope at least that the good Lord will spare our children." He winked at the medicus. "In any case, I don't think you're here for a boring house call. But do come with me to the library. There's a nice warm fire in the stove, and if you are lucky, there will be some of this black devil's brew left."

Simon followed him upstairs, animated by the prospect of a cup of hot coffee. He had introduced Jakob Schreevogl to the pleasure of this trendy new beverage. Two years ago, the young medicus had first purchased the brown beans from an Arabian street vendor and since then had become addicted. And now he had apparently hooked the patrician Schreevogl on it as well. Together, they had enjoyed veritable coffee orgies in the library. After the third pot, even tedious theologians like Johann Damascenes or Petrus Lombardus began to make sense.

Simon entered the library and looked around. A little cast-iron stove was glowing in one corner of the wood-paneled room, and book after book lined the walls on gleaming cherrywood shelves. Jakob Schreevogl was well-to-do. His father had taken a small stove-fitting business and grown it into the leading one in the area. Since the death of his father, young Schreevogl had invested a considerable portion of his money in his book collection, a passion he shared with Simon.

The patrician offered him a chair and poured him a steaming cup of coffee. Jakob Schreevogl was a big man and, like all Schreevogls, had a pointed, slightly hooked nose that nearly hung down into his coffee. As the young alderman slurped the hot brew, Simon inquired about the aldermen's meeting that had taken place that morning. He knew that important topics had been on the agenda.

"So, did the city council make any decision on how to proceed with these gangs of murderers?"

Jakob Schreevogl nodded earnestly. "We'll no doubt send out a patrol to search for the robbers."

"But you've done that once before!" Simon interjected.

"I know, I know," Schreevogl sighed. "But this time it has to be well thought out and needs a competent leader. We're still considering who might be the right person for that."

Simon nodded. The matter was too serious to be entrusted to a few drunken village constables. For weeks, a band of robbers had been ravaging the countryside. A merchant and two farmers had been attacked. The highwaymen had slain the merchant, and the two farmers had just managed to escape. There were at least a dozen men, they reported, some with crossbows and a few with muskets, even. In other words, a real danger, if not for the city, then at least for the surrounding area.

"If the aldermen can't get their hands on these scoundrels soon, we'll have to ask Munich to send soldiers." Jakob Schreevogl cursed under his breath and blew into his hot cup of coffee. "But the council wants to avoid that at all costs. Soldiers cost money, as you know. But forget about politics," he said, waving his hand dismissively. "It bores me. You have certainly come for a different reason."

"Indeed," Simon replied. "I'm looking for a book—or rather, for a quotation in a book that I think I've read here."

"Aha, a book!" Jakob Schreevogl smiled. "I'm pleased that you enjoy my library so much. So tell me, how does the quote go?"

"*Non nobis Domine, non nobis, sed nomini tuo da gloriam,*" Simon repeated from memory.

The patrician stopped to think. "Where did you read this?"

"In the little church of Saint Lawrence in Altenstadt."

"*Not to us, o Lord, not to us, but to Thy name be the honor,*" Jakob Schreevogl mumbled, furrowing his brow. "Strange. I believe that's the motto of the Knights Templar."

Simon had to cough when his coffee went down the wrong way. "The Templars?" he asked finally.

Schreevogl nodded. "It was their battle cry."

Suddenly, the alderman's brow furrowed again—he seemed to remember something. Quickly, he stood up and walked over to a shelf near the stove. "Now I know the book you mean!" he said. After a few minutes of searching, he took out a little leather-bound book no larger than the palm of a hand. "Here!" he exclaimed, handing it to Simon. "It's in this treatise by Wilhelm von Selling. *Ordinis Templorum Historia.* An ancient, strange book. Selling was an Englishman, a Benedictine monk who, in contrast to the church, tried to keep the memory of the Templars alive. He wrote this book more than two hundred years ago, but even at that time, the Templars had been confined to history for a century.

Simon nodded as he leafed through the well-worn tome. Some pages apparently had been ripped out, moisture had curled others, and some were scorched. The book was written in Latin with embellished initials and was not printed, but handwritten. It looked like the book had been through a lot in its long life.

"At that time, I just skimmed the book," Simon said, "but I remember the words. Tell me more about these . . . Templars."

Jakob Schreevogl sat down again and sipped his coffee. It was a while before he began to speak. Outside an ice storm beat against the windowpanes.

"Their full name is a bit longer—The Poor Knights of Christ and of Solomon's Temple. Much that we know of them is, perhaps, only a legend." The patrician settled back in his chair as he continued speaking. "One thing is certain, however. The Templars were the most powerful and richest organization that the world has ever known. They started out as a small order of knights during the Crusades whose actual purpose was to protect pilgrims on their way to Jerusalem. Until then, the order was a unique mix of knights and ascetic monks. But through clever tactics and the right support, the group spread across all of Europe in a few decades. Branches were everywhere. If a person wanted, he could purchase a bill of exchange in Cologne and redeem it in Jerusalem or Byzantium. The order answered only to the Pope and was thus, in fact, sacrosanct. Through clever financial policies, the Templars gradually became richer than kings or emperors, and that would finally be their undoing . . ."

"What happened?" Simon asked curiously, pouring himself another cup of coffee.

"Well, it happened as it so often does." Jakob Schreevogl shrugged almost apologetically. "The French King Philip IV had designs on their fortune. In the dead of night, he was able to arrest every Templar in all of France. He accused them of engaging in sodomy and satanic rites, bought witnesses, and extracted the necessary confessions through torture. Finally, even the church dissociated itself from the Templars. The pope could no longer support them and, in the end, let them fall. Their last Grand Master, to the best of my knowledge, was burned at the stake in Paris, and within a few years, the mightiest lords and masters of Europe became powerless victims. The Templars who were unable to go into hiding in time were pursued and killed. And all that after they had helped to shape the destiny of Europe for nearly two hundred years!"

"And what happened to their money?" Simon asked. "The French king no doubt grabbed that, didn't he?"

The patrician grinned. "Only a small portion. The rest disappeared and has never been found—gold, jewels, religious relics . . . It is said that the Templars hid it somewhere. Some people think they took it to the New World; others say the Holy Land or the British Isles. Whoever finds it can no doubt buy himself any throne in the world."

Simon whistled through his teeth. "Why have I never heard anything about this?"

Schreevogl was shaken by another fit of coughing. After a moment, he continued. "Because the church didn't want its complicity in the matter exposed. The noblemen, too, politely stayed silent and confiscated the Templars' territories. Only a few people, like Wilhelm von Selling, broke their silence."

The medicus nodded. "But that still doesn't explain what this Templar battle cry is doing in the Saint Lawrence Church."

Schreevogl hesitated. "I once heard that the Saint Lawrence Church used to be a Templar church," he said finally.

"A Templar church? In Altenstadt?" Simon almost choked again.

"Yes, why not?" the patrician said, shrugging. "The Templars had branches everywhere. And isn't there even a Templar Lane in Altenstadt?"

"You're right!" Simon cried. "The narrow little Templar Lane just before the bridge over the Schönach. It's strange, but I've never wondered about that street's name . . ."

"You see? But certainly the priest of the basilica in Altenstadt can tell you more. There have to be records from the little church next door. If they're not in the Saint Lawrence Church itself, then they'd be in Saint Michael's Basilica. Would you care for some more coffee?"

Simon stood up and grabbed Jakob Schreevogl's hand. "Thank you, but I think I have to go and see my father. There are a few tedious treatments to perform—coughs, fevers, bloodletting, just the usual. But you have helped me a great deal." He hesitated for a moment. "Could I ask for one more favor?"

The patrician nodded. "Yes, what is it?"

Simon pointed to the little leather-bound book on the side table. "This book about the Templars. Could I borrow it?"

"Of course. But be careful, it's very valuable."

Simon took the book and hastened toward the door. On the threshold, he stopped again briefly and turned around. "There's another quote I can't make sense of. It concerns two witnesses and a beast that does battle with them and finally kills them. Have you by chance ever heard of that?"

The patrician thought for a moment, then shook his head. "It rings a bell somewhere, but for the life of me I can't remember what it is. I'm sorry. Perhaps I'll think of it later." He looked at the medicus skeptically. "Simon, you're not rushing headlong into another adventure with the hangman, are you? For heaven's sake, be careful!"

Simon grinned. "I'll try. But do let me know if you remember."

He bowed briefly, then ran down the staircase with the book in hand. The patrician stood at the window upstairs and watched Simon vanish into the snowstorm swirling through the market square of Schongau.

The stonemason Peter Baumgartner was standing half naked, his muscular body stripped to the waist, in the middle of the hangman's living room. He was so terrified that he almost pissed in his pants. Despite the icy wind that whistled around the pig bladders stretched out and nailed over the windows, sweat was running down his face. He kept asking himself whether he shouldn't have forked out a few kreuzers more and gone to the medicus rather than the hangman. Or perhaps he shouldn't have gone to either. Yes, that was it exactly; instead, he should have stayed at home, washed the pain down with an Ave Maria and a glass of brandy, and then hoped that, with God's help, his shoulder would heal by itself. But now it was too late.

All sorts of tools lay on the table in front of him, and he couldn't say if they were intended as instruments of torture or medical devices: long pincers, presumably for prying out teeth; sharp, brightly polished knives in all sizes and shapes; and a small handsaw with a few rust-colored spots—spots of dried blood, no doubt, Peter Baumgartner thought.

What terrified Baumgartner most, however, was the gigantic figure of the Schongau hangman standing directly before him. His huge hands were immersed in a pot of white, greasy paste, which he was smearing slowly and methodically over him.

"Is that . . . human fat?" the mason gasped. Even though Baumgartner tried hard to hide his fear, he couldn't prevent his voice from trembling slightly. He knew that the Schongau executioner neatly flayed the corpses of the people he executed and scratched the fat off their skin. From that he made a paste that was supposed to work wonders. Baumgartner wanted very much to believe in miracles, but the thought of being rubbed down with the slimy remains of a criminal made him nauseous.

"You stupid bastard, do you think I'd waste my good human fat on somebody like you?" Kuisl grumbled, without looking up. "This is bear fat mixed with arnica, chamomile, and a few herbs you've never heard of. And now come here, it's going to hurt a bit."

"Kuisl, stop . . . I think I'd rather go to old Fronwieser . . ." the mason mumbled when he saw two huge dinner-plate sized hands in front of him dripping with fat.

"And let him charge you two guilders so that you'll never be able to move your arm again. Don't put up such a fuss, just come here."

Baumgartner sighed. He had fallen from the scaffolding in the St. Lawrence Church a week ago, and since then his shoulder had been discolored with bruises. The pain throbbed all the way down to his right hand so that he could no longer even hold a spoon. He had hesitated for a long time before going to the hangman, but in the meantime, he worried that he might never be able to use his right arm again. So he had scraped together some money he had saved and set out at noon for Schongau. Jakob Kuisl was famous far and wide as a healer. Like all executioners, Kuisl earned his money less through executions and tortures, of which there were just a handful at most during the year, than through healing and the sale of salves, pills, and ointments. He would also sell you a piece of the hangman's rope or a thief's thumb. A mummified finger in your money pouch was supposed to protect you from thieves, but naturally only when you sprinkled the purse with holy water every day and firmly believed in it. Jakob Kuisl didn't believe in it, but he earned good money from it anyway.

Like many other patients before him in the hangman's house, Peter Baumgartner was torn between fear and hope. It was generally known that most people left Kuisl's house no worse off than before, at least, and in many cases even better—something you couldn't always say of doctors with university training. On the other hand, Jakob Kuisl was the Schongau hangman. A mere glance from him brought misfortune, and speaking with him was a sin. If Baumgartner confessed to this visit the next time he went to church, he would surely have to say a hundred Lord's Prayers as penance.

"Come here, damn it, or I'll dislocate your other shoulder, too."

Jakob Kuisl, his hands smeared with fat, was still standing in front of the burly mason. Baumgartner nodded in resignation, made the sign of the cross, and then stepped forward. The hangman turned him around, carefully palpated the swollen shoulder, then suddenly seized Baumgartner's right arm and yanked it back and down. There was a loud cracking sound.

The scream could be heard all the way up in the marketplace.

Baumgartner collapsed onto the stool by the table and nearly passed out. He was about to throw up and let out a stream of curses when he cast a glance down at his right hand.

He could move it again!

The pain in his shoulder seemed better, too. Jakob Kuisl handed him a wooden box.

"Tell your wife to massage your shoulder with this three

times a day for a week. In two weeks you'll be able to go back to work again. You owe me a guilder."

Baumgartner's joy at being relieved of his pain was short-lived.

"A guilder?" he gasped. "Damn, not even old Fronwieser asks that much. And he has studied at the university."

"No, he'll bleed you, send you home, and three weeks later, saw off your whole arm for three guilders. That's what he studied."

Baumgartner wrung his hands, thinking it over. He really did seem cured. Just the same, he began to haggle.

"A guilder, eh? That's more than a miller earns in a whole day. How about half and we'll call it a deal?"

"Let's say a whole one, and I won't dislocate your other shoulder."

Baumgartner gave up with a sigh. He rummaged about in his purse and counted out the coins neatly on the table. The hangman picked up half of them and pushed the other half back across the table to Baumgartner. "I've given it some more thought," he said. "Half a guilder if you can tell me something in return."

Baumgartner looked at him in astonishment but then hurriedly put the coins back in his purse.

"What do you want to know?"

"You're the mason up the Saint Lawrence Church, aren't you?"

"Indeed," Baumgartner replied. "That's where I took a fall from that damned scaffolding."

Jakob Kuisl pulled out his tobacco pouch and began slowly and carefully to fill his pipe.

"What are they building up there?" he asked.

"Well . . . Actually, they aren't building anything," Baumgartner said with hesitation. He watched the hangman with fascination as he filled his pipe. Pipe-smoking was a completely new fashion. The mason had never met anyone except Kuisl who did anything like it. To be on the safe side, the Schongau priest had declared it a vice in one of his last homilies.

"We're just renovating the church," Baumgartner continued finally. "Both on the outside and on the inside—the whole balcony. It was close to collapsing. The church is said to be a good five hundred years old."

"Did you notice anything out of the ordinary during your renovations?" Kuisl asked. "Drawings? Figures? Old paintings?"

The mason's face brightened. "Yes, there was something unusual! Up in the balcony, the wall was full of bright-red crosses. The whole left-hand wall was covered with them!"

"What did they look like?"

"Well, different from the cross of Our Savior. They were rather . . . May I?" Baumgartner pointed to one of the sharp knives on the table. When the hangman nodded, Baumgartner carved a cross into the wood. The arms were of equal length and became narrower toward the center. The mason nodded with satisfaction. "They looked something like that."

"And what did you do with the crosses?" Kuisl continued.

"It was strange. The priest told us to paint them over. That was shortly after he got so upset about the cellar."

"The cellar?" The hangman frowned.

"Well, on New Year's Day, while moving the slabs, Johannes Steiner noticed that under one grave marker there was a hollow space. We then moved the cover aside. We needed three men to do that—it was a huge thing—and from there, steps led down below."

Jakob Kuisl nodded, lighting his filled pipe with a glowing wood chip. Baumgartner looked at him with growing enthusiasm.

"Did you go down into the cellar, too?" Kuisl asked, puffing on his pipe.

"No . . . Only the priest went down, and soon he came back all excited. The next day he told us to paint over the crosses, and we did."

The hangman nodded slowly. "Are you sure none of you went down?" he asked again.

"I swear by the Virgin Mary, no!" Baumgartner cried. "But why is that so important?"

Jakob Kuisl stood up and walked to the door. "Forget it. You can go now."

Peter Baumgartner straightened up, relieved. He didn't know why Kuisl was asking all these questions, but at least it had saved him half a guilder. Besides that, he was happy he could leave the executioner's house. He was sure he could see evil lurking in every corner of the room. Still, he was itching to ask just one last question.

"Kuisl?"

"What do you want to know?"

"This pipe of yours. How does it taste? It smells . . . well, really not so bad."

Jakob Kuisl expelled a huge cloud of smoke that almost completely enveloped his head.

"Don't get started with it," his voice rang out from behind the cloud. "It's like with drinking. You enjoy it, but you can't ever quit."

When the mason had left, Magdalena came down the narrow staircase into the main room. After the strenuous night, being thrown out of the Hainmiller house and meeting Benedikta Koppmeyer, she had lain down for a rest and had had weird dreams in which Simon and Benedikta rode past her in a sleigh, laughing and waving. Simon's face was a grotesque mask that dissolved and dripped to the ground like melting snow. She was finally awakened by Peter Baumgartner's scream. Through the thin floor, she overheard the rest of their conversation.

"Why do you think the priest wanted to have the crosses painted over?" she asked as she descended the staircase. "Do you think they had something to do with the crypt? And by the way, what did you find down there, anyway?"

"It would be better for you not to know," her father grumbled, "or you'll just start snooping around again."

"But, Father," she said with a look that had always bewitched him since she was a little girl, "if you don't tell me, Simon will. So tell me!"

"You'd better keep a close eye on your Simon."

"What do you mean by that?"

"You know exactly what I mean. He's doing more than just making eyes at this woman from the city."

Magdalena blushed. "How can you say something like that? You have hardly ever seen them together," she cried. "And besides . . . I don't care who Simon flirts around with, anyway."

"Then it's all right." He walked over to the stove and threw another piece of wood on the fire, sending sparks into the air. "It's much more important for us to learn who the workers were in the church."

Magdalena had trouble focusing her thoughts on anything but Simon. They had been a couple for more than a year, even if they couldn't act like one openly. She cursed her father for suggesting that Simon might have something to do with another woman.

"Why are you concerned with the workers?" she said finally, trying to pick up the thread of the conversation. "You certainly don't believe that—"

"You heard it," her father interrupted. "The workers opened the crypt, and even if Baumgartner swears up and down that none of them were down below, I don't believe it. Someone poked around down there."

"And then killed the priest?" Magdalena gasped.

"Rubbish!" Kuisl exclaimed, spitting on the floor, something he only dared to do when his wife, Anna Maria, wasn't home. At the present, she was up at the market in town with the twins.

"Naturally, none of them is responsible for what happened to the fat priest," he continued. "But they weren't able to keep their mouths shut, either. We've got to find who they spoke to, and I'm sure we'll have the murderer then."

Magdalena nodded. "The murderer learned about the crypt and was afraid Koppmeyer would find out too much, and that's why he killed him. That could be what happened," she said, mulling it over.

The hangman opened the door so that clouds of tobacco smoke and fumes from the stove could drift out, and an ice-cold breeze blew through the room.

"So what are you waiting for?" he asked.

"What do you mean?" Magdalena said, with some irritation.

"You wanted to help me snoop around, so go find the workers who were in the Saint Lawrence Church and talk with them. Talking with men and making eyes at them is something you can do, can't you?"

Magdalena grimaced at him, then put on her cape and walked out into the cold.

When Simon walked in the front door, he realized it would probably be some time before he would be able to continue reading the little book about the Templars. Sitting on the bench by the stove were three citizens of Schongau, all of whom looked like they needed more than just a few words of consolation and a cheese compress. Simon knew them all. Two were farmers from the area whom he had often seen in the marketplace. The third was the Schongau blacksmith's journeyman. He was coughing up reddish-yellow mucus, which he thoughtfully spat into some brown rags. Nevertheless, some kept spattering onto the wooden floorboards, which were only sparsely covered with dirty reeds. The faces of the patients were drawn, beads of sweat stood out on their foreheads, and all of them had dark rings around their eyes and faces the color of wax.

To drive away the poisonous miasma, old Fronwieser had been burning lavender and balm, and it smelled like Easter mass in the little room. Simon didn't think these vapors did any good. He had read, in fact, that diseases were carried by dirt and bodily fluids, but his father considered this to be just newfangled nonsense. As the blacksmith's journeyman on his left went into a new fit of coughing, Simon cautiously moved one step to the side.

"Isn't it nice that the young gentleman finally showed up. What kept you so long in Altenstadt? A nice little supper with the priest?" Bonifaz Fronwieser entered from the adjacent room holding a smoking pine chip and a few more sprigs of lavender. At one time, as a dashing young army surgeon in the Great War, he had been an imposing figure and had made eyes with many a pretty girl, but now, stooped over with thinning gray hair, he looked older than his fifty years, and all that remained of his former self was his piercing, alert eyes. And his harsh tone.

"I've been waiting for you for hours!" he snapped softly enough that the three patients on the bench couldn't hear. "I have to pay a visit to Master Hardenberg, a member of the city council. He's come down with it, too! And instead, here I am fooling around with a few farmers who can only afford to pay me with a few eggs, at best!"

He poked his withered index finger at Simon's chest. "Tell me the truth—you've been keeping company with the hangman again and sticking your nose into those filthy books! People are already gossiping, and you're giving them a reason to."

Simon rolled his eyes. Bonifaz Fronwieser hated the hangman, who he thought was corrupting his son with books and his unorthodox methods of healing.

"Father, the priest—" he said, trying to interrupt his father's harangue, but his father cut him off nevertheless.

"Aha, so that's it! No doubt you were partying with the fat old codger, eh? Hope you enjoyed your meal, at least," he croaked. "His housekeeper at least is supposed to be a good cook!"

"He's dead, Father," Simon said softly.

"What?" Bonifaz Fronwieser seemed irritated. For a moment, he wanted to continue his litany of complaints, but now he hesitated. He hadn't reckoned with this news.

"Koppmeyer is dead, so there were some things that had to be done," Simon repeated.

"I'm . . . I'm really sorry," the older physician grumbled after a short pause. "Did he have this fever, too?"

Simon eyed the three patients, who looked at him partly out of curiosity and partly out of fear. Then he shook his head.

"No . . . It was something else. I'll tell you later."

"Very well," his father grumbled, falling back into his familiar role. "Then get to work. As you can see, there are still a few of the living here and they need to be treated."

Simon sighed, then helped his father in examining the patients. There wasn't a lot to do: fetch a few dried herbs for a potion, listen to a few chests, check tongues, the usual sniffing and observing of urine samples. Simon had no illusions—most of this was just cheap playacting performed to give sick people false hope and take their money. Even doctors with university degrees couldn't usually tell very much. The two Fronwiesers were just as helpless in the face of this fever, which had been spreading around Schongau for a full two weeks and had killed a dozen people. People were getting chills and pain in the joints, and some died suddenly overnight. Others survived the first onslaught, only to be overcome with terrible coughing fits soon after.

It made Simon furious to stand by helpless in the face of this epidemic. His father, on the other hand, seemed to have resigned himself to it. The relationship between them was tense, to put it mildly. As the town doctor of Schongau, Bonifaz Fronwieser hoped his son would someday follow in his footsteps. But Simon didn't want anything to do with his father's old-fashioned methods—enemas, bloodletting, sniffing old men's urine. The young medicus preferred to occupy himself with the books that the Schongau hangman was always lending to him. He had long ago worked his way through the box of leather folios that Jakob Kuisl had given him as a present almost a year ago, and he longed for more. Even now, as he was occupied with treating the three patients, he couldn't help but think again about the theories of controversial scientists. Currently, he was rereading the work of an Englishman named William Harvey, which dealt with the circulation of blood in the human body. Was it possible that blood consisted of tiny animalcules . . . ?

"Why are you standing around daydreaming, you good-for-nothing!" his father snapped, interrupting his reveries. "Here, take some blood from Johannes Steringer! I'm going to the alderman now. Bleeding is something you can do by yourself!"

He handed Simon the sharp little stiletto they used for slitting a patient's veins. Then, after briefly wishing them a good recovery, he set out on his way. "And don't let them put you off with a few eggs and a loaf of bread," he scolded Simon as he walked past him.

Simon looked down at Johannes Steringer, who was sitting on the bench in front of him, coughing and shaking and spitting up reddish-yellow phlegm into a ratty handkerchief. He knew the blacksmith's journeyman from a few previous house calls, a strong, solid fellow who was slumped over now, hardly able to move, and staring blankly into space. The idea of letting blood from this sick, weakened body seemed outright foolish to Simon. He knew that bloodletting was a tried-and-tested remedy for almost any sickness; nevertheless, he put the stiletto aside.

"It's all right, Steringer," he said. "You can go home now. Have your wife make you some sage broth and lie down next to the stove until it gets better."

"And the bloodletting?" the journeyman gasped.

"We'll do that another time. For now, you need your blood. Go home."

Steringer nodded and set out for home, as did the two farmers. Simon gave each of them a little jar of wild thyme. As payment, the young medicus pocketed a few old discolored coins and half a leg of smoked ham. He thanked them and closed the door behind them as they left.

Simon took a deep breath. Finally, he had time to devote to the little book the patrician had given him. He sat down excitedly on the bench next to the stove and leafed through the yellowing pages.

There was a lot to learn about the rise and fall of the Templars. He read that they had even lent money to the Pope and that they had been almost invincible in battle, a band with strange rites and customs whose members had sworn allegiance to one another, who had flung themselves headlong into battle for God, and who were even admired by their enemies for their bravery. He read about the great battles in the Holy Land, the destruction of Jerusalem, the flight of the Templars to Cyprus, and their continuing power in Europe. He was astonished to learn that, in the end, the knightly order owned more than ten thousand castles and estates, from England to Byzantium! Had there also been a branch here in Schongau? Which Templar's bones had they found under the St. Lawrence Church? Had he left a message to posterity on the marble slab?

Two witnesses who prophesy . . . the beast that arises from the depths that fights, conquers, and kills them.

But even after studying the book a long time, Simon still couldn't find the strange saying engraved on the marble slab in the coffin. The book also said nothing about the Templars' legendary treasure. Was it possible it had never existed? Simon rubbed his tired eyes and went to bed. The wind continued whistling through the shutters, while in his room a thin layer of ice slowly formed over the bedposts.

3

MAGDALENA KNOCKED AT THE DOOR OF THE CARpenter Balthasar Hemerle's house and listened for the sound of steps inside. It was early in the morning, but she had already visited the masons and the stonecutter in Altenstadt the day before. The men all looked at her distrustfully at first—nobody was comfortable with the daughter of the hangman at their door. It was quite possible that her presence might make the cattle sick the next day. When she explained that she wanted to ask them about the dead priest in Altenstadt and the renovation work in the St. Lawrence Church, they let her in reluctantly, often under the suspicious eyes of their wives. Magdalena was not just the hangman's daughter, but with her thick black hair, bushy eyebrows, and full lips, she was also an attractive woman who was quite capable of exciting passions. She knew very well that men stared at her behind her back. Still, none of the young fellows ever asked her for a dance. No one except Simon.

Her conversations on the previous evening had not revealed anything new. All the workers agreed they had found the crypt, but only the priest had gone down into it. He looked pale when he came back, went to fetch some incense, and burned it there, and then immediately had the entrance sealed. They also mentioned the strange crosses on the walls in the balcony, but they all said they hadn't told anyone else about it. The visit to the carpenter's house was Magdalena's last try. Balthasar Hemerle led her into the living room. He was a large, good-natured man with a full, shaggy beard, a twinkle in his eye, and a face distorted by pockmarks. Unlike many other men in town, he was never troubled by the fact that Magdalena was just a dishonorable hangman's daughter. On the contrary, he had smiled at her at the last church fair and even tipped his large carpenter's hat mischievously to her by way of greeting. But Magdalena knew that he made eyes at other girls, too, and his wife had scolded him once or twice about it. Fortunately, Katharina happened to be at the market in Schongau at the moment.

"Well, young lady, what do you need from me?" Hemerle grinned, pushing a mug of mulled wine across the table to her. "Does the city need a new gallows? The old one looks pretty rotted, don't you think? I'll bet that it will snap at the next hanging, and your father will look like a damn fool."

Magdalena smiled and shook her head, sipping on the invigorating drink. She took another gulp and then finally got around to explaining why she was there. Balthasar Hemerle looked at her for a long time, thinking about it.

"The word going around is that the fat old Koppmeyer was poisoned. Does this have anything to do with that?"

Magdalena shrugged. "That's just what we want to find out."

Hemerle nodded. "I don't know how you have gotten involved in this," he began, "but it's true that none of us went down into the crypt. And the workers painted over the crosses just as they were told."

"Have you spoken with anyone about it?" Magdalena asked as she kept sipping on her mulled wine. She could feel its warming effects; she absolutely could not empty the whole mug, or she'd never make it home again.

"Who could we have talked to?" Hemerle said. "But wait . . ." He paused. "We were all talking about it last Sunday after church when our group was sitting at our regular table at Strasser's Tavern in Altenstadt. The priest had seemed nervous delivering his homily, and we did notice a few strangers in the tavern."

"Who were they?" Magdalena could feel her heart beginning to race, and not just from the strong wine.

"Strangers . . . I don't know," Hemerle grumbled. "Didn't look at them that closely. They sat at the next table with black cowls, like monks, and didn't even take off their hoods."

"Did you notice anything else?"

The carpenter knitted his brow. Finally, he seemed to remember something.

"There was an odor in the air like an expensive perfume," he said, "and three black horses standing just outside the door — not mares like your father's, but big jet-black horses. Could put a real fright into you . . ." He shook his head and laughed.

"But come now . . . Let's talk about something else," he said, leering at her. "I just finished making myself a new bed out of spruce. It's over there in the other room, and it's nice and big and warm. Would you like to see it?"

Magdalena smiled. "So that your wife will wring my neck? No thanks."

She emptied the mug in one long gulp and headed out the door. Swaying slightly, she stomped through the snow on her way back to Schongau.

Balthasar Hemerle waved to her as she left, but suddenly he looked serious again. He couldn't help but think of the men with the black horses. For a brief moment, he thought he could smell a whiff of perfume in the cold winter air. But no doubt it was just the aroma of mulled wine.

• • •

Early the next morning, Simon headed out to Altenstadt again. Before dawn, he tiptoed past the room of his snoring father. Bonifaz Fronwieser didn't get home until late last night, and Simon had to assume he had immediately exchanged the pay from his house call to Alderman Hardenberg for wine and brandy. The bartenders of the taverns behind the Ballenhaus permitted some guests to stay on after the eight o'clock curfew if they had enough change in their pockets. And the esteemed patrician Hardenberg certainly had paid more for his checkup than all the sick farmers put together that week. Enough, at least, for three glasses of the best burgundy.

Simon carefully closed the door and hurried toward the Hof Gate at the end of the street. Leaning against the ruined walls of the ducal castle, the city watchman Josef had already opened the gate reinforced with iron and was staring wearily at the approaching figure.

"Up so early, Simon?" he grumbled. They knew each other well, the young medicus having recently cured Josef's son of scabies—at no charge, of course. It was always good to befriend one of the city watchmen. That way you could slip into the city through the emergency gate from time to time, even after sunset.

"I've got to go to Altenstadt again," Simon said. "Another patient needs my help there."

"Is it the same coughing and sweating?" Josef asked, knowing that, in the little town of Altendorf, many people had fallen ill with the strange fever, too. Simon nodded slowly and hurried through the gate. Nobody had to know what he was really doing in Altenstadt. As the watchman watched Simon leave, he drew a Druid's cross in the snow.

"God forbid the plague should come back to Schongau," he called to the medicus. "God forbid!" He thanked the Virgin Mary for sparing him the sickness until then.

The road wound up the mountain, and soon Simon felt comfortably warm despite the dry cold. As he walked along, he wondered why he had set out at the crack of dawn to investigate the death of someone who was almost a total stranger to him. He could have stayed in bed, gotten up for a cup of coffee when the church bells rang nine o'clock; he could have sat by the fire roaring on the hearth and watched snowflakes twirling down outside. But, as so often was the case, he was overcome with curiosity, an innate urge to get to the bottom of things. And then, of course, there was Benedikta Koppmeyer. Ever since he had first seen her the day before, he couldn't get her out of his mind. Was he perhaps doing her a little favor by going on this mission?

Simon was headed for the basilica of St. Michael in Altenstadt. It towered above the little houses, a reminder of a time when this small village had been an important commercial center on the Via Claudia August, the old Roman military road. Built of heavy stone blocks, surrounded by a high wall, and flanked by two sky-high towers, the basilica looked more like a castle than a church.

Simon climbed the broad flight of steps to the main portal. Directly above the double doors, a magnificent relief depicted a knight, armed with a shield, helmet, and sword, fighting a dragon. In the mouth of the dragon was the body of a second man. Simon shook his head. Unlike many of his fellow countrymen, he had never felt comfortable with the bloody, monstrous figures and scenes depicted in churches. Such images were no doubt intended to remind people of the horrors of hell, but to Simon they felt more like messengers from a very distant past.

His anxiety subsided only when he stepped inside the church and turned his eyes upward. In the apse over the altar was the most beautiful and largest crucifix in their part of the country. The "Great God of Altenstadt" was known far beyond the borders of this little town in the Priests' Corner, and even the otherwise rather sober-minded medicus could not deny its appeal. The figure, carved of larch wood, was huge, surely three yards long and just as wide. On either side stood life-size figures of

Mary and John. But most striking was the face of the Savior. It looked down on the faithful, not distorted with pain or crying out condemnation, but gently, almost a bit sadly.

When Simon looked down again, he spotted a figure in one of the front pews that he had not noticed before. Perhaps because the person was kneeling, head bowed in prayer. A scarf fell over the figure's shoulders, and before Simon could say anything, the person stood up, made the sign of the cross, and turned around toward him. Simon was stunned. It was Benedikta Koppmeyer! Her face was even paler now than the day before, and it seemed she had not slept very much. Nevertheless, she exuded an aura of strength unlike anything Simon had ever seen before in a woman. Once the merchant's widow recognized Simon, she smiled at him wanly.

"I . . . I didn't expect to find you here in the church," the medicus stammered as she walked toward him. In the milky light of dawn, she almost seemed to be floating in space. "I thought you had a room in Schongau at the Stern."

"I do," she said softly, holding out her ringed hand for him to kiss. "But I couldn't sleep, so I came here to pray. This church . . . is something very special, don't you think?"

Simon nodded. Apparently, Benedikta could not resist the magical appeal of the basilica, either. Then it occurred to him that she must have made the trip from Schongau even before daybreak.

"You shouldn't be traveling alone," he remarked with concern. "A band of robbers is marauding about the countryside at present. A defenseless woman like yourself—"

"I am not as defenseless as I appear," she interrupted him dryly. Then she pointed to his empty hands and changed the topic. "But you don't have your bag with you today. Aren't there any sick people to heal? What else brings you here? Have you come to pray?"

Simon couldn't suppress a smile. "Unfortunately not. Although I do believe the priest wished I would come to church more often." He hesitated before continuing. "No, it has to do with your brother."

"My brother?" Benedikta looked at him with surprise.

Simon nodded, looking around to see if there were other parishioners praying in the church.

"It seems your brother discovered something down in the crypt of the Saint Lawrence Church," he whispered finally. "Perhaps he was silenced for this reason."

"But what are you looking for in Saint Michael's Basilica?" she persisted.

"Well, I hope the priest here can tell me more about the Saint Lawrence Church. After all, it's part of his parish."

Benedikta nodded. "I understand," she said. After hesitating a few moments, she continued. "Would you mind if I came along with you to see the priest? I'd like to learn more about my brother's death."

Simon shrugged. "Why not?" he said. "Come along. He's probably just now preparing for mass."

They came across the priest in the vestry, holding a dripping chalice to his mouth. Apparently he was sampling the wine to be used in the mass.

"The blood of Christ," Simon murmured, loud enough so the priest could hear him. "What a blessing that the Savior left us such a delicious legacy."

Pastor Elias Ziegler was startled but quickly pulled himself together. He turned toward the uninvited guests, noticeably angered. He was small and stocky, with a fleshy face and a crooked nose covered with spider veins. Indeed, it looked as though he often found it necessary to test the quality of the communion wine.

"As you surely know, the communion wine turns into the blood of Christ only after it has been consecrated," he declared dryly. "In its present condition, it is only wine, though a relatively good one." The priest wiped his mouth and put the chalice down on a silver tablet next to the hosts. Then he wiped his wet fingers on his cassock. His speech sounded a bit slurred. "I assume there is a reason why you have come to disturb me in my preparations for the mass. And with a woman, too, here in the vestry."

"We'll make it brief, Your Excellency," Simon said. He introduced himself and Benedikta. When the priest heard the name *Koppmeyer,* his ears pricked up.

"Andreas Koppmeyer?" he asked. "The priest at Saint Lawrence Church? I have heard of his death. My condolences to his sister. Does anyone know yet what—"

"I would like you to arrange my brother's funeral," Benedikta interrupted. "Is that possible?"

"But . . . of course." The priest, too, seemed impressed with her genteel, assured manner. As the head of the largest church in the region, he was accustomed to acting in a high-handed, arrogant manner. But this woman demanded respect. A single sentence from her sufficed to shrink him back to normal size.

"I'll make all the necessary preparations," he mumbled. "Don't worry. When do you want the burial to be?"

They agreed it would be on the following Saturday. Finally, Simon asked the priest the question that got to the heart of his visit. "The Saint Lawrence Church . . ." he began. "Benedikta Koppmeyer, as sister of the deceased, would like to know more about the church he worked in for so many years. And about its past. Are there documents here in the basilica?"

Pastor Ziegler shook his head. "I'm sorry, there aren't. The church doesn't belong to Saint Michael's parish. You would have to inquire in Steingaden."

"Steingaden?" Simon asked with surprise.

The priest nodded. "The Saint Lawrence Church belongs to the Premonstratensian Diocese in Steingaden. So far as I know, the diocese purchased the church many years ago, and if the

Swedes didn't burn the relevant papers, then they would have to be there still."

"And who did the church belong to before that?" Simon asked, trying to sound as innocent as possible. "The parish of Saint Michael?"

The priest laughed. "I shall have to disappoint you once again. We really never had anything to do with the Saint Lawrence Church. No, if the rumors are correct, the church formerly belonged to the Knights of the Teutonic Order, the Templars. But that was very long ago. Why are you so interested in that?"

"My brother always loved his church," Benedikta said. Her smile could have melted the January ice outside. "I only wanted to know more about the place that had meant so much to him. Perhaps you'd learn something you could use for the funeral sermon."

"Oh, of course." Elias Ziegler nodded solicitously. "I'll see what I can do. Does anyone yet know why—"

"Please excuse us now," Benedikta mumbled. "I am still overwhelmed with grief and need to be left with my prayers."

The priest nodded respectfully and watched as the two left the vestry and disappeared outside. Then he turned back to sampling the wine. It was too bad he had to use such good wine for the Eucharist, only to transform it into the blood of Christ.

"We must go to Steingaden," Benedikta whispered as they hastened through the basilica. "Today, if possible."

"Do you want me to come along?" Simon asked, uncertain what to make of this plan.

"Naturally. I want to know why my brother had to die. Is that so difficult to understand?"

"No, no. But today?" In the meantime, they had left the church and were standing in front by the portal. Snow blew in their faces. Simon pointed up. "It's snowing again. It will be hard for us to make progress," he said with concern.

"Well, I have a horse that will get me there safely and comfortably, even through knee-deep snow," Benedikta said, then looked at him questioningly. "And you? As the town medicus, you must surely have a horse as well. You are the town physician, aren't you?"

"Ah, sure, sure, but . . ."

"Well, then that's that," Benedikta said before running down the steps. "Let's leave in two hours."

Simon looked at her perplexed, then shrugged and followed her.

"Do you always make such rash decisions?" he asked when he caught up with her.

"I wouldn't be a successful businessperson if I always weighed and debated everything," she said. "I'll leave that to the men when they get together for their night out at the pub."

Simon grinned. "I hope I never have to do business with you. You would probably palm three barrels of overpriced wine off on me in a blink of an eye." This was the first time Simon had heard her laugh, and he could feel how much he wanted to please this self-confident, worldly woman.

But now he needed a horse, and he had an idea where he could get hold of one.

Not far from St. Michael's Basilica, Magdalena was standing on a street corner watching as the two walked down the little road on their way back to Schongau. Only a few minutes before, slightly tipsy, the hangman's daughter had left the house of Balthasar Hemerle, and now she intended to pay a visit to the tavern keeper in Altenstadt to ask him about the strangers who were there the previous Sunday.

The sight of Simon together with the strange woman from the city hit her like a blow to the stomach. The two seemed to be having an animated conversation, and after a while Simon even placed his cloak over Benedikta's shoulders. Magdalena thought she could hear soft laughter in the distance. And as much as she tried, she was unable to dispel her suspicions.

The alcohol in her body added to that feeling, overwhelming her with a grim wave of hatred, jealousy, and sadness. Furious, she pulled her bodice tighter and trudged off in the direction of the tavern. Her father had suggested she make eyes at the workmen. He could depend on her doing just that.

"You want *what?*" The hangman took his pipe out of his mouth and gave Simon a look of disbelief. Simon had found the hangman in the stable next to his house, cleaning out fresh, still-steaming manure. At the hangman's side, the cow, Resl, watched the nervous young medicus with a dumb stare as he tried not to lose his balance while hopping through the clumps of manure and frozen puddles of urine on the ground. Simon was nervously clutching a felt hat with ostrich feathers and was wearing his best Sunday clothes—a wool coat he had hastily brushed off and, under it, petticoat breeches, a shirt with shiny cuffs, and a knee-length jacket of the finest French cloth. Now he was standing in front of the hangman, nervously repeating his question.

"Would it be possible for you to lend me your horse?" he mumbled. "Only until tomorrow."

Jakob Kuisl looked at him, thinking it over. Then he broke out in laughter. "My old Walli? That dumb critter? She'll eat your fine hat like celery and throw you before you even know what happened." He shook his head, grinning.

Simon glanced nervously at the skinny mare sullenly chomping on some hay at the rear of the stable. It was quite possible that the hangman was correct.

"And just where do you intend to go, all dressed up like that? To Venice, to the carnival?" Kuisl asked, examining Simon's clothing from top to bottom.

"I . . . I'm going to Steingaden, to the monastery. Maybe I'll learn something more there about the hidden crypt in the Saint Lawrence Church."

In halting words, he told the hangman of his visit to St. Michael's Basilica and what he had learned there. When he was finished, he casually added, "Benedikta Koppmeyer will accompany me, by the way. She wants to learn more about the death of her brother."

"Ah, I see." Jakob Kuisl nodded. He spat into the manure, then picked up the rake and started spreading fresh straw in the stable. "That explains the fancy costume. Go ahead, then, and as far as I'm concerned, you can take Walli. I need her only to drive condemned people up the hill to the gallows. And there aren't any hangings at the moment. But watch out. The beast is as stubborn as a mule—and mean!"

"I . . . know how to handle horses," Simon reassured himself. Now, in any case, it was too late to bow out. Benedikta was waiting for him in front of the Stern and he was already late. It had taken him longer than expected to get dressed. Simon was proud of the wardrobe he managed to maintain despite his pathetic salary. Often, the daughters of rich patricians would slip him some money or give him some fine cloth. In spite of his small stature, he was considered a man of the world in Schongau, even though Magdalena kept telling him that it didn't mean very much in a little Bavarian city.

"Well then, thank you very much!" he exclaimed, a bit too cheerily as he groped his way toward the back of the filthy stable, carefully trying not to soil his jacket.

Walli was waiting for him in her stall. The old, emaciated horse stared at him angrily, stoically chewing on some bits of straw. She appeared not to want to have anything to do with the two-legged creature in front of her. As Simon approached, the horse snorted briefly, reared up on her hind legs, and started drumming nervously against the wooden siding of her stall with her front hooves.

"The bridle is hanging in the corner," the hangman mumbled, without looking up. "I hope you can manage by yourself. I have to leave. Lechner wants to talk with me about something. Orders from higher up." He put the pitchfork away, brushed the dirt from his callused hands, and turned toward the door leading to the living room. "Probably one of the aldermen has complained to him again about my selling medications to people illegally. Damn fools!" Then he turned around again. "By the way, if Walli is bad and snaps at you, just pull her ears. Then she'll calm down for sure." Cursing under his breath, he stomped out of the stable and into the main room of the house.

Simon stared at the horse in front of him, and the horse stared back with little, evil eyes. The medicus gulped. Finally, he took the bridle from a hook and opened the door to the stall with soothing gestures and gentle words. Benedikta would just have to wait a bit.

Jakob was still cursing as he made his way up to town with clean hands and a fresh shirt. It always spelled trouble when he was summoned by the court clerk, Johann Lechner. Lechner was considered the big wheel and the secret man behind the scenes in Schongau. On the city council, four aldermen alternated as chair every quarter, but the court clerk was the official representative of the elector's caretaker in town. And since the caretaker, Count Sandizell, rarely came to town—to say nothing of the elector himself—Lechner could rule like a king without a throne. He was actually only responsible for the elector's interests but, through careful maneuvering, had always been able to meddle in the affairs of the town.

The hangman entered the town through the Lech Gate and turned right into the Hennengasse. Snowflakes were blowing in his face, making him squint. He stayed clear of the main streets, as he was not a welcome sight in town. The few people he passed in the driving snow looked away and made the sign of the cross, muttering. As executioner, Jakob Kuisl was not allowed to marry in the Christian church, would never receive a Christian burial, and his children would not be baptized. When he drank his beer in the dark taverns behind the Ballenhaus, he sat at a table by himself, ostracized. Nevertheless, people often came to him in secret to be treated for various ills or to obtain surefire magic amulets. Jakob Kuisl sighed. He had long ago given up trying to figure out human behavior.

Finally, the hangman stood before the ducal castle that directly bordered the western city wall. The building was in disrepair: One of the guard towers was missing a roof, and snow was falling directly onto the charred rafters. A bridge with rotting railings spanned a moat overgrown with weeds and led into the interior of the compound.

Just as Kuisl was about to cross the bridge, he heard a whinnying and hoofbeats. From the interior courtyard, a black steed emerged, heading right for the hangman at a fast gallop. The rider was dressed in a black habit and cowl that almost completely concealed his face. He seemed not to notice Jakob Kuisl and continued galloping directly toward him so that he could avoid a collision only by jumping aside at the last moment. A corner of the rider's coat brushed Kuisl's face, and just as the hangman's nose detected the fragrance of an expensive, exotic perfume, the figure disappeared around the next corner. The hangman cursed the unknown rider, then continued the few steps across the bridge to enter the building.

Jakob Kuisl arrived at the clerk's office on the second floor and was preparing to knock on the massive wooden door when he noticed that it wasn't closed, just slightly ajar. The door squeaked as it swung inward, and in front of him sat Johann Lechner, armed with a quill pen and ink, reviewing some papers by candlelight while his right hand moved vigorously and erratically across the parchment. For a while, the only thing audible was the scratching of the pen.

"You can take a seat, Kuisl," the clerk said finally, without looking up. His face was pale, almost waxen, an impression accentuated by his black goatee. He wore a flat, dark velvet cap and a plain jacket that was just as dark. When Lechner finally looked up, Kuisl found himself staring into two black eyes that seemed to be in constant motion and appeared remarkably large in relation to his narrow face behind his pince-nez.

"I said sit down," the clerk repeated, pointing to a stool in front of the stained oak table that took up practically the entire width of the room. "I have a job for you."

"Did you finally catch one of the bandits?" Jakob Kuisl grumbled, settling onto the stool. The wooden stool groaned under the weight of his massive frame but didn't give way.

"Well, not exactly," the clerk replied, playing with the goose quill in his hand. "That's the reason I called you." He leaned back in his chair. "As you may know, a group of citizens has been formed to hunt down this band of murderers, and I'd like you to lead them."

"Me?" Jakob Kuisl almost choked. "But—"

"I know, as a hangman, you are dishonorable and cannot give orders to citizens," the clerk interrupted him, "but they're afraid of you, and they have respect for you. Those are pretty good qualifications for a leader. Besides, you're the only one I would entrust with a job like this. Didn't you kill that huge wolf just last year? And the matter with the mercenaries in the spring . . . You are strong and clever, you can fight, and you know this riffraff better than people like us."

"Why don't you appoint one of the aldermen as a leader?" the hangman joked. "They know how to push people around."

Johann Lechner laughed. "You mean Semer? Or old Hardenberg? I might as well send my mother. Fat, effeminate moneybags! Even the Swedes wouldn't have accepted them as hostages. No, Kuisl, you're the one. You have proved often enough that you're good for more than just stringing people up. And as far as giving orders . . ." He grinned at the hangman. "Don't worry, I'll tell the gentlemen that the executioner is calling the shots this time. It will be good for them. Do you still have your weapon from the war? You were in the war, weren't you?"

Jakob Kuisl nodded. Images floated through his mind like poisonous clouds. *More than you can imagine,* he thought.

"Fine," said the clerk. "The hunt will begin the day after tomorrow at eight in the morning. I've got to let everyone know first. Please show up at the marketplace at the appointed time. You'll receive a half guilder each day, plus a guilder for each robber you catch." Lechner hunched down again over his documents. "You can go now."

Jakob Kuisl started to reply, but when he saw the intense expression on the clerk's face, he knew objections were pointless. As he turned to go, he suddenly heard Lechner's voice again behind him.

"Oh, hangman! One moment!" When Jakob turned around, he saw the clerk was staring at him directly through his pince-nez. "I've heard that the priest in Altenstadt passed away and that you yourself were there shortly thereafter. Did anything happen there that seemed . . . strange?"

The hangman cursed to himself. How had the clerk learned so quickly about the events in the St. Lawrence Church? Obviously, nothing escaped Lechner. Jakob Kuisl reflected for a moment and then decided to tell the truth.

"It looks like someone poisoned the priest."

"Poisoned?" The clerk frowned. "Hmm, that's not good news. But if I know you, you already have a suspicion about who it could have been."

Jakob Kuisl shook his head. "No, sir. I have no idea."

"That's all right. The people of Altenstadt need to figure that out themselves." He frowned again. "Do you think maybe the fat priest just overate again?"

"No, sir. I believe—"

"Believing is something you do in church," Lechner interrupted him. "I want you to concern yourself only with this band of murderers out there. *Exclusively,* do you understand? That's an order. The city needs your expertise and your strength, not in Altenstadt, but here in Schongau. Everything else can wait. Is that clear?"

Jakob Kuisl remained silent.

"I want to know if that's clear."

The hangman nodded and, without another word, disappeared into the dark hallway. Behind him, he could once again hear the scratching of the quill pen.

Furtively, the clerk carefully extracted a document from the pile of papers he had concealed just before the hangman entered, and glanced at it once more. The seal seemed genuine, and the man who had delivered the letter believable.

Lechner scratched the tip of his nose with the goose feather. It wouldn't be wise to refuse the request of such a powerful person, even if he couldn't figure out the meaning of this official document. Lechner actually wanted only to ask the hangman about the murder of Father Koppmeyer, but the stranger he'd just seen made it unmistakably clear that further investigation into the Koppmeyer case was not desired. To support his demand, he had left behind a tidy sum. Lechner toyed nervously with the coins in his desk drawer. They felt cool and solid. The money would come in handy for necessary repairs in the city, above all to the ducal palace, which was in a pitiful shape. And the stranger had held out the prospect of more money if the hangman kept his mouth shut . . .

Just the same, it troubled Lechner. Why would such a powerful person be interested in preventing the Schongau hangman from snooping around in Altenstadt? Well, Lechner would have to make his own inquiries, and in the meanwhile, he'd just have to keep the hangman busy doing something else. Lechner chuckled to himself. The idea that Jakob Kuisl would soon be bossing around the fat old aldermen was just too precious. That alone was worth the little lie.

Benedikta was waiting impatiently in the driving snow in front of the Goldener Stern Tavern, just next to the Ballenhaus. Her horse, a splendid sorrel, pranced around nervously. When the merchant woman caught sight of Simon, a narrow smile crossed her lips.

"Do you usually travel on foot rather than by horse, Doctor?" she asked.

In fact, Simon didn't make the best impression sitting on his nag. On the short trip from the Lech River up to town, the beast had almost thrown him twice. Putting on the bridle had been a struggle, and Walli had bitten his hand several times. Sweat was pouring down his brow, and his hat, with the coquettish ostrich feather, sat at a crooked angle on his head. He had even slipped once in the stable, and now a light yellow-brown spot adorned his jacket. Nevertheless, Simon tried to laugh.

"Walli is a horse with a mind of her own," he said as the horse attempted to rear up again and tugged at the reins. "And I have a special liking for stubborn women."

The merchant woman smiled. "That's commendable, but perhaps the horse needs to have a little woman-to-woman talk."

Benedikta dismounted and slowly approached the snorting horse. When she reached the horse, she held her by the head, pulled her mane down, and whispered in her ear. At once, the horse settled down, stopped snorting, and stood there calmly.

"How . . . how did you ever do that?" Simon asked incredulously.

"Just *un secret de femmes,* a secret between us women."

Benedikta smiled and swung up onto her horse again. "We have to leave," she said, "or we'll never get to Steingaden before nightfall. It's already noon."

They rode out through the Lech Gate in the direction of Peiting. The snow was heavier now, and Simon had to squint to see the road in front of them, orienting himself by the wagon tracks that were now almost covered again with snow. On the gently ascending road, they met the occasional hiker or team of oxen, but once they had passed the houses of Peiting, they were finally alone. Stillness prevailed as the snow dampened all sounds.

The few towns they went through seemed inhospitable. The windows and doors were closed, and only occasionally could they see light shining through a crack in the window or a shy child peering around the corner of a house. At regular intervals, the two riders passed small frozen ponds, where frightened ducks flapped up out of the reeds and disappeared into the winter sky.

Alongside him, Benedikta was humming a little French song.

Belle qui tiens ma vie, captive dans tes yeux . . .

Simon noticed how hearing her voice warmed the cockles of his heart. True, he understood only half the words, but the mere sound of the foreign tongue was enough to overwhelm him with wanderlust. Here in the Priests' Corner, everything was so . . . God-fearing. So rigid and sleepy. Nothing changed. In Paris, on the other hand, people knew how to live! He heard there were theaters and tailors on every street corner; that people smelled of perfume, lavender, and forget-me-nots; and the best doctors in all of Europe taught at the Sorbonne!

He was so lost in thought that he didn't see the highwaymen until they were almost standing in front of them.

Three figures stood waiting at the side of the road in the heavily falling snow. Two of them were leaning on long, rough-hewn clubs, and the third had a dagger dangling at his hip. Now Simon noticed a fourth man. He was crouching in a thicket, his musket supported casually on the branch of a tree and pointed at them. All four of them looked famished. Their faces were drawn, and little icicles hung from their shaggy beards. They were dressed in threadbare jackets and soiled army coats, and the boots on their feet were nothing but shreds.

"Well, well, what do we have here?" asked the man holding the dagger, with a salacious grin. He was evidently the leader. "A pretty woman and her beau traveling all alone, and both dressed so elegantly!" He made a low bow, and the others broke out in raucous laughter. By now Simon was cursing his dandyish attire. Here in the forest, he probably looked like a pheasant searching for a mate.

"How about a little charity for a few poor sinners who had a hard time in the war and can't afford such finery?" the leader said. Still bowing, he held one hand out as he fingered the dagger with his other.

Simon could see one of the robbers at the side of the road looking Benedikta up and down and running his tongue over his lips, while the man with the musket examined Simon's expensive coat. His eyes reminded the medicus of a wild beast's, expressionless and lustful, lacking even a spark of humanity. Simon opened his mouth to defend the woman at his side—if not with a weapon, then with words—but all that came out was a hoarse squawk. He knew that these men would rob them and slaughter them like animals, but first, one after the other, they would attack and violate Benedikta. He reached into his coat pocket for the sharp stiletto he always carried with him, along with some medical paraphernalia, but what good would a knife be against four armed robbers? To make matters worse, Walli began prancing around nervously, and he wouldn't be able to restrain the old mare much longer.

"Get out of my way, or I'll slit you open from your belly right up to your throat, *espèce de pourriture!* You piece of garbage!"

Simon thought at first that he had heard wrong, but it was,

in fact, Benedikta who had spoken. Coolly, she eyed the leader of the gang of robbers in front of her, hands resting calmly on the pommel of her saddle, watching and waiting.

The robbers were just as astonished at her audacity. The head of the gang opened his mouth wide, but a moment passed before he could say anything. "You arrogant little bitch," he grumbled finally. "You'll be whimpering when I'm through with you. And then my comrades will get their turn, and this little peacock can sit there and watch."

"For the last time, I'll tell you to step aside." Benedikta's voice remained cool. Her horse snorted, and a cloud of steam emerged from its nostrils.

"That's enough, you damned whore." The robber chief reached out to seize the reins of her horse. "I'll show you what—"

The shot resounded like the crack of a whip through the snowy forest. For a moment, the robber could only stand there, mouth open, looking at the hole in his chest. The bullet had shredded the coat, the jacket, and the flesh beneath it, and a thin jet of blood spurted out. With a gurgling sound in his throat, the dying man tipped backward.

Simon looked around frantically to see where the shot had come from, and only then did he notice the smoking pistol in Benedikta's hand. She must have pulled it out from under her coat in a fraction of a second. And it was loaded!

In the next instant, a number of things happened simultaneously. Spurring her horse on, Benedikta sped down the road, Simon heard a shot and felt something cold whistle past his left cheek, the two robbers ran toward him swinging their cudgels and screaming, and Walli, terrified by the uproar, whinnied and rose up on her hind legs.

"Benedikta!" Simon shouted, struggling to stay in the saddle. "Wait for me!"

He managed to hold on as the horse bolted, branches lacerating his face, and he felt a heavy blow on his thigh where one of the robbers must have hit him with a cudgel. A sinewy, grimy hand reached for his horse's reins, and instinctively, Simon pulled out his stiletto and plunged it into the hand. He heard screaming, the hand disappeared, and Walli galloped off.

Only now did the medicus dare to sit up a bit in the saddle and look around. The road had disappeared, and Walli was galloping, as if possessed, deeper and deeper into the forest. Pine branches struck Simon in the face. He struggled to turn around, hoping to at least see behind him, but he couldn't find a road, not even a path, and it seemed as if Benedikta had vanished from the face of the earth! He was alone in the forest on a horse that seemed headed straight for hell. For a moment, he looked down and considered jumping, but when he saw the ground rushing past, he just clung tighter to his horse. Where was Benedikta? Again, he looked around frantically. The pine trees behind him seem to get thicker and thicker. He noticed that he had lost his expensive hat. It had cost two guilders! But then it occurred to him that, perhaps, in the future, he wouldn't need a hat anyway because his head would be gone . . .

As he was about to turn around again, he heard a soft hiss; then something hit him in the side of the head.

The world turned black, and Simon could feel himself falling into the snow. It felt strangely warm, *like a bed of feathers,* he thought. Hands seemed to reach out for him, but then he was swallowed up in a dark, billowing cloud.

4

MAGDALENA STOMPED TOWARD THE DOOR TO Strasser's Tavern. She could still feel the effects of the strong mulled wine at the carpenter's house, but she would need a lot more alcohol to forget seeing Simon and Benedikta together. How could he do something like that to her? A slut from the city! But perhaps she was being unfair to Benedikta; perhaps they had just happened to meet in the basilica and had been heading back to Schongau together and nothing more. But why, then, did Simon place his coat over her shoulders? And the way he laughed . . .

She opened the door to the tavern and was met by a warm, sticky mass of air. A fiddle was playing and someone was marking time to it with his foot. More than a dozen workmen had already gathered for lunch in the gloomy, low-ceilinged room lit by only a few torches. Some of the masons she had queried just the day before were among them. They looked at Magdalena suspiciously, then returned to their mugs of beer. A young fellow was sitting at a wobbly table in the middle of the room playing a fiddle while a few bystanders stood around clapping and dancing.

The hangman's daughter smiled. The men had probably already had more to drink than they should have. Work slowed down in the wintertime, and the workers struggled to get by with part-time jobs, squandering their meager earnings on booze and waiting for the arrival of spring. When the merry group of men saw that a woman had entered the tavern, they raised their glasses to her and made a few smutty remarks.

"Girl, come over here! I'll buy you a beer if I can have a look at your tender breasts!"

A short, stooped carpenter's journeyman sidled over to her, bowed deeply, and tried to take her by the arm.

"Come dance, hangman's girl. Make my back straight and my rod bigger with your black magic!"

Magdalena broke free from him, laughing. "I can't do any magic when there's nothing to charm. Bug off!"

She sat down at a table in an alcove off to the side. For a while, the men kept leering at her; then they started drinking again and swaying to the beat of the music. It was not customary for women to go to a tavern alone, but as a hangman's daughter, Magdalena was no ordinary middle-class woman; she was dishonorable, an untouchable. *More like a cross between a woman and a thing,* she told herself angrily, before her thoughts turned back to Simon and Benedikta again. What was the medicus doing with someone like that? Benedikta, however, was a refined lady . . .

She had almost forgotten why she was here when suddenly the tavern keeper appeared in front of her holding a foaming mug of beer.

"This is from an anonymous admirer," he said with a grin, setting the mug down hard on the table. "If I understand him right, he won't just stop at this one round."

For a moment, Magdalena considered turning down the beer. The alcohol she drank earlier was still pulsing through her veins, and her pride wouldn't allow a stranger to treat her to a beer, anyway. But then thirst won out, and she reached across the table and sipped from the mug. It tasted delicious and fresh. She wiped the foam from her lips and turned to the tavern keeper.

"Hemerle told me that, on Sunday, there were three strangers here wearing black cowls. Is that right?"

The tavern keeper nodded. "They must have been monks from somewhere, but not ordinary ones. They arrived on handsome black horses, the kind you rarely see around here, and tied them up outside the tavern. I could see right away that they were rich, educated people."

"Was there anything else special about them?" Magdalena asked.

Strasser knit his brow. "There was something strange. When I brought their beer, they suddenly all fell silent. But I heard a bit of their conversation anyway, and I think they were speaking in Latin the entire time."

Magdalena looked at him wide-eyed. "Latin?"

"Yes, just like our priest in the church," replied Strasser, making the sign of a cross. "God rest his soul. Not that I understood anything, but it sounded like Latin, I swear by the Virgin Mary."

"Were you able to understand anything at all?"

Strasser stopped to think. "Yes, one phrase, and it came up again and again—*crux Christi . . ."* His face brightened. "Yes, *crux Christi!* That's what they said!"

"*Crux Christi* means the cross of Christ," Magdalena murmured, more to herself. "Not exactly unusual if they were monks. Anything else?"

Strasser turned to leave. "What do I know? Why don't you just ask them yourself? One of them is standing back there at the bar, and he was just inquiring about your father."

Magdalena jumped up from the table. "And you're only telling me that now?"

Franz Strasser raised his hand apologetically. "He only wanted to know who the big man here in town was who smokes that stinking weed." He grinned. "No doubt he wanted to buy some from Kuisl. I also told him about you."

"About me?" The hangman's daughter almost choked on her beer.

"Well, because you do sell herbs, don't you? And perhaps this tobacco, or whatever it's called. Come along," he said, leading the way. "He seems to have a bit of money to spend. You can see he's a fine gentleman."

Magdalena jumped up and followed the tavern keeper through the bar, which was becoming more and more crowded. She looked around in hopes of picking the stranger out from the many people from Altenstadt who were there, but when they got to the bar, they found only familiar faces there. A mason tried to grope her, she gave him a smack in the face, and he walked away, moaning.

"Strange," Strasser mumbled. "He was here just a moment ago." He stepped behind the bar. "I'm sure he just went to the place that even the Pope has to go to. Just wait a bit."

Magdalena returned to her seat and sipped absentmindedly on her beer. Three men in black cowls conversing in Latin . . . The strangers were surely traveling monks, but why, then, the expensive black horses? And why had one of them inquired about her father?

She took another big gulp. The beer was delicious, perhaps somewhat bitter, but it stimulated the senses. Her head felt light, and thoughts came and went before she could get a grip on them. The music and laughter of the men sitting at the bar blurred into a single pulsing hum. Could that be the effect of the alcohol? She really hadn't had that much to drink . . . It didn't matter; she felt free, and a smile spread across her face. She tapped her feet in rhythm with the fiddle and continued drinking her beer.

• • •

The man in the black cowl stood outside and watched her through a small crack in the shutters. He'd have to wait until the henbane began to have an effect. Sooner or later, this woman would have to come out, and she would surely need help then. Who could harbor any suspicions at the sight of a gentleman offering to escort a drunken girl home? What was the name of the girl, again?

Magdalena.

His whole body began to tremble, and he couldn't figure out why.

Jakob Kuisl loved peace and quiet, and nothing was as peaceful as a winter evening after it had snowed all day. It felt as if the snow had swallowed up every sound, leaving emptiness that overcame any thoughts, worries, strivings—leaving only space for quiet meditation. Sometimes Jakob Kuisl wished that eternal winter would come over the world and finally put an end to all its chatter and gossip.

He walked along the snowy road toward Altenstadt. In the distance, he could hear the bells of the basilica sounding. He was looking for his daughter. She had been missing since early that morning, and now it was almost after noon. Magdalena had promised to help her mother mend some old clothes and linens, and Anna Maria Kuisl kept going to the door all morning, looking for her daughter. Her grumbles and complaints gradually turned to anxious silence, and when the hangman finally confessed that he had sent Magdalena to Altenstadt to make some inquiries for him, she threw him out of the house. The words she shouted after him were unmistakable: He couldn't set foot in the house again unless he came back with Magdalena.

The hangman loved his wife, he respected her, and some people even said he feared her, which was nonsense, of course, because a hangman fears nothing and no one, least of all his wife. But Jakob Kuisl had learned that talking back was pointless and meant only the end of the peace and quiet he longed for so much in his house. And so he left to look for Magdalena.

In Altenstadt, he could hear music coming from the only tavern in town. The windows of Strasser's Tavern cast a warm glow, and laughter, the stamping of feet, and the sound of an out-of-tune fiddle could be heard. Jakob Kuisl approached, peeking inside through a slit in one of the windows.

What he saw made his blood run cold.

On a table in the middle of the room, a few young men were dancing and singing a crude peasant song in raucous voices. A circle of onlookers gathered around with glasses raised, laughing and cheering them on. Among the young men on the table, a girl was dancing and stretching her arms up in a suggestive pose. Then she tilted her head far back while one of the men poured beer into her mouth from a huge beer stein.

It was Magdalena.

Her eyes were rolling wildly while one fellow reached out lustily toward her skirt and another pulled on the strings of her bodice.

Jakob Kuisl kicked the door and it swung inward with a loud bang. Then he stormed in and headed for the group. He grabbed one of the young men, yanked him off the table, and flung him in the direction of the onlookers, where he landed headfirst against a stool that splintered on impact. A second fellow hit the hangman hard over the head with his mug of beer. That was a serious mistake, as he found out only too soon. Kuisl grabbed him by the arm, pulled him down off the table, slapped him hard, and tossed him backward into two other men, all of whom landed in a tangle of arms and legs on the floor. The mug shattered, and a pool of beer spread across the floor at the feet of the astonished spectators.

Jakob Kuisl picked up his daughter like a sack of flour and threw her over his shoulder. She fought back and screamed as if she had lost her mind, but his grip was as solid as a vise.

"Would anyone else like a good thrashing?" he growled, looking around expectantly. The young men rubbed their aching heads and glanced at one another nervously.

"If anyone touches my daughter again, I'll break every bone in their body. Do you hear?" he said softly, but firmly now. "She may be a hangman's girl, but she's off-limits."

"But she said herself she wanted to dance," one of the carpenter's journeymen said sheepishly. "She probably had a little too much to drink . . ."

One look from the hangman silenced him. Then Kuisl tossed a few coins at the tavern owner, who had retreated against a wall, along with a few respectful others.

"Here you are, Strasser. For the mug and a new stool. If there's anything left, treat the boys to a few beers. Now, goodbye."

The door slammed behind him. What remained was a group of young men who felt as if they were awakening from a dream. After Jakob Kuisl had disappeared around the corner with Magdalena, the men started to whisper to one another, and then general laughter broke out.

"Are you crazy, Father?" Magdalena shouted. By now the two had arrived at the main street. She was still draped over her father's shoulder like a sack. She spoke with a slight slur. "Stop . . . Put me down at once!"

The hangman flung his daughter in a wide arc into a snowdrift. Then he came plodding after her and rubbed snow in her face until it glowed bright red. Finally, he took out a vial and poured a bitter liquid down her throat until she started to spit and cough.

"For God's sake, what is that?" she groaned, wiping her mouth. She was still dazed, but she could at least think somewhat clearly again.

"Ephedra, enzian, and a broth made from those brown beans Simon has," her father grumbled. "Actually, I wanted to take the tonic to Hans Kohlberger because his wife is always so tired and just sits around staring out the window. But it will do for you, too."

Magdalena shuddered. "It tastes horrible, but it helps."

She made a face at first, but then suddenly turned serious. What was the matter with her? She could just barely remember sitting down at the table and drinking a beer. She had felt more and more lightheaded. Then she joined the workers dancing, but at this point, her memory blurred. Was it possible that someone poured something into her beer? Or had she just had too much to drink? She didn't want to worry her father, so she remained silent and just put up with his lecture, which was now reaching its climax.

"It was disgraceful, shameless, the way you behaved in there, you hussy! What are people to think? You . . . you . . ." He took a deep breath, trying to calm down a bit.

"Oh, people . . ." she muttered. "Let the people talk. I'm just the hangman's daughter; they'll talk about me, anyway."

"And Simon?" he growled. "What do you think Simon will have to say about that?"

"Oh, you can just stop with Simon!" she replied, turning her head aside.

The hangman grinned. "Aha, I see that's what this is all about. Well, you won't get your Simon back acting like that."

He didn't want to tell her he had lent his horse to Simon for the trip to Steingaden with Benedikta, so he switched the topic. "Did you learn anything about the church?"

Magdalena nodded and told him what she had heard from Balthasar Hemerle and the tavern keeper Strasser.

The hangman seemed to mull this over. "I think I have seen one of those monks already . . ."

"Where?" Magdalena asked, curious.

Her father turned away suddenly and started marching off

in the direction of Schongau. "What does it matter?" he grumbled. "What does it matter to us who killed Koppmeyer? Your mother was right when she said that's no business of ours. Let's go home and eat."

Magdalena ran after him and seized him by the shoulders.

"No, you don't!" she shouted. "I want to know what happened there. Koppmeyer was poisoned! There's a dusty old grave in the crypt and some strangers prowling around the area, speaking in Latin or some other secret language. What does it all mean? You can't just go home and put your feet up by the fire."

"Oh yes I can," Jakob Kuisl said, marching forward.

Suddenly, Magdalena's voice became soft and cold. "And suppose they pick up some innocent man for Koppmeyer's murder and throw him in the dungeon? Just like they did back then with Stechlin?" Magdalena knew this was a sore spot for her father. "It was really poison that killed the priest, wasn't it?" she added. "So it's quite possible they'll have you torture someone, just like the midwife the last time, only because she knew something about poison. Is that what you want?"

The hangman stopped in his tracks. For a while, the only sound that could be heard was the cawing of a crow.

"Very well," he said finally. "We'll have another look around the Saint Lawrence Church. Right away. Only so you'll be able to sleep soundly again."

The stranger watched the two as they walked down the main street toward the St. Lawrence Church. He struggled to calm himself by reciting the Lord's Prayer. His plan had failed. He was dying to pry information out of the hangman's girl about what her father had found in the crypt.

Magdalena . . .

A distant memory flashed through his mind, then vanished.

He shook his head. He would have to talk again with this

clerk. After all, he had paid good money to make sure the hangman stayed out of their way. It certainly appeared now that this stinking butcher from Schongau could do as he pleased.

Under his black coat and white tunic, the man fingered a golden cross that hung directly over his heart. He would need strength. His brotherhood had never approved of the common folk learning to read—you could see what that led to. The people became rebellious and didn't do what they were supposed to. He had learned in the tavern that the hangman, despite his origins, was smart and educated, and that made him dangerous. More dangerous, in any case, than that nosey little doctor's assistant who kept running after his master like a little poodle.

The stranger kissed the cross and put it back under his tunic. He had made a decision: He couldn't rely on the clerk; he would have to act himself. They would get rid of the hangman at once. The danger that he would meddle in their affairs was too great. Now the man would have to tell the others.

The sound of his steps was muffled by the soft, powdery snow.

The hangman and his daughter walked toward the St. Lawrence Church, its wind-battered tower almost obscured by rising clouds of fog in the gathering darkness. Though there was no wind, it was bitter cold. Magdalena could see light from torches inside the rectory through slits in the shutters. The housekeeper and the sexton were evidently still awake. Jakob Kuisl headed directly toward the church while Magdalena tugged nervously at his arm.

"Look over there," she whispered, pointing at the church.

The door to the church was chained shut, but for a moment the light from a torch appeared in the windows. It was just a brief flicker, but Kuisl had seen it clearly.

"What in God's name . . . ?" he grumbled. He walked around

the church, Magdalena at his heels. They discovered fresh footprints leading from the cemetery gate toward the apse.

The hangman stooped to examine the footprints. "There are two of them," he whispered. "Solid shoes, good boots. They're not workers or farmers from around here." His eyes followed the footprints, which led to a shaky scaffold the workmen had constructed back in autumn and, high above, to a church window that had been forced open.

"We need to go and get help," Magdalena said anxiously.

Her father laughed softly to himself. "Who shall we ask? Magda? The skinny sexton?" He walked over to the scaffolding. "I'll have to deal with it myself," he said, turning around once again to look at Magdalena.

"You stay here, do you understand? No matter what happens. If I'm still inside when the bells toll again, you can go and get help if you want. But not before."

"Shouldn't I come along with you?"

"Nothing doing. You're no help to me. Go and hide behind the gravestones and wait for me to come back."

That said, he began to climb the bars of the scaffolding. It creaked and swayed, but it held. In a short while, the hangman reached the second platform and was working his way across the icy boards to the window that had been forced open. Then he slipped inside.

Though darkness was just beginning to fall outside, it was already pitch black in the church. Jakob Kuisl squinted; it took a while for his eyes to get accustomed to the dark. He could feel the smooth, freshly planed flooring of the balcony beneath his feet and hear hammering and whispering voices from somewhere below. Finally, he could vaguely make out the flooring and walls of the church. Just one look showed that the mason, Peter Baumgartner, had spoken the truth—up here in the balcony, the wall was emblazoned with the red *cross pattées* of the

Templars. The crosses had recently been painted over, but in a few places someone had taken the trouble to wipe off the white lime wash.

As if he wanted to check to see what was behind it, the hangman thought.

Looking down from the balcony, he could see that the stone slab had been pushed aside again, even though he had replaced it the last time he was there.

He reached under his coat for the heavy, larch-wood cudgel that he always carried with him. He had avoided using it in the tavern, knowing that one blow from this weapon could smash the skull of any opponent like a walnut. Now he took it out and weighed the warm wood in his hand. He would need it today —that much was sure.

His feet groped for the flight of steps that led down from the portal. As silent as a cat, he slipped down and scurried over to the hole in the floor. He could hear voices below, echoing strangely —the intruders were no doubt in the back part of the crypt, where the sarcophagus stood.

The hangman paused for a closer look at the heavy stone slab, which lay on the floor off to one side. Whoever was down below must have just arrived; after all, he and Magdalena had just a few moments ago seen the light of torches in the church.

The hangman looked around again in the darkness, then climbed slowly down the stone steps until he reached the storeroom.

The oaken table along the opposite wall had been moved aside, and through the low entryway behind it, he could see the flickering light of a lantern and hear the voices clearly now.

"Damn! There has to be some hint here—something!" one of them hissed. His voice sounded strangely hoarse, as if the man had difficulty speaking. "This is the right grave, so he hid it here somewhere."

A second, darker voice replied with a Swabian accent. "There's nothing here, by God, nothing but bones, dust, and this marble slab with the inscription." His voice fell to a low whisper. "I swear, I hope God does not punish us for disturbing the rest of the dead."

"Don't waste your time thinking about that . . . Think instead about solving this blasted riddle. That's the only reason the Master summoned you to help us here. Don't forget that, you fat, mollycoddled old bastard! If it had been up to me, you'd still be dusting off books in some cellar. So stop your whining and keep looking! *Deus lo vult!* God wills it!"

Not until that moment did Jakob Kuisl notice an unusual accent in the first stranger's hoarse voice. He had to be a foreigner.

"All right, then, let's have another look around the next room," the anxious Swabian voice said. "Maybe I overlooked something in one of the boxes. The heretic could have hidden it there among all the rubbish."

By the sound of the voices, Jakob Kuisl could tell that the figures were heading now toward the exit. He stepped back against the wall right next to the doorway. As the steps came nearer, a warm circle of light slowly moved in his direction. A sinewy hand, then the sleeve of a black cowl, emerged with an iron oil lamp.

Jakob Kuisl reacted fast. He brought the cudgel down hard on the hand so that the lantern fell to the ground and went out. The monk carrying the lantern barely had time to shout because Kuisl yanked him forward and struck him directly on the back of the head with his cudgel. Groaning, the fat man sank to the ground. For a moment, it was quiet; then the hoarse voice spoke up again from the other room.

"Brother Avenarius? What is the problem? Are you . . ."

The voice broke off, and all that could be heard was a soft rustling sound.

"Your Brother Avenarius is not feeling very well," Kuisl called back into the silence. "But still, he's better off than Koppmeyer. You killed him, didn't you?"

He waited for a reaction, but when no sound came from the other side, he spoke again.

"I don't like it when people are poisoned in my district. There's only one person here allowed to kill other people, and that's me."

"And who are you that you think this is any business of yours?" the voice with the foreign accent hissed back at him from the other side.

"I'm the hangman," Kuisl replied. "And you know what fate is reserved here for people who poison others. The wheel. But first I'll string you up and probably cut you up, too."

There was hoarse laughter in the other room.

"And how does the hangman die? Well, no matter, you'll find out soon enough."

Jakob Kuisl growled. He had had enough of this idle banter. The man on the ground next to him groaned—apparently the blow hadn't been hard enough and he would come to soon enough. Just as the hangman was preparing to strike him again, he felt a draft of air. A shadow sprang out of the doorway and swung at him from the side. Kuisl jumped back and felt a curved blade slice into his left forearm. He took a swing with the cudgel again, but the heavy larch-wood club whizzed past his opponent's head, just missing him. Kuisl picked up his foot and kicked the man hard right between the legs. He was happy to hear the man groan in pain and step back. In the darkness, Kuisl could see nothing but a black outline. The man in front of him seemed to be wearing a monk's cowl and gripping a curved dagger like the ones Kuisl had seen before carried by Muslim warriors. But there wasn't any time to look at him more closely, as he was preparing to attack again and this time lunged toward the hangman's chest. Kuisl stepped back and drove off his opponent with his cudgel. When he took another step forward, he stumbled over something soft and large—the fat Swabian he had put down earlier, still lying on the ground in front of him.

He was about to fend his opponent off with a few more blows when he heard a soft scraping sound behind him. In the next moment, a thin rope came down around his neck.

But weren't there only two of them?

Kuisl put his hands up to his neck, but the leather cord was already cutting deep into his skin. He gasped for air like a fish out of water, and everything turned black. In a desperate move, he threw his whole weight backward and could feel how he hit against something—the wall! He planted both feet firmly on the ground and tried to crush the man behind him between his broad back and the wall. Finally, the pressure on his neck decreased and air started streaming into his lungs again. He gasped and coughed, then with a loud roar, wheeled around, ready for the next blow. His left hand clawed at a piece of soft, velvety material and then tore it to pieces. With his right hand, he searched for the cudgel he had lost earlier. Then he crouched down, looking frantically around the dark room.

Everything became indistinct, and individual shadows blurred into others—a single, huge form.

Suddenly, he felt a numbness pulsating from his injured left arm into every corner of his body. He tried to move his fingers, but he couldn't. He was paralyzed.

The curved dagger was poisoned!

As he slid down the wall of the crypt behind him, he noticed a strong perfume that reminded him of violets, or a large, colorful field of flowers. Wide-eyed, but unable to move even his little finger, he could only watch as three men in black cowls bent over him, whispering.

The third man . . . must have followed me . . . Where is Magdalena?

Jakob Kuisl felt the two strangers pick him up and carry him away.

When Simon awoke, he was lying in a bed covered with fresh sheets and staring at a ceiling made of freshly planed spruce. From somewhere outside, he could hear the muffled sound of construction: hammering, sawing, men calling back and forth to one another. Where in the world was he?

He sat up and felt a sharp, stabbing pain in his head. Reaching for his forehead, he could feel a fresh bandage, and the memory came back to him. He had been attacked by robbers! Benedikta had . . . Yes, that's right, Benedikta had shot them; then he remembered the wild ride through the forest and how, finally, everything went black. He must have struck the branch of a tree. Strong arms had helped him back up on his horse, and he remembered the voices, but then everything went black again.

Thirsty, Simon looked around and spotted a knee-high nightstand on one side of the bed with a clay pitcher on top. Not only the wooden ceiling, but also the night table seemed freshly constructed, as did the wide bed. There was a fragrance of resin and fresh-cut wood in the air. A small stove was crackling in a corner, but otherwise the room was empty. The shutters were closed, but judging by a narrow, bright ray of light entering the room, it had to be daytime.

Simon reached for the pitcher and tested the contents: something bitter and aromatic, a bit like mint—apparently a medicine that someone had put out for him. He was drinking in deep gulps when a creaking sound announced a visitor. In the doorframe stood Benedikta, smiling.

"Well, have you had a good sleep?" She pointed to his bandage. "We didn't have a doctor here to do that, but I think the canons here know how to sew things up with needle and thread."

"The canons?" Simon looked at her, bewildered.

Benedikta nodded. "The Premonstratensian canons. We're at the monastery in Steingaden. As we were fleeing from the robbers, you hit your head against a tree. I put you on the horse and brought you here—it was only a few miles."

"But the men . . . the voices . . ." Simon could feel the stabbing pain in his head getting worse. Benedikta looked down at him sympathetically, and he felt how he was starting to blush. He must be a pathetic sight: pale, bandaged up, and dressed only in a dirty linen shirt.

"What voices?" she asked.

"When I was unconscious . . . Who helped me back on the horse?"

Benedikta laughed. "It was me! But if it makes you feel any better, it was the monks who undressed you later."

Simon smiled. "If it had been you, I would surely have remembered."

She raised her eyebrows in feigned indignation and turned to leave. "Before we cross the boundaries of decency, it would probably be better if we stop and think about why we are actually here," she said. "The abbot is waiting to see us, but naturally, only if your injury permits," she added with a slightly derisive smile. "I'll wait outside for you."

The door closed, but Simon lay still a moment to collect his thoughts. This woman . . . confused him. When he finally got up and dressed, the headache was still bothering him, but after checking the bandage with his hands, he could see that the monks had done their work well. He could feel a neat suture; eventually a little scar above the hairline would be all that remained.

The medicus carefully opened the door and was at once blinded by the dazzling winter light. The sky was blue, the sun was shining, and the snow sparkled and glittered in such bright light that it took a while for his eyes to adjust. Then he looked out at the largest construction site he had ever seen.

Before him lay the Steingaden Monastery—or rather, what was being rebuilt in new splendor after the attack by the Swedes. Simon had heard that the current abbot, Augustin Bonenmayr, had ambitious plans, but only now could he see with his own eyes just how ambitious they were. Tall newly built structures stood all around. Many of the buildings sported new roof timbers, most were still covered with scaffolding, and white-robed monks and numerous workers scurried back and forth with trowels and wheelbarrows full of mortar. On Simon's left, three men were calling loudly back and forth to one another as they tugged on a pulley, and somewhat farther away, an oxcart approached on a newly paved road, bringing freshly cut boards. The air smelled of resin and mortar.

Seeing Simon's astonishment, Benedikta explained what was going on. "One of the foremen showed me around a bit. In the area where we were sleeping, they are building a new tavern, and right next to it will be the Latin school . . ." She pointed to a small building on the other side of the park. "There's even a plan to build a theater here." She walked ahead as she continued speaking. "I had a talk with the prior this morning. Abbot Bonenmayr plans to make the monastery the most beautiful in the entire region—at least as beautiful as the one in Rottenbuch, he says. He's over there in the abbey and will receive us at noon."

All that Simon could do was nod and jog along behind her. Benedikta had taken charge of everything as a matter of course, and Simon could see now why her brother would seek her advice. Behind her refined facade, Benedikta had an extremely direct way about her. He thought about the pistol and the shots she had fired the previous afternoon.

They met the abbot in the cloister between the abbey and the church. Augustin Bonenmayr was a gaunt man with a narrow face. On his nose he wore a pince-nez rimmed in brass, which he was using at the moment to study frescoes in a passageway leading from the chapel. In one arm he was carrying a bundle of parchments, and on his belt dangled a gigantic bundle of keys, along with a plumb line and a carpenter's square. He looked more like a master builder than the leader of a great monastery.

When he heard the footsteps of the newcomers, he turned around to greet Simon and Benedikta.

"Ah, the young lady with the question! I have been informed of your arrival," he said, removing the pince-nez. His deep voice resounded through the cloister. "And you must be young Fronwieser." The abbot approached the medicus with a warm smile and extended his hand. Like all members of the Premonstratensian Order, he wore a white tunic, and a purple sash around his waist identified him as the abbot of the monastery. Simon knelt down and kissed a golden signet ring decorated with a cross.

"If you will permit me to say it," Simon mumbled, still kneeling, "I have never seen such a magnificent monastery."

Augustin Bonenmayr laughed and helped him to his feet. "Indeed, we shall rebuild everything—the mill, the brewery, a school, and of course, an abbey. We intend this to be a place of pilgrimage for the many who seek the closeness of God."

"I am certain that Steingaden will be a showpiece in the Priests' Corner," Benedikta said.

The abbot smiled. "People again feel the need for places worthy of a pilgrimage, places where we can feel just how great God really is." He stepped out of the chapel into the cloister. "But you have not come to talk about pilgrimages, have you? I have heard that you are here on a far sadder mission."

Simon nodded, then briefly stated the purpose of their visit. "Perhaps the reason for the priest's death has something to do with the history of the Saint Lawrence Church."

The abbot frowned and turned to Benedikta. "Do you really think your brother was poisoned because of some dark secret having to do with his church? Isn't that a bit far-fetched?"

Before Benedikta could answer, Simon interrupted. "Your Excellency," he said matter-of-factly, "it is said that the Saint

Lawrence Church is the property of your church. Are there any building plans? Or does someone know at least who the former owner was?"

Augustin Bonenmayr rubbed the bridge of his nose where the pince-nez had rested. "The monastery owns so many properties that I really don't know about each individual one, but perhaps we can find something in our archives. Follow me."

They walked along the cloister wall toward the abbey. On the second floor, they came to an unmarked, low door with two huge locks. As soon as the abbot opened them, Simon was confronted with the musty odor of old parchment. The room was at least twelve feet high. Individual shelves were recessed into niches and filled to the ceiling with books, folios, and rolls of parchment bearing the seal of the monastery. The room itself was covered with cobwebs, and a thin layer of dust had settled on a finely polished walnut table in the middle.

"Our centuries-old monastery library," Bonenmayr said. "A miracle that it has survived and not fallen victim to fire. As you can see, we are rarely here these days, but the order is still the same. Wait . . ."

Taking a ladder from a corner, he climbed to the top of the next-to-last shelf.

"Lawrence Church, Lawrence Church . . ." he muttered to himself, looking around at the individual shelves. Finally, he called out in surprise. "Well, good heavens, here it is right in front of me." He came down with a tattered roll of parchment with bits of red sealing wax still clinging to it.

Simon looked at the broken seal in surprise. "The roll has evidently been opened already," the medicus said, passing his finger over the edges of the parchment, "and not too long ago. The wax is still shiny where the pieces broke off."

Augustin Bonenmayr examined the brittle parchment thoughtfully. "Indeed," he mumbled. "It is strange. After all, the roll is several hundred years old. Oh well, but . . ." He walked over to the table and unrolled the parchment. "But perhaps it was just recently copied because of the bad condition it's in. Let's have a look."

Each standing to one side of the abbot, Benedikta and Simon stared at a document that was beginning to crumble at the edges. The writing was faded, but still legible.

"Here it is." Bonenmayr pointed with his right index finger at a passage in the middle. "The monastery of Steingaden purchased the following properties in the year of our Lord 1289: two properties in Warenberg, two in Brugg, one in Dietlried, three in Edenhofen, one in Altenstadt, and . . . Indeed, that's the Saint Lawrence Church in Altenstadt!" Bonenmayr whistled appreciatively. "Really a big transaction. It cost us two hundred and twenty-five denarii. That must have been a tidy sum back then."

"And who was the seller?" Simon persisted.

The abbot's finger moved up to the top of the parchment. "A certain Friedrich Wildgraf."

"What was he?" Simon asked. "A merchant? A patrician? Please tell us."

The abbot shook his head.

"If what I see here is correct, Friedrich Wildgraf was no less a person than the provincial master of the Order of the Knights Templar in the German Empire, an extremely powerful man at the time."

Bonenmayr raised his eyes and looked into Simon's petrified face.

"What is the matter?" he asked anxiously. "Are you not well? Perhaps I should explain to you first who the Templars were."

"That won't be necessary," Simon said. "We know about them."

Just half an hour later they left the monastery. From a safe hiding place, a figure watched as they disappeared with their horses into the trees. Turning away, the man fingered a rosary in his sweaty hands once again, one pearl after the other. Many years had passed, but now he felt they had almost reached their goal. God had chosen them.

"*Deus lo vult,*" he whispered, then fell to his knees to pray.

5

AN UNPLEASANT ODOR BROUGHT JAKOB KUISL back from his nebulous nightmares and into the present. A musty smell of dust and earth, somewhat moldy and damp, like in a trench, he thought.

Where am I? What happened?

The memory came surging back—and with it, the anger and pain. He had failed to notice the third man! He must have come down the stairway to the crypt behind him. The stranger, who smelled of violets, had nearly strangled him with a leather strap. Jakob Kuisl knew that people who were strangled lost consciousness in a minute's time and that death followed just a few minutes after that. He knew this well, as he himself had executed some people in this fashion. Some of those condemned to death at the stake had paid him to strangle them and spare them the painful death by fire. In the heavy smoke, onlookers couldn't see that the person in the flames was already dead.

Jakob Kuisl remembered the poison dagger that paralyzed him down in the crypt in a matter of minutes. Some interesting poison that he had never heard of. The plant or berry no doubt came from another part of the world. Carefully, the hangman tried to wiggle his fingers and toes. They moved—a good sign. The effect of the poison, whatever it was, had started to wear off, and for the first time, he was able to open his eyes now.

And saw nothing.

He blinked a few times. Was he blind? Had the men blindfolded him? Or was it really so dark in this cellar? He tried to reach up and touch his face.

He couldn't.

After a few inches, his hand bumped into something cold and hard. He tried the other hand, but the same thing happened. He tried to sit up, but his head bumped into a stone slab. He broke out in a sweat, and his mouth felt dry. He turned this way and that, but on all sides there was nothing but cold stone. He felt his heart beginning to race and struggled to control his breathing.

They've buried me alive. In the sarcophagus . . .

Jakob Kuisl counted his heartbeats. He struggled to breathe regularly, and finally he felt how the time between heartbeats was lengthening until it was beating normally again. And then he began to scream.

"Hey! Can anyone hear me? I'm here!"

He sensed that his voice reached no farther than the stone slab, where it was completely swallowed up. Considering the huge weight of the stone, it was likely that even someone standing directly next to the sarcophagus would not be able to hear him. He had to help himself.

Perhaps Jakob Kuisl could have raised the slab with his strong arms, but the cover was so close to him that he couldn't raise his arms any higher than his chest. Perhaps he could . . .

Taking a deep breath, the hangman pressed his whole body upward so that his broad forehead touched the slab.

It felt as if he were trying to push his way through a wall with his head.

The veins on his temples bulged, and blood surged through his head. He pressed and pumped, his muscles as hard as rock. He could hear his bones crack, but the slab was as unmoving as if had been cemented in place.

Then, finally, he heard a soft grating sound.

A ray of light appeared in a narrow crack—actually, not a ray of light at all, but a darkness not quite as dark as the interior of the sarcophagus. He continued pushing his upper body against the stone, knowing that if he gave up now he wouldn't regain the strength to raise the slab again for a long time. Perhaps forever. His lower back felt like a mighty oak that was ready to splinter, but finally he moved the slab far enough that he could raise his arms to his chest and push them up against the cold stone above him.

With a loud cry, he pushed away the six-hundred-pound stone.

The slab hovered above him for a moment like a serving tray, then tipped to one side and crashed to the stone floor, where it broke into pieces. Like a corpse rising from the dead, Jakob Kuisl sat up in the coffin. His body was covered with stone dust and crushed bone. Human bones and scraps of cloth were scattered all over the room, and in one corner lay the slab with the inscription.

Jakob Kuisl climbed out of the sarcophagus and reached for the marble slab. Only now did he notice that he was still holding in his left hand a scrap of the black cowl he had seized just before losing consciousness. He held it up to his nose and smelled a fragrance of violets, cinnamon, and something else that he couldn't quite place.

He would never forget this fragrance.

With the scrap of cloth and the marble tablet in hand, he climbed out of the crypt. They would find out that it was a mistake to pick a fight with the hangman.

• • •

Magdalena had a bad night behind her. She had waited a full hour in front of the St. Lawrence Church, but her father still hadn't returned. Finally, three figures in dark robes had crept out of the same church window they had pried open before and disappeared into the darkness. Magdalena could hear from far off the whinnying and hoofbeats of their horses as they left.

Where was her father?

Finally, she hurried to the rectory to awaken Magda and the gaunt sexton. Together they opened the door to the church, while Magda, terrified, kept making the sign of the cross, praying, and staring up into the night sky. If someone was really still lurking around in there, the shock would probably kill both of them, Magdalena thought. But the church was empty. The stone slab above the crypt had been moved aside, but even after Magdalena had descended the stairway—despite Magda's praying and moaning—she had not been able to find anything. Evidently, there had been a struggle in both underground rooms, which were littered with refuse. In the back room, the sarcophagus had clearly been examined again. Bones and scraps of material lay around the room, but the sarcophagus stood just as her father and Simon had left it, with its lid closed. A strange fleeting feeling came over her as she looked at the sarcophagus, but she couldn't figure out what it was. It almost seemed as if she could sense the presence of her father. But he was still nowhere to be seen.

Fearful, she finally spent the night in the rectory and returned home early the next morning. Her mother was already up and standing in the doorway, her eyes red with tears.

"Where were you?" she asked. "And where is your father?"

For a brief moment, Magdalena was tempted to lie to her mother: She had been called to work overnight as a midwife in Altenstadt, and her father was sleeping off a night of carousing at Strasser's Tavern. But then it all came out.

"I . . . I just don't know," was all she could say, sobbing, before burying her face in her mother's bosom. Sitting at the table inside, Anna Maria Kuisl finally learned the whole truth about her husband's uncertain fate.

"How often have I told your father not to meddle in other people's affairs!" she scolded. "Don't we have enough problems already? But no, he won't listen. He pokes his nose in books and other people's garbage, and now he's putting his own daughter in danger once again! To hell with him!"

Anna Maria Kuisl's unique method of conquering her fear for her husband was by scolding and cursing. The more she cursed, the more relief she got. In the end, she often told him just to drop dead—although she really loved him. Anna Maria Kuisl herself came from a family of hangmen in Kempten. Death and horror were nothing new to her, but no one could take away her fear for her family. On the other hand, she simply couldn't imagine that Jakob had been killed and buried by three dastardly murderers who were just passing through. They couldn't do this to Jakob Kuisl, the hangman of Schongau, that goddamned pigheaded smart aleck!

Of course, Jakob Kuisl picked the most unfavorable of all possible moments to return home. The door creaked and his broad frame appeared in the doorway, still covered with stone dust, dirt, and crushed bone. His forehead and arm were bleeding, his hands badly skinned, and every one of his muscles was painful and stiff as a board. No doubt that was the reason he couldn't duck when the pot of porridge came flying through the air at him.

"You bullheaded clod! How often have I told you to keep your daughter out of this when you go poking your nose around?"

Jakob Kuisl wiped the warm porridge from his shirt and stuck his finger in his mouth. "You got any more, or was that all for today? Doesn't taste half bad . . ." he muttered.

A clay cup came flying through the air at him, but this time he was ready. Though his upper body was stiff, he managed to turn away so that the cup smashed into pieces against the wall behind him.

"How dare you even show up here," his wife shouted. But her anger already seemed to have cooled somewhat. Besides, she didn't have any more ammunition. "I've been worried sick about you two."

The patter of little feet could be heard coming down the stairs. The seven-year-old twins, Georg and Barbara, stood there in their nightshirts, blinking at them from behind the railing.

"Mama, why does Papa have porridge all over his jacket?"

"Because Mama was scolding him." Anna Maria Kuisl went up the stairs. "Because you have such a stubborn damned father. It's outrageous. Now put some clothes on before you freeze to death."

She disappeared upstairs with the children while Jakob grinned and pointed to Magdalena and to the pot on the floor.

"What do you say? Would *you* at least make me a pot of porridge? Or are you going to throw the spoon at me, too?

Magdalena smiled. "Well, Father, the main thing is that you're back." Then she picked up the battered pot, took it back to the kitchen, and put fresh water on to boil.

Early that afternoon, Simon Fronwieser stopped by the hangman's house and reported what he and Benedikta had learned. The return trip from Steingaden to Schongau had been uneventful. Just after they'd left, they came upon an armed party of merchants who accompanied them to Schongau. The merchants hadn't seen a trace of robbers. Perhaps they looked too well armed for them, Simon thought. Or they still remembered Benedikta and preferred to hide in the forest and lick their wounds.

Benedikta stayed at the Goldener Stern Inn, where she hoped to finish some important correspondence. Anna Maria Kuisl had taken the twins into the forest to gather firewood. She was still angry at her husband and, for that reason, was staying out of his way. Jakob knew that this would all pass over by the next day, at the latest.

Now Jakob and Simon were sitting at the table in the main room, thinking about everything that had happened the day before. A roughly mortared tile stove in the corner spread a pleasant warmth, and on the table a piece of wood was burning in a torch holder, bathing the low-ceilinged room in a gentle glow. Under the bench, a few chickens were scratching around in their cages.

Magdalena made an herbal broth that the men sipped morosely. Simon yearned for a cup of coffee, but Magdalena had refused to serve him the stimulating beverage. In his present condition, she said, a calming herbal drink would be just the right thing for him. In general, Magdalena seemed sullen and uncommunicative, and Simon had the feeling that she also refused him the coffee because he had traveled to Steingaden with Benedikta. At some point, when he touched her skirt, she retreated to the stove and avoided looking him in the eye.

Both the hangman and the physician had bandages on their foreheads. Jakob Kuisl had a bandaged hand as well, but that didn't keep him from holding a cup in one hand and a smoking pipe in the other. He told Simon briefly about being attacked in the crypt, and now they were discussing what to do next.

"Let's summarize what we know, again," Simon began. "In the crypt under the Saint Lawrence Church are the bones of a Knight Templar; that's at least what we can assume from reading the inscription on the sarcophagus." He slurped listlessly on his herbal brew before continuing. "The church itself once belonged to the Knights Templar many years ago before the latter sold it to the Premonstratensians. The seller was a certain Friedrich Wildgraf, the local master of the Order of the Knights Templar in the German Empire. Benedikta assumes—"

"Oh, just stop already with this Benedikta!" Magdalena interrupted angrily. "Maybe you weren't really in Steingaden until noon today; maybe you were making love in some stable, then showed up here holding hands this morning, and the whole story about the robbers is one big cock-and-bull story — "

"Be quiet, Magdalena, and stop talking such nonsense. Help us figure this out; that would be more helpful."

Her father's voice was calm and composed, but Magdalena knew she couldn't take this much further. She and Simon had already had a heated argument earlier in the afternoon, and Simon had assured her that nothing had happened between him and Benedikta. But the way he looked down when he spoke to her made her fear the worst.

"Maybe the remains in the crypt belong to this Friedrich Wildgraf," she suggested.

"That's also what Benedikta assumes," Simon replied, shrugging.

"Nonsense." From a flask under the table, the hangman poured something strong into his cup of herbal brew. "This Templar sold the property. Why would he want to be buried there? Anyway, such a noble gentleman has certainly found a better place to bide his time until Judgment Day than in our dilapidated Saint Lawrence Church, of all places."

Neither Simon nor Magdalena could argue with that.

"Whatever the case," Simon continued, "what's down there is certainly the grave of a Knight Templar. That old fart Koppmeyer finds it, talks too much, and suddenly he's dead."

"Probably poisoned by the three men that Magdalena and I saw in the church yesterday," Jakob Kuisl grumbled. "They were looking for something there. What the hell could it be?"

"In any case, these men are still around here somewhere," Magdalena added. "They have been wandering about here for days, talking in Latin with each other in the tavern." Once more, she told them what she'd learned in Altenstadt. "Strasser, the tavern keeper, thinks they are monks," she said, "refined, educated people. One of them stank of perfume, he said, like a whole gang of Frenchmen."

"Damn! What was I thinking?" Jakob Kuisl said, slapping himself on the forehead. Then he pulled out the bit of cloth he had brought back from the crypt.

"I almost forgot. This is a piece of the cloak I tore off one of the thugs in the Saint Lawrence Church. I'm sure it's from the same bastard who visited Lechner in the castle that morning. He nearly ran me down."

"Are you quite sure?" Simon inquired.

"Just as sure as I am that the devil has a cloven hoof. It was the same perfume. Nobody can tell me different!" He kneaded the scrap of black cloth in his hand, as if he were trying to squeeze out its fragrance.

"Lechner—a part of the conspiracy that cost the fat priest his life . . . ?" Simon shook his head skeptically. "The clerk may well be an unscrupulous schemer, but this doesn't sound like him at all."

"Anyway," Kuisl grumbled, "he ordered me to stay out of this. As of tomorrow, I'll be leaving to catch the gang of robbers in the Schongau forest."

"You? Why you, Father?" Magdalena stood there with her mouth open.

"Because Lechner thinks I'm the only one who can do it. And because that way he can get rid of me."

Jakob Kuisl told them briefly what the clerk had demanded of him.

"He wants to get me out of the way—that much is certain," he grumbled. "But I can't be put off that easily. I'm going to find the bastard who did this to me as sure as Jakob Kuisl is my name."

Simon swallowed hard. He didn't want to think about what the hangman would do with the three assassins if he actually caught them.

"Until the hunt's over, you've got to be my tracking dog around here," Kuisl said, turning to Simon. "I don't give a damn about Koppmeyer, but now they've gone too far. Nobody locks the hangman inside a coffin, no one, and certainly not bums and beggars like these!"

With a sweeping gesture, Jakob Kuisl pulled out the marble slab, which he'd kept under the bench until this point.

"The solution is right here somewhere," he said, tapping the slab with his bandaged finger. "This smart-aleck knight hid something while he was still alive, and we'll find it if we can solve this riddle. I'll bet my fat ass on it."

"But maybe it's just an inscription, an epitaph, and nothing more," Simon objected.

"Not at all!" The hangman was adamant. "The assassins were interested in the slab as well; in any case, it was no longer in the coffin. The solution is right here before our eyes!"

Once more, Simon looked at the strange inscription.

> And I will tell my two witnesses to prophesy. And when they have ended their testimony, the beast that arises from the depths will fight, conquer, and kill them.

He racked his brain trying to figure out what these words might mean. If it referred to a place, then it had to be somewhere they knew about, and if there was ever a chance of finding it, it had to still exist today, three hundred years later.

Two witnesses . . . a beast that fights them and kills them . . .

Images passed through his mind, only to vanish again: warriors, knights, monsters, dragons. Suddenly, a new image came to mind, and this time, it stuck.

Two witnesses . . . A beast . . .

"I have it!" he shouted suddenly. "It's so simple when you know. It was always right in front of us."

"What do you mean?" Magdalena asked.

Simon hopped excitedly around the table. One of the cups fell over, spilling herbal brew across the table. The hangman, too, gave Simon a bewildered look.

"Come on now, tell us," he said. "And please don't act like the incarnation of Beelzebub."

Simon paused, but he didn't sit back down. "First . . . first, I have to check something," he said gasping for breath. "Do you have a Bible here in the house?"

Jakob Kuisl stood up, went to his room, and came back with a well-worn book.

"God also has a place in the hangman's house," he growled, tossing the Bible to Simon. The physician leafed through it until he found the page he was looking for.

"Here!" he said, pointing triumphantly at a passage. "The Revelation of Saint John, Chapter Four. Here's the verse!" He began reading the line out loud: "*I will tell my two witnesses to prophesy . . .*" He looked at the two of them excitedly. "The two witnesses are Enoch—the son of Cain—and the prophet Elijah! When they arrive to fight the beast, the Day of Judgment is close at hand!"

Magdalena shrugged, obviously bored. "Nice that you're so well versed in the Bible. But where can we find these . . . witnesses? I, for one, have never seen them here in Schongau."

Simon grinned broadly.

"Not here in Schongau, actually," he said. "But you can see them magnificently portrayed over the portal to the basilica in Altenstadt. I think we should pay a visit to this beautiful church today."

When they saw the relief above the portal, they were surprised they had not noticed it earlier. Directly above the entrance, it depicted a knight fighting a dragon with a shield and sword, as well as a second man who was being devoured by the beast. How many times had each of them passed under this relief on entering the basilica?

"I have seen images like this in other churches," Simon muttered. "A priest in Ingolstadt explained to me that it at one time stood for the approaching Judgment Day."

"Then Judgment Day has been a long time coming," Magdalena said. "After all, we're still waiting for it."

"You were never in a war," Kuisl said, pondering the dragon's claws and wings, its foaming mouth, "or else you would know that the Four Horsemen of the Apocalypse have been among us for a long time."

"Stop this silly talk, Father," Magdalena said. "Just help us figure this out." Then she turned to Simon. "So here are the two witnesses. And now what?"

"There has to be a clue somewhere here," Simon said softly, "in or around the basilica. I suggest we separate. You, Magdalena, look around the outside of the building, and your father and I will go in."

Jakob Kuisl headed toward the portal, with Simon close behind. On entering St. Michael's, a shiver ran down his spine, as so often before. The Great God of Altenstadt was looking down on him benignly from a huge cross more than nine feet tall. Now, in the late afternoon, they were almost alone in the church except for a few old women fingering their rosaries with arthritic hands. There was a strong smell of incense in the air. Simon forgot for a brief moment why he was here, and folded his hands to pray. Comparing the splendid new buildings at the Steingaden Monastery with the basilica here in Altenstadt, he had the feeling that this was God's true home.

While Simon, lost in thought, was pondering the mighty crucifix, the hangman walked straight through the nave to study the frescoes in the chancel. After that, he proceeded down the side aisles. On the south side, a long-dead artist had painted a mural of the Fourteen Holy Helpers. Over the entrance, a larger-than-life statue of St. Christopher looked down sternly at the hangman.

"Nothing," he grumbled. "I'm not finding anything. Damn! I think you were wrong."

"We have to keep looking," Simon insisted. "There is *certainly* something here; it's just well concealed. Perhaps—"

He was interrupted by a shout from outside. *Magdalena!* They rushed out to find her standing at the edge of the snow-covered graveyard surrounding the basilica. She was facing the south wall of the church and pointing at a small, chest-high plaque almost completely covered with ivy. Magdalena had pulled the ice-covered vegetation aside.

"Here!" she exclaimed. "Here it is! You were right, Simon!"

The stone plaque, old and weathered, was cemented into a recess in the wall. On it an inscription was engraved.

> Fridericus Wildergraue, Magister Domus Templi in Alemania. Anno domini MCCCXXIX. Sanctus Cyriacus, salva me.

"Friedrich Wildgraf's memorial plaque," Simon whispered. "Master of the Knights Templar in Germany. Deceased in the Year of Our Lord 1329. Saint Cyriacus, save me."

"But why is this plaque here when the grave of the Templar is in the Saint Lawrence Church?" Magdalena wondered.

Simon shrugged. "By the year 1329, the Templars had been banned in Germany for more than twenty years," he said. "Maybe it was just too dangerous to bury the German provincial master here. It's possible that the priest at that time could get approval for this small tablet." He ran his hands over the inscribed letters. "But perhaps this tablet is only intended as a clue to put us on the right track . . ."

"Before we beat around the bush any further," the hangman said, "let's just figure out a few things." He pulled out his knife and began scraping away the mortar around the tablet.

"But, Father!" Magdalena whispered. "What if the priest sees us—"

"The priest is busy preparing for mass and probably getting stoned on the wine," Jakob Kuisl said and continued scraping. "But feel free to ask him, if you wish."

Soon he had made a little groove around the tablet, then inserted his dagger to pry it out, and it fell into the soft snow.

Behind it there was nothing but gray stone.

Simon tapped on it, but it was solid, a part of the enormous block of stone and as immovable as the other stones the church was made of.

"Damn!" he exclaimed. "This can't be it! Is this Templar just making fools of us?"

The medicus kicked the icy wall, which seemed to make no impression on the church. Only his frozen toes hurt. Finally, he took a few deep breaths.

"Very well. The riddle has led us here to the basilica," he murmured. "Here's the memorial plaque. What have we overlooked?"

The hangman bent over and picked up the plaque lying in the snow in front of him.

"*Sanctus Cyriacus, salva me.* Saint Cyriacus, save me," Kuisl repeated. "Isn't it strange that he chose this saint for the inscription? As far as I know, Saint Cyriacus was a martyr who was burned in boiling oil and then beheaded."

"St. Cyriacus is the patron saint for those tempted in the hour of death," Simon said. "For a Templar accused of treason and sodomy, not a bad patron to have."

"Aren't those the Fourteen Holy Helpers depicted in the basilica?" Kuisl asked. "I've never seen a Saint Cyriacus there . . ."

A sudden thought flashed through Simon's mind. The saints in the south aisle! How could he have been so blind?

Without waiting for the others, he raced around the church, stormed through the portal, and finally, stopped in front of the Fourteen Holy Helpers in the south aisle. They were positioned in groups of two, one above the other. At the very top was Barbara, the patron saint of the dying and helper in cases of lightning and fire. After her was St. Christopher, St. Margaret as patron saint of women in childbirth, St. George, and St. Blaise, who helped in cases of illness of the throat. Nine other patrons were immortalized on the wall of the church, but St. Cyriacus was not among them.

But there was another saint pictured there whose name was noted in small letters beneath the picture.

St. Fridericus . . .

Simon almost laughed when he read the inscription. Apparently, none of the church's many visitors had ever noticed the error. The painting depicted a man in a bishop's robe with a miter and staff. His right hand was raised protectively over a castle sitting atop a forested mountain, and on closer examination, one could see he was touching the castle with his index finger.

In the meantime, Jakob Kuisl and his daughter had also arrived in front of the picture of St. Fridericus.

"He fooled us all for many hundreds of years," Simon exclaimed, laughing. Some of the women praying turned around with admonishing glances. "St. Fridericus!" he added, whispering, but still grinning. "He simply used his own name! What magnificent blasphemy!"

"But what is this Templar trying to tell us?" Magdalena asked, puzzled, as she considered the fresco. "Is he just mocking us?"

Kuisl approached the painting to within a few inches. He

tapped the castle beneath the picture of the saint, where he'd noticed a brown spot not much larger than a flyspeck.

"Here," he said. "Here it is."

He fished out a magnifying lens from deep inside his pocket and held it over the spot. Suddenly, he was able to make out two words painted in thin, shaky brush strokes.

Castrum Guelphorum . . .

"The old castle of the Guelphs," Simon whispered, "up on the Castle Hill above Peiting. My God, all that stands there now is ruins!" He sighed and rubbed his tired eyes. "I am afraid the search will last longer than we first expected."

The stranger with the black cowl and the sweet smell of violets was standing outside in the cemetery of the basilica. With trembling hands, he held up the Templar's stone plaque, which Jakob Kuisl had left lying there.

How was that possible? The hangman was not only still alive, but had also apparently discovered a clue! Perhaps it was an act of providence, after all, that this Kuisl had not suffocated in the sarcophagus. The stranger had thought this a suitable way of dying for someone responsible for killing so many others. In any case, the man was alive and had solved the riddle—he, his daughter, and that brash young medicus. Why hadn't *they* been able to figure this out? Didn't the monks have a specialist in their own ranks? They had read the same words on the marble plaque in the crypt but hadn't been able to make sense of them.

For days they had been hiding like itinerant riffraff in local barns to avoid arousing suspicion. They lived on nothing but dry bread and their faith; they froze, they prayed, and the only thing that kept them going was the knowledge that *they* were the chosen ones, those sent by God.

Deus lo vult . . .

The stranger cursed in Latin and, at once, murmured a short prayer asking the Lord to forgive this little sin. Then he started putting his thoughts together.

Everything now was actually very simple. They would track these three like bloodhounds, they would find the treasure, and the Master would give them his blessing. Their place in paradise was assured, even if the path to it was cold and stony.

The stranger made the sign of the cross and smiled. Carefully, he put the stone plaque down on the ground again and hid behind the gravestones, waiting for the three to come back out of the basilica.

Simon's initial elation at finding the clue in the basilica quickly turned into confusion and anger, and the reason was walking along defiantly beside him. Without speaking a word, he and Magdalena descended the narrow pathway back down to Schongau. The hangman's daughter nearly slipped a few times, but when Simon reached out to help her, she brushed his hand aside. Just what was wrong with her? Not a word of approval about his find, just this silence.

Jakob Kuisl had gone his own way back in Altenstadt, grumbling about having to pick something up from the blacksmith down on the Mühlenweg as he disappeared into a narrow lane. The clerk had ordered him to report to the marketplace with a group of citizens the next day to begin a search for the robbers in the Schongau forests. For that reason, Simon knew he wouldn't be able to count on the hangman in the next few days. He also suspected Kuisl stayed behind in Altenstadt for another reason—sensing that there were bad feelings between Magdalena and himself. Kuisl wanted to give them some time alone. But his plan had backfired. Ever since they had started the hike back to Schongau, they had not exchanged a word, and just as they were arriving at the Hof Gate, Simon blew his top.

"Magdalena, just what is wrong with you?"

"What's wrong with *me?*" She glared at him. "You should ask yourself, instead, what's wrong with *you!* Flirting with this Benedikta. I'm good enough for cleaning and cooking, but this Benedikta is a fine lady!"

Simon could only roll his eyes. "Magdalena, we have already talked about this. There is nothing between me and Benedikta Koppmeyer," he tried to convince her, choosing his words carefully. "She saved my life; she is an amazing woman, but— "

"An amazing woman! Bah!" Magdalena stopped and glared at him. "She can talk fine, the amazing woman. She has beautiful, expensive clothes, but underneath it all, she is nothing but a dolled-up tramp!"

"Magdalena, I forbid you— "

"No, you can't forbid me from doing anything, you scoundrel!" Magdalena worked herself into a rage. "Do you think I can't see how you flirt around with other girls behind my back? But because I'm just the hangman's daughter, it doesn't matter. People are bound to gossip, anyway. I'm telling you, Benedikta is a slut!"

"Aha! A slut?" Simon lost his patience now, and his voice took on an icy tone. "This . . . slut has more decency and education than you'll ever have in three lifetimes. She knows how to behave, she speaks proper German without stammering and stuttering, and she can even speak French! She is a refined lady and no foul-mouthed hangman's girl!"

The chunk of ice hit him right on the nose so that, for a brief moment, he felt faint. When he gathered his wits again, he felt warm blood flowing down his face, forming a pattern of red dots in the snow.

"Magdalena!" he shouted, still holding his nose and snuffling. "Stay here. I didn't mean it that way!" But the hangman's daughter had already passed through the Hof Gate and vanished.

Cursing under his breath, he hurried toward town, taking care that the blood didn't drip onto his expensive petticoat breeches. Why did Magdalena always have to be so ill-tempered? He knew that what he had said was pretty stupid, and he wanted to ask her forgiveness, take her in his arms, and tell her that she was the only one he really wanted. But the hangman's daughter was nowhere in sight.

"Magdalena!" he shouted over and over, looking everywhere in the little side streets. "Come back! I'm sorry!"

Passersby gave him strange glances, but he held his head down and hurried along. She had to be somewhere! At the next street corner, he stumbled over a little dog and it ran off whimpering. On and on he went, passing ox carts and glancing nervously at heavily clothed figures, shadowy figures barely visible in the snow that was starting to fall. Magdalena had simply disappeared. As he turned into the Münzgasse, he heard a familiar voice behind him.

"Simon?"

He turned around. Standing in front of the portal of the Church of the Ascension was Benedikta, eyeing him with concern. Apparently, she was just coming out of the Schongau parish church.

"You're bleeding!" she exclaimed. "What happened?"

"Nothing," he muttered. "I . . . fell, that's all."

"Let me have a look." She walked over to him and started to dab determinedly at the blood on his face with her lace handkerchief. And although her touch burned, it felt good, too.

"A sheet of ice in front of the Hof Gate," he sniffed softly as she continued to wipe his nose. "I slipped."

"You need hot water to clean the wound. Come." Like a mother, she took his arm and pulled him along behind her.

"Where are we going?" he asked.

"To Semer's Tavern, where I'm staying," she said. "In the

restaurant we can surely get a bowl of water and a cup of mulled wine for you. And then you can tell me if you have found out anything in the meanwhile."

Simon hesitated. Actually, he wanted to keep looking for Magdalena, and his father would be waiting for him at home. This damned fever was claiming more and more victims who needed treatment. But how could anyone object to a cup of mulled wine? Magdalena had probably already made it back to the tanners' section of town and was sitting in her father's house and sulking. It was probably better anyway to wait until the worst of her anger had passed.

There was also a lot to tell. So much had happened in the last few days, and Simon simply needed someone to talk to. In happy anticipation, he staggered along behind Benedikta toward Semer's Tavern. When she opened the door, his swollen nose took in the fragrance of freshly baked pastries and warm wine.

Magdalena wiped the tears from her eyes as she ran half blind through the streets of Schongau, not even noticing people she passed along the way. She was just so . . . furious. How could Simon be so cruel to her? Perhaps it was true they were not a good match—she, a hangman's daughter, a butcher's girl, the offspring of a dishonorable family; he, an educated medicus, someone who could speak well and wore polished boots and a coat with shiny buttons, and who was adored by the women in town. But he, too, came from a poor family! His money and his clothes were borrowed or donated by one or another of his fawning admirers. Magdalena clenched her teeth. She had watched this spectacle far too long, and this was finally the limit. She might well be a dishonorable, dirty hangman's daughter, but she still had her pride.

The sound of a child coughing and whining tore her from her thoughts. Without paying much attention to where she was going, she had turned off into a small side street just after the Hof Gate and wandered through narrow lanes into the Women's Gate area, where the poorer residents lived. The air reeked of tanning solution. Acrid clouds of steam billowed from a dyer's cottage where freshly dyed gray linen smocks hung out to dry on wooden frames. Magdalena looked around and listened. The crying was clearly coming from the workshop. As the hangman's daughter walked by the ramshackle thatch-roofed hut, she saw a pale woman with sunken cheeks standing in the low doorway.

"You are Kuisl's daughter, aren't you?"

Magdalena could find nothing hostile in the way the woman looked at her, so she stopped and nodded.

"They say you're a good midwife," the woman continued. "You helped the dairyman's wife in the birth of her twins, and both are still alive. And you gave a powder to the blue-dyer's daughter, the young hussy, to get rid of the fetus . . ."

Magdalena looked around carefully in all directions. "I don't know what you're talking about," she said softly.

"Oh, come now." The woman made a dismissive gesture. "In this part of town, you can speak openly. Every other woman here has gotten something from your father to keep from having a kid, or a love potion he brewed up." She giggled, revealing a few black stumps of teeth between her dry lips. "Only the fat cats can afford the fancy physician, or those who flirt with him. But I don't need to tell you that . . ."

"What do you want from me?" Magdalena asked. "I have no time for your silly talk."

The woman's face suddenly turned dark.

"My little Lisbeth is sick. I think she has this fever. But we don't have any money for the doctor. Perhaps you'd like to come in and have a look."

She gestured for Magdalena to enter and at the same time curtsied clumsily. Her scornful look had completely vanished, and all that remained was a despairing mother who feared for the life of her child.

Magdalena shrugged. “I can have a look at her, but I can’t promise anything.”

Entering the smoke-filled house, she found a kettle standing on a rusty tripod over an open fire and emitting thick, acrid steam. The smoke was so thick that it wasn’t possible to see much more of the cabin. Magdalena could make out a wobbly table, a churn of rancid butter, a stool, and a few sacks filled with straw in a corner. This was the same corner the whining was coming from. Moving closer, Magdalena caught sight of a little child on the ground, a girl perhaps ten years old, with a pale face and sunken cheeks. Rings like black half-moons circled her eyes, which flitted around anxiously. She was coughing, shaking, and spitting up red mucus. The hangman’s daughter realized at once that it was the same fever that had killed so many Schongauers in recent weeks. She bent down over the girl and stroked her hot forehead.

“Everything will be all right,” she murmured. The child’s eyes closed, and her breathing became more regular.

“Give me some hot water,” Magdalena called out over her shoulder, and the anxious dyer woman hurried away, then returned with a steaming cup. The hangman’s daughter pulled out a leather purse from a deep pocket in her skirt and shook a gray powder into the cup.

“Have her drink one swallow of this mornings and evenings for three days,” she said, “but three swallows right now. It’s arnica, evergreen, St. John’s wort, and a few herbs that you don’t know. It will help her sleep and forget the cough. That’s all I can do,” she said with a shrug.

The dyer woman clutched the cup and looked at Magdalena anxiously. “Will she recover? She’s all I have left. My husband, Josef, died last summer when tanning fumes burned his insides. He was spitting blood at the end, just like Lisbeth now.”

"Don't you have any other children?" Magdalena asked sympathetically.

"Smallpox took every last one, and Lisbeth is the last . . ."

The woman's eyes filled with tears. She pressed her lips together tightly and stared fixedly into space. The girl seemed to be sleeping now, but with every breath her frail chest rattled.

In a moment of inspiration, Magdalena reached for a chain around her neck decorated with amulets attached at regular intervals: a wolf's tooth in a tin setting, a bloodstone, a silver arrow like the one that pierced St. Sebastian, a mole's paw, a rock crystal, a tiny cloth pouch that had been blessed . . . It was a so-called "Fraisen chain," a charm necklace meant to ward off evil spirits and black magic. The hangman's daughter tore the wolf's tooth off the chain, bent down to the girl, and pressed it into her limp hand. The little girl's hand closed in her sleep.

"What is it . . . ?" the mother asked anxiously.

"It will protect her," Magdalena said, trying to console her. "My father cast some powerful charms on it."

That was not really true, but the hangman's daughter knew that faith, love, and hope could often do more than the strongest medicine. Her father had given her the charm necklace when she was still a child, and whenever she was afraid or felt threatened, she would clutch it tightly in her hand. It gave her strength, and she hoped that some of this strength would be transferred to the little girl now.

"I will never be able to pay you," the woman objected. "I am a poor dyer woman."

Magdalena stopped her with a wave of her hand. "It's the wolf my father shot last year. We have enough teeth in our house for all of Schongau." She winked at her conspiratorially. "The important thing is the magic charm it possesses. You won't betray me, will you?"

The woman shook her head, still speechless over the gift from the hangman's girl. Then something occurred to her, and her face brightened. "Though I have no money," she said, "perhaps I can help you. Your father was over in Altenstadt because of the dead priest, wasn't he?"

Magdalena pricked up her ears. "How do you know . . . ?"

The woman shrugged. "People talk. They say he was poisoned. Now listen . . ."

She looked around carefully and lowered her voice.

"I went to see Koppmeyer a few days ago—had to give him some dyed fabric for the mass. I'm standing there in front of the rectory and see a man talking with the priest inside. A monk it was, with a black cowl, and under the cowl was a fine, white cloth, not the sort of rags that people like us wear."

"Please continue," Magdalena urged her.

"The monk was speaking softly, but very intensely with the priest. I could see that Koppmeyer was really afraid. His eyes were bulging as if they might almost fall out of their sockets. Then the man shouted at him and went outside for his horse. I hurried over to hide behind the woodpile."

"What did he look like?" Magdalena asked.

"There wasn't much to see because of his hood and the robe . . ." The woman hesitated. "But one thing was very strange."

"What? Tell me!"

"He had to bend forward as he mounted his horse, and underneath his robe I saw a golden chain dangling down with a big, beautiful cross. But it looked different from the crosses we have in church."

The excitement practically took Magdalena's breath away. "What . . . what did it look like?"

"Well, it didn't have just one crossbeam, it had two; the upper one was shorter, and the whole cross was made of gold. I have never seen one like that before."

Magdalena thought for a moment but couldn't remember ever seeing a cross like that, either.

"What happened then?" she finally asked.

The dyer woman shrugged. "I took the cloth to Koppmeyer. He was still pretty upset. He handed me two pennies too much and sent me on my way. I've never in my life seen the fat priest so frightened. I mean, the man was as strong as a bear!"

Magdalena nodded. "You have helped me a lot, and I am grateful." She headed toward the door, deep in thought. "Don't forget the potion for your daughter," she said as she left. "If she doesn't get better in three days, come over and see us at the hangman's house." She grinned. "If you dare . . . But my father kills only people who have done something to deserve it."

The dyer woman watched as Magdalena vanished into the next alleyway. The girl started to cough again. Praying quietly to herself, the mother returned to the house and to her daughter.

Simon was sitting alongside Benedikta at a table in the back of the tavern at the Goldener Stern Inn, sipping on a mug of mulled wine. His nose had finally stopped bleeding, but he could feel it swelling by the minute. He was probably already completely disfigured. He glanced around at the other guests. Now, as evening set in, the tavern was filling slowly with merchants, wealthy craftsmen, and a few aldermen who would overnight there. The tavern belonged to Karl Semer, the city's presiding burgomaster. It was the best place in town and thus attracted a wealthy clientele. A fire was burning in the large stone fireplace in the corner, lending a cozy atmosphere to the room, and a chandelier bathed the low, wood-paneled room in a subdued light. The aroma of cinnamon, cloves, and stew hung in the air.

Simon rarely came here, preferring the cheap saloons in the area behind the Ballenhaus, where the wine and the beer were cheaper but also caused bigger hangovers in the morning. He loved it when one of the journeymen or apprentices picked up a fiddle and started to play while the other guests stamped their feet and the girls' skirts whirled around. Here at Semer's Tavern, things were much more civilized. At the table next to them, two merchants were talking in hushed tones about their recent sales, and farther back, the alderman Johann Püchner tried flirting with one of the servers by inviting her to join him for a glass of wine. The perky young woman put a glass of the best Alsace wine down in front of him, then disappeared into the kitchen, giggling.

Until that moment, Benedikta had refrained from asking questions, dabbing away now and then at the blood beneath Simon's nose. She appeared lost in thought as she nipped on her cup of diluted wine and, like Simon, seemed to be carefully observing the other guests. Finally, she turned and spoke to him.

"I have decided to stay in Schongau for a few more days. My manager can handle the business in Landsberg just as well as I can, and besides, I was able to make some good contacts today with a few wine merchants from Augsburg." She sighed. "But of course it's primarily my brother that keeps me here. I won't rest until they catch the damned murderer. Have you been able to learn more about his death?"

Simon hesitated for a moment, then told her about the solution to the riddle, what they had found in the basilica in Altenstadt, and how he planned to search the ruins of the Guelph castle for further clues.

Benedikta's face darkened. "But what does that all have to do with my brother? It's not possible that he knew about all these things."

Simon took a long sip before continuing. "Your brother certainly did not know the entire truth, but he knew about the grave under the church. He told someone about it, and that someone wanted to keep the information to himself."

"So that no one else would know about it?" Benedikta looked at him in disbelief. "What have you found up to now except a few silly riddles, a joke played by an aging knight?" She shrugged. "Perhaps this Wildgraf was just a man with a sense of humor and all you'll find in the castle ruins is a coarse rhyme about how nosy some people are."

Simon shook his head. "The Templars didn't think that way. They were an order of knights that combined the virtues of a Christian life and knighthood; they didn't go around tricking people. The first riddle comes from the Revelation of Saint John, and the second refers to an ancient noble family, the Guelphs. It can't be an accident. It almost looks as if our dead knight wanted to test us to see if we were worthy. Clearly, he was looking for men who were well versed both in the Bible and in the life of the nobility. Templars . . ." He hesitated, then stopped speaking.

"Is something wrong?" Benedikta looked at him and smiled. "Has the wine gone to your head?"

Simon shook his head, then pulled out the little guide he had borrowed from Jakob Schreevogl and was still carrying around in his jacket pocket.

He laid it on the table and started leafing through it excitedly.

"What is that?" Benedikta asked, trying to get a glimpse.

"It's a book about the Templars," Simon replied, but then he stopped flipping through the pages and sighed. "For a moment, I thought I had remembered something, but I must be mistaken."

He told Benedikta briefly what he knew about the Templars.

"This Friedrich Wildgraf, who was buried down there in the crypt, was a master of the Order of Teutonic Knights," he concluded. "According to the contract we saw in Steingaden, he was the commander for the entire German Empire. He was a member of the inner circle of power. But in just a few years, the Templars were pursued and wiped out all over Europe. Their huge fortune, however, vanished . . ." He looked Benedikta straight in the eye before continuing. "Why would a powerful master of the order pose riddles like this if not to conceal something? First there was the quotation on the sarcophagus, now the clue in the basilica . . . There must be a reason for all that!"

"Do you think . . . ?"

Simon nodded. "I think Friedrich Wildgraf may have hidden the Templars' treasure somewhere around here. Or at least a part of it."

"A treasure?" Benedikta picked up her handkerchief and wiped a few drops of wine from her lips. "Why would the Templars want to hide something in this godforsaken spot, of all places? According to what you have told me, they had headquarters in Paris, in Jerusalem, in Rome! What would lead them to the Priests' Corner, of all places"—she spat the name out like a piece of rotten fruit—"to bury a treasure in the remotest part of Bavaria?"

Simon pounded his fist on the table. "That's just the point! Nobody would think to look for the treasure here. The French king probably couldn't have found the Priests' Corner on a map, even if the duke had drawn a circle around it. Mountains, forests, swamps, and a few illiterate, but well-mannered peasants—the perfect hiding place!"

Benedikta was silent for a while; then she nodded slowly. "Perhaps you're right." Her eyes, so often alert, took on a glassy sheen. "How much do you think . . . ?"

"Money?" Simon shrugged. "It's hard to say, but in any case, more than we can imagine. Don't forget, the French king ordered the extermination of the Templars just because of this fortune. Even if only a part of it is here . . ." He broke off in the middle of his sentence and looked around. "In any case," he whispered, "we had better be careful. People have been killed for a lot less money."

"But people have also risked their lives for far less," Benedikta replied with a wink. "Don't ever tell a businesswoman about hidden treasures; you'll have a hard time getting rid of her.

In my opinion, we should take this risk," she said, raising her wine glass. "To your health! *A la vôtre!*"

"*A la vôtre,*" replied Simon, and they clinked glasses. This woman from Landsberg surprised him again and again, but she was right: If only a fraction of the Templars' treasure were buried somewhere in the Priests' Corner, he would never have to worry about his future again. He would be able to buy crates full of coats, petticoat breeches, new shoes, hats with peacock feathers, a fast horse, and a trunk full of the latest medical instruments. His standing in town would change dramatically, and not only that . . . Who could forbid him then from marrying the hangman's daughter? He would build a house for Magdalena and himself! Who knows, maybe they would open an apothecary together in Schongau. He, the physician, and she, the wife, an expert in the healing herbs and poisons in the region—a perfect couple!

He was so absorbed in the joyful anticipation of his future life that he didn't notice a haggard figure in the back of the tavern standing up and heading toward the door. As the man left the tavern, he exuded a soft aroma like a gentle whiff of spring.

6

MAGDALENA STOOD IN THE BITING COLD IN FRONT of the parish church and pulled her woolen shawl tighter around her shoulders. After her visit with the dyer woman, she had wandered aimlessly through the narrow streets. Where could she go? After her angry outburst, Simon would certainly be looking for her at her parents' house. But even now, after her anger had somewhat subsided, she didn't want to see him. Perhaps at that very moment he was standing in front of their house in the Tanners' Quarter and worrying about her. As well he should! How dare he rave to her about this woman! It would be good for him to fret a little. Perhaps it would awaken his guilty conscience. Nobody could treat a Kuisl that way!

Deep in thought, she wandered across the market square. Night was falling and a traveling merchant was hawking scissors, knives, and all sorts of bric-a-brac. The fragrance of honey-roasted hazelnuts filled the air. Magdalena looked around, rubbing her hands together to keep warm. It was snowing lightly now, but at this time of day, there were only a few Schongau residents passing through the square, anyway. Wrapped in more or less ragged clothing, they walked stooped over so snow wouldn't blow directly in their eyes. Magdalena looked into their empty, gaunt faces. The Great War had ended just a few years before and people were still suffering the consequences. The residents of the once-wealthy city had fallen victim to pestilence, sickness, and hunger. Even now, only the snow covered the crumbling masonry on the walls and the frozen piles of excrement in the streets. Interspersed among the houses were ruins of buildings whose roofs had caved in, silent witnesses to whole families wiped out by the plague. In recent decades, the city had lost more than a third of its inhabitants to the plague, and almost every family had mourned the loss of at least one member. As a child, Magdalena had often seen carts filled with dozens of corpses heading toward the new St. Sebastian Cemetery. The old cemetery by the parish church had filled up long ago and now this new fever had come over the city!

On the spur of the moment, Magdalena decided to go to Semer's tavern. She still had a few coins in her pocket, and a warm drink would certainly do her some good after all the day's aggravation. The very thought of it raised her spirits. Her hand was already on the doorknob when she glanced through the bull's-eye window to the left of the entrance.

What she saw hit her like a slap in the face.

Behind the glass, slightly blurred, she could make out Simon and Benedikta sitting at a table. The two seemed engrossed in something or other, and in the dim light of the candles, she thought she could see Simon put his arm around her. Magdalena shuddered. At first she was tempted to tear open the door, grab a heavy mug off one of the shelves, and throw it at Simon. But instead, she just ran across the marketplace, unable to think clearly, tears running down her cheeks before turning to ice.

When she came to her senses, she was standing near the Kuh Gate. The midwife's house was just a few yards away, and without giving it a further thought, she tore open the door and stormed in.

Martha Stechlin looked up in astonishment. She was sitting at a table in the main room, crushing some dried herbs in a mortar. She was about to give the young woman a tongue-lashing but changed her mind when she noticed how pale Magdalena was and how she was trembling.

"Girl, what is wrong with you?" she asked with concern. "This isn't because of the Steigenberg woman, is it? You don't have to worry; the child is well and you don't have to . . ."

Magdalena shook her head, then broke down in tears again. The midwife guided her over to the table, sat her down gently on one of the wooden stools, and stroked her hair.

"What is wrong, my dear?" she murmured, handing her a cup of a hot peppermint tea, which had just been bubbling on the hearth.

Magdalena poured out her heart to the midwife in bitter words, and when she was finished, Martha nodded compassionately.

"That's just the way men are," she whispered, "never content with what they have. But sooner or later, they always come back. My Hans . . . God bless his soul . . ." Her voice broke and she wiped her eyes as if trying to brush away a tear.

"What about your husband?" Magdalena asked, happy to turn attention away from her own troubles. "You never told me about him."

"He was always flirting with the girls," Martha said. "He was never home; he always hung out in the taverns, the dirty swine . . ." A smile crossed her lips. "But I loved him. Even when we couldn't have children and people began to gossip, we stayed together. No random strumpet was going to come along and change that." She winked at Magdalena.

"What became of him?" The hangman's daughter wiped the tears from her eyes as the warmth of the fire spread up her legs.

The midwife was staring off into space. "He caught the

plague. I buried him more than ten winters ago, and since then, I have been alone."

In the silence that followed, the only thing audible was the crackling of the fire on the hearth. Magdalena bit her lip. Why had she asked? Embarrassed, she sipped on the steaming cup.

Finally, the midwife arose and walked over to her shelves, which extended from the shrine in the corner of the room all the way to the hearth. "So be it!" she said. "Life goes on." Her gaze wandered along the line of jars and pots on the shelves. The jars were all freshly glazed and labeled according to their contents. The midwife opened a few of them and shook her head.

"I'll need some dried melissa," she murmured. "And ergot, if nothing else works."

"What for?" Magdalena asked, walking over to her. "Are you expecting another difficult birth?"

Magdalena had been Martha Stechlin's apprentice for half a year, and in that time Magdalena had assisted in five difficult births. Only in difficult cases did people call for the midwife. Often women gave birth without help, alone, or with only the immediate family present, whether in a warm living room, in the stable, or sometimes even in the field. If Stechlin was looking through her jars now, there had to be another critical case pending.

"Frau Holzhofer . . ." Martha Stechlin started to say.

Magdalena gasped. "The wife of the second burgomaster?"

The midwife kept searching through the jars. "Holzhofer's wife is already past due," she said. "If the child doesn't come by next week, we'll have to give her ergot."

Magdalena nodded. Ergot was a fungus that grew on rye and oats, a strong poison that caused the notorious St. Anthony's fire, but in small doses could induce labor.

"And now you don't have any more?" she asked.

Martha Stechlin had now arrived at the last row of jars. "No, no ergot, melissa, artemisia, or sundew. And your father has none left, either!" She sighed. "It looks like I'll have to make a trip to Augsburg in this awful cold! The apothecary there is the only place I can get ergot or artemisia in the winter. But what can I do? If anything happens to his wife, Holzhofer will blame it on me, and then they'll throw me out of my house or set it on fire . . ."

Suddenly, the hangman's daughter had an idea. She smiled broadly at the midwife and announced, "I can go!"

"You?" The midwife made an incredulous face, but Magdalena nodded eagerly.

"I'd like to get away from Simon for a while, in any case. I'll leave with the first ferry tomorrow morning, and we'll see how he gets along without me." The more Magdalena thought about it, the more she liked the idea. "Just write down for me what you need and where I'm supposed to go in Augsburg," she continued, speaking rapidly. "My father certainly needs a few pills and herbs as well, so I can spare you both a trip."

The midwife stared at her, mulling it over. Then she shrugged. "Why not?" she muttered. "After all, you want to become a midwife. It can only be a good thing for you to see what an apothecary looks like from the inside. And Augsburg . . ." She smiled at Magdalena. "Well, the city will take your mind off things. Just be careful that you don't go haywire. You have never in your life seen so many people," she said, clapping her hands excitedly. "But now, let's get to work! The marigold leaves must be finely ground and the lard rendered, because Kornbichler's wife wants her ointment this evening!"

Magdalena smiled and proceeded to pour the fragrant dry leaves into a mortar. The air smelled of hot goose fat, and Stechlin's chatter sounded like a trickling watermill. Simon, her father, and the dead priest suddenly seemed far, far away.

When Jakob Kuisl opened the trunk, memories of a completely different life came flooding back.

The box had been stored for years in the attic of the hangman's house, hidden behind rolls of rope and broken barrels where no one could see it. The hangman had carried it down into the main room of the house and opened it now with the key he had been keeping safe. Putting aside a folded, moth-eaten army uniform, he took out first the dismantled barrel of a matchlock musket, then its polished inlaid handle, a pouch of lead bullets, and a chain holding wooden powder kegs, also known among mercenaries as the "Twelve Apostles." He pulled the bayonet out of its sheath and tested its sharpness with his thumb. After all these years, the steel was still just as sharp and shining as the executioner's sword, which had been hanging in the devotional corner of his house for ages.

At the very bottom of the trunk lay a little cherrywood box. Jakob Kuisl unsnapped the lock and opened it carefully. Inside were two well-oiled wheel lock pistols. The hangman passed his hand over their polished handles and cool iron cocking hammers. These pistols had cost a fortune, but at that time, money was of no importance. In a drunken frenzy, you just grabbed whatever you wanted, helped yourself. Kuisl's eyelids twitched. Suddenly, a shadow fell over his memory.

Legs wriggling up in the branches of a tree, a flickering fire, the crying of a little girl coming from the blackened ruins. The sound of laughing men playing dice around a mountain of bloody clothing and glittering trinkets . . . a charred baby's rattle . . .

He had been a troop leader, a so-called "sword player" who always fought on the front lines with a double-edged sword, as his father had. He received double pay and the largest portion of the spoils.

He had been one of the best, the perfect killer . . .

A charred baby's rattle . . .

With a shake of his head, the hangman tried to wipe away the memory. He closed the cherrywood box before any further dreams could pour forth.

Hearing the door squeak, he wheeled around as Magdalena came storming in, her face beet red. She had hurried back from Stechlin's house just in time, before the watchmen closed the gates to the city. Now she was eager to tell her father the news.

"Father, I must leave for Augsburg tomorrow morning on an errand for Stechlin! Please allow me . . ." She stopped short when she saw the trunk. "What is that?"

"Nothing that concerns you," her father grumbled. "But if you really want to know, they are weapons. Tomorrow the hunt for the robbers begins."

Magdalena examined the bayonet, the soiled mercenary's uniform, and the gun, all of them set out neatly side by side on the table. She stroked the copper-reinforced barrel of the musket.

"Where did you get these?"

"From before."

The hangman's daughter turned away from the weapons and looked her father in the eye. "You've never told me about *before.* Mother told me you were a brave soldier, is that right? Why did you go to war?"

Jakob was silent for a long time. "What do you want to do with your life?" he asked finally.

Magdalena shrugged. "Do I have a choice? As your daughter, I either marry a butcher or an executioner. You don't have the choice of doing anything else, either."

"War is cruel, you know," the hangman replied, "but it makes people free. Anyone can kill, and if he's smart about it, he can even become a sergeant or a sergeant major and will have more money than he can ever waste on liquor."

"Then why did you come back?" Magdalena replied.

"Because with killing, it's just like with everything else in life . . . Everything has its place."

And for the hangman, that was the end of the matter—he had

nothing further to say. He closed the trunk and gave his daughter a challenging look. "So you want to go to Augsburg? Why?"

Magdalena explained that the midwife needed some important ingredients and wanted to send her to the big city to get them. "And she wants me to get a bezoar for her, too!" she said excitedly.

"A bezoar?"

"A stone from the stomach of a goat, which helps with infertility and difficult births and—"

"I know what a bezoar is," the hangman interrupted harshly. "But why does Stechlin need it?"

Magdalena shrugged. "The wife of the second presiding burgomaster, Holzhofer, is pregnant, but the child won't come. She asked Stechlin for a bezoar."

"The Holzhofer woman is going to have to fork out a heap of money for that," the hangman grumbled. "A bezoar is not cheap, and that means you'll have to carry a lot of money with you to Augsburg."

Magdalena nodded. "Stechlin will give it to me first thing in the morning."

"And what if you're robbed?"

Magdalena laughed and gave her father a kiss on the cheek. "Are you worried about me? Don't forget I'm the daughter of the Schongau hangman! People are more afraid of me than I am of them." She smiled. "Please let me go! Mother said I'd have to ask you. I'll take the ferry first thing tomorrow morning, and there will be a group of Augsburg merchants on board on the way back. What can happen?"

Jakob Kuisl sighed. It was always hard for him to deny his daughter anything. "Very well," he said finally. "But only if you also bring something back for me. Let's see what I need . . ."

He crossed the room, where, on the opposite wall, a huge cupboard reached right up to the ceiling. The drawers and shelves were overflowing with parchment scrolls and books, and some drawers were open, revealing countless pouches, crucibles, and phials. Though it was the middle of winter, the entire room smelled like summer—rosemary, ginger, nutmeg, and cloves. The hangman's apothecary, passed down in his family from generation to generation, was known all around Schongau. Not even the midwife—to say nothing of the physician—had a collection of herbs, medicines, and poisons to rival the Kuisls'.

On a wobbly table in the middle of the room, a flickering torch smoked in a rusty holder. In its dim light, Magdalena noticed a few books open on the table, among them Dioscorides's work on medicinal plants and a book she had never seen before in a foreign language.

"Are you looking up something because of Koppmeyer's poisoning?" she asked inquisitively.

"Maybe." Without another word, Jakob Kuisl examined his stock of herbs and powders and put together a list for Magdalena.

"I also need a few things you won't get from an apothecary," he said. "Dried belladonna and thorn-apple seeds. Also, some alum, saltpeter, and arsenic. I know the fellows there, and if you just hand them a few extra kreuzer, they'll give you the stuff without any problems. And if they don't . . ." He grinned. "Just say the Schongau hangman sent you. That has always worked." Suddenly, his face darkened.

"But you're leaving so suddenly . . . That doesn't have anything to do with Simon, does it?"

Magdalena scowled. "I don't give a damn about Simon. He can get along without me for once."

Jakob Kuisl turned back to his list of medicines. "Well, if that's what you think, at least you'll miss all the killing." His face darkened. "You don't have to get pulled into all this, but it's clear to me that we haven't seen the end of it."

Magdalena moved closer to him. "Do you know now who the men could have been who attacked you in the church?"

The hangman shook his head. "I'll find out eventually, then God help them." The candle cast flickering shadows across his face.

In moments like this, Magdalena feared her father. *That's the way he looks,* she thought, *when he wraps a noose around someone's neck or breaks his bones on the wheel, one by one.*

"I know that at least one of the men visited Koppmeyer before his death," she said finally. She told him about her conversation with the dyer woman and the strange golden cross the woman had seen around the stranger's neck. When she had finished speaking, her father shook his head.

"Templars, Latin verses, a golden cross with two crossbeams . . . The whole thing is getting more and more confusing!" He pounded his fist on the table so hard the pages of the book flew up. "In any case, Simon is going to the castle on the hill above Peiting tomorrow morning to see if he can find any clue there. Perhaps we'll know more then about the people who are chasing us or about these confounded Templars who are making fools of us all."

For a moment, Magdalena was tempted to reconsider her plans. What if Simon actually found a treasure up in the old ruins? Or if the strangers were lying in wait for him there? Wouldn't he need her help? But then she thought about the trip on the ferry, the big city, the new smells and faces. She wanted to get away from everything—and from Simon, too.

She kissed her father on the forehead and went upstairs, where her mother and the twins were already asleep.

"Take good care of yourself, Father," she whispered. "And of Simon, too." Then she disappeared into her bedroom.

In the flickering light of the torch, Jakob Kuisl hunched down again over his books. Belladonna, nightshade, wolfsbane . . . There were many drawings of poisonous plants here, but none had an effect like the one that had made him as stiff as a corpse in the crypt. That preparation had to have come from some distant land—that much was certain. But how did those men get a hold of a poison like that? Did they themselves come from this distant place? Were they itinerant monks from a far-off monastery? One had spoken a peculiar dialect.

And Latin.

Suddenly, the strange words that he overheard in the crypt came back to him.

Deus lo vult . . . God wills it . . .

With a sigh, he closed the book and began cleaning the musket. He would have to get up early the next morning for the hunt. Johann Lechner had summoned the men to report to the marketplace on the ringing of the six o'clock bell. Young Fronwieser could go ahead and deal with the Templars, riddles, and assassins. Jakob Kuisl would chase the thieves; that was something the hangman could do better than anyone.

Leonhard Weyer cursed and whipped his horse. The animal whinnied, reared up on its hind legs, and pushed its rear hooves even deeper into the snow. Night was falling, and the Augsburg merchant had to squint to see through the heavy, blowing snow.

They were too late! They had left Schongau at the crack of dawn, but by noon, they should have known they would never make it to Füssen by nightfall. Weyer had decided to take the old road through the forest, which was longer but mostly unused, particularly now in wintertime. Bandits preferred to lie in wait along the broad military road along the Lech River, and the Augsburg clothier was certain that no bandit would sit here, freezing his ass off all day on the off chance he'd meet a solitary farmer with a wagonload of fodder for his livestock. Besides, Weyer had told only his closest friends in Augsburg and Schongau that he'd be taking this route, and in contrast to other times, he had taken just a simple wagon for this trip, leaving his comfortable well-sprung carriage behind in Augsburg. Who would ever suspect anything? Weyer felt safe, but that didn't change the fact that night was falling and they still had not reached a village.

Around noon, snow had begun to come down harder, and his four servants made almost no progress getting the wagon through snow drifts that were three feet deep in places. Now, as night was falling, they could hardly see their hands in front of their faces. On both sides, the road was lined with tall pines that reached up like black fingers to the sky. Their two packhorses snorted and struggled to pull the wagon through the knee-high snow. Again and again, the servants had to climb down and push when the wheels got stuck in the slush and half-frozen puddles. The servants flailed away at the tired Haflingers, but no matter how hard they beat them, they wouldn't move any faster. And now the wagon was stuck again in a drift. Shoveling and cursing, two servants tried to dig it out while the other two pushed the overloaded wagon from behind.

"Damn, can't you go any faster? In an hour it will be pitch black here!"

While his gray horse pranced around nervously, Weyer stood there in his fur-lined mittens, panting and rubbing his cold hands together. He was wearing a snow-covered bearskin hat and a knee-length coat of smooth, shiny fur, but still, he was cold to the bone. His breath formed little white clouds in front of him and hoarfrost settled on his eyebrows and his freshly trimmed goatee.

He looked around anxiously. Like a black shroud, darkness had enveloped the pine trees at the edge of the road and was advancing slowly toward the small group. He cursed again and shouted at the servants, who were wearily pushing the wagon through the snowdrifts. It was at least half an hour to the nearest town! He had already given up on reaching Füssen that day and would be happy just to reach the safety of a cheap village inn. His plan had been perfect! Because of the bandits along the highway, no other large-business owner in Augsburg had dared to leave the safety of the city walls. When they did, it was in a large group guarded by dreadfully expensive mercenaries. Because Weyer had set out for Schongau alone, before everyone else, he would be able to dictate prices—if he ever got to Füssen. Nervous, he reached under his coat for the loaded pistol hanging on his belt. He had brought along four of his strongest men, and all were armed with sabers and clubs. Even the coachman was armed with a crossbow. But would all this be enough to hold off a ferocious, hungry band of highwaymen? Weyer shook his head. But really, would bandits be wandering around on such a lonely stretch of road? Nobody knew he was traveling here with such valuable cargo.

"Giddyap! Go, you damned mare!"

Joseph, his first servant, whipped one of the Haflingers so hard that it jumped and the wagon finally lurched forward, over the snowdrift. The journey could resume.

Wagon tracks with only a light covering of snow appeared on the road in front of them. Leonhard Weyer smiled. They would make it. He'd be doing business in Füssen before anyone else, and the profit would be considerable. Perhaps after he'd concluded this deal, he could finally retire and leave everything to his sons. A warm hearth, a good drink, a fat roast capon—what more could a person want?

A sound came from the right, a faint crackling in the icy branches. Leonhard Weyer squinted into the darkness in front of him, but all he could make out were the dense thickets of pines. His servants had heard something, too. They whispered and looked around warily in all directions. Something was lurking out there. Now Weyer heard a whistle from a tree nearby. Looking up in the tree, he could see branches moving as if they were alive, swaying back and forth in the almost windless air.

He noticed the eyes much too late.

They were gleaming white on an otherwise ashen face, and below the eyes, a crossbow was aimed directly at the merchant. Leonhard Weyer heard a soft click, then felt a searing pain in his right shoulder. Tumbling from his horse, he instinctively reached for his pistol but couldn't find it. All around him, chaos broke out: There was shouting in the gathering darkness, shots, and the groans of men fighting. A shrill cry became a gurgle; then someone fell to the ground with a thud. He looked to the side and saw Joseph, his first servant, his eyes bulging in terror. Blood gushed from a broad wound across his neck onto Weyer's expensive fur coat. The merchant gazed at the slaughter in disbelief. How was this happening?

Who, in God's name, could know that we were taking the old road?

He pushed the corpse in front of him to one side and reached into his coat. The fur was so heavy he couldn't find the opening. Where were his damned pistols? Finally, he felt their cold steel and slipped them out through the opening. He ignored the pain in his shoulder and sat up carefully. From this position, he could see that two of his servants lay bleeding on the ground and another was struggling with three robbers, one of whom struck him on the back of the neck with an ax. Out of the corner of his eye, Weyer noticed a shadow approaching from the left. He wheeled around to see a man running toward him. He had tied pine branches to his arms and legs, his face was blackened, and in his right hand, he held a polished pistol. He was short in stature, and his movements were sleek, like a cat's. Despite the disguise, Weyer had the feeling he had seen this man before.

But where?

There was no time to think about it, however. Weyer pointed his loaded pistol at the bandit and pulled the trigger.

There was a click, nothing else.

Damn, the powder got wet, Leonhard Weyer thought. *God help me!*

The figure slowly moved closer, obviously enjoying this moment, and pointed the barrel of his pistol directly at Weyer's forehead. Just before the cock came down, igniting the powder, Weyer finally recalled where he'd seen the figure.

Was it possible? But why . . .?

The sudden realization couldn't help him now. The world flew apart into a thousand stars, and behind them was nothing but unending blackness.

They met on the market square before dawn, shadows in the darkness that only gradually took shape as Jakob Kuisl approached.

The hangman knew most of them: The gatekeeper, Jakob Rauch, was there as well as the powerfully built smith, Georg Krönauer, and Andre Wiedemann, an old war veteran leaning wearily on his musket, suspiciously eyeing the newcomers shuffling into the square in heavy overcoats, their breath turning into white clouds in front of them. Farther back, Kuisl saw the sons of aldermen Semer and Hardenberg standing with Hans Berchtholdt, whose father represented the bakers in the Outer Council. They whispered among themselves, pointed at the hangman, and played apathetically with their shining sabers. From time to time, as the remaining men arrived, Kuisl heard laughter coming from that group.

Nearly two dozen men had formed a circle around the hangman—aldermen, tavern keepers, and tradesmen, all honorable citizens, eyeing him with a mixture of distrust and hostility, as if they were just waiting for him to give them some reason to contradict him. Jakob Kuisl suddenly realized how futile Lechner's plan was. He was nothing more than a dishonorable hangman, a torturer and butcher. How could he give orders to these people?

He cleared his throat and was about to speak when a voice rang out in the fog behind him.

"Gentlemen, I have some sad news for you all."

Johann Lechner had appeared like a ghost out of the gloom. He looked as if he'd been awake for hours: Elegantly coiffed with a cleanly clipped beard, his jacket and coat neatly buttoned, he had the bearing of someone accustomed to giving orders. He directed his piercing eyes at the crowd.

"A few dead bodies have been discovered in the forest just on the other side of Lechbruck," he continued. "They were the Augsburg merchant Leonhard Weyer and his servants, who departed from Schongau just yesterday morning." He raised his voice, scrutinizing the men standing around him armed with scythes, flails, and rusty muskets. "The next time it may be one of us they rob and murder. My fellow citizens, it is finally time to crack down on this gang."

There was whispering in the crowd and curses here and there.

"Quiet, please!" The clerk clapped his hands, and immediately, the crowd fell silent. "Kuisl was a mercenary in the Great War," Johann Lechner began, pointing to the middle of the group, where the hangman stood completely outfitted with saber, rifle, and pistols. "An able and clever leader, as I have heard. He has had experience with these sorts of scoundrels, and he knows better than any of us how to handle weapons. I want you to follow his commands, for the good of us all."

"And if we don't want to, eh?" It was Hans Berchtholdt, the baker's son, who struck a defiant posture across from the clerk. "My father thinks you don't have any right to give us orders. This is still a free city! A Berchtholdt won't be bossed around by a dirty butcher!"

A swish could be heard as Jakob Kuisl pulled his saber out of its sheath, gripping the handle tightly.

"Your father is an old fool." The voice came from the right, where Jakob Schreevogl materialized out of the heavy morning mist. The patrician nodded in the direction of the clerk and

Jakob Kuisl. "If you'll allow me, I wish to join the group." The young alderman put his well-oiled pistol back in his belt and took a stand next to the hangman.

"I'm pleased that another fighter has joined our ranks," Johann Lechner responded with a smile. "And now, to your question . . ." He glared at the baker's son, and Berchtholdt stepped back, intimidated. "The attack on the Augsburg merchant was a dastardly murder and thus no longer a concern of the town but of the elector," Lechner continued. "I am the representative of the elector in Schongau, and I am directing the hangman to lead this group. Would you like to discuss this matter with me before the court in Munich?"

Hans Berchtholdt stepped back into the ranks again, and the two other patricians' sons looked away, distraught.

"No . . . of course not. I . . ." Berchtholdt stammered.

"Good. Then we can finally begin." The clerk turned to Jakob Kuisl. "The hangman will explain how we will proceed."

Jakob Kuisl grinned. You could say what you wanted about Lechner, but he had a firm grip on his town. Grimly, the hangman rammed his saber back into its sheath, looking each of the men in the face, one after the other. Then he briefly explained his battle plan.

As Simon slammed the door behind him and set out to inspect the castle ruins in Peiting, he could hear his father cursing and carrying on behind him. It was just before eight in the morning, and the first farmers and tradespeople were up and about with their carts in the streets of Schongau.

Bonifaz Fronwieser had insisted that his son stay home to help with the patients who would be coming in for treatment. Just the night before, two more Schongauers had come to the house complaining of coughing and chills. The old doctor had talked them into buying a syrup of linden blossom extract and, for an exorbitant fee, also examined their urine. Then, with a few words of assurance, he had sent them on their way. Simon was so happy he wouldn't have to watch this foolishness that day. They were so powerless! People were dying like flies, and the doctors here couldn't think of anything better to do than to bleed the patients and administer enemas. In Paris, London, and in Leiden in the Netherlands, doctors were far more advanced. Some renowned scholars there even asserted that illness was transmitted from person to person—not by bad air and miasmas, but by creatures too small to be seen with the naked eye. In Schongau, they still thought snot was mucus draining from the brain and that a common cold could cause a person to wither up inside and become a zombie.

Simon cursed. Until just the week before, he'd held onto a bit of Jesuit's powder, which was extracted from the bark of an exotic tree that grew on the other side of the Great Ocean. The fever was receding, but he'd used up the last bit of it now, and the next Venetian merchant would not be coming north over the mountain passes to Schongau until spring.

When Simon turned the corner onto Weinstrasse, he could no longer hear his father's screams. No doubt, Bonifaz Fronwieser was already washing down his anger with a glass of cheap white wine. Simon hoped that by nightfall his father would have calmed down again, and that Magdalena would have come to her senses, too. He'd stopped by at her house the day before and banged on the door several times, but no one had answered. Finally, Anna Maria Kuisl dumped a chamber pot out the window, an unmistakable sign that his presence was not desired. In a few days, the blizzard would no doubt die down, and maybe by then he would have learned more about the riddles concerning the Templars' treasure. Possibly, he might get a better idea that very day after his visit to Peiting.

As he was leaving through the Lech Gate in the frosty morning fog, a figure approached him that, until that moment, had been hidden behind the town wall. It was Benedikta.

"I think our conversation yesterday ended much too abruptly," she said, smiling. She wore a woolen cap and a heavy, coarse woolen coat that didn't quite suit her dainty figure. She must have bought the clothing in town after realizing that she would be staying a bit longer. Seeing the surprised look on Simon's face, she shrugged apologetically. "My brother's burial is not until tomorrow, so I thought I might come along with you. For your own protection . . ." She winked at him.

Simon could feel himself blushing. *Protected by a woman. I hope the hangman never hears about this . . .*

Only now did he notice a bulge under Benedikta's heavy coat at about hip level. He suspected that was where she stowed the pistol she had used to finish off the robber.

"Why not?" he said. "But please, let's not take horses this time. Every muscle in my body still aches."

Benedikta laughed aloud and walked ahead, crunching through the snow so fast that Simon had difficulty keeping up with her.

"Don't worry," she said. "I gave my Aramis a day off today. And in any case, it's not far, is it?"

Simon nodded. He had caught up and was walking alongside her now. "Do you see the big hill?" He pointed across the Lech River. "Beyond that is Peiting, the closest town, and right next to that is the castle on the hill with the old Guelph ruins—at least whatever the Swedes didn't destroy."

"Doesn't anyone live up there on the hill anymore?" Benedikta asked.

Simon laughed. "Just a few castle ghosts. It was once inhabited by the Guelphs, a family of princes that reigned here. But that was long, long ago. In the Great War, people took refuge up there, but the Swedes destroyed the last remnants of the castle.

Now, you'll meet only an occasional farmer up there looking for stones for building his walls or barns."

"And do you think we'll actually find something up there?"

Simon shrugged. "Probably not, but then, at least we'll have tried."

The path along the Lech climbed gently. Soon they were surrounded by trees. The walls and houses of Schongau could be seen intermittently over the tops of the trees, until finally they were enveloped in dense forest. Simon looked around carefully. Peiting was less than an hour's walk from town, yet after everything that had happened in the past three days, Simon thought he could see a highwayman behind every tree. Except for a tired farmer driving an oxcart, however, they didn't meet a soul.

When the first houses of Peiting were in sight, they came upon a narrow path leading up to the top of Castle Hill. Simon walked ahead. The snow here was significantly deeper and not yet packed down, so progress was slow and difficult. They kept sinking into the snow, sometimes up to their hips. After a while, they discovered a trail animals had made in the snow, and walking became easier. The path climbed steeply now and was lined by ancient oak trees, which at one time must have flanked a boulevard built by the dukes but had since been reclaimed by the forest. About half an hour later, they reached the crest of the hill and the forest receded, revealing a clearing where the ruins stood.

The Swedes had done a thorough job. The outer walls had been torn down, and all that remained of the once stately buildings were scorched black skeletons, sooty beams, and rubble covered in snow. Only the ancient keep towered up from the ruins, like an index finger warning the visitors. Eerie silence lay over the clearing, as if the snow up here, three feet deep in places, had swallowed every sound.

"Wonderful," Benedikta said, rubbing her frozen hands together. "This Templar certainly couldn't have found a better place to hide something."

Shrugging, Simon surveyed the chaotic scene, not sure where to begin. "When the Templars still lived in Schongau, this must have been an imposing castle. But at some point, the duke disappeared, the castle fell into ruin, and then the Swedes arrived . . ." He climbed up to the top of a pile of rubble, trying to get a better view of the entire site. From up there, he could see Schongau, the Lech that flowed out of the mountains toward Augsburg, and in the distance, the peak of Hoher Peißenberg peering out of the morning fog. Directly beneath them lay rubble and ruins. Simon sighed and carefully climbed back down to join Benedikta. "It would be just as easy to find a needle in a haystack," he said. "But since we're here . . ."

They decided to split up. Benedikta would take the southern side and Simon the northern. He trudged through rubble, glancing into the buildings as he passed; though all that remained, for the most part, were the walls. Now and then, he stumbled over bones and grinning skulls dispersed among blocks of stone. In one corner, he found a skeleton wrapped in the ragged remains of a Swedish uniform. Twice he broke through the snow, and one of those times he struggled to free himself when his boot became wedged in a hidden fissure.

"Did you find anything yet?" he called out toward the place he thought Benedikta must be. Strangely, his voice sounded both loud yet muffled to him.

"There's nothing here," she shouted back. "Do you really think we should keep looking?"

"Just a bit longer!" He climbed over another large pile of rubble and saw the ruins of a little chapel on a rise in front of him. He continued over rocks and snowdrifts toward the ruins of the nave, where he guessed the Guelphs probably had come to pray. Now all that remained were bare, sooty walls. Even the lead-framed church windows had been broken and the lead likely melted down to make bullets. Snow drifted down through the remains of the roof truss onto the stone altar, and burned beams were strewn around everywhere in heaps.

On a whim, Simon entered the chapel and climbed over a pile of wood to reach the altar. The Templar's previous two riddles had to do with churches—first the little St. Lawrence Church and then the basilica in Altenstadt. Perhaps that was the case here as well. He just had to—

With a loud crack, the beams under him gave way. Splinters ripped at his overcoat and jacket as he fell with a muffled cry into a deep hole. He tried desperately to break his fall by gripping a piece of wood that jutted out, but it gave way, too, and followed him, crashing down into the darkness.

The landing was hard and painful. He could feel hard stone and something thin splintering beneath him. As he struggled to his feet, he heard a *whoosh* above him. Instinctively, he threw himself to one side before a whole batch of beams crashed down, landing on the ground right beside him. A few feet farther to the right and he would have been buried beneath them.

Simon took a deep breath and carefully tested his arms and legs. Nothing seemed to be broken. His new jacket from Augsburg was ripped from his shoulder down to his hip, and a few tiny splinters had pierced his clothing in places, but otherwise he was unhurt.

Only now did he have the chance to investigate what it was he had fallen into. Reaching over to one side, he picked up a pale, broken femur, and between his legs a toothless skull grinned up at him.

Simon jumped up in horror and looked around. Decayed, partially discolored skulls and bones were strewn all across the floor. Apparently, he had fallen through the rotted flooring into the crypt. A few rays of light streamed in through an opening above him. On the western side of the crypt, a narrow stone staircase led to a trapdoor in the ceiling that no doubt was once used as an entrance. Plaques with inscriptions on them were set into the stone walls here, showing knights with swords and on horseback. Simon looked closer. The men pictured there were probably Guelph rulers or members of the House of Hohenstaufen, which had inhabited this castle after them. The physician remembered that the castle had once served the Romans, too, as a fortified tower. *Just how old were these bones?*

"Is everything all right?" Benedikta's voice came from the opening above, where he could see her anxious face now. "I heard the crash and came over right away. What happened?"

Simon grinned. "I probably shouldn't have helped myself to so many dumplings at the Epiphany feast. I fell through like a sack of potatoes." He gestured to the plaques and the bones scattered around him. "With a little less luck I would be lying here along with the others."

Benedikta looked down at him. The floor of the crypt lay about thirty feet below the church. "We'll need to get a beam for you to climb up on," she said, looking around.

Simon nodded. "Look over there on the right, by the altar. I think I saw some big boards there. But for heaven's sake, be careful, or we'll both be down here together."

Benedikta smiled at him. "Is that the worst thing that could happen?"

She disappeared, and Simon could hear her cautiously walking across the rotting floor of the church. As the medicus waited for help, he examined the plaque closer. The Latin inscriptions gave the names of the deceased, and the stone reliefs showed knights in armor, standing, lying, and on horseback. One plaque even portrayed two knights on a horse. The physician stopped short.

Two knights?

Something bubbled up inside Simon, a fuzzy image, something that had lain dormant in his subconscious until that moment. Hectically, he fished the little guidebook by Wilhelm von Selling out of his jacket pocket and leafed through it. About halfway through the book, he found the solution.

Two knights. One horse.

"Benedikta! Benedikta!" he shouted, hoarse with excitement. "I think I've found something, the solution to the riddle—it's here!"

Benedikta's face appeared again in the opening. "What?"

"The Templars!" Simon shouted. "They must have been here. There's a Templar's grave plaque down here. The seal of the Grand Master always showed two knights on horseback. There's an old illustration of it here in Selling's book!"

Simon waved the book around as Benedikta carefully lowered a beam.

"For the Templars, riding horseback together was considered a sign of great confidence, a symbol that they shared everything, and for that reason, they put it on their seal. Now I can read the inscription." He moved closer to the plaque and passed his finger over the raised letters along the edge of the plaque.

"*Sigillum Militum Christi,*" he whispered. "Seal of the Warriors for Christ. It is, in fact, their seal."

In the meantime, Benedikta had slid down the beam and was standing alongside him.

"Another grave plaque," she groaned. "This is getting boring."

"There has to be something behind it." Simon pulled out a stiletto that he occasionally used for minor surgical procedures and began to scratch away at the mortar along the edges of the plaque. Benedikta worked along with him for a good quarter-hour until the plaque came loose and fell to the ground.

There was nothing behind it.

Only a bare wall on which someone had, in fact, chiseled a few lines into the rock. Unlike all the other inscriptions in the crypt, these sentences were in German, though in an archaic one. Simon quietly read them to himself.

> "This is what I discovered among men as the greatest wonder, that the earth did not exist, nor the sky above, nor trees, nor mountains, nor any other thing, and the sun did not burn, the moon did not shine, and the beautiful ocean did not sparkle."

"For heaven's sake, what does that mean?" Benedikta whispered. "Another riddle from the Bible?"

Simon nodded. "That's what it looks like. But I've never heard this passage before. And there's something else remarkable . . ."

"What?" Benedikta looked at him questioningly.

"Well, if it's from the Bible, it actually should be in Latin. At that time, so far as I know, there was no German translation—at least nothing sanctioned by the church. But the inscription is in German."

Moving in for a better look, Benedikta pointed to a word in the second line.

"The word *tree* is all in capital letters. But why?"

Simon once more ran his index finger over the letters. "Perhaps this word is especially important," he said. "Perhaps the treasure is buried under a tree."

Benedikta scoffed. "But which one? It's a forest out there."

"It would have to be a very old tree, one that was standing here more than three hundred years ago. And there must be something special about it so you could recognize it again." Simon hurried over to the charred beam and began to pull himself up. "Come, let's have a look around. Perhaps we're close to solving the riddle!"

Benedikta sighed and climbed up after him.

They searched all morning and half the afternoon for old trees, or unusual crippled trees, or oaks with something carved into the trunk, or beeches that stood apart, on hills. They looked for hidden signs and stone plaques on the ground; they searched in knotholes, in the crevices among roots, in old badger holes.

And found nothing.

After five hours of searching in vain, Simon sat down on a large snow-covered stone block that had fallen out of the wall, rubbing his ice-cold hands together. "This isn't getting us anywhere," he said, his breath turning to clouds of steam in the frigid air. "Even if the treasure, or whatever it is, lies hidden under a tree here, the ground is frozen and much too hard for us to dig."

Benedikta sat down beside him on the stone block, her face chafed from the dry cold. "Do you still believe there's a gold treasure buried up here somewhere?"

Trying to warm up, Simon stood and began pacing. "Perhaps it's not money at all. It could be gold, jewelry, diamonds, something very small and valuable. But it could also all be rubbish, and I'm just getting carried away."

Angry, he tossed an egg-size stone down the hill. It knocked over a little mound of snow, setting off a small avalanche that came to rest among the trees below.

"Let's go home," he said, turning to Benedikta. "You have to prepare for your brother's funeral, and for the time being, I have had enough of these Templars."

Together, they tramped back through the snow into the valley. Neither noticed the three figures hiding behind a wall, staring after them with spiteful eyes.

Brother Avenarius rubbed the thick bandage on the back of his head where the hangman had hit him with the club.

"It doesn't look like they found anything," he said in his Swabian dialect. "Perhaps the young man is not as smart as he thinks he is. *Sapientia certa in re incerta cernitur* . . . True wisdom is found in an uncertain situation."

"He's smarter than you, wiseass!" The man with the scarred face and the rasping voice fiddled with the curved dagger in his hand. "What have your erudite maxims done for us so far, eh? They've given us nothing but a dead priest and a heap of trouble!"

"I had nothing to do with the priest!" the Swabian shouted angrily. "He didn't have to be killed right away. It would have been enough to . . . well, silence him."

"Well, he's silent now," the scarred man replied. He threw his dagger and it lodged in a rotted stump, quivering.

"Brother Nathanael is right," replied the third, a monk dressed in black who gave off a strong scent of violets, even here outside. He was as gaunt and haggard as a dried-out, cracked log. He was the only one of the three monks who hid his face under his cowl. "The priest was too dangerous. *Deus lo vult!*"

"Where's all this leading?" the Swabian lamented. "First the priest, then the hangman . . . The Master didn't send us out to do that!"

"The Master's words were more than clear." The tall, haggard monk leaned in to Brother Avenarius now. While the perfume nauseated the fat Swabian, Avenarius would never dare to say anything about it. The haggard man was their leader, even though he seemed to act stranger with each passing week.

"The Master has ordered us to bring the treasure back to where it belongs," the man with the violet scent whispered. His mouth looked like a red spot in the depths of his black cowl. "Nothing else matters. In any case, the hangman escaped. He's alive. I saw him just yesterday with the others at Saint Michael's Basilica."

"You *what?*" The monk with the scar jumped up, but the haggard one restrained him.

"It's fine. God obviously did not want the hangman to die.

He needs him still as some small part in His great plan. We can assume that his daughter, the hangman's girl, got away from us for the same reason. An astonishing woman . . ." He stopped as if he were reflecting. "Her name is Magdalena. It's strange, I once knew someone by that name . . ."

Suddenly, he clapped his hands. "Now let's report to the Master."

The gaunt man jumped over the wall and beckoned the others to follow. Seeing a disappointed look in the face of his scarred colleague, he tried to cheer him up. "If they really find the treasure, their work is done, Nathanael. God won't allow the heretics' sacrilege to spread again. We destroyed them once and we shall succeed this time as well. Every memory of it must be destroyed. Your time will come."

The monk with the curved dagger nodded grimly; then the three set out like tracking dogs after a fresh scent.

7

JAKOB KUISL WALKED ALONG THE STEEP SLOPE of the Ammer Gorge, looking down at the rushing river over two hundred feet below. Ice floes drifted along the surface, bumping into one another, piling up in bizarre formations that reminded the hangman of a crooked, worn-out flight of stairs. Below, darkness was already approaching, and before long the temperature would drop. Slowly, the sun dipped below the tree line, bathing the faces of the search party in the last rays of golden sunlight.

"We need to stop for today," Hans Berchtholdt mumbled behind him. "It's like hunting for a needle in a haystack."

Almost from the very start of the hunt, the baker's son had expressed doubts about the undertaking, and then the other patrician sons had followed suit. How would they ever find a band of robbers in the vast Schongau forest? Wasn't this a job for soldiers and simple constables, anyway? Even if some of the young men had been keen on the idea at first—they hoped to finally have a chance to play real war games—the cold, strenuous march had robbed them of their last bit of enthusiasm. Now all they wanted was to go home.

Jakob Kuisl kept a careful eye on the other bank of the river, hoping to spot any sign of suspicious movement. Highway banditry had always plagued the Bavarian forests, but since the Great War, it had become practically impossible to travel from city to city without an armed escort. Several times a year, Kuisl strung up a few thugs on Gallows Hill, some no older than fourteen, but it did no good. Hunger and desire trumped fear of the hangman. And this winter, the gangs of robbers were larger than they had been in many years. Their leader, Hans Scheller, had rallied almost two dozen of his cronies, among them former mercenaries, but also farmers whose fields, barns, and livestock had been destroyed in the war, as well as their women and children.

"Hey, Kuisl, I'm talking to you! Let's go home. You can keep looking by yourself."

Kuisl gave the baker's son a scornful look. "We'll check out one last hiding place; then you can go home to your warm feather bed. You do look completely frozen, or does the red nose come from the boozing?"

Hans Berchtholdt turned even redder. "Don't get smart with me, butcher!" he shouted, putting his hand on his sword. "I won't let someone like you lecture me. It's a disgrace that Lechner put you in charge!"

"Watch your tongue, Berchtholdt!" said Jakob Schreevogl, who up to that point had been walking ahead silently with the hangman. "You heard yourself what the clerk said. Kuisl knows what he is doing better than any of us, and so he's the leader."

"Berchtholdt is right, Schreevogl!" This time it was Sebastian Semer, son of the presiding burgomaster. In a tight-fitting doublet with copper buttons and an elegant round hat adorned with a rooster feather, he looked quite out of place here in the forest. In addition, the cold seemed to be getting the best of the young patrician in his thin leather boots. His voice trembled—whether from the cold or out of some unconscious anxiety about confronting the hangman, Jakob Kuisl couldn't tell. "It's unheard of that a butcher and executioner is ordering around honorable citizens," Semer finally said. "I . . . I . . . shall complain to my father!"

"Yes, yes, do that, and get started before nightfall."

Kuisl stomped ahead, hoping that the group would follow. He could feel his authority slipping away. He could count on the fingers of one hand the men who trusted him in this endeavor: Jakob Schreevogl; old Andre Wiedemann, whom he had known since the war; perhaps the blacksmith, Georg Kronauer; and a few workers. The rest followed him because the clerk ordered them to and because they feared the hangman.

Kuisl sighed under his breath. Most people didn't consider executioners honorable citizens because the job involved things that no one else wanted to do: torturing and hanging criminals, removing dead animals from town, sweeping up the streets, and preparing magic drinks and extracts. For the sons of the aldermen, the very idea that such a person should give them orders was an abomination. Kuisl could sense clearly that resistance was brewing.

Under his breath, he cursed Lechner for having put him in this situation. Was it possible that Lechner just wanted to get rid of him? For far lesser reasons people had lynched hangmen. If the next hideout was empty like the rest, the hunt for robbers was over for him, too.

When he stepped out from behind the next dense grove of pines, however, he knew at once that they were on the right track this time.

From down below in the gorge, smoke rose toward them —just a thin column, but easy to see in the cold winter air. Kuisl grinned. He had been sure the scoundrels were hiding out somewhere around here. When he planned the hunt, he knew there was little point in just stumbling through the forest hoping to happen on individual bandits. The region around Schongau was a wilderness of forests, gorges, and steep hills. Around each town, only small areas were farmed, and beyond them the primeval forest took over, endless and profound.

The hangman knew this area better than anyone else. In recent years, he had combed miles of the forest for healing and poisonous plants. He knew every major cave, every ruin, every hiding place. They had already been to three possible hideouts that day, and now, at the fourth, their luck seemed to have changed. From the beginning, Kuisl suspected he would find something here at Schleyer Falls.

The smoke rose through a crevice in the rock near the steep slope. The hangman knew that, below, huge limestone formations had been hollowed out by water over a period of thousands of years, concealing an extensive network of caves with entrances behind the waterfalls. Here, at Schleyer Falls, the water flowed over green moss, down to the Ammer River in the summer; now, in the winter, icicles hung down like a white curtain in front of the entrances.

Kuisl bent down to inhale the smoke, which smelled like roasted meat and burned fat. It was coming up through a natural chimney in the rock and had to be from a large campfire.

"Hangman, what's wrong? Why—"

Kuisl motioned to the baker's son to be silent, then pointed to the column of smoke and a small path about a hundred and fifty feet in front of them that led down into the gorge. He was about to move ahead when he caught sight of a few iron rungs that lead downward in the rock wall next to him.

"Their escape route," he whispered. "We have to split up. You take the main body of men down the path," he said, addressing Jakob Schreevogl. "I'll climb down the rungs with a smaller number of people, just to make sure they don't slip away from us like rats through this escape hatch."

He reached into a sack he had been carrying over his shoulder, took out some torches, and distributed them to Andre Wiedemann and Georg Kronauer. "We'll smoke them out from behind," he said to the others. "You'll be waiting by the entrance, and when they come out, capture as many as you can, but if anyone resists, kill him."

The old war veteran Andre Wiedemann grumbled his approval, while Hans Berchtholdt's face turned as white as a sheet. "Shouldn't a few of us wait up here just in case someone slips by you?" he stammered. Like his friend, Sebastian Semer was suddenly no longer as outspoken as he had been moments before. An owl hooted somewhere, and he glanced anxiously in all directions.

"Nonsense," Kuisl said as he stuffed his two freshly oiled wheel lock pistols with powder, still chewing on his cold pipe. "We need every man down below. Now, off you go!"

He nodded at Jakob Schreevogl once again, then put both pistols in his belt and, with the loaded musket slung over his shoulder, climbed down the rungs with Wiedemann; the blacksmith, Kronauer; and two other workers. For a moment, he wondered whether it might have been better to leave the two patrician boys up above. It was possible they would panic, do something rash, and blow the group's cover. But when he thought of their shining sabers, dapper hats, and polished rifles, he couldn't help but smile.

They wanted to play soldier. Now they'd have a chance to see what it was really like.

Magdalena felt as if she were flying. Standing at the very front of the raft, she watched water rush against the rough-hewn logs to her right and left. Now and then, the raft bumped into shattered ice floes or broken icicles that eddied and sank to the bottom of the Lech. They rushed past slopes on both sides that fell steeply down to the river from hilltops of snow-covered beeches. The raftsmen's laughter and commands sounded like an unending song. Farther downriver, the Lech exited the narrow gorge and wound its way through a snow-covered landscape dotted with darker spots marking the locations of towns and small groves of trees.

On the left, the little town of Landsberg appeared. Its formidable town walls and towers had been partially dismantled and taken away during the Great War. The hangman's daughter had heard stories about how the little town had suffered much more than Schongau in the war. Many Landsberg girls, fearing they would be raped by marauding soldiers, jumped from watchtowers into the Lech and drowned. Magdalena remembered now that Benedikta, too, came from this town. These thoughts of the war and of her rival suddenly cast a pall over a trip that had been so pleasant up to then.

"Some girls staring into the waves have fallen in." The deep voice tore her out of her musings. She turned to see the Augsburg merchant Oswald Hainmiller, who was gnawing on a goose wing and offered her a second piece. Fat dripped from his lips, soiling his trimmed Vandyke beard and white pleated collar. The fat merchant was going on forty and wore a silver buckle and a wide belt that strained against his paunch. The red rooster feather on his hat fluttered in the breeze. Magdalena thought it over for a moment, then reached for the goose wing and took a healthy bite. Except for a few spoonfuls of oatmeal, she hadn't eaten anything all morning.

"Thanks very much!" she said with a full mouth before directing her gaze back to the turns in the river ahead.

Hainmiller grinned. "How long are you staying in our beautiful city?" he asked, wiping grease from his cheek with his lace-trimmed sleeves. "Will you have to go right back to your shabby little town?"

Hainmiller spoke in the broad Augsburg dialect that Schongauers hated so much because it reminded them of the free imperial city's snobbishness. Magdalena had booked passage that morning from the merchant. Oswald Hainmiller was bringing wine, oil, tin, spices, and a large cargo of lime with him, and Magdalena's presence was a welcome opportunity for him to while away the time and to boast a bit until they arrived in Augsburg that evening.

Magdalena sighed. The fat merchant had been trying to strike up a conversation with her ever since they left Schongau. It didn't look as if he would ever give up. Even when Magdalena told him she was the daughter of the Schongau hangman, he kept hitting on her. In fact, that seemed to excite him only more. Magdalena resigned herself to her fate and smiled back.

"I'll be able to stay only a day," she said. "Tomorrow, I'll be heading back."

"One day!" the merchant cried, gesturing heavenward as a sign of despair. "How will you be able to appreciate the beauty of this city in just one day? The new town hall, the bishop's palace, all the fountains! I have heard about Schongauers who were so overwhelmed when they first arrived they had to sit down—the sight was just too much for them."

The sight of you *is too much for me,* Magdalena thought, trying to concentrate on the whitecaps in front of her. This fat braggart was already spoiling her visit to Augsburg with all this talk. She was truly looking forward to seeing the city, which had been one of the greatest and most beautiful in Germany before the war.

"Do you know yet where you are going to sleep?" The merchant's face took on a ferret-like appearance.

"I . . . My father gave me the name of a good inn by the river," she said, and could feel her blood beginning to boil. "Food and lodging for only four kreuzers per night."

"But in return, you'll have to share your bed with a whole army of fleas and bedbugs." Oswald Hainmiller stepped very close to her now and was petting her skirt. She could see goose fat forming droplets in his beard. "At my house there is a four-poster with white linen, and you'd have to share that only with me. Perhaps I'd even pay *you* four kreuzers for the night," he whispered in her ear, moving so close now that she could smell the alcohol on his breath.

"Cut it out!" Magdalena snapped, pushing him away. "I may be just the hangman's daughter, but I'm not available."

The merchant didn't back off. "I know you girls," he slobbered. "First you resist, but then you're all the more willing."

The wine, combined with the sight of Magdalena, had clearly made Hainmiller more and more lecherous during the last hours of the trip. "Don't make such a fuss," he said, grabbing her bodice.

Magdalena pushed his hand away, disgusted. "Wash your mouth out before you say another word," she replied. "You stink like a dead rat."

She struggled to free herself from his grip and ran to the middle of the raft, where two Schongau raftsmen were guiding the vessel with long poles. She knew them by sight from Semer's tavern. They looked over at her hesitantly but didn't intervene. Magdalena cursed. She was probably nothing more in these men's eyes than the hangman's tramp getting her just deserts.

For Oswald Hainmiller, the whole thing became more and more of a game. He ran after her, grinning, while she fled past the raftsmen toward the back of the raft. She clambered over crates and packages, past millstones and sacks of marble and salt. Finally, she reached the back of the raft, but the merchant was still close behind her.

"Very good," Hainmiller purred, tugging at her bodice. "Here, at least we won't be disturbed."

Magdalena looked around. To her left, she spotted a large wooden cart full of quicklime, shrouded with a makeshift linen cover. Thinking quickly, she removed the waxed tarp, hoisted herself up, and skipped along the edge of the cart, smiling and swaying her hips suggestively.

"Come on!" she called to the merchant, who by now was out

of breath. "If you want me, you've got to come up here and get me."

Oswald Hainmiller hesitated a moment, then pulled his fat body up onto the side of the cart and edged his way toward her. "In just a second . . . just a second . . . I'll have you," he groaned.

When he'd gotten just an arm's length away, Magdalena suddenly gave him a shove, and he waved his hands wildly in the air trying to catch his balance.

"You damn slut!" he roared before falling headfirst into the cart.

A cloud of white dust covered him, and before long, he started to scream. The quicklime was in his eyes, in his mouth, and in every little open cut. Writhing, he coughed and finally pulled himself out of the cart. His coat and the jacket underneath were covered with white spots that started eating away at the cloth wherever there was any moisture. Magdalena jumped down from the cart and grinned. At the very least, Oswald Hainmiller would need a new wardrobe before his next tryst. And perhaps a new face.

After hesitating briefly, she took two handfuls of the white powder and carefully filled the side pockets of her overcoat, being careful that the strong, caustic powder didn't get wet and eat through her clothing, too. Who knows, maybe she could use it again.

"I'll . . . I'll make you pay for this, you hangman's wench!" Hainmiller, panting and half blind, leaned over the back of the raft to wash his burning eyes in the water. Seconds later, he was squirming and screaming on the floor of the raft as the powder, hissing and smoking, reacted with the water. "You damned slut!" he howled, crawling across the logs in search of a clean rag to wipe his face. "You won't enjoy anything in beautiful Augsburg, that I promise you!"

"From now on, leave me alone," she shouted, moving to the

front again, where the Schongau raftsmen stared at her curiously. "You, too," she shouted, "you lecherous, cloven-hoofed scum! You're all trouble!"

Sitting down on a crate in the bow, she wrapped her arms around her knees and stared straight ahead. Her mother always warned her that most men were either horny fools or unfeeling blocks of ice. It was best to have nothing to do with them. Magdalena started to cry, but not wanting any of the nosy people standing around to see how sad she was, she brushed away her tears.

At this moment, like a little child, she wished her father were there.

Jakob Kuisl slid down the bank until his feet came into contact with the first rung. An iron railing ran along the rock face before disappearing into a fissure after about fifty feet. For a moment, the hangman considered lighting the torches he'd brought along, but he decided against this, lest he warn the bandits. Inside the fissure, everything was black, but soon his eyes grew accustomed to the dark. Above him, daylight was cut off briefly as each of the men squeezed his way through the crevice. There were only five of them, but Kuisl knew he could count on each, particularly Andre Wiedemann, who had fought with him near Augsburg in the battle against the Swedish invaders. But the blacksmith and the two other men looked like seasoned veterans, too.

After another fifty feet, the railing ended at the foot of the rock chimney. In one corner, Kuisl could make out a narrow passageway and hear the sound of muffled voices and laughter inside. The men slipped to the ground carefully on both sides of the passageway, and the hangman ventured a quick glance.

Behind the knee-high entrance, a short tunnel opened onto a large cave a few feet away. Over a crackling fire, a few rabbits sizzled on a spit. Now and then a ragged figure walked past the fire. Jakob Kuisl could see more men sitting on the other side of the flames, huddled in fur and rags against the cold. Someone belched loudly, others laughed, and two others still were quarreling loudly. Jakob could also hear the whine of a small child and smell sweat, gunpowder, and burning meat in the air.

Smoke stung Kuisl's eyes; he blinked. He had been right. They had found the winter quarters of the Scheller gang, and it looked now as if most of them had returned in the evening from their daily forays. The hangman smiled grimly. There could hardly be a better moment to put a stop to their game. From the voices, Kuisl could only guess how many there were—perhaps around thirty, among them many women and children.

He nodded to Wiedemann, Kronauer, and the others; then he cut off six of the twelve wooden powder flasks from the chain around his shoulder. In each, there was enough powder for one charge. With a leather cord, he tied six of them together so tightly they could all fit in one hand.

He squinted, estimating how far away the thieves were, and raised his arm. With one smooth gesture, he tossed the self-made bomb through the tunnel and directly into the fire.

The explosion was so strong it threw Kuisl back a full yard into the tunnel. The blast reverberated from the rocky walls of the caverns and corridors, a thundering echo so loud it seemed the mountain might collapse. Jakob Kuisl felt a faint tingling in his ears, and it was a while before he could hear the screams, coughing, and cursing coming from the robbers' den. He gave a sign to the four other men, and they crawled through the low tunnel, entering the inferno with their sabers drawn.

The explosion had blown embers and burning logs throughout the cave and caused rocks and boulders to fall from the ceiling. Ragged men and women crawled around, trying to get their bearings despite the heavy smoke. A few lifeless figures surrounded what was left of the fireplace, and agonized screams and the cries of children resounded through the smoke-blackened cave.

The hangman hesitated. Deciding against an attack, he shouted in a loud, deep voice that could be heard everywhere in the cave. "It's over, you dirty thieves. Now put down your weapons and leave, nice and easy, with your hands up. There's a small army of well-armed citizens waiting for you outside, and if you behave and surrender, then—"

A dark shadow flew at him. At the last moment, he ducked and the blade only brushed his cheek. The man in front of him was at least a large as he was, and though his face, framed by a shaggy beard, was blackened with soot, his eyes flashed like glowing embers.

Kuisl's voice sounded deep and threatening. "Put down your weapons and go outside. You'll only make this worse."

"Go to hell, you bastard," the man snarled, and raised his saber again. This time the hangman was ready. He jumped back, pulling out a loaded pistol and pressing the trigger in one motion.

The bullet hit the robber in the shoulder and threw him back against the wall. As he stared in disbelief at the bloody mass where his right arm had once been, the hangman took out his larch-wood cudgel and struck the giant so hard that he tumbled to the floor against the rock wall.

"I warned you," Kuisl grumbled, wiping a trickle of blood from his cheek.

Out of the corner of his eye, the hangman could see Wiedemann fighting one of the robbers, too. The other three men had run outside behind the fleeing highwaymen.

Wiedemann's back was to the wall, and despite the cold, pearls of sweat formed on his brow. The man in front of him swung at him with a jagged saber as if he were splitting wood. The veteran was struggling to fend off his opponent, and it looked as though he was about to collapse under a hail of blows.

Outside, shots could be heard. Jakob Kuisl hesitated. What was going on out there? Hadn't the scoundrels surrendered?

"Surrender!" the hangman shouted at the robber fighting with Wiedemann. "You're the last one!"

But the man didn't even seem to hear him. He kept slashing away at Andre Wiedemann with a look in his eyes that reminded the hangman of a wild beast, a mixture of hunger, desire, and naked fear. The boy was probably not even twenty years old.

Jakob Kuisl kicked the boy in the side with his right boot. When he fell to the ground, panting, Kuisl pointed his second loaded pistol at him.

"Now get out, and be quick about it! Then nothing will happen to you."

The young robber seemed to be thinking it over. He looked the hangman up and down, then threw the saber away and ran toward the exit with his hands in the air.

"I'm leaving," he shouted. "Don't hurt me, I'm—"

As he crossed the cave entrance, a shot rang out.

The boy's body was thrown back inside, and he landed on the ground, quivering. Once more, he raised his head and looked at the hangman in disbelief, then collapsed.

"Damn! What's going on out there?" Kuisl shouted. "The man surrendered!"

He hurried to the exit, which was framed on both sides by icicles so big they looked like columns. When he looked outside, he saw the flash from a gun to his right. He ducked behind one of the icicles and, at the same moment, felt a dull pain in his left upper arm.

"You damn fools!" he cried out. "It's me, the hangman! Stop at once!"

He leaned against the rock face, looking for cover. When he heard no further shots, he poked his head out carefully and saw a gruesome scene outside the cave.

A wave of anger came over him.

The Schongau men formed a half circle around a pile of dead bodies—young, old, men, women, and children. Blood flowed in streams over the white snow.

Several muskets were still directed at the entrance, and only gradually did the citizens lower their weapons. Hans Berchtholdt's musket was still smoking. With a mixture of confusion and bloodlust, he stared at the hangman, who emerged from the cave now looking like the devil incarnate.

"I . . . I . . ." Berchtholdt stuttered.

"You dirty bastard, you almost killed me!" shouted Jakob Kuisl. Then he ran to the baker's son and grabbed the barrel of the musket with his right hand. With a loud curse, he rammed the butt of the gun into Berchtholdt's stomach so hard he sank to the ground, gasping.

"And what is this?" the hangman roared, pointing to the pile of corpses. "You were supposed to disarm and arrest them, not slaughter them!" For a moment, he was tempted to hit Berchtholdt over the head with his own musket, but Kuisl broke it over his knee instead and threw it as far as he could.

"They . . . they just started shooting." Jakob Schreevogl stepped forward now. His face white, he was trembling and looking down sheepishly. "I couldn't help myself."

"How many?" Kuisl whispered.

Schreevogl just nodded. "We were able to capture a dozen, and the rest are dead, shot down like dogs."

Berchtholdt stood up and spoke again, groaning. "You ought to be glad—that saves you work; you won't have to string up so many."

"It . . . was very simple," Sebastian Semer added, a kind of fire burning in his eyes that the hangman knew all too well. "Just like hunting."

Behind them, other voices joined in: "Why wait? Let's string the rest of them up on the beech tree over there!"

Jakob Kuisl closed his eyes. His wounded left arm ached. Bloody scenes passed before his eyes, memories of days long gone.

Silence, only the cawing of the ravens strutting around on the bloody uniforms and pecking at the eyes of the dead women . . . a knotty tree full of twitching bodies that hang like plump apples on a tree . . . the men—my own men—looking at me, eyes wide with fear. I grab the next one, toss the noose around his neck, one after the other. One after the other . . .

The baker's son seemed to notice Kuisl's distress. "Since when has the hangman been afraid of death, huh?" he jeered, tottering about unsteadily. "All we did was make less work for you."

Kuisl ignored him. "You're just animals," he whispered softly to himself. "Every one of you is worse than the hangman."

He pushed the crowd aside and walked over to the trembling prisoners who were tied up, awaiting their fate. There were around a dozen of them, including four women. One of the women carried a screaming infant in a sling on her back. Two emaciated boys, around six and ten years of age, clung to their mother. Most of the men had fresh wounds, had been struck by a sword or grazed by a bullet, and many of the haggard faces were beaten black and blue.

One member of the anxious group stood out. He was almost as large as the hangman and wore a full beard, torn breeches, and a filthy leather cape collar. Blood seeped from a wound on his forehead, but despite his impoverished appearance, there was an aura of strength and pride about him. He looked at the hangman with an alert, steady gaze.

"You must be Hans Scheller," Kuisl said.

The gang leader nodded. "And you're nothing more than a filthy, murdering band of thugs," he said.

Cries and angry shouts came from behind the hangman.

"Watch what you say, Scheller!" one of the workers shouted back. "Or we'll rip your belly open right now and hang your guts up in the branches!"

"Nobody's going to rip anyone's belly out," Kuisl said. His voice was calm, but there was something in it that caused the others to fall silent.

"We'll take the marauders along with us back to Schongau now," he continued, "and then the city council will take care of them. You all have done enough damage here already." He turned aside with a disgusted expression. Snowflakes fell on the lifeless bodies piled up at the cave entrance like so many slaughtered animals.

The hangman shook his head. "Now let's at least give them a decent burial."

For the time being, he bound up his left arm with a dirty rag and used his right arm to move aside a few stones lying in a hollow near the cave.

"What's the matter?" he growled. "Doesn't anyone want to help me? After you nearly shot me to death, too?"

Silently, the Schongauers moved in to help him clear a space for the icy stone graves.

Jakob Kuisl's left arm was so painful that he left the men to finish the bloody work on their own. With clenched teeth, he went back into the cave to look around.

The two robbers lay dead right where he'd left them, but the smoke was still so thick he couldn't see farther than a few steps. He climbed over rubble, burning tree branches, and blackened logs until he reached the rear of the vault. Strewn about here were the robbers' few belongings: tattered coats, stained copper plates, a few rusty weapons, even a roughly carved wooden doll.

Farther back still, directly along the sooty rock wall, the hangman came across a wooden box reinforced with iron bands.

Its padlock took only five minutes of the hangman's time. The lock snapped open, and Jakob Kuisl put his lock pick back in his bag, opening the trunk cautiously, well aware that some boxes like this were booby trapped — poisoned needles and pins could come shooting out. But nothing happened.

At the bottom of the trunk lay a few shining guilders; a silver pitcher; a corked, unopened bottle of brandy; furs; and a golden brooch that at one time must have belonged to the wife of a rich merchant. There wasn't much there, but that didn't surprise the hangman. The robbers had evidently bartered most of their treasure away or hidden it somewhere, which Kuisl doubted. He would certainly discover the truth in the tower dungeon. The hangman hoped that Hans Scheller would be reasonable and spare him having to tie hundredweight stones to his feet, as he had done with the highwayman Georg Brandner two years ago. Kuisl had had to break every bone in Brandner's body before he finally told him where he had buried the stolen coins.

Underneath a lice-ridden fur coat and bearskin cap, the hangman finally came upon a laced-up leather bag. He opened it and couldn't help laughing — it was exactly what he needed now. Evidently, either the robbers had at one time attacked a barber surgeon or one of them had held onto the surgical kit from his military service. In the bag, a needle, thread, and forceps were neatly arranged by size and still relatively free of rust.

Kuisl uncorked the bottle of brandy with his teeth and took a long swig. Then he rolled up his left shirtsleeve and felt for the wound. The bullet had passed through his coat, leather collar, and shirt and had lodged in his upper arm. Fortunately, the bone appeared uninjured, but Kuisl could feel that the bullet was still lodged in his flesh. He found a piece of leather in the bag, clenched it between his teeth, and groped for the bullet with the forceps.

The pain was so severe that he felt himself getting sick, so he sat down on the trunk to take a few deep breaths before continuing. Just when he thought he was going to faint, the forceps met a firm object. He carefully drew it out and viewed the small, bent piece of lead. After taking another drink, he poured the rest of the brandy over the wound. Once again, he was almost overcome with pain, but the hangman knew that most soldiers didn't die from bullets themselves, but from the gangrene that followed a few days later. During the war, he learned that brandy could prevent gangrene. While most barber surgeons recommended cauterizing the wound or pouring hot oil into it, Kuisl preferred this method and had had good experience on some of his patients with it.

Finally, he wrapped the arm with material he'd ripped from the shirt of a dead robber and listened for voices outside the cave. The men seemed almost finished with their work, so Kuisl would have to remind them soon of the two corpses in the cave. And they would have to take the trunk along, too. The owners of the stolen objects were no doubt rotting away somewhere in the forests around Schongau, but the city could put the money to good use, if only to pay the hangman for the upcoming executions. Kuisl earned one guilder for each robber he hanged, four guilders for each blow to a man on the wheel, and two guilders and thirty kreuzers for torturing prior to the execution. It was quite possible that this was exactly the fate in store for robber chief Scheller.

Just as Kuisl was about to stand up, he caught sight of a large, glossy leather bag behind the trunk. It was made of the finest calfskin, and the front was embossed with a seal that the hangman didn't recognize. Was it possible, after all, that the robbers had other treasures stashed away? He set the bag in front of him and looked inside. What he saw puzzled him.

What in the world?

Lost in thought, he stuffed the bag into his sack and headed toward the cave entrance.

He would have some questions to ask Hans Scheller. For both their sakes, Kuisl hoped the robber chief would answer them quickly and honestly.

Night was falling on the Tanners' Quarter just outside the town walls when Simon knocked on the door to the hangman's house.

He'd spent the last hour stomping back to Schongau through a light snowfall. The businesswoman had proceeded directly to Semer's inn. Simon assumed she had to make preparations for her brother's funeral the following day, but she also seemed exhausted. The medicus, too, was tired and freezing after the long search. Despite the cold and approaching nightfall, however, he wanted to talk with Jakob Kuisl about what they had found in the castle ruins. He was also curious about how things had gone in the hunt for the highwaymen. His hands and feet felt like blocks of ice, so he was more than happy when Anna Maria Kuisl finally came to the door.

"Simon, what in the world has happened to you?" she asked in astonishment, looking at his snow-covered overcoat and stiff, frozen trousers. She seemed to have already forgiven him for the disturbance late the previous night, when Simon had been calling loudly for Magdalena. The hangman's wife shook her head sympathetically. "You look like the snowman that the kids built in the backyard."

"Is your husband here?" Simon's voice trembled. His whole body was frigid now.

Anna Maria shook her head. "He's out hunting for the robbers. I hope he comes home soon. But come in now; you look like you're freezing," she said as she led Simon into the warm room.

She poured some hot apple cider for Simon and handed him the cup. The room was filled with the aroma of steaming onions and melted butter.

"Here, this will be good for you." She smiled cheerfully at him as he sipped on the cider sweetened with honey.

"I'm sorry I can't offer you coffee, but perhaps you'd like to wait for my husband in the other room. I've got to go back upstairs and have another look at the children." They could hear a dry cough and the cries of little Barbara upstairs.

"Georg has it in his chest," she said anxiously. "Let's hope it's not this fever that's going around." She'd climbed the steep flight of stairs before Simon could ask if Magdalena was home.

She was probably still feeling hurt. Well, he had learned that women needed time. She'd be back, and then he would have a chance to say he was sorry.

Fortified by the sweet apple cider, Simon entered the adjacent room. In the course of the last year, he had become accustomed to visiting the hangman's library at least once a week, and Jakob Kuisl allowed him to browse through the old folios and leather-bound books in his absence. In the process, Simon had often stumbled upon things that were interesting for his work as a doctor. For example, the hangman had the complete works of the English doctor Thomas Sydenham, in which every known illness was listed and described in detail—a compendium not even found in the library in Ingolstadt!

The book he held in his hand at the moment, however, didn't have the slightest thing to do with medicine. Titled *Malleus Maleficarum* (*The Witches' Hammer*), it was written by two Dominicans—Heinrich Kramer and Jakob Sprenger. Some pages were soiled and worn, and some had a brownish sheen that looked like dried blood. Simon had frequently browsed through the so-called *Witches' Hammer.* On the page he had open at the moment, the authors tried to prove that the Latin word *femina* (woman) came from *fides minus,* meaning "of less faith." Another chapter described what witches looked like, the type of magic they used, and how one could protect himself from them. Then, Simon became engrossed in a detailed passage that described how to make the male organ disappear by magic.

"A bad book," a voice behind him said. "It would be better for you to put it away."

Simon turned around. In the doorway, the hangman stood wearing a bandage over his left arm, while snow melted from his fur trousers and formed a puddle at his feet. He tossed his musket in a corner and took the volume from Simon's hands.

"This book belonged to my grandfather," he said as he placed it back on one of the tall shelves along with the other books, parchment rolls, notes, and farmers' almanacs. "He used it in interrogations back in the days when more than sixty women were burned at the stake in Schongau. You can make anyone out to be a witch if you just badger them long enough."

Simon felt a chill, and not just because of the unheated room. Like all other Schongauers, he'd heard a lot about the notorious witch trials three generations ago that had made the city a name for itself all over Bavaria. In those days, Jakob Kuisl's grandfather Jörg Abriel had come into a lot of money and dubious notoriety. With his attendants, he traveled by coach to a number of places where executions were to be held and extracted a confession from every witch.

"These Dominicans . . ." Simon asked after a pause. "Aren't they often inquisitors at witch trials?"

The hangman nodded. "*Domini canes* is another name for them—the dogs of the Lord. They are clever and well read and do the dirty work for the Pope." He spat on the floor, which was covered with fresh reeds. "Let's hope that no one from this despicable order ever comes to Schongau. Where the Dominicans are, there is fire. And who gets his hands dirty then? Who do you think? Me! That filthy, accursed gang! Unscrupulous smart-asses and bookworms who revel in the suffering of others!"

Having worked himself into a frenzy, he pulled out the bottle of brandy from under his overcoat and took a deep swig.

Then he wiped his mouth with the back of his hand and took a deep breath. Only slowly did he regain his usual composure.

"Do you yourself use that . . . book?" Simon pointed hesitantly to *The Witches' Hammer* on the shelf.

The hangman shook his head and headed toward the heated room. "I have other methods. But tell me now what you found up at the castle."

They made themselves comfortable by the stove, where a stew of onions, carrots, and bacon was simmering. Suddenly, Simon realized how hungry he was, so when the hangman filled up two plates, he dug in gratefully.

After they had eaten in silence for a while, Simon pointed to the hangman's bandaged arm. "Did that happen while you were chasing the robbers?" he asked.

Jakob Kuisl nodded, wiped his mouth on his sleeve, and pushed the plate aside. Then he started filling his long-stem pipe.

"We caught them," he grumbled. "Down in the Ammer Gorge near Schleyer Falls. A good number of them are dead, and the rest are cooling their heels up in the dungeon. So I'll have plenty to do in the next few days, too, and won't be able to help you." He lit his pipe with an ember and eyed Simon sternly. "But stop stalling and tell me now . . . What happened up on Castle Hill? Or do I have to apply the thumbscrews to you first?"

Simon grinned inwardly. Even if the hangman was crabby and uncommunicative, he was just as curious as Simon. The physician wished he could get more out of the hangman about the fight with the robbers, but for now, he related what he had found in the crypt under the chapel and everything else he had learned in his search with Benedikta. "The inscription," he concluded, "must be a riddle. And the word *tree* is carved in capital letters. But I swear we examined every tree in the whole damned forest up on that mountain and couldn't find a thing!"

"An inscription in German . . ." the hangman murmured. "Strange, you would think the Templars would have written in

Latin at that time. At least that's the way it is in all my old books, only pompous-sounding Latin, no German and certainly not Bavarian German. Well, so be it . . ." He puffed big black clouds of smoke from his stem pipe, eyeing them intently in the flickering light of the embers. "This damned Templar is sending us on a wild goose chase," he muttered. "First the crypt in the Saint Lawrence Church, then the basilica in Altenstadt, and now the castle ruin in Peiting, which doesn't seem to be the last riddle, either. I wonder what else lies in store for us."

"I think I know," Simon said. He explained his suspicion that Temple Master Friedrich Wildgraf had concealed part of the Templar's treasure here. The hangman listened without saying a word. "This treasure is more than anything we can imagine," Simon finally concluded in a whisper, as if he feared someone could be listening in on them. "Enough to buy whole cities, I believe, and fund wars. Such a treasure would also explain the murder of Koppmeyer, the presence of these monks in Strasser's Tavern, and the attempt on your life. Someone is doing everything he can to eliminate anyone else who might know about this."

"But what's the point of all this rubbish with the riddles and the game of hide-and-seek?" grumbled the hangman, drawing on his pipe. "A simple clue in the crypt, a testament would have also sufficed."

"Up to now, all the riddles have had something to do with God," Simon interrupted, struggling not to cough through the clouds of smoke. "The Templars no doubt wanted to make sure only a true believer would find the treasure. The inscription from the castle ruins also seems like a sort of prayer." He pulled out a parchment roll on which he had noted the lines.

"*This is what I discovered among men as the greatest wonder,*" the physician mumbled, "*that the earth did not exist, nor the sky above, nor* TREE . . ." He hesitated. "Why in the world is 'tree' capitalized? Did we overlook something up there?"

"*Deus lo vult,*" the hangman murmured suddenly.

"*What?*"

"*Deus lo vult*—it's the will of God. That's what the man with the dagger said to the fat Swabian down in the crypt. It almost sounded like a battle cry. What the devil does that mean?"

Simon shrugged. "A man with a strong scent of perfume, another with a curved dagger, a fat Swabian . . ." The medicus rubbed his tired eyes, which were tearing up from the smoke. "What an odd group! And how did these men ever learn about the Templar's grave? From the construction workers?"

The hangman shook his head. "I don't think so. I actually have another idea, but it's too early to say yet. Now I'm tired."

He rose to accompany the physician to the door. Suddenly, it occurred to Simon that, with all the excitement, he had completely forgotten to ask the hangman about Magdalena.

"Your daughter . . ." he began saying at the doorway. "I . . . I must speak with her. I think I have to apologize. Is she upstairs in the house or still with Stechlin?"

The hangman shook his head. "Neither. She left for Augsburg this morning on the ferry to get a few supplies for me and the midwife. It's probably best if you don't see each other for a while."

"But . . ." Simon suddenly felt forlorn.

Jakob Kuisl pushed him outside, slowly closing the door behind him. "She'll come back, don't worry," he grumbled. "She's just a stubborn Kuisl like her mother, and now, good night. I have to go upstairs and have a look at little Georg."

With a creak, the door clicked shut on Simon, leaving him alone with the darkness. Snowflakes were falling on his head, and it was as silent as the grave. Carefully, he threaded his way through the fresh snow toward the lights of the town. Slowly, a feeling crept over him that he had made a great mistake.

• • •

The merchant stopped bothering Magdalena for the rest of the way to Augsburg. Once or twice, he cast a glance at her with reddened, spiteful eyes, but otherwise, he was busy washing off the quicklime with icy water from the Lech and rubbing lotion on his burning face. Oozing red pustules were breaking out around the edges of his beard, and he cursed softly as he sipped from a bottle of fruit brandy to calm himself down.

The six o'clock bells were about to ring when Magdalena spotted a number of sparkling lights in the darkness ahead—just a few at first, but as time passed, more and more appeared until they eventually filled the entire horizon.

"Augsburg," she whispered, full of awe.

Until now, Magdalena had known the city only from what people had told her—that it was a metropolis more lively and colorful than little Schongau. Here Protestants and Catholics lived peacefully side by side in a free city, subject only to the emperor. Its wealth was legendary before the Great War, and even now, the city seemed to have lost little of its former splendor.

The view helped the hangman's daughter forget her anger and sadness for the time being. The ferry landing was a short way outside the city, near the Red Gate. Even at this late hour, there was more activity on the pier than Magdalena had ever seen in Schongau. Barrels and sacks were being offloaded by the dozen, and a crowd of dockworkers were bent over as they carried the heavy cargo to storage sheds nearby. The glow of innumerable torches and lanterns made it possible for work to continue even now, after darkness had fallen. Harsh commands, but also crude words and laughter, could be heard all over the landing.

Fortunately, Magdalena had already paid for her passage in Schongau, so she could disembark without having to deal with the merchant anymore and disappear in the noisy crowd. She kept checking to make sure the little linen bag was still hanging over her shoulder. It contained instructions from Stechlin and her father—but above all, the money the midwife had given her. Twenty guilders! She had never had so much money in her life! Most of it came from the pregnant Frau Holzhofer, who was waiting in Schongau for her bezoar.

When Magdalena looked around again, she noticed that Oswald Hainmiller, along with two men dressed all in black, had been trailing her. He was whispering to them and pointing at her. His face, disfigured with pustules and a red rash, seemed to flare with hatred.

Magdalena boarded one of the little boats that ferried people over a canal to the Red Gate. It was a rough trip, and passengers were pressed close together. Out of the corner of her eye, she noticed that the two men had boarded the boat as well, but she decided to ignore them for the time being.

Shortly thereafter, she arrived, freezing and hungry. The Red Gate would be closing punctually when the six o'clock bell rang, and merchants dressed in furs, as well as ragged day laborers and wagon drivers, were crowding into the city. Magdalena jumped aside to let a horse-drawn coach pass, and promptly tripped over a street vendor behind her, holding a sales tray around his neck.

"Can't you watch where you're going?" the man snapped at her as he picked his tinderbox, shears, and whetstone up off the street.

"I'm . . . I'm dreadfully sorry," Magdalena stuttered. Feeling something tug at her, she turned around just in time to see a boy, about ten years old, trying to cut off the strap to her purse with a little knife.

Magdalena slapped him so hard that he fell back into filthy slush.

"You'd better not try that again!" she growled at him, grabbing the purse even tighter, and hurrying through the slowly closing gate. When Magdalena turned around again to look at the boy, she was shocked to see the two men from the landing just a few steps away, carefully observing her.

"What's the rush, dear?" one of them growled. He was wearing a tattered overcoat and a patch over one eye. "Let's look for a place to stay together tonight. We'd be warmer together." A gust of wind blew his coat open a bit, revealing a heavy dagger about a foot long. The other man, who was as fat as a wine barrel, was swinging a big polished stick.

Without waiting to hear what the other might have to say, Magdalena raced off. She slipped into the crowd, then gradually worked her way through it. Behind her, she could hear suppressed cursing. The crowd in front of her was so dense that it was hard to make progress. She knocked down a few day laborers, bumped into some peddlers, and tipped over a basket of firewood.

Finally, she had worked her way through most of the crowd, and the street grew markedly quieter. Just as she was about to breathe a sigh of relief, she heard the hurried footfalls of someone behind her. She looked back as she ran and caught a glimpse of her pursuers, who had been able to slip through the crowd as well. The fat man waved his cudgel in the air and panted. The man with a patch over one eye was faster, and gaining ground. Magdalena looked around, desperate for help. Why hadn't she stayed hidden in the crowd? The men would never have dared to attack her in public. But here? Night had fallen and the houses and streets were just barely visible. There were hardly any people in this part of town, and the few who saw the men pursuing Magdalena ducked into entryways or anxiously peered out at the pursuers from behind tiny recessed windows.

Thinking fast, Magdalena turned into a narrow side street. Perhaps she could shake off her pursuers in a labyrinth of little lanes. She ran past clattering millwheels, over rickety bridges, and through tiny cobblestone squares, but the two men were right on her heels. She was a good runner and, in the forest or fields, probably could have shaken off the two easily, but here, in the streets and alleys, the men had an advantage. They knew the location of every stairway, every row of parked wagons that she would have to run around.

Coming around the next corner, she was suddenly confronted with a wall. Frost-covered ivy spiraled down from the top of the ten-foot-high wall, and a pile of fetid garbage lay in one corner. Bare walls rose up to the left and right. Seized with panic, Magdalena looked for a way out.

She had run into a cul-de-sac.

Her two pursuers caught up with her. She felt like a trapped animal as the men slowly approached her, smiling.

"You see, you little tart, now we've found a place all to ourselves," the man with the eye patch said. He looked around as if he were inspecting a room at an inn. "Maybe it's not so comfy, but I do like it. How about you?"

The fat man with the cudgel now approached from the left. "Don't make it harder than necessary," he growled. "If you scratch and bite, it's just going to hurt more."

"Oh, let her go ahead," the other said. "I like it when they scratch and bite." He swung his saber through the air. "Hainmiller gave us a tidy sum so you wouldn't forget him so soon. Just what did you do to his face, girl? Did you give him a bad shave? Well, in any case, we're going to shave *you* now."

The fat man looked at her almost sympathetically. "It's really too bad; you have such pretty lips. But what can we do? Let's get it over with." He moved closer.

Magdalena scrutinized the men, considering her options. She was alone, and this didn't look like the kind of area where anyone would come running out to help if she shouted. On the contrary, people would probably close their shutters and hope to steer clear of trouble themselves. Both thugs were powerfully built and looked like seasoned street fighters. It was clear that she had no chance for a fair fight.

But perhaps there was a way to trick them.

She dropped her arms, lowering her head meekly as if resigned to her fate, just waiting for the men to attack her. "Please don't hurt me . . ." she whimpered.

"You should have thought about that before, slut," said the man with the eye patch as he approached her with his sword raised. "Now it's a little too— "

With a sweeping gesture, Magdalena took aim at the thug, flinging a handful of the quicklime at him that she had been keeping in her jacket pocket. The powder formed a cloud in front of the man's eyes. He screamed and rubbed his face, trying to wipe away the lime with the arm he was using to hold the sword, but managed only to rub it deeper into his eyes. Shrieking loudly, he fell to the ground.

"You damned whore! I'll make you pay for that!"

He crawled toward her on his knees, swinging the sword wildly through the air, while the fat man with the cudgel approached. Magdalena reached into her jacket pocket again. Even though she knew it was empty now, she held her arm up again as if about to throw the next handful at the fat man's face.

"What do you say, fatso?" she snarled. "Do you want to go blind like your friend?"

The fat man stopped and looked down at his comrade moaning on the ground.

At that moment, Magdalena pretended to fling the powder in his face. The man ducked, and the hangman's daughter ran toward the pile of garbage.

Her feet sank into the slimy half-frozen garbage and feces, but she was able to jump up and get a handhold on the top of the wall. Her fingers dug into the ice and snow as she pulled herself up.

She had almost reached the top when she felt something pulling her back down again. The fat man was tugging on her shoulder bag, and the strap was tightening like a noose around her neck, cutting off her breath. She had just two choices: surrender and fall back down or be choked to death.

Of course, there was a third option—to let go of the bag—but she didn't even want to think about that.

As the strap tightened around her neck, Magdalena couldn't help but think of the people sentenced to die on the gallows. Is this how it felt when one was hanged? Dark clouds passed before her eyes, and she began to lose consciousness.

The third possibility . . .

She ducked suddenly, slipping the strap over her head, and the fat man fell back with a groan into the pile of garbage. She was free!

Ignoring the curses and cries of pain behind her, she jumped down the other side of the wall and ran along the street ahead, struggling to catch her breath. She ran through icy alleys and over slippery bridges, fell once or twice in muddy slush, and finally, gasping for air, came to a stop at a street corner.

She leaned against the wall of a house, sobbing, then collapsed on the cold ground. She had lost everything. Twenty guilders! Money that Stechlin and her father had entrusted to her, money *only borrowed* by the midwife from a patrician woman! She could never return to Schongau—the shame was too great—and she didn't even have a few coins for shelter that night. She was completely alone.

Magdalena was crying when she sensed someone standing nearby.

She looked up to see a young man leaning against the side of a house a few feet away. It was the little pickpocket who had tried to steal her purse. He watched her silently.

Finally, Magdalena lost her patience. "Why are you looking

at me like that?" she shouted. "Mind your own business, and get out of here!"

The boy shrugged and turned to leave.

Suddenly, Magdalena remembered that there was, indeed, someone who might help her. She could at least get shelter for the night, and perhaps he would have a suggestion about getting the money back. Magdalena had hoped she wouldn't have to go there, but as things stood now, it was her last chance.

"Wait!" she called to the boy, who turned around with a questioning look.

"Take me to Philipp Hartmann," she whispered.

"Who?" the boy asked, anxious. Faint light fell on his face from a window nearby, and he suddenly looked as white as a sheet. "I don't know any—"

"You know exactly who I mean." Magdalena stood up and wiped the saliva and tears from her face. "I want to go and see the Augsburg hangman—and hurry up about it, or I'll see that he strings you up by the Red Gate. I swear I will, as sure as my name is Magdalena Kuisl."

8

AT SIX O'CLOCK THE NEXT MORNING, JAKOB KUISL headed up to town. At this time of year very few people were out and about so early in the day, even on the busy Münzgasse. The few wine and cloth merchants he did meet crossed to the other side of the street when they saw him coming or made the sign of a cross. It was never good news when the hangman came up the hill from the Lech to Schongau. People tolerated him as long as he stuck to executions and carting away dead animals, but otherwise, they preferred that the executioner stay down below in the stinking Tanners' Quarter.

Jakob Kuisl could sense the townspeople watching. Word had gotten around that he'd smoked out the Scheller Gang, and no doubt his dispute with the young patricians was no longer a secret. Without paying any attention to the whispers behind him, he headed to the tower dungeon—a squat, three-story tower with soot-stained walls situated right along the city wall—where the watchmen had locked up the bandits the night before. Wrapped tightly in a coat that was much too thin, a bailiff stood guard in front of a heavy wooden door. He had propped his spear against the wall in hopes of warming his frozen hands in his pockets. He looked astonished as the hangman approached with a broad smile.

"Here, Johannes," Jakob Kuisl said, handing the bailiff a few warm chestnuts he'd been concealing under his coat. "My wife put a few of these aside for you and sends her best wishes."

"Well . . . thank you . . ." The bailiff sneezed and rubbed the warm chestnuts between his frozen fingers. "But you didn't come here just to bring me something to eat, did you?" he asked, peering out from under his rabbit-fur hood. "I know you, Kuisl."

The hangman nodded. "I've got a score to settle inside there with Scheller. Just let me in for a moment. I'll be right back."

"But what if Lechner hears about it?" Johannes muttered as he hungrily shelled the warm chestnuts. "He'll give me hell."

Jakob Kuisl dismissed the thought with a wave of his hand. "Oh, Lechner, he's turning over in his bed right now and going back to sleep. Go down to see my wife today after the noon bells, and she'll give you a pine liniment for your cold."

The bailiff grinned, popped a steaming chestnut between his rotten yellow teeth, took out a large rusty key, and opened the door to the dungeon.

"But don't rough up Scheller," he called to the hangman with a full mouth, "or he'll keel over before we have a chance to break him on the wheel, and that would be a pity."

Jakob Kuisl didn't answer but headed to the cells in back. The men and women had been split into two groups. Some of the robbers lay around listlessly on the cold stone floor, their wounds largely untreated. The six-year-old boy Kuisl had noticed the day before seemed to suffer from a high fever. His whole body trembling, he looked toward the ceiling vacantly while his mother rocked him in her lap. As Kuisl approached, some of the men who could still stand started rattling the rusty bars of their cells.

"So soon, Hangman?" one of them shouted. "Just when it's getting comfy here! Didn't you at least bring along a last meal for us?"

Others laughed. The air was filled with the stench of excrement and damp straw.

"Goddamn you!" one of the two women prisoners shouted, holding a screaming child out to him. "Who will take care of my little boy when I'm no longer here? Who? Or do you want to string him up along with us?"

"Oh shut up, Anna!" said a voice from the adjacent cell. "If the kid survives, they'll give him to the church. The boy is better off than any of us. If you didn't live with dignity, you can at least die with some."

Hans Scheller struck a defiant posture in the middle of the cell, his muscular arms folded across his chest. He looked like a rough-hewn, immovable block with facial features chiseled out of hard walnut. His cheeks were black and blue and swollen from being struck, and his left eye was glued shut with dried blood. With his right eye, however, he stared Jakob Kuisl down attentively and proudly.

"What do you want, Kuisl?" he asked. "You're not coming to take us to the gallows. You'll make a big deal out of that, with wine, dancing, and laughing, and if Scheller screams loud enough when you break him on the wheel, you'll get an extra guilder. But I won't scream; you can count on it."

"There's never been anyone who didn't scream," the hangman growled. "You've got my word on that."

Jakob Kuisl noticed a flash of fear in Scheller's eyes. The wheel was one of the cruelest forms of execution. After the executioner broke every bone in the condemned man's body with an iron bar, he tied him to a wagon wheel. If the prisoner was lucky, the executioner was merciful and broke his neck. If the prisoner wasn't, the executioner set the wheel up outside and let him die a slow miserable death in the blazing sun. That could take several days.

Jakob Kuisl winked at Scheller. "But we'll see. Perhaps it will be very different this time."

"Ha-ha!" jeered a neighbor in the next cell. "The hangman will let us go when the Pope wipes his ass with leaves!"

"Shut up, Springer!" Hans Scheller shouted. "Or I'll cut off your nose even before the hangman gets around to it."

The robber fell silent, and the others slowly moved back from the bars, too, settling down in the filthy, damp straw.

"So, Kuisl, what do you want?" the robber chief whispered.

The hangman was close enough to the bars now that he could smell the robber's foul breath. Hans Scheller's stubbled face was scarred, black and blue, and coated with dried blood.

"If you tell me where you've stashed your loot, I might be able to arrange a more lenient punishment," Kuisl said softly.

"Loot?" Hans Scheller feigned surprise and stared at him innocently. "What loot?"

In a lightning-fast motion, Jakob Kuisl reached through the bars to grab the robber chief's hand, bending his fingers back until they cracked. Hans Scheller turned white in the face.

"Let's not play games, Scheller," Kuisl growled. "This is just a little foretaste of what you can expect if you keep this up. Tongs, thumbscrews, the rack—I can show it all to you today. So what do you say?"

Hans Scheller tried to pull his hand back, but the hangman just applied more pressure. The cracking was now quite audible.

"The loot . . . is buried near the cave, over by the dead beech tree . . ." he groaned. "I would have told you, anyway."

"Excellent." Kuisl grinned and let go. Hans Scheller pulled his hand back and looked at his little finger, which was bent away from his hand at an odd angle.

"Go to hell, Hangman," he whispered. "I know people like

you. You'll grab the loot for yourself and let us all suffer a long time before we die."

Jakob Kuisl shook his head. "I'm serious, Scheller. I'll appeal to the town for you. No torture, no wheel. A nice, clean hanging. I promise."

"And the children and women?" Scheller asked. There was almost a look of hope in his face.

The hangman nodded. "I can't promise anything, of course, but I'll do my best. But in return, you have to tell me a few things."

Hans Scheller looked at him suspiciously. "What?"

"First, this attack a few days ago on our medicus and his companion. Was that you?"

Scheller hesitated for a moment. Finally, he replied, "Not me personally, but a few of my men. They were getting bored, so they ambushed him, and then the woman blew them away." He grinned. "She must have been a hell of a woman, according to what I've heard."

The hangman grinned back. "I'd say so, too, if a woman beat me to the draw in a gunfight. But I have something else here—this bag." From under his overcoat, Kuisl pulled out the embossed leather satchel he had found in the robbers' hideout. "Where did you get this?"

The robber chief hesitated. "Let's see . . . We took that from some other bandits."

"Other bandits?"

Scheller nodded. "They were tough customers. We surprised them some time ago sitting around their campfire at night, but they fought back like the Swedes. Before they fled, they slit open the bellies of two of my men. They're a really bad bunch—be careful before you get mixed up with them. They left the bag behind." Hans Scheller looked surprised. "But why do you want it? There's nothing of value there. We went through it twice."

The hangman didn't answer but continued his questioning. "What did the men look like? Were they wearing black cowls, like monks? Were they carrying curved daggers?"

"Curved daggers?" The robber chief shrugged. "No, they were just ordinary bandits—dark coats, wide-brimmed hats, sabers. Quick and experienced fighters. I presume they used to be mercenaries."

"And what sort of loot did they have?" Kuisl continued.

Scheller's battered face twisted into a grimace. "We got whole bags full of it, quite a bit. They must have been as busy as hell around here." He stopped to think for a moment. "But one thing was strange. They left a lot of things behind at the campfire—dishes, pots, spoons, tablecloths, things like that. A set for four people, but we saw only three of them." He continued smiling. "The fourth was probably out in the woods taking a piss and took off when we arrived."

"A fourth man . . ." Jakob Kuisl said, thinking aloud and looking at the purse in his hand. Then he threw it over his shoulder like an old, unwanted toy and headed for the exit.

"Remember your promise!" Hans Scheller called out as the hangman left.

He nodded. "You've got my word."

He looked in on the sick boy, who was trembling, feverish, and raving incoherently. "After the noon bells, I'll stop by and bring you a drink of ivy and juniper brandy, which will help the boy's fever."

As Kuisl opened the door to leave, he came face-to-face with the severe countenance of Johann Lechner. Behind the clerk stood the bailiff, shrugging apologetically.

"Kuisl," Lechner snarled. "You owe me an explanation. I came here to observe the prisoners, and what do I find? The hangman was already here before me. Let's just hope you haven't wrung their necks already."

Jakob Kuisl sighed. "Your Excellency," he said, "you'll get

your explanation, but let's go up to the office in the castle to do that. Only the robbers need to freeze their asses off down here."

The funeral bells tolled at exactly ten o'clock, and the funeral began. In spite of the cold, many people had come to say their last farewells to Father Andreas Koppmeyer, among them many simple folk, workers, and day laborers, who counted the fat, fatherly priest as one of their own. Because the old St. Lawrence Church was under renovation and in no way equipped to handle such a huge crowd, the citizens of Altenstadt had moved the funeral service to the great basilica at the last minute.

Simon was one of the last to arrive. He had been up half the night thinking about the riddle in the chapel, leafing through the little guide by Wilhelm von Selling, but he'd made no progress. He was also tormented by the thought that Magdalena had set out for Augsburg without even saying good-bye. Would she ever forgive him? Why was she always so stubborn?

He had fallen asleep just before daybreak and was awakened just a few hours later by his father, who was extremely reluctant to give him time off to attend the funeral. Simon jumped into his trousers, pulled on a new jacket of fine Augsburg cloth, and on the way out the door, drank what remained of the previous night's coffee, straight from the pot.

As he carefully opened the portal to the basilica, the sermon had already begun. The door squeaked loudly and a blast of cold air came in from outside, so that some of the mourners turned around with disapproving looks. Simon mumbled a few words of apology, took off his hat, and sat down in the back of the basilica on the right, where pews were set aside for the men. In the front, on the opposite side, he could see Benedikta. She was wearing a loosely pleated black skirt and, over that, a lap jacket that accentuated her tightly laced bodice. Her red hair was almost completely hidden under a black hood, and she seemed even paler than usual. All around her sat the well-to-do citizens of Altenstadt. Simon recognized the innkeeper Franz Strasser, the carpenter Balthasar Hemerle, and Matthias Sacher, who, as a rich miller, represented the Altenstadters in the Schongau town council. The physician's gaze wandered to the red upholstered seat of honor behind the altar. There, sitting up straight and murmuring a silent prayer with his eyes closed, was Augustin Bonenmayr, the abbot of Steingaden. As Andreas Koppmeyer's superior, he had evidently not hesitated to take the long trip and pay his last respects to the Altenstadt priest.

The dead priest lay in an open coffin in front of the altar, and the church was so cold a thin layer of ice had formed on his face.

Pausing in his sermon for a moment to cast a disapproving eye at the late arrival, Father Elias Ziegler now continued. His nose was as red as a ripe apple, and Simon guessed he'd already helped himself to the communion wine that morning.

"Andreas Koppmeyer was one of us," the priest said unctuously, "a bear of a man who understood well the cares and fears of his flock, because these were concerns he shared with them."

A whimper sounded from one of the pews in back, and Simon turned around to see Magda, the fat housekeeper from the rectory, who took out a large, dirty handkerchief and blew her nose loudly. The skinny rector, Abraham Gedler, seemed close to tears, too, and clutched a prayer book tightly, as if trying to squeeze blood out of it.

"But the Lord alone knows when our hour is at hand," the priest continued, "and so we lay all our hopes and cares in God's hands . . ."

Simon's thoughts wandered to Magdalena and her trip. No one was safe from robbers, even on the Lech—to say nothing of the way back by road. He hoped nothing had happened to her. Her father should never have allowed her to go! She was much too young and naive for such a trip, Simon thought. Unlike Benedikta. The woman from Landsberg might be only a few years older, but she seemed so much more mature. Simon looked straight ahead. Even now, in the face of her brother's death, Benedikta Koppmeyer seemed composed. The physician couldn't find anyone else in the congregation who might be a relative. Presumably, Benedikta and Andreas were the only siblings, and the woman had no children. At least she hadn't spoken of any. Simon was both fascinated and irritated by this elegant lady, who could speak French and, only minutes after, kill a robber in cold blood. He was both attracted and repelled by her. He sighed, knowing that this mix could have fatal consequences.

Simon glanced up at the Great God of Altenstadt, who looked down benevolently and all-knowingly on the faithful. He couldn't help the physician with his problems, either.

"Let us pray."

The priest's words tore Simon from his reveries, and he stood up with the others to recite the Lord's Prayer.

"Pater noster, qui es in caelis, sanctificetur nomen tuum . . ."

When Pastor Elias Ziegler had finished, he raised his head to the Great God of Altenstadt and spread his arms as if in benediction. Then he spoke in a clear voice.

What the priest said next nearly knocked Simon over, and he struggled to get a grip on the arm of the pew.

"*This is what I learned among mortal men as the greatest wonder. That there was neither the earth nor the heaven above. Nor was there any tree nor mountain. Neither any star at all, nor any other thing . . .*"

The voice of Elias Ziegler echoed through the dome of the basilica like that of a prophet. Here was the riddle from the crypt in the Castle Hill chapel.

"You are demanding *what* from me?" Johann Lechner looked at the hangman in disbelief and dropped the pen he was about to use to sign a few papers. His lips formed a narrow, bloodless line in a pale face, and his eyes darted nervously back and forth. The endless paperwork and, above all, his growing worries about the town had kept him awake the last few nights. Lechner's skin sometimes looked as transparent as a blank sheet of parchment, but the strength of his will and tenacity were legendary—and feared—far beyond the borders of Schongau.

With Jakob Kuisl and a retinue of two bailiffs, he had hurried back to the ducal palace after their meeting in the dungeon. He walked ahead the entire time, and the guards struggled to keep up.

In his office, Lechner gestured to Kuisl to take a seat and then went back to working on his documents. Only after some time had passed did he ask Kuisl what had happened during his conversation with the robber chief. When Jakob Kuisl told him, the little artery on Lechner's pale forehead swelled up and turned a fiery red.

"Naturally, we'll set an example and break Scheller on the wheel. Anything else is out of the question!" he exclaimed angrily as he continued signing his papers. "I'll go to the city council today and urge a speedy execution."

"If you do that, we'll never learn where Scheller hid the loot," Kuisl said, taking out his pipe.

"Then squeeze it out of him. Start with the thumbscrews, put him on the rack, and stretch him with millstones. Stick burning matches under his fingernails . . . It doesn't matter how you torture him. You'll think of the right method."

Kuisl shook his head. "Scheller is a tough customer. It's likely he won't talk, even when I torture him. So why waste your time and money?"

The clerk glared at Kuisl. "What kind of loot would they have?" he said finally. "A few guilders and farthings, maybe a lice-ridden fur coat. Who cares about that?"

Kuisl's gaze wandered almost apathetically around the room.

Documents were piled up on tables and shelves, awaiting action by the clerk. Lechner's breakfast—a mug of wine and a piece of white bread—lay untouched on a stool.

Finally, the hangman spoke up. "I'm guessing it's a lot more than just a few guilders. Scheller stole from another band of robbers."

"Another band of robbers?" Johann Lechner could barely keep from jumping out of his seat. "Do you mean there's another gang of thugs roving around out there?"

Slowly and methodically, the hangman filled his pipe. "All the attacks recently—from the Hoher Peißenberg to the Landsberg region—can't have been the work of just one gang. I believe Scheller. First let me track down the others as well; then the day after that, I'll string up the robber chief and his men for you, if that's what you want. If we do that, we'll know where the loot is hidden and finally be able to bring peace again to the Priests' Corner."

Lechner looked at the hangman, thinking. "And if I insist on torturing them on the wheel?" he asked finally.

Kuisl lit his pipe. "Then you can look for your robbers yourself. But I doubt you'll find them. I'm the only one who knows all the places they might be hiding."

"Are you threatening me?" Lechner's voice was suddenly as cold as a January morning.

Jakob Kuisl leaned back and blew little rings of smoke toward the ceiling. "I wouldn't call it a threat; I'd call it an understanding."

For a long time, only the sound of Lechner's fingers drumming on the desktop was audible.

"Very well, then," the clerk said finally. "You catch these other robbers for me, and for all I care, Scheller can be hanged instead of broken on the wheel. But first he'll have to tell us where the loot is hidden."

"Let the women and children go," the hangman said softly. "Give them a whipping and banish them from the town—that should be enough."

Lechner sighed. "Why not? After all, we're all human beings." Then he leaned forward. "But you've got to do one thing for me in return."

"What's that?"

"Put out your damned pipe. That disgusting smoke comes straight from hell. In Munich and Nuremberg they outlawed the vice years ago. And if things continue as they have been, I'll have to make drunkenness a punishable offense here in Schongau as well, and then you can whip yourself."

The hangman grinned. "As you wish." He extinguished the pipe with his thumb and started toward the door.

"Oh, Kuisl," the clerk added.

The hangman stopped. "Yes?"

"Why are you doing this?" Lechner looked at him suspiciously. "You could make a pile of money breaking him on the wheel—ten times what you get for a hanging. So why? Are you getting a little soft in your old age, or is there some other reason?"

Jakob Kuisl shrugged. "Were you in the war?" he finally replied.

Lechner seemed irritated. "No, why do you ask?"

"I've heard enough screaming in my life, and now I'd rather do a little healing."

Without another word, the hangman left, closing the door behind him.

Inside, the clerk continued perusing his documents, but he was having trouble putting his mind to it. He would never understand this Kuisl. So be it. He had promised the wealthy messenger he'd get the hangman out of the way for a long time, so if there was a second gang, all the better. That would take time, and Lechner would also save himself the sixteen guilders it cost to break the prisoner on the wheel—two guilders for each blow—not to mention the additional money that might be added to the city coffers if they retrieved it.

Satisfied, he signed another document with a flourish. They could always break the leader of the second group on the wheel. For the sake of justice.

Simon drummed his fingers nervously on the armrest of the pew, waiting for the last amen from Elias Ziegler. He felt like jumping up during the service, running to the front of the church, and demanding some explanation from the drunken priest. Benedikta, too, had started fidgeting and shifting around in her pew, turning back to look at Simon with a wide-open mouth when Ziegler mentioned the riddle they'd seen in the crypt. But before the service was finally over, there were two prayers in Latin and what seemed to Simon like an endless *Kyrie eleison*.

The citizens of Altenstadt now formed a line to offer condolences to Benedikta, who took a seat on a small wooden stool alongside the bier. At her side, the pastor nodded piously to the guests as they walked past the coffin and expressed their sympathy. Some of them placed dried flowers in the coffin, crossed themselves, or made signs with their fingers meant to ward off evil spirits. By now, most of them believed Andreas Koppmeyer had died simply from overeating, but thanks to the housekeeper, Magda, the rumor was still going around that the devil's minions had poisoned him because he had done too much to promote good in the world. The housekeeper collapsed in tears in front of the bier and had to be taken outside by the sacristan, Abraham Gedler.

Simon stared at Benedikta. Even now, the Landsberg wine merchant preserved her composure. She thanked each person individually and reminded everyone about the funeral feast to follow. That really wasn't necessary; Simon assumed that many Altenstadters came to the funeral only so they could gorge themselves on a big meal afterward.

"Well, Fronwieser, have you made any progress in your investigation?"

Simon spun around. It was Augustin Bonenmayr who had joined him in line. The tall, gaunt abbot from Steingaden was wearing his brass pince-nez here in the basilica as well, and from behind them, his tiny, alert eyes peered out at the physician.

"Unfortunately not, Your Excellency."

"If you ever should consider leaving Schongau, then do come to Steingaden," he said, his eyes twinkling. "The monastery needs another smart, open-minded physician like you, especially now that we are rebuilding and expanding. When the construction is finished, thousands of people will be making a pilgrimage to Steingaden each year—people with illnesses and infirmities. God can't heal them all." The abbot smiled benignly. Then his gaze fell on the coffin and he became serious again. "A great loss for us all," he said. "Koppmeyer was a man of the people. The church needs more like him."

"You're right, Excellency." Simon looked ahead nervously. There were just three mourners in front of him; he would be able to ask Elias Ziegler about his prayer. In his excitement, he had trouble concentrating on Augustin Bonenmayr's words.

The abbot of Steingaden took off his pince-nez and polished it with a lace handkerchief. "Do you still think he was poisoned?" he asked softly. "Perhaps the good man truly just ate something that didn't agree with him, or too much. Everyone knew he was not averse to the pleasures of this world. But then, if it really was a murder . . ." He kept polishing his glasses, though they were already as clear as limpid water. "Have you ever asked yourself who would benefit most from Koppmeyer's death? As far as I know, he had only one relative, his sister." The abbot turned away. "Good day to you, and God be with you."

Simon stood there, gaping, the abbot's words resounding in his ears. Could Benedikta have poisoned her brother? He couldn't for the life of him imagine that, but there was no time to think about this, as he had arrived at the bier that very moment. Inside lay the body of Andreas Koppmeyer, his face waxen and peaceful and his hands folded around a crucifix. In the narrow box, he suddenly looked much smaller than he had been in life. The corpse already seemed slightly bloated. In spite of the cold, it was clearly time to put him in the ground.

Simon nodded to Benedikta, who was still standing at the coffin accepting expressions of concern. He mumbled some condolences, then turned to the priest.

"A wonderful sermon, Your Excellency," he whispered. "So full of compassion."

"Thank you." Father Elias Ziegler smiled.

"I especially liked the closing words, the prayer about the greatest miracle, humankind, at a time when there was no earth, no heavens, and not a tree standing . . . Where does it come from?"

"Ah, the Wessobrunn Prayer." The priest nodded appreciatively. "Did you know it is considered the oldest of all German prayers? There is something especially magical about it, I think. I'm glad you liked it. I haven't used it in my sermons for ages."

Simon nodded. "The Wessobrunn Prayer," he murmured. "Why is it called that?"

The priest shrugged. "Well, because it has been safeguarded for many years in Wessobrunn in a monastery only a day's trip from here. The monks keep it in a shrine, like a relic."

Simon's mouth suddenly turned dry. "Is this prayer more than three hundred years old?" he asked in a hoarse voice.

"Indeed, much older, even." Elias Ziegler looked worried. "Are you ill? You're so pale."

"Oh, no, it's just that—"

Benedikta smiled sympathetically at the priest. "You must

know he was very fond of my brother. This has all been a little too much for him."

Elias Ziegler nodded earnestly. "Isn't that true for us all?" he said. Then he turned to the next mourner.

Simon paused at Benedikta's side. "The Wessobrunn Prayer," he whispered. "I should have known! So the treasure is hidden in the Wessobrunn Monastery."

"Or the next riddle," Benedikta whispered, holding her head erect while accepting condolences from the mourners. "In any case, we'll have to go to Wessobrunn. I hope in the meantime you've learned a little more about riding a horse," she said, with a slight smile, "or we'll never find out if this Templars' treasure really exists."

Simon returned the smile but felt a queasiness in his stomach. The Steingaden abbot had sown a seed of suspicion that took root in his mind. Nodding, he bade farewell and left the cold basilica.

The young boy led Magdalena through the narrow lanes of Augsburg, down into the Weavers' Quarter. Little icy gutters lined the paved streets. Everywhere, there were millwheels that drove the weavers' looms during the warmer part of the year but now were silent, covered with icicles and half submerged under ice where a number of brooks came together. Most houses didn't have windows but just tiny peepholes, and Magdalena had the feeling that behind each of them a pair of eyes was staring at them as they walked by.

It was well past nightfall, and she kept looking around to see if the two thugs might be waiting around the next corner for her as she passed by with the boy.

Finally, they came to a large house directly along the city wall. With whitewashed stone walls, green shutters, and a heavy wood front door, it seemed almost elegant in comparison to the rundown weavers' cottages, though it was nowhere near as magnificent as the three-story mansions closer to the city hall. Magdalena could hardly believe this was the hangman's house, but the boy stopped and knocked. Shortly, steps could be heard, a little slit opened beside the door, and a bearded face appeared. As the man raised his lantern to get a look at his visitors, Magdalena could see the reddish-blond hair of his beard and two eyes sparkling in the dim light. The man looked at Magdalena and the boy with suspicion.

"No more customers today," he growled. "Come back tomorrow if you're still alive and kicking."

The boy crossed himself, mumbled a brief prayer, and took off into the darkness. Magdalena stared at the hangman behind the peephole. Apparently, he hadn't recognized her.

"Are you deaf, or what?" The man's voice sounded threatening now. "Beat it fast, or I'll come and get you, you goddamn harlot!"

He was just about to close the little hatch when Magdalena addressed him.

"It's me, Magdalena Kuisl from Schongau. Don't you recognize me?"

Eyes wide in astonishment, he opened the door. His massive frame was illuminated by the light from the room.

Philipp Hartmann was almost as big as the Schongau hangman. He had a long, thick, reddish-blond mane, which, along with his beard, framed a wrinkled face. His arms were as thick as tree trunks, and a massive paunch with a dense growth of hair spilled out from under his shirt. He could be mistaken for a day laborer or hired thug, except that his shirt was made of the finest fustian and the black jacket over it didn't show a single patch. Philipp Hartmann sized her up with the narrow little slits of his eyes—the eyes of an intelligent but extremely proud man.

Finally, he grinned. "Indeed, Magdalena Kuisl!" he cried,

and his deep voice echoed through the streets. "What a surprise! Come in before you freeze to death standing outside the hangman's house."

He put his hand on her shoulder and guided her into the warm house. A fire rumbled softly in a tile stove, and some leftovers from supper were still on the table: roast pheasant, a half wheel of cheese, and a sliced leg of ham, alongside a pitcher of wine and a plate of sliced white bread. Magdalena felt her mouth water, reminding her she had eaten nothing substantial since the night before. Philipp Hartmann noticed her gaze and gestured for her to sit down. "Come and eat; it's too much for one person."

Magdalena sat down to eat. The bread was still warm, and the fine, white pheasant leg delicious. It was like Easter and a church fair combined. The Kuisls could afford a meal like this only when there were a lot of executions—and even then, only when the pay was good. Philipp Hartmann looked at her, impressed with her beauty, but kept his silence.

Suddenly, footsteps could be heard on the stairs, the door squeaked, and a little girl peeked in. She was about five years old, wore a nightshirt, and had reddish-blonde pigtails.

"Go back upstairs, Barbara," the hangman said. "We have company. Magdalena will certainly stay overnight, so you can play with her tomorrow morning." He smiled, a facial expression that clearly did not come naturally to him. "Perhaps she'll even stay longer."

Magdalena swallowed the rest of the pheasant, but suddenly the meat had lost its taste and seemed dry. The little girl nodded, scrutinized the hangman's daughter from head to toe again, and then disappeared up the stairs.

"You can have more, if you like," Philipp Hartmann said, pouring her another cup of wine. "I've also got some nuts and other delicacies. We're not hurting for money."

Magdalena shook her head in wonderment and admired the

whitewashed walls, the brightly polished copper kettles, and the enameled pitchers and plates. Philipp Hartmann's wife had died more than a year ago, and still, the house was in remarkably good condition. The reeds and straw on the floor smelled fresh, and Magdalena couldn't find a single cobweb anywhere. In the devotional corner, an oil painting of the Madonna, which looked as if it had just been framed, hung next to a polished executioner's sword. Beneath this, fresh linen and colorful clothes were stacked on the brass-studded cover of a walnut chest. Magdalena nodded to herself. Her father had been right; the Augsburg hangman would, in fact, be a great match for a girl, but even in her wildest dreams, she couldn't even consider marrying him.

Philipp Hartmann sat down next to her, poured himself a cup of wine, and raised his glass to her. "And now tell me what you're doing in Augsburg at this time of year. Actually, it's the man who is supposed to be the suitor and pay a visit to his intended—or do you do things differently in Schongau?" Again, he tried to smile.

"It's . . . not exactly what you think," Magdalena began hesitantly. It was wrong for her to come here; she knew that. She was leading him on by coming here, but what other choice did she have? Even as far away as Schongau, people knew the Augsburg hangman's wife had died of consumption the year before. Since that time, Philipp Hartmann had been looking for a new wife and a good mother for his little girl, Barbara. The only possible match for him as a hangman was the daughter of a butcher or a hangman.

Three months had passed since Philipp Hartmann had paid a visit to the Kuisls in order to get to know Magdalena a little better. The men had quickly come to an agreement, and her father had described the life of the Augsburg hangman's wife to her in glowing colors. In contrast to the Schongau hangman,

Philipp Hartmann was well-to-do. Admittedly, he was also a so-called dishonorable man whom people avoided, but with hard work and ambition, Hartmann had made a name for himself in recent years. He was viewed not just as an experienced hangman, but as an excellent healer who was consulted by well-off citizens as well as the simple people. Workers, merchants' daughters, and patricians all came to him for treatment and they all left behind decent sums of money.

For hours her father had tried to reason with her, tried to explain she would never be allowed to marry Simon and that all she would achieve would be mockery and, in the worst case, banishment from town. But in the end, all his arguments were in vain and Philipp Hartmann finally left empty-handed, taking his dowry in a safely guarded little chest back to Augsburg with him.

And now Magdalena was here at his house, eating his food and asking for a place to stay the night. She felt dirty and wrong, and only slowly and hesitantly did she tell him what had happened to her.

The hangman listened to her silently, and when she finished, he said, "So it isn't a suitor's visit, after all . . ."

He paused for a moment. Magdalena had a heavy feeling in her stomach.

"Well, be that as it may"—he stood up to stir the fire—"your money is, in any case, gone," he called back to her. "I know the two guys. Bad apples. I've put them in the stocks a couple of times and whipped them in public, too. They actually were banished from town some time ago and shouldn't be here. I poked out the eye of the big fat fellow because he came back to Augsburg, and if I catch them again, I'll string them up." He returned to the room and wiped his large sooty hands on a fine white towel. "Now, what were you supposed to get for your father and the midwife?"

Magdalena, who'd always had a strong memory, recited the

individual herbs and other ingredients. The hangman nodded, thought for a moment, then replied, "I have melissa, sundew, and most of the other herbs right here. You can get ergot in the apothecary."

"But I have no money!" Magdalena wailed, burying her face in her hands. "Twenty guilders—where can I get all that money?"

Philipp Hartmann hesitated, then walked over to a chest in the corner and opened it with a key from a chain on his belt. Magdalena listened to the clinking, and when the hangman returned and opened his hand, ten shiny guilders rolled across the table toward her.

"You'll need this for the apothecary," Hartmann said. "The rest you can get from me."

Magdalena looked at him in disbelief. "But . . ." she started to stay.

Something else rolled across the table toward her—a black, shining ball the size of a child's fist made from a strange material she had never seen before. She held it in her hand and could hear something rattle inside.

"A bezoar," the hangman said. "If you ask me, a useless magic thing for superstitious wives. You can keep it; I have no use for it anymore, in any case."

"I'll never be able to pay you back," Magdalena whispered.

The hangman shrugged. "I could give you fifty times as much as a dowry. I'm not a poor church mouse like your father. In a few years, I'll be able to purchase my citizenship rights, and who knows . . ." He tried to put on a cheerful face, but his face twisted into a grimace. "Perhaps you'll think it over some more. I'm not a bad catch, and Barbara urgently needs a mother." He stood up and walked to the door. "You can sleep here in the main room on the bench. Go to the apothecary tomorrow and then have a look around Augsburg. You'll see that it's a not a bad place to live."

As Magdalena listened to his heavy footsteps going back up the stairs, her stomach sank. She felt as if she had swallowed the bezoar.

The wagon driver lay on a bed of straw and screamed like a stuck pig. Startled, Bonifaz Fronwieser, who had just been tapping his abdomen, withdrew his hand.

"Hmm, so this is where it hurts," the older physician said, looking at his son apprehensively. Anton Steingadener's wife knelt alongside the two doctors, wiping sweat from her husband's brow with one hand, fingering a rosary in the other. Just an hour ago, the elderly couple had arrived at Fronwieser's house, where several patients had been waiting since noon. Most were suffering from the fever that had been going around Schongau for weeks, but this case, Simon thought, looked even more serious, if that were possible. He was already certain that it was hopeless.

"What's wrong with him, Herr Doktor?" Agathe Steingadener wailed. "Was it the food? Our bread is not the best, I know. We add milled acorns to the dough because we never have enough flour. But these pains . . . What is wrong with him?"

"How long has he been like this?" Bonifaz Fronwieser asked, examining Anton Steingadener's eyes under a magnifying glass. They were dilated and glassy, and the man's severe pain had driven him half crazy.

"Let's see . . . three days, I think," Agathe Steingadener replied. "Can you help him?"

Bonifaz Fronwieser stepped back, letting his son palpate the man's abdomen again. It was rock hard and swollen above the pelvis. Simon pressed lightly, and the man screamed again as if he were being impaled on a stake.

"My God, what's wrong with him? Just what does he have?" shouted Agathe Steingadener, clutching her rosary tightly. "Has the devil taken possession of him, just like he did with the priest in Altenstadt?" She broke out in tears. "Holy Mary, Mother of Jesus! The devil is taking our poor souls and won't even spare God-fearing citizens and priests! My husband went to mass every third day, and we often prayed together at home—"

"Your husband has a tumor," Simon replied, interrupting the litany. "It has nothing to do with the devil. But prayer can't hurt."

He didn't tell the woman that prayer was probably the only thing that could still save her husband. Simon knew that such tumors were sometimes removed at big universities, but here, in Schongau, they had neither the knowledge nor the tools to carry out such a complicated operation. Simon cursed as he rummaged through the shelves in the medicine cabinet, looking for some poppy seed extract, and in so doing, he knocked over a few small phials. It would only partially relieve the man's pain, offering him, at best, a slow decline into unconsciousness. Everything else was in the hands of God.

When Simon finally found the bottle, he noticed something moving behind him. His father's fingers closed around his wrist.

"Are you crazy?" old Bonifaz Fronwieser hissed in his ear, quietly so the wagon driver's wife couldn't hear him. "Do you know how expensive this medicine is? The Steingadener woman will never be able to pay for that!"

"Shall we let her husband die a miserable death like a beast?" Simon whispered in reply. "He's in great pain; we must help him."

"Then send him to the hangman," his father replied, in the same low voice. "Kuisl will give him one of his elixirs, and then it will be over. It's high time for Lechner to forbid that quack from practicing medicine before he poisons half the town with his herbs and elixirs."

"Half the town has already been to him, and he's got more

patients than you can ever imagine!" Simon replied in a clear voice.

Taking the phial of poppy seed extract from his father's hands, he gave it to the Steingadener woman.

"Here, give your husband two spoonfuls of this a day in a glass of wine," he said in a comforting tone. "The drink won't make the tumor go away, but at least the pain will be more bearable."

"Will he get better?" the woman asked anxiously, looking down at her husband. Josef Steingadener seemed to have fallen asleep out of exhaustion. He trembled and twitched, but was otherwise quiet.

Simon shrugged. "Only the Lord knows that. We'll help you take him home now."

Bonifaz Fronwieser stared angrily at his son but nevertheless gave him a hand in carrying the heavy wagoner out the door and lifting him into a wagon. Agathe Steingadener gave them a few coins, then sat down in the coachman's box and drove off. She did not wave good-bye. No doubt she was already wondering how she would make out financially without her husband.

On this day, Simon and his father had three more patients who all came to them with the fever. They were well-to-do citizens, and Bonifaz Fronwieser prescribed them theriac, a wickedly expensive potion made of poppy seed extract and angelica root, which probably wouldn't help but would at least not make the patients any worse. Simon knew this wasn't true of all of his father's medicines.

While the young physician examined the phlegm his patients coughed up and checked their urine, his thoughts kept turning back to the Templars' treasure. Could it be hidden in Wessobrunn? Or would they find only another riddle there? In any case, though he was deeply troubled by what the abbot of Steingaden had said, he decided to set out with Benedikta the following day. Just what was it Bonenmayr had said at the funeral? *"Have you ever asked yourself who would benefit most from Koppmeyer's death?"*

One thing clear was clear to Simon. Even though he could never imagine this happy, enlightened businesswoman poisoning anyone, from now on he'd keep a closer eye on Benedikta.

Simon wished the hangman could come along with them the next day, but Kuisl would have to stay in town to prepare for the upcoming trial. Simon was excited to share with the hangman what they had learned right after the funeral, but Kuisl had been strangely brusque in response, as if he were suddenly no longer interested in solving the riddle. When the physician told him he was departing for Wessobrunn the next day with Benedikta, Kuisl just shook his head.

"Are you sure it's safe to do that?" he grumbled.

"The road is secure," Simon replied, "now that you've caught the robbers."

"Have we really caught them all?" Kuisl asked, grinding a few dried herbs in his mortar. He wouldn't say any more than that. The hangman, completely enveloped in clouds of pipe smoke, continued grinding the herbs to a powder. Simon shrugged and walked back up to town to help his father.

He was about to turn to the next patient, a scrawny farmer from the neighboring town of Peiting who was suffering from consumption and coughing up sputum, when he heard shouting from the Lech Gate. It sounded like something bad had happened, and throwing on his coat, Simon ran down the street to see what the trouble was.

A few men had already gathered at the gate, staring at an oxcart just now rumbling down the icy street into town. On top of the wagon filled with straw were the disfigured bodies of two young wagon drivers from Schongau whom the physician knew from his frequent visits to the taverns behind city hall. To the best of his recollection, they were employed by Matthias Holzhofer, the second presiding burgomaster and an influential local merchant. The heads and chests of both men had been hastily wrapped in blood-soaked bandages, and with pale faces, they seemed to be not long for this world.

A farmer, who drove the oxen with a switch, had trouble moving the wagon forward. "Clear the way!" he shouted. "A new attack! I found them lying in their blood up on the high road above Hohenfurch. Damned robbers, may the devil take them all!" When he caught sight of Simon running alongside the wagon, he stopped and exclaimed, "You've been sent by God! See what you can do!" He put the reins in Simon's hand. "Take the wounded men to your father. I'd prefer the hangman, but I think he's needed somewhere else at present."

Followed by barking dogs, children, and wailing women, Simon drove the oxcart to his father's house. He glanced again at the two pale, groaning wagon drivers, the blood-drenched straw, and the filthy bandages, and cursed himself for having given away the whole bottle of poppy seed extract a while ago. This was another case where probably only the dear Lord could do anything to help them.

Johann Lechner drummed his fingers impatiently on the table, waiting for the murmuring to stop. The aldermen looked nervous. The emergency meeting of the city council on the second floor of the Ballenhaus hadn't allowed the city patricians enough time to get attired in a manner befitting their station in life. Their fur caps sat askew atop bald heads, and their faces were red with excitement. Some were still wearing nightshirts under heavy coats made from dyed wool. The members of the Inner Council, which appointed the four burgomasters, seemed the most agitated of all. In their midst sat Matthias Holzhofer, shaking his head again and again. His round face, usually so cheerful, was pale and drawn, and he had large rings under his eyes.

"My most valuable shipment!" he exclaimed, pounding his fist on the polished oak table. "Around a thousand guilders!

Cloth, fustian, silverware—to say nothing of all the spices! How can this be? Goddammit! I thought the hangman had smoked out the accursed band of robbers!"

The aldermen started grumbling and Johann Lechner admonished them, tapping his signet ring against a full glass of port wine, demanding silence. "Gentlemen, I've called the council together to make an important announcement. Silence!" He pounded the table with his hand. "Quiet, for God's sake!" The murmuring stopped at once, and all eyes turned to the clerk. As the representative of the elector in the absence of the administrator, Lechner really had no business being in the city's town hall, but as things turned out, he'd become the chairman of the meetings. During the Great War, people were glad to have a strong hand in charge, and since that time there had been no reason to change what was tried and true.

After things had finally quieted down, the clerk proceeded. "I actually wanted to call this meeting of the council to inform you that the band of robbers has finally been caught and commercial traffic can resume. The hangman, along with many honorable citizens, has done an outstanding job."

"Truly an outstanding job," the patrician Jakob Schreevogl murmured. "Honorable citizens have created a bloodbath!"

Nobody was paying attention to him, however. All eyes were directed now at the clerk, who continued speaking in an earnest tone. "But now it appears there's more to it. As much as I regret to say so, there seems to be a second band of robbers. The executioner has already questioned the head of the first group, Hans Scheller, about it."

At once, the general whispering resumed. Michael Berchtholdt, who, as a baker, sat in the Outer Council, spoke up. "I hope Kuisl introduced the scoundrel to the hot irons! He should break every bone in his body, one by one."

"Well, the hangman has used . . . his own methods." Lechner replied, and Michael Berchtholdt, as well as the other aldermen, seemed pleased with that answer. It was good to have someone like Jakob Kuisl take care of the dirty work.

"A second gang of robbers!" Matthias Holzhofer lamented. "Will there be no end to this highway robbery?"

"Master Holzhofer, please excuse me for asking," young Jakob Schreevogl interrupted. As owner of Schongau's largest stove-fitting company, he had been a member of the Inner Council for only a short time. "Isn't it extremely risky to send such a valuable shipment to Füssen in troubled times like these? Whether there is one gang of robbers out there or several, you are positively asking for trouble!"

Matthias Holzhofer shrugged. "The word was that the Scheller gang had been captured—and anyone sending out a wagonload of goods under these conditions gets the best prices." He grinned and twirled his clipped Vandyke. "There's not much competition in this wretched cold. Moreover . . ." He hesitated before continuing. "We took a route through small villages, avoiding the main roads. It takes longer but avoids the woods along the major roads where the bandits lie in wait. Who would ever suspect that there, too . . ." He stopped short and shook his head.

Johann Lechner cleared his voice before beginning to speak again. "It's not the first time a band of robbers has attacked travelers on back roads," he began. "The Augsburg merchant Leonhard Weyer was killed by robbers a few days ago the same way. I happened to be in Semer's Tavern just the night before when he told me about his plan to take the old cow path to Füssen."

Burgomaster Karl Semer, owner of the tavern on the market square, interrupted him. He was breathing heavily under a red velvet jacket, and his eyes bulged with emotion. "Oh, God, two of my drivers told me recently that they were taking a route different from the usual one, too," he gasped. "At least one of them has been reported missing, and I haven't heard a thing about the other yet . . ." He wiped the sweat from his brow and took a deep gulp of port wine. Despite the bitter cold outside, a huge green tile stove made the town council chambers almost unbearably hot.

An anxious murmur came from the back of the room, where the members of the Outer Council and other ordinary residents sat. Almost all of them had sent a wagon with goods to other Bavarian cities in recent days and weeks. Those who could not go by river ferry depended on the Schongau wagon drivers, who had been in bitter competition with those from Augsburg for years. What would happen if other wagons were attacked?

"Just a moment!" said Jakob Schreevogl, raising his voice. "If I understand correctly, all these wagon drivers have decided to take an unfamiliar route. Nevertheless, they were attacked. That means either that highwaymen are roaming all the roads now, which I doubt, or . . ." He gazed out at the other members of the council. "Someone out there has been spying and giving specific directions to the robbers."

"Who would that be?" Matthias Holzhofer interrupted. "My men have discussed it only with me."

"And mine, too," said Burgomaster Semer. "Nobody here knew this fellow Weyer from Augsburg. Who might he have spoken with?"

"Maybe it was the Augsburgers themselves who killed our people!" cried out the baker Michael Berchtholdt from the back of the room. "Our wagon drivers have always been a thorn in their side. If they had their way, they would be the only ones transporting goods from Venice and elsewhere."

"Nonsense," replied Jakob Schreevogl. "Weyer was himself an Augsburger. They aren't going to kill their own people."

Berchtholdt shrugged. "Perhaps he was a maverick. Who knows? Someone other Augsburgers had a score to settle with? Those damn Swabian punks!"

There was a murmur of approval in the room.

Johann Lechner tapped his signet ring against his wineglass

again. "Quiet! We won't get anywhere like this!" he shouted. "We can only hope that the two injured wagon drivers can give us information about the bandits. Perhaps that way we can learn who's behind this." Before proceeding, he examined the face of each member of the council. "It must be our common mission to put an end to this second gang of robbers as well. I suggest, therefore, sending the hangman out with a group of men again."

"What? Put the hangman at the head of a group of honorable men again?" Burgomaster Semer shook his head in disbelief. "My son told me about the hunt. It's outrageous that an executioner was put in charge of honorable citizens. Chasing and executing people is the job of hangmen, bailiffs, and court officers. If they hear of this in Munich or Landsberg, participants in this hunt will quickly lose their rights of citizenship."

"They'll lose their rights of citizenship when they ignore directions and slaughter a gang that includes women and children!" Jakob Schreevogl interrupted. "Your son and Berchtholdt's have blood on their hands—more than the hangman in his entire life!"

"What an outrageous insinuation!" Berchtholdt shouted. "My son kept things from getting worse. Scheller and his bloodthirsty companions were about to kill us!"

"Silence, for God's sake!" Johann Lechner shouted, louder than usual. Quiet quickly returned to the room. It was rare for the clerk to lose his composure, and after a few moments, he got a hold of himself again. He took a deep breath. "Arguing and brawling won't get us anywhere," he finally said. "I'll send the hangman out again. He has shown that he understands what he's doing. But this time, only the men who are actually suited for the job will go with him." He cast a sideways glance at the burgomaster. "Your son and the son of the baker certainly are not; they've already demonstrated that. As far as the Scheller gang is concerned . . ." Lechner paused as if thinking it over. "Hans Scheller has already confessed. In my opinion, further torture is not necessary. With the agreement of the council, I can begin the trial as representative of the elector in the next few days. The execution will take place shortly after — the sooner the better — as an example to the other gangs."

The aldermen nodded. As so often, the remarks of their clerk seemed sound and logical, and a general feeling of satisfaction reigned immediately after he spoke. "You'll see," Johann Lechner said, packing his goose quill and inkpot in his leather briefcase. "When Scheller is strung up on Gallows Hill, peace will return to the town. You have my word on that."

9

THE FOLLOWING DAY, A SNOWSTORM SWEPT OVER the entire Priests' Corner, as if the good Lord wanted to bury all life under a white cover. People stayed inside their houses and cottages, and when they did peek outside, it was only to briefly mumble a short prayer and shut their doors against the rattling wind. Traffic on the river, as well as on the roads, came to a halt, and the blizzard took a number of wagon drivers by surprise, leaving them to die lonely deaths, struggling to free their horses from snowdrifts several yards deep. They were not found until days later, frozen stiff alongside their wagons, some torn to shreds by the wolves, their horses having run off in the vast expanse of white.

The blizzard hit Augsburg, too. Since the day after Magdalena's arrival, she had not been able to leave the hangman's house for even a minute. Of course, time was of no importance, since a leisurely stroll through town was out of the question, in any case. The apothecary was surely closed in such weather, and the next commercial convoy to Schongau would have to wait until the weather cleared. Magdalena knew that traveling on her own would be suicide.

Thus, during the day, she made friends with little Barbara, who quickly captured her heart. Sitting by the fire, Magdalena whittled a wooden doll for her, singing the same children's songs she had for the twins at home. She could sense the girl needed a mother. Barbara stared at her with her big eyes, running her hands over Magdalena's cheeks, and pleaded "Again!" whenever Magdalena got tired and stopped singing. Magdalena often thought about the fact that little Barbara was a hangman's daughter just like herself, except she had no brothers or sisters and, above all, no mother. How often had she herself sat just like this long ago in the lap of her father? How often had her own mother sung her to sleep with the same children's songs?

During this time, Philipp Hartmann was working in the room next door, tying together bundles of herbs, making new ropes, and distilling herbal brandy in dark flasks. The aroma of alcohol drifted through the room, almost intoxicating Magdalena. From time to time, the hangman dropped in and patted his daughter on the head or gave her and Magdalena a prune or a dried apple. He avoided touching or making any unseemly advances on Magdalena, but she could sense him staring at her back. When he did so, a chill came over her despite the warmth in the room. Philipp Hartmann was certainly a good man and a good father, and well-to-do, but she loved someone else.

But did she really still love Simon? After the whole business with Benedikta, she noticed how her feelings had cooled—whether out of anger or disappointment, she couldn't say. It would take time for her heart to warm to him again.

The blizzard raged into the next day, not letting up until evening, so the stores remained closed. Not until the third morning after her arrival could she finally get out to the apothecary. Along the way, she passed the enormous Augustus Fountain, now draped in icicles a yard long, and looked up at the five-story city hall on her left. Magdalena shuddered. How could men make such huge buildings? Patricians wrapped in heavy fur coats streamed out of the portal, absorbed in deep conversation. The snow was still knee-high, but city watchmen were already shoveling narrow lanes through the town square and the surrounding streets. Homes and shops were coming to life. People had been confined for two days, and now they could go out shopping again. They bought fresh bread and meat or fetched pitchers of foaming brown beer from the innkeeper. Magdalena made her way through crowds of quarreling cooks, each trying to buy a rabbit or pheasant for his master, and a group of choirboys on their way to the Augsburg Cathedral.

Finally, she arrived. Straight ahead, between Maximilianstraße and the magnificent St. Moritz Church, was the Marienapotheke, the oldest apothecary in Augsburg. That morning, Philipp Hartmann had told Magdalena that the owner, Nepomuk Biermann, worked closely with him and had the best selection of herbs and other ingredients in town. Hartmann bought several ingredients there that he couldn't prepare himself, and in return, Nepomuk Biermann ordered from the hangman human fat and leather to treat joint pain and tight muscles.

"Biermann is a strange fellow," Philip Hartmann said, "but he really knows what he is doing and tries to treat you fairly. Be sure you get to see the herb room — it's huge."

Nepomuk Biermann's place was a narrow four-story gabled building that could have used a new coat of paint. Situated among patrician homes, it looked a little like a neglected stepchild. Magdalena passed under a sign that displayed the name of the shop in flowing letters. Opening a narrow but solid door, she was immediately enveloped in a cloud of fragrances — dried herbs and exotic odors that reminded her of their own medicine chest at home. She closed her eyes and inhaled the strange aromas, many of them from another world of plants and spices far across the ocean, from ancient forests where lions and other monsters dwelled, or from distant islands inhabited by cannibals and mythical creatures with feet attached to their heads. There was an aroma of cinnamon, muscat, and black pepper.

When Magdalena closed the door behind her, a little bell rang. Shortly thereafter, a man appeared. Stooped over, he was small and mostly bald, except for a fringe of hair around the sides like a monk. From behind an eyepiece resting on his nose, he stared out at the hangman's daughter with a disgruntled expression. Evidently, he'd been occupied with something more important than the menial work of waiting on customers.

"Yes?" he asked, looking her up and down as he would an annoying insect. "How can I help you?"

"I was sent by Philipp Hartmann," Magdalena said. "I'm supposed to pick up a few herbs."

At once, the man's expression changed. His toothless mouth broadened into a smile. "Hartmann, huh? Did the Augsburg hangman manage to get a woman, after all?"

"I'm . . . just helping him at present," Magdalena stammered, handing Nepomuk Biermann the list of ingredients. Gripping his eyepiece, the pharmacist studied the piece of parchment. "Aha, I see," he mumbled. "Ergot and artemisia, also daphne, belladona, and thorn apple. What are you going to do with this—send the hangman off into the other world or ride away yourself on a broomstick?"

Magdalena struggled for words. "I . . . uh . . . We're expecting a difficult birth," she finally said. "The child won't come and the mother's in great pain."

"Aha, I see, severe pain," Nepomuk Biermann said, holding the glass up to his eye again. "But be careful you don't give her too much of it all at the same time, or the good woman won't suffer any pain at all. Ever again." He grinned and winked his right eye, which peered out like that of a giant fish from behind the eyepiece. "You know, *dosis sola venenum facit*— it's only the dose that makes the poison. Even old Paracelsus knew that. Did the hangman tell you about Paracelsus, eh?"

Magdalena nodded quickly, and the little man left it at that. Nepomuk Biermann walked toward a low doorway that led from the shop counter to the rear of the building. He motioned for her to follow. "Come along, girl, you can at least help me collect the herbs."

Magdalena hurried after him. She found herself in a room cluttered with shelves and drawers. High wooden walls divided the room into sections and doubled as shelves. Nepomuk Biermann scurried like a dervish through the narrow corridors, carefully opening labeled drawers here and there. He checked the contents of each drawer against the list in his hand, spooning out a portion and weighing it on a scale that stood on a marble table in the center of the room.

"Ergot, artemisia . . ." he mumbled. "Just where do I have the damned daphne . . . ? Ah, yes, here it is."

Biermann couldn't help but laugh as he watched Magdalena, standing wide-eyed in the midst of the six-foot-high shelves. "Well, you never saw anything like this before, eh?" With a sweeping gesture, he announced, "This is the largest collection of herbs from here all the way to Munich, you can take it from me. Probably not even the venerable Paracelsus had an apothecary shop like this."

He had just opened another drawer when the little bell up front in the shop rang again. He stopped, annoyed. "Please excuse me," the little hunchbacked man said to Magdalena, placing the bag of herbs he had already weighed in her hand and scurrying out of the room. "I'll be right back."

The hangman's daughter stayed behind and looked around in wonderment at the fragrant labyrinth.

It was the voice that caught her attention, the demanding

voice of a man who was clearly annoyed; he was talking with the pharmacist, and this was not a friendly conversation. Out of sheer curiosity, she walked over to the door leading to the shop up front and listened in.

"I need the same thing that I got once before from you," the stranger growled.

"The . . . the same?" Nepomuk Biermann asked. "You know it's hard to get, and actually, I'm not supposed to sell it. That . . . could cost me my business."

Magdalena could sense the pharmacist's anxiety. Carefully, she stepped back against the wall in order to hear better.

"I'll pay you well," the man said to the sound of jingling coins. "But I'm depending on it really working right this time! The last time death came much too fast. This time it has to be slow so no one notices, or else . . ."

"You must always use it in small doses," Nepomuk Biermann insisted. "If you use only small doses, no one will become suspicious, I swear by God!"

"Then swear by the Savior," the stranger said, and laughed raucously. "*Deus lo vult.*"

Magdalena gasped when she heard these last few words—the same words the man in the crypt had spoken to her father shortly before they'd stabbed him.

Was it perhaps the same man?

Although Magdalena was aware of the danger she was in, she moved closer to the door. Sidling up to it, she slowly turned her head toward the front of the store. From here, she could see only a small section above the counter, but it was enough to cause chills to run up and down her spine.

Magdalena glimpsed a black cowl and, dangling from a golden chain, a golden cross with two crossbars. Not until now did she notice that a new scent had joined the mix in the apothecary.

Violets.

"I need something else," the stranger said, scratching his chest. "Quicksilver. As much as you can get hold of."

Nepomuk Biermann nodded. "I . . . understand. Give me until tomorrow—"

"I shall be here tomorrow morning," the man interrupted. "The other preparations I'll take along with me right away."

The stranger reached out for a little silk pouch the pharmacist offered him, then without a further word, turned to leave, slamming the door behind him.

Magdalena hesitated briefly, then gathered up the herbs that Biermann had already packed for her and stuffed them into her linen bag. Out of the corner of her eye, she noticed other herbs lying out on the table. Quickly, she grabbed these as well and put them in her bag. *Who knows what I might be able to use them for?* she thought.

With the bag in hand, she hurried back to the sales room and, from there, out the door.

"Hey!" Nepomuk Biermann called after her. His face was as white as a sheet, and pearls of sweat had formed on his forehead. "What are you doing? You have to pay! Stay here. That man is dangerous! You don't understand . . ."

Whatever else he said was drowned out in street noise. Magdalena hurried after the priest's murderer, past snowdrifts and astonished pedestrians. She didn't know what she was going to do when she caught up with him, but she wouldn't be a Kuisl if she allowed this chance to slip by.

In Schongau the blizzard raged, too, and people stayed inside their warm houses, hoping they wouldn't run out of firewood. In the surrounding forests, the howl of wolves could be heard now and then, and on the rooftops snow piled up, making the beams creak. Even the oldest Schongauers had rarely seen a storm like this, and it was certainly the worst since the Great War had ended.

The streets and narrow lanes in town were empty except for a single figure making his way through the blizzard, up from the Tanners' Quarter, toward the dungeon. Jakob Kuisl held onto his wide-brimmed hat with his right hand, shielding his eyes with his left and trying to see ahead through the chaos. He looked like a black giant in a sea of white. He cursed under his breath. His pipe had gone out in the blizzard, and though he needed it to concentrate now more than ever, it would no doubt take a long time for him to relight the wet pipe.

Immediately after the council meeting, Johann Lechner had told the hangman he would send him out to hunt for the second group of thieves. This time, however, he would be allowed to pick out his men himself. The hangman decided to keep the company small. From what the robber chief told him, he knew that there were probably only four bandits roaming around out there, but they were all experienced fighters. Somehow they had managed to find out the planned routes of individual merchants, even though the victims all claimed they had discussed their plans only among themselves. Was there a leak somewhere among the Schongau patricians? Could one of them be involved in the raids?

Matthias Holzhofer's injured drivers had been questioned but revealed little. The attackers were disguised, they said, wrapped in black coats and armed with crossbows, muskets, and rifles. They were clearly a small but ferocious group and far superior to the ordinary highway bandits.

To learn more about this mysterious group, the hangman decided, despite the blizzard, to visit the dungeon and question Hans Scheller again.

There was no watchman standing guard at the door to the massive tower, and Jakob Kuisl assumed the bailiff was either in the tavern or inside the dungeon. Who could blame him in such weather? The hangman knocked loudly on the iron-reinforced door and heard steps coming from inside.

"Who's there?" a voice asked.

"It's me, Jakob Kuisl. Open up before the storm blows me away."

There was a grinding sound as a key turned in the lock. The door opened a crack, and the pinched face of the city bailiff Johannes peered out. "What do you want, huh? Your last visit cost me a fine of eight kreuzers and an extra day of guard duty. Lechner's not happy when somebody crosses him."

"Let me talk with Scheller once more." The hangman gave the door such a shove that the bailiff was pushed aside.

"Hey, Kuisl, you can't do that!"

Kuisl tossed him a little bag. "Take this and be quiet."

The bailiff looked inside curiously. "What is it?"

"Chewing tobacco. From the West Indies, where the snakes are as fat as the trunks of oak trees. Chew it, but don't swallow. It will keep you awake and warm."

Withdrawing to a stool in the corner with his little bribe, Johannes sniffed at the dried weed. "Chew it, huh?" He looked at the hangman again. "But don't crush Scheller's other hand, or he'll die on us in the dungeon, and it'll be my fault."

"Don't worry. I know what I'm doing."

The hangman approached the cells in the rear, where the robbers were detained. In contrast to his last visit, they appeared listless now. The men and women crouched in the corners on filthy straw. They had wrapped themselves in threadbare coats and tried to keep each other warm against the January cold. In their midst lay the feverish boy, trembling all over. The wind whistled through the barred window behind them. Alongside the robbers sat a bowl of moldy bread and an apparently empty pitcher of water. A bucket of excrement stank so badly that Kuisl had to step back. Hans peered out at him from behind the bars with an empty gaze, his small right finger festering like a bloated sheep intestine.

"It's you again," he whispered. "What else do you want?"

The hangman spun around. "What kind of a pigsty is this?" he shouted at the bailiff, who was still absorbed in the exotic, fragrant plant. "These people have nothing to eat or drink, and there are no blankets or fresh straw! Do you want them to die before they are executed?"

The bailiff shrugged. "You can see for yourself what the weather is like outside. I've asked twice for food, but none arrives."

"Then go and get it yourself."

"Now?" Johannes looked bewildered. "But the storm—"

"At once!" The hangman walked over to him, grabbed him by the collar, and lifted him off the stool so that his feet dangled in the air. His face turned bright red, and his eyes bulged.

"That's the way Scheller is going to feel soon," Jakob Kuisl growled, "and so will you, by God, if you don't do what I say at once. Fresh water, bread, warm blankets—do you understand?"

The bailiff nodded, and Kuisl let him down again.

"And now get out."

Without even turning around, Johannes rushed out. Snow and wind blew in through the open door, but as soon as the hangman closed it, silence prevailed once more in the dungeon. The only sounds now were the soft whine of the baby and the distant howling of the wind. The robber chief looked at Jakob Kuisl in astonishment. Just as he was about to ask a question, the hangman spoke up.

"Did the medicine I gave you help the boy?"

Scheller nodded, still speechless about what he had just witnessed. "Why did you do that?" he asked finally.

Jakob Kuisl didn't answer. "I spoke with Lechner," he said. "No torture on the wheel, a quick, clean hanging, and the women and children will be let go."

Scheller broke into a wide smile, but soon he turned serious again. "How long do we have?" he asked.

Jakob Kuisl took a draw on his cold pipe. "If the weather permits, the trial will be in a few days. After that there will be three more days—that's the custom. Semer, the tavern keeper, will serve you your last meal: bacon, dumplings, sauerkraut, and for each of you, a jug of muscatel to keep you warm on your last walk."

Hans Scheller nodded. "A full week, then." He stopped. "It's good it's over," he said finally. "This wasn't really any way to live."

The hangman changed the topic. "There's still something I have to ask you about the other gang of robbers. You said there were four of them. Four plates, four cups, four knives . . ."

Hans Scheller nodded. "As I said, the fourth probably had just gone out into the woods to relieve himself."

"But the fourth plate," the hangman continued. "Was it dirty? Did it looked used?"

The robber chief stopped to think. "Now that you mention it . . . actually, no. You're right . . . Three plates that had been used were around the fire, but the fourth was stashed away in one of the saddlebags along with a cup."

Jakob Kuisl chewed on his cold pipe stem, cursing to himself because it had gone out. "That must mean that the fourth man hadn't been with the others for a while. Perhaps he was in town."

Hans Scheller shrugged. "Who cares where the fourth man was? Perhaps he had run away earlier."

The hangman told him about the town clerk's suspicion that information about the merchants' secret routes had been leaked to someone. The robber chief nodded.

"I understand. The fourth man hangs around in town and informs his comrades about the routes. Then all they have to do is help themselves. After all, the wagons are not very well guarded, and the merchants are not afraid of anything. Not a bad plan." He grinned, and Kuisl could see that almost all of his top teeth were missing. "Sounds like a plan I would make up." Suddenly, he stopped. "I just thought of something."

"What is that?"

"Alongside the leather bag that you have now, something else was lying there by the campfire—a little bottle made of blue glass. It looked quite valuable, and when we opened it, it smelled like the whole damned palace of the French kings."

Jakob Kuisl forgot about his pipe. "Perfume, you mean?"

Scheller nodded. "Yes, exactly. It stank like a whole field of spring flowers."

"And this perfume . . ." The hangman chose his words carefully. "Did it smell like . . . violets, perhaps?"

Scheller shrugged. "I don't know anything about these things. We poured it over our horse. He smashed the bottle the next day in the cave, the stupid beast."

Jakob Kuisl contemplated this a few more minutes, then turned to leave. "Thanks, Scheller. You've been a lot of help to me. When we meet the next time, I'll see to it that it goes fast. I promise."

"Kuisl." Hans Scheller's voice had a faraway, dreamy sound. The hangman turned around.

"What is it, Scheller?"

The robber chief seemed to be struggling for words. Finally, he began to speak. "Do you really want to know what I've learned, hangman?"

"Tell me."

"I was a carpenter, a good one, down in Schwabmünchen. But then the Swedes came and raped my wife and cut her throat. They bashed my boy's head against the door and set my house on fire. I fled into the woods, and now it all ends here." He tried to smile. "Tell me, hangman. If you were in my shoes, what would you have done?"

Jakob Kuisl shrugged. "You always had a choice." He walked to the door, but then turned around again. "I'm sorry about what happened to your wife and the boy. At least you'll be together again soon."

The door closed and Scheller remained alone with his thoughts. He would have cried like a little child if he hadn't long since forgotten how.

Outside, the blizzard lashed Jakob Kuisl's face with sharp pellets of ice. He pulled his hat down and forged ahead through the wall of white. His head was spinning as if the storm were also raging inside him.

A perfume that stank like a meadow in springtime . . .

Had the man with the violet perfume paid a visit to the robbers? Or was *he* the fourth man? Magdalena told him that the stranger had been sitting with his friends in the Altenstadt tavern. Had they overheard the merchants' conversations about the route? But even if that was the case, what did any of this have to do with the Templars' treasure? The hangman cursed. He needed to finally put all those pieces together.

Another day would pass before the good Lord would send someone to help Jakob Kuisl solve at least one of the riddles.

The blizzard brought new patients, so Simon hardly had a moment to even think about the Templars or the Wessobrunn Prayer during the day. He and his father had been able to save only one of the two wagoners employed by the alderman Matthias Holzhofer. The other had quietly passed away the same evening.

In other respects, too, Simon and his father never had a chance to rest. They passed the hours stirring new medicine, bleeding patients, and examining urine. Among the victims of the "Schongau Fever," as the epidemic had come to be known, were a carpenter's journeyman whose whole body had broken out in blue pustules, another patient whose foot was crushed by an oxcart, and a wagon driver with frostbite on both hands. The man had attempted to drive from Schongau to Landsberg in his wagon and was discovered lying in a ditch only a mile from town. He had been trying in vain to pull his wagon out of the snow when he was finally overcome by the cold. Simon and his father agreed that three fingers on the left hand would have to be amputated—a job that Bonifaz Fronwieser regarded as one of his specialties since his days as an army doctor.

Old Fronwieser had traveled around with his family during the Great War, following the Bavarian foot soldiers. He had sawed off innumerable arms and legs that were riddled with bullets, and he cauterized the stumps. It was during this time that his wife died, so after the war, Bonifaz Fronwieser settled down in Schongau with his son. He'd never forgiven his son for dropping out of an expensive medical school in Ingolstadt a few years ago, partly because he was short of money, but also because he lacked the interest. Even back then, Simon was attracted more to the latest fashions and games of dice than to Hippocrates, Paracelsus, and Galen.

His father became even more displeased when Simon started consorting with the Schongau hangman, borrowing books on medicine from him and often looking over his shoulder when he was treating patients. Simon then used what he had learned from the hangman on patients in Fronwieser's own practice.

Simon was also critical of his father during the amputation of the wagon driver's three fingers, an operation Bonifaz Fronwieser could do in his sleep. They had sedated the patient with a bottle of brandy and shoved a board between his teeth. When old Fronwieser picked up his surgical pincers to nip off the black stumps that had once been fingers, Simon pointed to the rusty cutting blades.

"You have to clean them first," he whispered to his father, "or the wound will become infected."

"Nonsense," said Bonifaz Fronwieser. "We'll cauterize the

places afterward with boiling oil—that's what I learned from my father, and that's the logical way to do it."

Simon shook his head. "The wound will become inflamed, believe me."

Before his father could answer, he'd taken the pincers and washed them off in a pot of boiling water on the stove, and only then did he start to operate. Watching silently, his father had to admit that Simon knew what he was doing and completed the job quickly. There was no doubt that the boy was talented. Why, for heaven's sake, had he ever dropped out of school in Ingolstadt? He could have become a great doctor, not a run-of-the-mill barber surgeon like himself, but a doctor with university training, a learned, esteemed physician whom people would respect and reimburse with silver coins—not with rusty kreuzers, eggs from the farm, and worm-infested corned beef. A Dr. Fronwieser, a first in the family . . .

Sullenly, the old man watched as Simon finally applied the white linen bandage. "Not bad work at all," he grumbled, "but what are you going to do with the dirty pincers? Are you going to throw them away and buy new ones?"

Simon shook his head and smiled. "I'll wash them off again in boiling water and use them again; that's what the hangman does when he clips off a thief's thumb or index finger, and nobody has died on him." He checked the wagon driver's breathing. "Just recently Kuisl told me about an old remedy. He smears sheep dung and mold on the wound and says there's nothing better for inflammation. The mold . . ." He stopped because he could see he had gone too far. His father's face had turned a bright red.

"Just cut it out with your damned hangman and his filthy drug collection!" Bonifaz Fronwieser shouted. "He just puts crazy ideas in your head. He should be forbidden from practicing! Sheep dung and mold—bah! I didn't send you off to school to study that!" He walked to the other room and slammed the door behind him. Shrugging, Simon watched as his father left, then poured a bucket of water over the wagon driver's face to wake him up.

A few more hours passed before Simon finally found time again to delve into the world of the Templars and the Wessobrunn Prayer. At six o'clock sharp, as the bells tolled, he closed the office and went down to the marketplace. When he opened the door to the Stern, where he'd arranged to meet Benedikta, he was greeted with the warmth and stuffy odor of wet clothing. At this time of day, the tavern was full of wagon drivers and merchants stranded by the storm and whiling away the time drinking and playing dice. Under the low ceiling of the taproom, about a dozen men were milling about, most of them engaged in serious, muffled conversations.

The merchant woman was sitting at a corner table in the very rear, engrossed in a parchment. As Simon approached, she rolled up the document and smiled at him.

Simon pointed to the roll. "Well? Are you taking notes on the damned riddle?"

Benedikta laughed. "No, this is just a terribly boring balance sheet. Business goes on in Landsberg even when it rains or snows. Believe me, the life of a merchant's widow is a rather boring one. And unfortunately, I haven't yet found a new husband who is clever and loving and also knows how to deal with this tedious stuff." She winked at Simon. "All my suitors up to now could do only one or the other." She stuck the parchment roll in a bag at the end of the table and gestured for him to take a seat. "But enough of this sad story. Have you studied this Templar's book some more?"

Simon nodded. "I actually do have some ideas." He took the little guide out of his jacket pocket and started leafing through it, while Benedikta snapped her fingers to get the attention of the innkeeper and ordered two cups of brandy.

"The Order of the Knights Templar was founded by a certain . . . Hugues de Payens, a Norman knight," the medicus began, his finger passing over the scrawled lines in the text. A small tallow candle on the table gave off so little light that Simon had difficulty continuing. "At first there were only nine men, a small fraternity, but the order soon spread, first to the Orient, along the routes to Jerusalem, and later to all of Europe—Italy, France, and England."

"But how about German lands?" Benedikta interrupted.

Simon shrugged. "Not so much here. In our countries, the so-called Teutonic Order of Knights was in charge, an order that attempted to convert the heathen in Eastern Europe with fire and the sword . . ." He shook his head. The medicus had never thought highly of trying to convince people of the true faith through force of arms. Simon believed in the power of words over the sword. "Be that as it may," he continued, "there were also German Templars and, naturally, German commanderies—that is to say, Templar settlements—here in Bavaria, in Augsburg, Bamberg, and Moosburg, for example. The settlement in Altenstadt must have been a part of the Moosburg commandery." He sighed. "The little Saint Lawrence Church is all that remains of it, however."

"And a certain Friedrich Wildgraf, who was no less than the German master of the Order of Templar Knights, sold this settlement, with all the land and the Saint Lawrence Church, to the monastery at Steingaden in the year 1289," Benedikta continued. "Years later, when the Templars were being hunted down all over Europe, he hid a treasure here . . ."

She paused while a server set down two cups of brandy, giving Simon a flirtatious glance. Teresa, like so many other girls, had a crush on the medicus. Benedikta didn't speak again until the girl left.

"All right, then, let's assume this treasure is really buried somewhere around here. Then tell me something . . . Why is the grave of this Friedrich Wildgraf located in Altenstadt if nothing around here belonged to the Templars anymore?" She shook her head. "His date of death is given as 1329 on the memorial plaque at the Altenstadt basilica, and that's long after the estate was sold. That doesn't make any sense."

Simon shrugged. "Or maybe it does. Let's just imagine that Friedrich Wildgraf sells this settlement for the Templars because it's just too remote, too far from the roads leading to Jerusalem. There's too little activity here; it just doesn't pay to keep the settlement. Twenty years later, the Templars are being hunted down all over Europe. Friedrich Wildgraf remembers this little remote commandery—"

"And decides to hide out here!" Benedikta interrupted him excitedly. "Naturally! No doubt he had compatriots here from back in the old days—loyal servants. Friedrich Wildgraf knew the aldermen in the area and influential citizens who were still well disposed toward him, and even the Templars' church still existed. A perfect hiding place for him and for the treasure!"

Simon nodded. "This time he probably didn't come as a Templar, but perhaps as a trader or the local priest—who knows? But he brought something to Schongau with him, something very valuable, and when he noticed that his hour of death was at hand, he decided to hide it in such a way that only a select group would be able to find it . . ."

"The Templars' treasure," Benedikta murmured. "It could have happened that way. Probably only a chosen few even knew that it existed! As the former master of the order in Paris, Wildgraf may have learned about the treasure and was given the assignment of finding a suitable place to hide it. He had already gone into hiding and his pursuers had lost track of him . . ."

The medicus smiled grimly. "Friedrich Wildgraf certainly went to a lot of trouble to hide his tracks. Only a small memorial plaque at the church in Altenstadt mentions his death." He nipped on his strong brandy, which tasted of pepper, cloves, and cinnamon, before continuing. "But his grave is actually located under the former Templars' church, and that's where Friedrich Wildgraf left his riddle. He chose Christian symbolism to prevent the treasure from falling into the wrong hands. Perhaps the grave was meant to be opened again on a specific date, and if that's the case, perhaps that was all forgotten—the date came and went unnoticed, with nothing happening. But perhaps, too, the riddle was meant to be solved only on Judgment Day. We'll never find out . . ."

Benedikta frowned. "Then, during the restoration work in the church, my brother finds the sealed crypt, opens it, and tells me and the bishop about it," she said, lost in thought.

Simon started. "The bishop?"

"Didn't I mention that?" Benedikta gave him a confused look. "My brother wrote in his letter that he would also tell the bishop in Augsburg about it. After all, the bishop was his superior."

The physician frowned. "Did he send a messenger to the bishop, or did he write?"

"I . . . I don't know."

The wind rattled the windows. Simon gripped the cup of brandy tightly to keep warm.

"Perhaps someone intercepted the messenger and learned about the treasure that way," he murmured, looking around carefully. "It's quite possible that someone was watching us when we went to the Altenstadt basilica and to the castle ruins." He leaned forward and continued in a whisper. "Benedikta, it's all the more important for that reason that no one learns where we are going now, because the next riddle is something known only to us at present. We have to leave for Wessobrunn without anyone noticing!"

Benedikta smiled at him. "Let me take care of that. Mysterious disappearances are my specialty . . . along with reading balance sheets . . ."

Simon laughed, and for a moment his gloomy thoughts receded. But then it occurred to him that he hadn't thought about Magdalena since the previous day. He sighed, washing his guilty conscience down with brandy that had become lukewarm in the meanwhile. Well, at least she was far from any possible danger she might encounter in Schongau. He grinned. Besides, a Kuisl never had any trouble taking care of him- or herself, anyway.

Magdalena ran out into the street just in time to see the stranger taking a left turn. He was swinging the silk purse of poison almost playfully as he strode along the broad main street.

For the first time, the hangman's daughter got a good look at him. Dressed in a black cloak and a white tunic, he was gaunt and his arms and legs seemed unnaturally long for his body. He was slightly stooped, as if carrying some invisible weight. With his cowl pulled down over his face and his arms swinging, he looked like a busy black bug scuttling for cover. The man was clearly a monk, though Magdalena couldn't say what order he belonged to. Carefully, she followed.

The only path through the snow was a track just wide enough for two people. Hurrying, he passed bundled-up councillors and maids carrying baskets; once, he gave a shove to a farmer leading a stubborn ox to the butcher's. The farmer landed in the snow, cursing, alongside the animal. Without paying him any attention, the stranger continued on. Magdalena had trouble keeping up, squeezing her way past grumbling people, forced to step into the knee-high snow to the left or right of the path. Soon her shoes and stockings were drenched. She needed to catch a glimpse of the man's face, but he was still wearing his cowl and didn't turn around once.

Deep inside, Magdalena hoped he would never turn around to look at her. That would probably mean certain death for her.

Farther ahead in the market square the path became wider. Market women, wrapped in layers of thick underskirts, were setting up their stands for the farmers' market. The monk walked straight past them without looking one way or the other. Finally, Magdalena could see where he was headed.

The Domburg.

The hangman's daughter knit her brow. The previous day, during the snowstorm, when Philipp Hartmann had told her some of the history of the imperial city, he had mentioned the Domburg. The center of Augsburg was a little city in itself, surrounded by a wall and gates. It was the site of the first Roman settlement, a military headquarters along the Lech River. Since then, the bishop's offices, the cathedral, and the bishop's palace were all located there, too, along with the homes of well-to-do tradesmen. What could Koppmeyer's murderer be looking for there?

On each side of the gate, two of the bishop's watchmen dressed in elegant uniforms leaned on their halberds. As the monk walked by, they saluted briefly, then went back to dreaming of mulled wine and warm gingerbread cookies. Magdalena paused for a moment. The man had entered the Domburg without being stopped! Had the watchmen recognized him?

She had no time to think about this. If she didn't want to lose sight of the stranger, she would have to walk past the guards. Closing her eyes and crossing herself, she approached the gate, smiling broadly. The two bailiffs looked at her suspiciously.

"Stop! Where are you going?" one of them demanded. It didn't really sound as if he was interested in knowing but was just doing his duty in asking the question. Magdalena smiled and showed the guard the bag of herbs she was holding under her coat. She also noted, with some satisfaction, the little leather bag of guilders from the Augsburg hangman still hanging at her side. Even if she lost track of the strange monk now, she still had done well in her business dealings. That little gnome of a pharmacist had it coming to him! Why was he selling poison to a murderer?

"Herbs from pharmacist Biermann," she said, addressing the

watchmen and pouting. "Sage and chamomile. The prior has a terrible cough."

The soldier glanced briefly into the bag, then let her pass with a nod. Only after Magdalena had passed through did he stop to think.

"Strange," he remarked to his colleague. "The prior looked the picture of health this morning. He was well enough to give his usual fire-and-brimstone sermon. Hey, girl!" But the hangman's daughter had already disappeared around the corner.

Magdalena had trouble finding the stranger again. The little streets, lined with the homes of goldsmiths, silversmiths, engravers, and clothiers, were narrower and more winding than in the lower part of Augsburg. On a hunch, she turned right, only to wind up at a dead end. She spun around, ran this time in the other direction, and found herself suddenly right in front of the cathedral, a structure at least three times higher than the church in Schongau. Bells echoed through the cathedral courtyard as pilgrims and others who'd come to pray streamed out through the mighty portal, making way for those entering. On the steps, tattered beggars held out their hands, pleading with passersby. A mass must have just finished. Magdalena had to hold her breath—how many people could fit inside this enormous dome? She looked around hastily but saw only a sea of unfamiliar forms and faces.

The stranger had disappeared.

She was about to give up when she saw something glitter among the churchgoers and beggars on the wide steps leading up to the portal. She ran up the steps and was just able to catch a glimpse of the man as he disappeared inside the cathedral. The golden cross on his chain sparkled briefly once more in the sun, and then he was swallowed up inside the enormous building. Magdalena ran after him at a brisk pace.

Entering the cathedral, she couldn't help pausing a moment.

It seemed as if she were in another world; she had never before seen such an imposing building. As she continued to move forward, she looked up at the towering columns, the balcony, and the bright, colorful stained-glass windows with the morning sun streaming in. On all sides, angels and saints stared down from richly decorated walls.

The monk strode through the cathedral and finally turned left toward the end of a side aisle. Here, he knelt down in front of a sarcophagus and bowed his head in prayer.

Magdalena hid behind a column, where she finally had a chance to catch her breath.

A murderer who prays . . .

Had he come, perhaps, to confess his sins? Magdalena considered this for a moment before rejecting it. After all, the stranger had just purchased more poison. A penitent sinner wouldn't do that.

She wanted to get a look at his face, but the haggard monk still hadn't removed his cowl, and the only thing visible was his protruding, pointed nose. The bag with the poison was still dangling from his wrist, and the cross hung down from his broad shoulders like a heavy padlock.

Magdalena couldn't see whose coffin the man kneeled at. Concealed behind the column, she watched him impatiently. When she realized the prayer might take a while, she looked up once more to admire the size of the cathedral. She studied the columns and side altars, the many niches, and the stairways that led up and down. On the left, a well-worn stone staircase led down into a crypt, and farther back, a small walkway branched off. On her right, above the stone altar where the stranger was praying, a row of paintings depicted some old men wearing mitres and capes. Each held a shepherd's crook in his hand and looked down benevolently on his followers. Magdalena noticed that the paintings on top left were old and faded, and their subjects had a strange gray hue, like messengers from a distant era. Farther down to the right, the paintings seemed newer and more colorful. Each painting was dated, and Magdalena realized these were portraits of all the Augsburg bishops. In the last painting on the bottom row, an astonishingly young man was depicted with thinning black hair, a hooked nose, and a strange penetrating gaze. Magdalena read the name beneath it.

Bishop Sigismund Franz. Appointed 1646.

The bishop up there seemed to be staring directly into her soul with his unpleasant piercing eyes.

She hesitated.

Something about the painting irritated her. Was it the black, almost impoverished look of the cloak? The cold gaze? The surprising youth amid all these old men? As she looked closer, she realized what it was, but it took a while to accept it.

Around the bishop's neck hung a golden chain with a cross —with two crossbeams.

Just like the one the monk wore!

Magdalena almost cried out loud. Thoughts raced through her head, but she had no time to organize them—the monk had finished praying. He stood up, crossed himself, and bowed now. Finally, he headed for the cloister and disappeared through an ancient stone doorway. He hadn't once turned around. Casting a final glance at the young bishop above her, Magdalena took off after the stranger. She felt as if Bishop Sigismund Franz's eyes were boring right through her from behind.

Just after the first cockcrow, there was such a loud pounding at Jakob Kuisl's door that it sounded as if he himself were being summoned for execution. Outside, it was still the dead of night. Kuisl lay in bed alongside the soft, warm body of his wife, who turned, blinking and groggy, to her husband after the visitor had pounded on the door a third time.

"It doesn't matter who it is . . . Wring his neck," she mumbled and buried her head under a down pillow.

"You can bet on it," the hangman groaned, swinging his legs out of bed, almost falling down the stairs when the knocking began again a fourth time. In the next room, the twins woke up and began to cry.

"All right, all right," the hangman growled, "I'm coming!"

As he stumbled down the ice-cold stairs barefoot and dressed only in his nightshirt, he swore to himself he would, at the least, apply thumbscrews to this disturber of the peace. He would probably also shove burning matches under his fingernails.

"I'm coming, I'm coming!"

Jakob Kuisl had had a strenuous night. The little ones had a terrible cough and couldn't be calmed down, even with hot milk and honey. Once Georg and Barbara had finally drifted off to sleep, Kuisl rolled around in bed for hours thinking about the second gang of robbers. He was brooding about the mysterious fourth man when he'd finally fallen asleep.

Only to be awakened what seemed like five minutes later by this fool trying to break down his door.

Furious, Jakob Kuisl ran down the steps, threw aside the bolt, tore open the door, and shouted at his visitor so loudly that the guest almost fell over into a large snowdrift behind him.

"What is God's name do you think you're doing, you stupid clod, coming here in the middle of the night . . ." Too late, he noticed it was Burgomaster Karl Semer standing there. "Confound it . . ." the hangman muttered.

The hangman stood a full head taller than the burgomaster, and the patrician looked up at Kuisl in terror. There were dark circles under Semer's eyes, he was pale, and his left cheek was badly swollen.

"Excuse my bothering you at such an early hour, Kuisl," he whispered, pointing at his cheek. "But I just couldn't stand it . . . the pain . . ."

The hangman frowned, then opened the door. "Come in."

Leading the burgomaster into the main room, he relit the fire in the hearth with a few pieces of kindling he kept in holders on the table.

In the faint light, Karl Semer looked around the hangman's quarters — the executioner's sword next to the devotional corner, the rough-hewn stool, the huge well-worn table, the gallows ladder in the corner. A few books lay open on the table.

"You're reading . . . ?" the burgomaster asked.

The hangman nodded. "Dioscorides's work. An old tome, but there's nothing better for learning about herbs. And this one here," he continued, holding up a newer book, "Athanasius Kircher, a damned Jesuit, but what he writes about the plague is first rate. Do you know his work?"

The burgomaster shrugged. "Well, to tell the truth . . . I read mostly balance sheets."

Lighting his pipe from a piece of kindling, the hangman continued. "Kircher thinks the plague is transmitted by tiny, winged creatures that he has seen with a so-called 'microscope.' He says nothing about vapors emanating from the earth, or God knows what else the quack doctors go on and on about, but creatures so small they're invisible to the naked eye, that jump from one person to another — " Kuisl's enthusiastic remarks were interrupted by his children's crying. His wife, too, could be heard complaining loudly up in the bedroom.

"What in God's name is going on down there?" she cursed. "If you want to go out and drink, go to Semer's tavern and let the children sleep in peace!"

"Anna," Jakob Kuisl hissed, "Semer is standing right down here."

"What?"

"The burgomaster is down here with a toothache."

"Toothache or not, please keep the noise down, for God's sake!"

A door slammed.

The hangman looked at Karl Semer and rolled his eyes. "Women," he whispered, but softly enough that his wife couldn't hear. Finally, he turned serious again. "So what brings you to me?"

"My wife thinks you're the only one who can help me," the burgomaster said, pointing to his swollen cheek. "I've had this toothache for weeks, but tonight . . ." He closed his eyes. "Make it go away. I'll pay whatever you ask."

"Well then, let's have a look." Jakob Kuisl guided the burgomaster to one of the stools. "Open your mouth."

He held up a small piece of burning wood to see into the burgomaster's mouth. "Ah, I can see it, the son of a bitch," he mumbled. "Does this hurt?" He tapped a finger on a black stump of a tooth far back in the burgomaster's mouth. The burgomaster jumped and let out a scream.

"Shh," Kuisl said. "Remember my wife. She doesn't have much understanding for these things."

He left for the adjoining room and returned shortly with a little bottle.

"What is that?" the burgomaster grumbled, half dazed with pain.

"Clove oil. It will ease the pain." The hangman put a few drops on a cloth and dabbed it on the tooth.

Karl Semer groaned with relief. "Indeed, the pain is better. What a miracle!"

Jakob Kuisl grinned. "I can inflict pain, and I can take it away. Everything at a price. Here, take it!" He handed the burgomaster the little bottle. "I'll give you the tincture for a guilder."

Kuisl poured the burgomaster a cup of brandy. He drank it in one gulp and gratefully took another cupful.

The two men sat across from each other for a while in silence. Curious, Semer looked around the room again, his eyes coming to rest on the gallows ladder.

"Scheller's trial will probably be tomorrow," the burgomaster said, pointing to the ladder. Relieved of pain, he now looked remarkably relaxed, even in the hangman's house. "Then, in three days, you can go to work."

But then he became angry. "This damned second band of robbers!" He pounded the table with his fist so hard that the brandy splashed out of the glass. "If it weren't for them, I could sell my muscatel easily in Landsberg and beyond. The Swabians love their wine, and I can't deliver it!"

"But perhaps you can." The hangman poured himself a big glass of liquor this time.

Karl Semer looked up at him in amazement. "What do you mean by that? Don't talk nonsense. As long as we don't know who's leaking information about our secret routes, it's extremely dangerous out there. Shall I let the same thing happen to me as Holzhofer and the others?"

Jakob Kuisl grinned. "I know roads that even the highway robbers don't. It would be easy to get through with a horse and sled. And besides, you could get an escort for the first few miles. With my men, I'll be out there chasing the thieves down the next few days, anyway."

"An escort, huh?" The burgomaster furrowed his brow. "And what will that cost me?"

Jakob Kuisl emptied the liquor in one gulp like a glass of milk. "Almost nothing," he said. "Just a little information." He leaned over the table. "All I'd like you to do on your way to Swabia is to ask around a bit for me. For a man like you, what I want to know should be easy to get." He explained to the burgomaster what he wanted.

Semer listened attentively and nodded. "I don't really know what good that will do, but if that's all there is to it, sure . . . And we could leave as early as tomorrow?"

The hangman nodded. "As soon as the snowstorm lets up. But until then . . ." He pointed to the burgomaster's cheek. "With a tooth like that, I wouldn't take any big trips, anyway."

The burgomaster blanched. "But the pain has stopped, and I have the clove oil . . ."

"That will work for a while, but believe me, the pain will return, worse than before, and eventually, even the cloves won't help anymore."

"Oh, God, what shall I do?" Karl Semer, seized by panic, held his cheek and gave the hangman a pleading look. "What shall I do?"

Jakob Kuisl went to the chest in the next room and brought back a pair of pincers as long as his arm, a tool he usually used only for torturing prisoners. "We'll probably have to pull it," he said.

Karl Semer looked close to passing out. "Right away?"

The hangman gave the burgomaster a stein full of liquor. "Why not? My wife has to get up, anyway."

The scream that followed awoke not only Anna Maria and the twins, but the entire Tanners' Quarter as well.

Magdalena followed the dark monk through the Augsburg Cathedral, seeking cover behind columns along the way. He disappeared into a cloister directly in front of her. The hangman's daughter then followed him through a portal leading to the atrium, just in time to see him walk past a wooden door and disappear around another corner. Two acolytes were walking toward her, giving her curious looks. She slowed her pace and smiled as she passed by them, swinging the bag of herbs as casually as possible. The pimply young men stared at her low neckline as if they'd never seen a woman before. *They probably don't see a low neckline in the cloister too often,* Magdalena thought, smiling stoically. Finally passing the acolytes, she picked up her pace, rounded the next corner . . .

And no one was there.

Magdalena uttered a curse she'd learned from her father. The damned monk had gotten away again!

She hurried on, circling the atrium until she was back again at the door leading into the cathedral. How was that possible? How had the man disappeared through the portal again? She would *have to* have seen him! Standing in the cloister, she looked around an inner courtyard surrounded by columns. There was not a soul to be seen here in the little herb garden or amid the low bushes, which lay dormant under a cover of snow. It seemed as if the stranger had simply vanished into thin air. Once more, she made the rounds of the cloister. Maybe she had overlooked a door somewhere, an opening, a hidden niche?

Until now, Magdalena hadn't had time to look around more carefully. The walls on one side were covered with memorial plaques from many historical periods. Knights in old-fashioned armor, grinning skeletons, and hook-nosed bishops stared out at her. But there was no door to be seen.

She had completely lost track of the man.

Exhausted, she leaned against one of the slabs and took a deep breath. At least she knew now that Koppmeyer's murderer was somehow connected with this cathedral. The watchmen at the gate had greeted him, he obviously knew his way around the cathedral, and he was wearing the same cross as the young bishop pictured over in the side aisle. A cross with two crossbeams.

The same cross . . . The thought that suddenly dawned on her was so dreadful and absurd that she didn't want to accept it at first.

Could it be that this monk and the bishop were one and the same?

Before she could think through the implications of this ghastly idea, the slab behind her began to speak.

Magdalena jumped away, dropping the purse and the herbs. She stared at the man engraved on the stone slab—a knight in armor with an open helmet, a broadsword at his side, and two dogs playing at his feet. He glared back at her with vacant eyes.

Magdalena held her breath and listened. From the knight's mouth, open in a mute cry, Magdalena thought she could make out an almost inaudible murmuring and hissing.

Carefully, she approached the stone relief once more. Pressing her ear against the cold plaque, she could hear a hum behind it, a continuous, mournful sound. Magdalena closed her eyes and listened. It was not a single voice, but the muffled choir of many men that came through the stone.

Was it possible . . . ?

She pressed both hands against the slab, but it didn't yield. She looked for a crack along the edges where she might get a handhold; she probed for some hidden mechanism.

All in vain.

Finally, she noticed two palm-size basins of holy water attached waist-high to both sides of the slab—two grinning stone skulls, each with a depression in the top serving as a basin. The skulls appeared old and weathered, and the holy water in the basins was frozen. Magdalena examined them more closely.

The skull on the right was bent at an odd angle and looked up at Magdalena with a teasing grin.

Like a man on the gallows whose neck my father has broken, she was thinking. She reached out for the skull and tried to turn it straight.

It moved.

With a grating sound, the heavy stone slab moved back, revealing a steep, worn stone staircase leading down into the darkness. Magdalena held her breath and listened. From far below, she could hear men singing a mournful chorale in Latin.

Mors stupebit et natura, cum resurget creatura . . . Deus lo vult . . .
Confutatis maledictis, flammis acribus addictis . . . Deus lo vult . . .
Deus lo vult. God wills it.

There they were again, those strange Latin words her father had told her about, the ones used by the Latin-speaking strangers in the Altenstadt tavern and by the murderers in the crypt.

God wills it . . .

It was time to go down and see what this was all about.

Magdalena stuffed the purse with the herbs back under her dress and started down the steep staircase, one step at a time. The steps spiraled around a weathered column, and the singing grew louder as she drew nearer. She noticed symbols carved into the walls now—engravings of fish here and there, the letters P and X. She passed niches in which there were flickering oil lamps lighting her way. She had the feeling this stairway was much older than the cathedral above.

She finally reached the bottom. A narrow, domed corridor led toward the singing, and farther ahead she could make out a bright light. As she groped through the dark corridor, her hand felt something smooth and dry that crumbled at her touch. Pulling her hand back, she gazed down on a neatly stacked pile of skulls on the floor next to her. She had stuck her hand straight in the eye socket of one of the skulls. On the opposite wall, bones were stacked up to the ceiling. The singing sounded quite close now.

Iudex ergo cum sedebit, quidquid latet apparebit . . .
Deus lo vult . . .

Magdalena had reached the end of the corridor. Kneeling down, she peered out from behind the little pyramid of skulls.

What she saw was terrifying. The high-vaulted room was the size of a church and had rough niches carved into the walls all around, reaching up to the ceiling and stacked full of bones. At the front of the room was a stone altar and, beyond that, a weathered cross on the wall. By the light of torches, Magdalena could see a group of at least two dozen men in monks' cowls and capes gathered around the cross, some kneeling and some standing and singing their chorale. Over their black habits, all of them wore white cloaks adorned with crosses in the same shape and color as the one behind the altar.

The crosses had two crossbeams, painted blood red.

Tuba mirum spargens sonum, per sepulcra regionum . . .
Deus lo vult . . .

After what seemed like an eternity, the men finished singing. Though Magdalena could feel her feet falling asleep, she remained crouched behind the pyramid of skulls, watching the proceedings. One of the cloaked men stepped up to the altar and raised his hands in blessing. He, too, had a cowl pulled down over his face. He turned around to face the group and spoke in a loud voice that echoed through the vault.

"Dear brethren," he began, "honorable citizens, clergy, and simple pastors who have traveled from afar to get to this place. Our brotherhood has always made it our mission to destroy heretics wherever they may be and prevent the spread of the accursed Lutheran heresy!" A murmur of approval rose from beneath the cowls, but the man motioned for his listeners to be silent. "You know that we are also trying to save our Master's treasures from destruction at the hands of heretics. Much has been returned to the fold of the Holy Catholic Church, the only church!" He paused dramatically before continuing. "I have convened this meeting to proclaim some happy news. We have succeeded in finding the largest treasure in all of Christianity!" Excited whispers coursed through the crowd. Their leader raised his hand again to silence them.

"The wretched Templars have hidden it in a place not far from here. But in his infinite mercy, God has sent us a sign that this treasure will soon be ours and we will soon be able to embark on our Holy War! We must not allow this Lutheran rabble to again sully the name of our Savior. It was here, in this city, that the heresy began to spread through German lands, and here it will end! I am certain that, with the help of this treasure, the Great War can begin again! Down with the heretics! Victory is ours!"

"*Deus lo vult! Deus lo vult!*" cried a number of the monks. Others fell on their knees and began to pray or flagellate themselves with their belts.

Again, their leader demanded silence.

"Most of you already know about the treasure, but now Brother Jakobus, a true servant of our brotherhood, will give you further details. I don't need to stress how important it is to maintain strict secrecy about everything he tells us. Traitors will meet a fiery death."

"Death to traitors!" someone shouted. "Death to the heretics and Lutherans!" Others joined in the shouting.

Magdalena gulped, crouching even lower behind the skulls.

Now a man dressed in a cowl and cloak stepped forward. As he started to speak, a chill ran up and down Magdalena's spine. It was the stranger from the apothecary! Somewhere down below here in the vault, he must have donned the white coat with the strange cross. But it was his voice she recognized.

"My brethren! He speaks the truth. Victory is close at hand!" Though he had a slight lisp, Magdalena understood every word. "It's a miracle, believe me! Many years ago, but just a few miles from here, the accursed Templars buried the greatest treasure in all Christendom. These heretics made up a few childish riddles to keep the secret from us, but just recently — "

Much too late, Magdalena noticed that she had leaned too far over the pile of skulls. She bumped one with her right elbow. Falling from the pyramid, it rolled noisily across the floor toward the vault.

Brother Jakobus paused and looked suspiciously in Magdalena's direction. He was about to resume speaking when the other skulls started tumbling forward as well. Frantic, Magdalena tried to stop them, but it was too late.

A centuries-old equilibrium disturbed, the skulls now started falling on all sides with a clattering and banging. Soon Magdalena found herself standing in the corridor in plain view. For a moment, time seemed to stand still.

"Seize her!" the leader shouted to his comrades-in-arms, who were just as shocked as Magdalena. The man's cowl slipped off the back of his head and Magdalena found herself staring into a spiteful face—the same face she had seen in the portrait up in the cathedral.

The bishop.

In a fraction of a second, Magdalena realized what this meant. The Augsburg dignitary was not the murderer of Andreas Koppmeyer. No, he was the leader of this insane group—a group presumably capable of far worse crimes, one that, barring a miracle, would torture her as a witch, strangle her, and commit her body to the fire. If she were lucky, they would tear her into pieces first.

Brother Jakobus was the first to get over his shock and run toward the hangman's daughter, who was rushing down the corridor, stumbling over bones, getting back on her feet again, and racing up the stairs. Behind her she could hear the monk's footfalls. She ran and ran, spiraling up the staircase as if trapped on a nightmarish merry-go-round, until she finally reached the door.

It was then she realized the door had no handle on the inside.

Gasping for breath, she threw herself against the stone, but this was like hitting her head against a wall. The door would not yield a bit.

She pounded and kicked the stone slab.

"Help!" she cried. "Doesn't anyone hear me out there? Help me!"

Smiling broadly, Brother Jakobus moved toward her, his

hands raised as if in benediction. Only at the last minute did she see the curved dagger in his right hand.

"I'll give you just a little cut, I promise," he whispered. "Just like your father. You'll sleep like the stone knight behind you." He feigned a blow from above, then thrust the knife at her from below. Magdalena reached for his hand, but the man was quicker. The blade came down, and even though she ducked to one side, it cut her upper arm, which she had raised to fend off her attacker.

"Divine providence has led you to us!" Brother Jakobus murmured. "I know your name, Maria Magdalena, the whore of Christ. You are much too precious to commit to the flames. I have great plans for you."

Magdalena could feel her body going stiff. When numbness reached her legs, she slid down the gravestone behind her and came to rest on the floor, her eyes wide in fear. From far off, she could hear an organ.

Maria zu lieben ist allzeit mein Sinn, in Freuden und Leiden ihr Diener ich bin . . . My heart is devoted to Mary, my queen, in joy and in sorrow to serve her I mean . . .

In the cathedral above, just a few yards away, mass had begun.

10

EARLY THE NEXT MORNING, SIMON AND BENEDIKTA set out for Wessobrunn on horseback. They avoided major roads leading north along the Lech River that might be under the robbers' surveillance. Instead, they crossed the bridge over the Lech to Peiting and, from there, headed directly toward Mount Hoher Peißenberg, which towered like a giant above the villages and little towns in the otherwise flat countryside. The blizzard of the last two days had passed, and the air was clear and pure. The sun shone so brightly in the blue sky that Simon had to close his eyes whenever he looked too long at the snowy fields and trees.

In the last hour, Simon had often glanced back. Whenever he and Benedikta left a clearing and entered the endless forests around the mountain, the feeling came over him that he was being watched. It felt like an itch between his shoulders, and Simon expected any moment to hear the twang of a bowstring or the rattle of a saber. Whenever he turned around, though, all he saw was an impenetrable thicket of pines. Occasionally, a startled bird flew away, squawking, or snow trickled softly down from branches. Otherwise, silence prevailed.

In many places, the blizzard had bent the trees down like

reeds, and from atop his horse, Simon looked down on wide swaths of downed trees in the forest. At least the farmers wouldn't complain this winter about a lack of firewood.

"Don't look so cross!" Benedikta called to him. "It doesn't go well with your beautiful eyes. The robbers are on the Lech, not here. What is there of any value here?"

In contrast to Simon, the businesswoman seemed carefree, humming a French tune and spurring her horse on across the wide clearings. Simon had trouble keeping up with her. He'd borrowed the hangman's old mare again for their ride to Wessobrunn. Walli seemed to have gotten somewhat used to him, but she stopped from time to time whenever something green poked its head out of the snow cover. Then even kicking her wouldn't get her to move. Occasionally, she snapped at Simon or tried to throw him off, but the medicus was determined to teach the beast some manners. The horse came to a dead stop again and tugged calmly at a weed poking its head up out of the snow. Simon tugged desperately on the reins and dug his heels into Walli's scrawny body, but he might as well have been sitting on a rock.

Benedikta watched him struggle, grinned, then put two fingers to her mouth and whistled.

"*Allez hop, viens par ici!* Giddyap, this way!"

As if the horse had just been waiting for Benedikta's command, it started to move again.

"Just where have you learned to deal with horses like that?" Simon asked, patting Walli on the rump and trying to catch up.

"My mother comes from a family of Huguenots who fled from the French Catholics." Benedikta brought her horse into a faster trot. "A respected family from the area around Paris with an estate and property. She learned to ride as a child and no doubt passed this love along to me. *Je suis un enfant de France!*" She laughed, racing off.

Simon dug his heels into Walli's sides, trying to keep up with Benedikta, and for a brief while they rode side by side.

"France must be gorgeous!" he cried to her. "Paris! Notre Dame! Fashion! Is it true that the city blazes with the light of a thousand lanterns at night?"

"In your Schongau, I'd be pleased to see even a dozen lanterns. And people smell better in Paris." She gave her horse a slap. "But now, enough of this foolishness. The last one to reach the edge of the clearing pays for the first round of muscatel in Wessobrunn! *Allez, hue, Aramis!*"

Her sorrel leapt forward and raced to the edge of the clearing, while Walli plodded along listlessly, clearly in the hope of finding a few tasty blades of grass at the forest edge.

As they approached Peißenberg, they turned left, heading north, and, two hours later crossed through a dense forest of firs interspersed with dark-green yews.

"Keep an eye on your horse. The trees are very poisonous, so make sure she doesn't eat the leaves or the hangman will wring your neck," Benedikta warned.

Simon nodded. He didn't want to think what Jakob Kuisl would do to him if he had to flay his own horse. Probably, he'd stick Simon up to his neck in a vat of tannic acid. The medicus was still lost in thought, pondering how indebted he really was to the hangman, when he suddenly felt the urgent call of nature.

"Benedikta, excuse me, but I . . ." He smiled with embarrassment and pointed to the yews on the left. "It will take only a moment."

"If you've got to go . . ." she said, winking. "But don't let the bad fellows catch you with your pants down."

Entering a thicket of yews, Simon squeezed past sharp branches and opened the buttons of his coat and trousers. When he was finished, he paused to enjoy a moment of peace and tranquility in the forest.

At this moment, Simon had the unmistakable feeling that someone was watching.

It was a warm, tickling sensation on his back; he was petrified when, a moment later, he heard a crackle behind him. Slowly, he buttoned up his trousers and moved farther back into the thicket. Instead of going back to the road, he turned left, jumped down into a ditch in front of him and crawled along on the ground parallel to the road. For protection, he picked up a branch about the length of a club, which had broken off in the blizzard. Finally, he crossed through another thicket and, in a wide circle, returned to where he'd started. Holding the club tightly, he moved forward, trying not to make a sound. Just behind a large fallen tree he came to a stop.

Ten paces in front of him, a man was leaning against a tree.

He was wearing the red Turkish trousers of a mercenary foot soldier and a gray jacket from which a sword and powder horn hung. In his right hand he held a musket like a walking stick. He was looking out at the road, where Benedikta was waiting. Suddenly, the man put his hand to his mouth and let out a very realistic-sounding caw like that of a jay. Another caw answered, then a third. The man nodded with calm satisfaction, pulled a dagger from his waistband, and began cleaning his fingernails, all the while keeping a close eye on the road.

Simon clutched the cudgel so tightly that his knuckles turned white and he had trouble swallowing. An ambush! Judging from the signals, there had to be at least three men. The physician looked around at the bushes and yews but couldn't see any other men. They were probably hiding on the other side of the road. Simon rose cautiously, trying to formulate a plan. He had to warn Benedikta and then ride away as soon as possible! He could only hope the highwaymen didn't have horses.

As quietly as possible, Simon crept back through the thicket of yews. The crackle of even a tiny branch sounded to him like a peal of thunder, but finally he reached the road. When he emerged from the ditch with twigs in his hair and trousers wet from the snow, Benedikta looked down at him in amusement.

"Did you find a badger hole to do your business? As far as I'm concerned, you could have just gone in the ditch." Then she noticed the anxious expression on his face and turned serious. "What happened?"

Simon mouthed his next words. "Robbers. On both sides of the street. We have to get out of here."

Again, one jay call followed another.

Benedikta hesitated briefly. "Don't worry," she whispered. "As long as we're on our horses and keep moving, they can't catch us." She grinned and pointed to her skirt pocket. "Don't forget, I'm not completely defenseless. *Allez!*"

Her horse bounded forward and galloped away, and to Simon's great relief, Walli promptly followed. The medicus thought he saw something move behind the trees. He expected to hear the crack of a shot, the whistle of a bullet, or the pain of one impacting his shoulder—but nothing happened.

Clearly, they had shaken off the robbers.

But how? Had he been mistaken? He'd expected that, at the very least, the men would shoot at them with their muskets or crossbows as he and Benedikta rode away. But there was no time to think. The horses raced off, and Benedikta was already entering another part of the forest far ahead. Her laughter dispelled his dark thoughts. Perhaps the highwaymen had simply decided to wait for a more promising victim.

Soon they left the yew forest and a large clearing opened up in front of them. The road climbed steeply, lined by houses on both sides. Simon breathed a deep sigh of relief. They'd reached the village of Gaispoint, and high above them, on a hill, was the Wessobrunn Monastery.

As the medicus looked around, it struck him how well maintained the houses looked. Many of them were built of stone and had obviously survived the war with little damage. Many stucco workers had settled in Gaispoint to take advantage of the booming construction business in the surrounding churches and monasteries. The physician had heard that the Gaispoint stucco workers were well known and highly regarded in Venice and as far away as Florence and Rome. At present, the stucco workers were engaged principally in restoring the neighboring Benedictine monastery to its former glory. Even though the Swedes had left the village largely untouched, they had plundered and set fire to the monastery itself.

Simon and Benedikta rode over a narrow bridge toward the rectory. The grounds seemed gloomy in the light of the setting sun. Parts of the encircling wall had collapsed, and many of the outer buildings had been burned down by the marauding soldiers. Loose stucco was crumbling from the church walls, and all that remained of the well house roof was the timber frame. Crows rose up from a heavy layer of ice covering the fountain and flew off. Only the squat bell tower standing off behind the parish church seemed to have weathered the tumultuous times.

Benedikta knocked on the heavy door of the main house, but it took a while before someone answered. A bald monk peered out at them suspiciously through a narrow crack in the door.

"Yes?"

Benedikta put on her sweetest smile. "We've ridden a long way to see this famous monastery. It would be a great honor for us if the abbot—"

"Abbot Bernhard is not available now. Go over to the tavern next door, and perhaps tomorrow—"

Sticking his foot in the crack, Simon pushed the door open a bit. The monk stepped back, startled.

"My companion has come all the way from Paris to view the famous Wessobrunn Prayer," the medicus said in a commanding tone. "Madame Lefèvre is not accustomed to waiting, especially as she is considering a substantial donation to the monastery."

Benedikta looked at him for a moment in astonishment, then joined in the game. "*C'est vrai,*" she mumbled. "*Je suis très fatiguée . . .*"

For a moment, the monk looked confused, then finally ushered them into the vestibule.

"Wait a moment," he said, disappearing through a doorway.

"A substantial donation?" Benedikta whispered. "What were you thinking? I don't have anything substantial to give."

Simon grinned. "It won't necessarily get to that point, Madame Lefèvre. All we want is to see this prayer. I do believe we shall have to leave tomorrow in a great hurry. *Compris?*"

Benedikta smirked. "Simon Fronwieser," she whispered, "it seems I've underestimated you until now."

At that moment, a side door opened on a tall black-robed monk with penetrating eyes. Breadcrumbs still clung to his mouth, which he wiped with his sleeve. His Excellency had clearly been disturbed at supper.

"I am Abbot Bernhard Gering," he said. He was at least two heads taller than Simon. Looking down, he asked, "What can I do for you?"

The abbot raised his eyebrows as if he were examining a bug in the monastery kitchen. Obviously, Father Bernhard was hungry and thus rather ill-disposed. His pronounced nose reminded Simon a bit of Jakob Kuisl's.

"*Ah, frère Bernhard,*" Benedikta sighed, extending her hand. "*Comme c'est agréable de faire la connaissance de l'abbé de Wessobrunn!*"

Father Bernhard hesitated, then smiled wanly. "You come from France?" he asked in a much softer voice as he shook her hand.

Benedikta smiled back. "*De Paris, pour être précis.* Business matters in Augsburg have brought me to your beautiful isolated region." She pointed to Simon. "My charming guide offered to show me the way to your monastery. In Paris, I heard of your . . . *comment dit-on* . . . Wessobrunn Prayer, and now I am dying to see it."

Suddenly, the abbot perked up. "Paris, you say? I spent part of my younger years in Paris! What a wonderful city! *Parlez-moi de Paris! J'ai appris que le Cardinal Richelieu a fait construire une chapelle à la Sorbonne.*"

Simon closed his eyes and said a quick prayer. Hearing Benedikta speak the purest Parisian French with the abbot, he opened his eyes again. Father Bernhard nodded and smiled, and now and then posed an interested question. He suddenly seemed years younger, as if he'd fallen under a spell.

After just a few moments, Bernhard Gering led them to his private quarters, where excellent French wine and tender chicken awaited them. The medicus grinned. It was astonishing how a foreign language could open doors. Then he feasted on the coq au vin.

Outside the monastery gates, two monks huddled in a niche against the biting winter wind. A blizzard was brewing again and tugged at their black cowls. A thin layer of snow had fallen on the backs of the horses standing next to them. These men were not Benedictines like the monks of Wessobrunn, and though they would never admit it, they despised their brothers inside the monastery. The Benedictines prayed, ate well, and drank. They spent their tithes on stucco and gold leaf and honored God by reveling in pomp and splendor. They'd lost sight of what was sometimes necessary—a strong hand to free the rose of God from the rampant weeds.

These two monks belonged to an order that thought of itself as Christendom's elite. For centuries, these brothers had been on the frontlines of the war against the heretics. Other monks quietly tended their cloister gardens and decorated their churches, but *these* monks were destined for higher things! Their third man had returned to Augsburg, and now they were waiting here in the cold, as they had promised not to let the two busybodies out of their sight. As God's watchdogs, they followed their master undeterred through storms and snow.

They didn't notice that they themselves were being observed.

"Up here?" Simon glanced up a steep staircase leading to the clock tower attic. Wind was whistling through the stairwell and shaking the entire roof truss, so that more than once the physician reached out and frantically grabbed hold of the railing.

"Just a security measure," the abbot remarked, wiping cold sweat from his forehead. He stopped for a moment to catch his breath. "During the Great War, we took all the monastery's books up here. It's the safest place around here. The tower is ancient and as solid as a fortified castle."

Groaning, he continued upward, followed by Simon and Benedikta. The medicus examined the unplastered walls in the light of their lantern. The walls were several feet thick and interrupted only by the occasional narrow embrasure.

During the meal, Benedikta had repeated her wish to Abbot Bernhard to see the Wessobrunn Prayer. Her father, who came to Paris from Germany, had often told her about the oldest prayer in the German language, with its simple yet stirring words. When she found it necessary to travel to Augsburg on a business matter, she decided to take a detour to Wessobrunn and make a donation to the monastery to support the library. The prospect of a pending windfall made it easy to convince the abbot to show them the prayer that very night.

After a few more turns on the clock tower's spiral staircase, they finally reached the attic. A trapdoor opened on the area directly under the roof. Simon peered in, moving the lantern around in a circle, and saw mountains of books and boxes scattered amid timber, trunks, and moth-eaten bundles of cloth, completely filling the attic.

With a barely suppressed cry of excitement, the medicus rushed to the first pile and began leafing through the books there. The first one was a yellow, faded copy of Seneca's *De vita beata,* and next to it lay an illuminated edition of Paracelsus's *Großer Wundarzeney* filled with detailed engravings and brilliant initials. Simon examined the books. Digging through the pile, he found a huge illustrated Bible and, right after that, the collected works of Aristotle, something he hadn't held in his hands since his days as a student in Ingolstadt. This was no cheap printed copy, however, but handwritten, with marginalia in an elegant script. When he took it in hand and opened the ribbon, a cloud of dust swirled up. He had to sneeze, and the light from the lantern flickered.

"Careful with the fire," murmured the abbot, who had disappeared behind some tall crates in a corner. "One false move and all of Western culture goes up in flames!"

Simon gingerly set his lantern down atop a pile of books and, sitting cross-legged on the floor, immersed himself in the world of letters. He felt neither the cold nor the wind whistling between the loose tiles of the roof.

It was Benedikta who shook him by the shoulder and roused him from his daydreams.

"Forget the books; we don't have time!" she whispered. "Once we have the treasure in hand, you can buy all these books, for all I care, and lock yourself up with them for the rest of your life. But come now!"

In the meanwhile, the abbot reappeared from the rear of the attic carrying a small trunk closed with a heavy padlock. He took a key out from under his habit and opened the box decorated with silver fittings. Resting on a red velvet lining inside was a simple cross and, at the bottom, a single book bound in bright calfskin.

With slender fingers, the abbot opened two golden clasps along the side of the book, then turned the brittle parchment pages until he found a certain passage in the middle. Simon leaned over to get a closer look. Some of the letters were red, the color of dried blood in the lantern light, and others were written in fine dark-brown flourishes and only slighted yellowed. Despite their age, they were quite legible. "The Wessobrunn Prayer," he whispered.

Abbot Bernhard nodded. "It's many hundreds of years old," he said, passing his hand gently over the page. "A treasure dating from the time the German Empire was still a primeval forest inhabited by heathens and wild animals. The prayer sounds like an ancient magic spell, and we Benedictines guard it like no other document."

He sighed, quoting the beginning of the prayer with his eyes closed.

> "This is what I learned among mortal men as the greatest wonder. That there was neither the earth nor the heaven above. Nor was there any tree nor mountain. Neither any star at all, nor any other thing, neither sun nor moon, nor the sparkling sea . . ."

Simon quickly read it through, but nothing stood out as a clue about where to turn next. Finally, he cleared his throat and interrupted the abbot's monologue.

"Yes, a wonderful prayer, Your Excellency. Where was it stored before?"

Abbot Bernhard stopped and gave him a bewildered look. "Before?"

"Well," said Simon, "I mean before it was brought to this tower during the Great War."

Bernhard Gering smiled. "Ah, that's what you mean. Well, it was in a little chapel in the rectory. We just barely had time to rescue the document. A few days later, the Swedes came to loot and pillage. The chapel, too, was burned to the ground."

Simon gulped, and Benedikta, who stood beside him, turned even paler than usual. "Completely?" she asked.

"Yes, completely. We even carted away the foundations, and now a little herb garden is there in the summer. But are you feeling well?" Bernhard looked at them anxiously. "It was just a little chapel, after all, with no holy relics or church treasure, and the prayer, as I said, we were able to save. Were you acquainted with the little church before the war?"

Benedikta came to Simon's aid. "My guide no doubt often prayed there as a child." She turned toward the abbot. "Was anything else saved from the church along with the Wessobrunn Prayer? A picture? A statue? Perhaps a memorial plaque?"

The abbot shook his head. "Unfortunately not. Everything was destroyed. And there were no memorial plaques in the chapel. Did you want to go there to pray?"

Simon nodded. His head was spinning. They had placed such great hope in the prayer, in finding something that would give them a clue in their search for the treasure, but all they found was an ancient parchment that didn't help at all. Was this the end of the search? Had the secret of the Templars' treasure been buried forever with the destruction of the Wessobrunn chapel?

One last time, Simon scanned the lines, silently mouthing the verse to himself.

. . . that there was neither the earth nor the heaven above.
Nor was there any tree . . .

Simon stopped short. They had overlooked something.

Tree . . .

Unlike the lines in the crypt of the ruined castle, the word here was not written in capital letters. So was there perhaps a certain tree here, and not in Peiting?

It was Benedikta who interrupted the silence. She, too,

seemed to notice the discrepancy. "Is there perhaps somewhere around here a tree with some special significance?" she asked, trying to seem casual.

"A special significance?" The abbot looked even more confused. "What do you mean—"

"*Ah, oui, excusez-moi,*" Benedikta interrupted. "This is a prayer about the miraculous powers of nature, the heavens, the mountains, and trees. I am a devout soul in search of a powerful place for my prayer. Perhaps a tree?"

Bernhard's face brightened. "Ah, yes, the old Tassilo Linden southeast of the monastery! An ancient tree blessed by God! Duke Tassilo is said to have dreamed there of the three wellsprings that later made this place famous. An excellent place to pray!"

"How old is this linden?" Simon asked.

"Certainly hundreds of years old. It has four trunks that have grown together, and some people consider this a symbol of the four elements. The Tassilo Linden is the most famous tree in our area."

"Your Excellency," Benedikta interrupted, "could you do us a great favor?"

"But of course."

"Would you take us to this tree tomorrow morning? I believe it would be the perfect place for me to open my soul to God at daybreak." She smiled at the abbot. "Surely, it will be revealed to me there what sum I should finally donate to the monastery."

"Under these circumstances," said the abbot, "I'll make sure that no one will be there to disturb you tomorrow. And please include the monastery in your prayers."

Simon nodded. "We shall do that. Your Excellency?"

"Yes, my son?"

"Might I borrow some books until tomorrow morning?"

The abbot smiled. "But of course. I'd be delighted if someone would read them again."

After assembling a stack of books, Simon staggered down the stairs with his hands full. It would be a long night.

Magdalena was lying in a ship's hold, being rocked gently side to side by waves that beat against the hull. She had difficulty keeping her eyes open as the sound of the water and the constant back and forth lulled her to sleep. A storm was brewing outside, however; the rocking became more violent, and she was thrown back and forth in the little ship like loose cargo. She would have to go up on deck to see what was wrong up there.

She stood up. Her head banged against a wooden wall, and with a cry of pain, she sunk back down again.

The pain woke her up, and the dream floated away like a cloud. She was not on a ship at all, but inside a tiny wooden crate. The rocking was from the movement of a wagon. Magdalena could hear the snorting of horses and a monotone hissing sound and, after a while realized it was the sound of runners of a sled being pulled through the snow. So it was not a wagon, but a sled that was taking her somewhere in a box. Now she could feel the cold coming through the slats of the box. A shaft of light entered through the cracks—too little to see more than a few indistinct figures rushing by. Her head pounded as if she had drunk a whole barrel of wine by herself.

Magdalena measured the narrow space around her with her hands and feet and quickly realized that the box was exactly the size of a coffin. Had she died perhaps and come back to life? Was someone taking her to the cemetery to bury her alive?

Or was she already dead?

"Help! Is someone there?" Her voice was nothing more than a soft wheezing sound. "I'm not dead! Get me out of here!"

The long, drawn-out call of a coachman was audible as he brought the sled to a stop. The shaking finally stopped and a crunching sound could be heard as someone trudged through the snow toward the box. Magdalena's heart began to pound.

Someone had heard her, and she was safe! In no time, the grave-digger would realize his error and break open the coffin. She would laugh in his face and tell him—

"Shut your damned mouth, Hangman's Daughter, or I'll dig a hole six feet deep and stick you in it, just like we used to do with sluts like you."

Magdalena fell silent. She recognized the voice at once—it was the man who had stuck her in the arm with the dagger, the man the other brothers had called Brother Jakobus. The name brought memories flooding back: the cathedral, the cross around his bishop's neck, the subterranean vault, the meeting. There must have been poison on the tip of the dagger that had paralyzed her and finally made her pass out—the same poison that had also made her father lose consciousness. Brother Jakobus was obviously taking her away somewhere to dispose of her.

But where?

"Listen, we'll soon be going by a security post." The man now sounded somewhat conciliatory. "Don't make a sound, do you understand? Not a sound! I don't mean to kill you, because we still need you, but if I have to, I will. Did your father ever tell you how long it takes to suffocate when you're buried alive?"

Brother Jakobus did not wait for the answer but climbed back up to the coach box, judging from what she could hear. With the crack of a whip, the sled moved forward again.

Magdalena tried to put her thoughts in order. The monk knew her and her father! He was probably the man with the violet perfume who had been watching her all along in Schongau and Altenstadt. By coincidence, he'd run into her again in Augsburg. He was apparently out to find the Templars' treasure, and clearly, there were many more people involved.

Magdalena shuddered. Only now did she remember she'd recognized the bishop among those disguised figures. It seemed clear he was the leader of this insane plot. The bishop had spoken of a brotherhood. What order could he have meant? And what treasure were these men looking for? What treasure could be so great as to turn pious, influential Christians into merciless killers?

Magdalena's thoughts were interrupted when the sled suddenly stopped. She could hear voices—apparently, the watch post.

"Where are you going with the coffin, Father? We don't need any plague victims in town!"

"Don't worry, my son. An elderly brother of mine has gone to join God. I'm taking him back to his hometown."

Magdalena was tempted to scream, but then she remembered what the monk had said.

Did your father ever tell you how long it takes to suffocate when you're buried alive?

She kept quiet. Finally, the guard let them pass, and the sled continued its journey. She could hear footsteps outside, laughter, and individual voices. Someone with a strong Swabian accent was hawking hot chestnuts. Where was she? Where was the man taking her? She had no idea how long the poison had knocked her out. One day? Two?

Again the sled stopped, and she could hear the muffled sound of Jakobus's voice. He was speaking with someone, but the conversation was too faint for her to understand anything. Suddenly, the coffin began to shake. Magdalena felt herself being lifted up and then carried down a flight of stairs. Imprisoned in her coffin, she slid from one side to the other.

"Careful, careful!" Brother Jakobus scolded. "Have some respect for the dead!"

"Where your brother is, it won't bother him anymore," she heard a deep voice reply grimly. Then the coffin fell to the ground, and Magdalena suppressed a cry of pain. She could hear coins being counted out, then heavy steps struggling up the stairway again. After that, only silence.

Magdalena waited a moment, then groped at the boards

above her. Certainly, Brother Jakobus wanted to rest and had put up for the night in some inn. Would she be able to loosen the boards a bit now? Her father said that coffins were often very carelessly nailed together. After all, nobody figured the dead would want to escape their last resting place.

Pressing with both hands against the top of the coffin to check how secure the boards were, she heard a ripping sound. Someone was prying a board off the lid! A moment later, a bright light shone into the coffin through the crack, and a head with a monk's haircut peered in above her. Brother Jakobus was shining his torch inside. His face was only a few inches from hers, but she wasn't able to reach up and seize him since her arms were still pinned beneath the cover. A strong scent of violets filled her nose.

"Well, Hangman's Daughter?" Brother Jakobus asked, passing his hand almost sympathetically over her cheeks. "How do you like your bed? Does it make you think of Judgment Day? Are you overcome with weeping and trembling? The wrath of the Lord catches up with everyone sooner or later."

In answer, Magdalena spit in his face.

The monk wiped the spittle from his cheek and his eyes narrowed to little slits. But then he smiled. "You slut. Women have always brought sinfulness on mankind, and you shall pay for it in eternity!" He closed his eyes briefly. "But you, too, are part of God's plans, at least for now . . ." He moved briefly out of her field of view and, seconds later reappeared with a wet sponge in hand. "Until then, I'll have to silence your fresh, malicious tongue. Our journey is not yet over, and before then, your shouts might betray our cause." As he spoke the last of these words, he pressed the sponge down over Magdalena's face. "And I will take no pity on your children, for they are sons and daughters of a whore . . ." the monk whispered.

The hangman's daughter writhed about, attempting in vain to call for help, but trapped beneath the boards, she couldn't pull her head away. She held her breath, whimpering, as Brother Jakobus pressed the sponge down harder and harder against her face.

The monk looked up to the heavens, murmuring quietly. "Your mother is a harlot, and she who gave birth to you is an abomination. Thus, behold, I will block your way with thorns and erect a wall that you may not find your way . . ."

When Magdalena was finally overcome by the need to breathe, she opened her mouth in a stifled cry and a bitter fluid filled her throat. She could smell poppy seeds and the fragrance of herbs that her father used in relieving the misery of condemned men on their march to the gallows. Paris quadrifolia, ranunculus, wolfsbane . . . Now the voice of the monk sounded like a distant, monotone chant.

"Mine is the vengeance, saith the Lord . . ."

Then her world turned black and she sank back into the coffin, which now felt like a bed of fine linen. The last thing she perceived was the sound of a hammer pounding on the wood.

Death is knocking at my door . . . They're coming to take me away to Last Judgment . . .

With vigorous blows, Brother Jakobus hammered new nails into the coffin.

Simon was awakened by the little bells sounding for the *laudes,* the Benedictines' morning prayers. Although he'd pored over the books from the Wessobrunn Monastery library late into the night, he was wide awake now. He quickly washed his face and hands with the ice-cold water in a basin alongside the bed and ate a piece of dry bread. Then he hastened outside. Benedikta, who had already gotten directions from Abbot Bernhard to the Tassilo Linden, was waiting for Simon in the monastery yard. Together, they walked through the gate alongside the parish church. To their left were the three ice-filled springs and the well house. Along the outside of the monastery wall, a path led down into the valley. It soon veered away from the wall, and the path became icy and slippery as they entered a snow-covered deciduous forest. A few times Simon nearly fell, cursing and grabbing hold of branches in the dense growth of trees. A little stairway with worn steps led down into the valley. Finally, they reached a shadowy clearing, and in the middle stood an enormous tree, larger than any they had ever seen. They stopped and gazed at it in awe.

"The Tassilo Linden," Simon whispered. "The word *tree* in the Wessobrunn Prayer! It must be this tree. In any case, it's surely the oldest and most striking one here, if not in all of the Priests' Corner."

The linden, at least one hundred feet tall, had four trunks that grew up out of one. In winter, stripped of its leaves, it looked like the withered hand of a giant witch, its clawlike fingers reaching for the sky.

Simon looked around. Once again, as in the yew forest the day before, he had the feeling he was being observed. He looked all around the dense forest surrounding him but couldn't see a thing. The monastery loomed up in the distance, somewhere a little rivulet was gurgling in an icy brook, and from far up in the branches of the linden tree came the lonely sound of an angry crow. Simon watched as it spread its wings and flew away. Suddenly, a ghostly stillness fell over the clearing.

Benedikta broke the silence. "There has to be a clue here somewhere!" she said, walking toward the tree. "Perhaps higher up," she said, craning her neck. "I suggest I look around down here and you climb up to the top of the tree."

"The top?" Simon followed her gaze upward. "That's a full hundred feet! I'll break my neck."

"Oh, come now!" Benedikta shook her head. "You don't have to climb all the way to the top. After all, it was at least several hundred years ago that this Templar hid something here. At that time, the tree was not as high. So come on, *allez hop!*"

She stooped over and began to examine the roots and knotholes at the base of the linden. Uncertain, Simon stood around for a moment, then sighed and looked for a something to grab on to.

The bark was icy and slippery, and he kept sliding back down. Finally, he got a good grip between the trunks of the tree. He pulled himself up from one branch to the next, stopping whenever he found a knothole. Holding on with one hand, he groped inside each hole with the other. He found wet, slippery foliage, acorns, and beechnuts that squirrels had stashed there for the winter, and a handful of slimy mushrooms.

But nothing else.

The crow returned, settling on a nearby branch, observing with curiosity this two-legged creature searching the knotholes for food. Simon felt like a little boy whose playmates had promised him a treasure and only now noticed he'd been hoodwinked. "This is going nowhere!" he called down to Benedikta. "Even if the Templars did hide something here, the ravens and magpies took it long ago." He looked down, where Benedikta was still searching around on the ground.

"Look in the other branches!" she called up to him. "We mustn't give up when we're so close!"

Simon sighed. Why did he always let women boss him around? He reached for a thick branch of the second tree trunk and moved forward slowly. Benedikta looked very far away now, a little dot of color almost swallowed up in the white snowdrifts down below. He tightened his grip on the icy branch. If he fell now and hit his head down below, it would burst like a wet snowball.

Finally, he reached the second trunk. The branches seemed strong, so he kept climbing until he was nearly at the top, with a view of the entire valley. In the distance, he saw the Ammersee sparkling in the sunlight and, on a hill even farther away, the tiny monastery of Andechs. On the other side, the Hoher Peißenberg rose up from the flat land, a distant foothill of the Alps peeking in and out of the clouds. Simon looked back at the monastery again and then around the forest surrounding it. Bare beech trees, snow-covered firs, a man in the branches . . .

A man?

Simon blinked, but his eyes had not deceived him. Barely a hundred feet away, someone was watching him from behind the branch of a fir.

At his side, the stranger held a crossbow, with the bowstring tightened and poised to shoot. He wore a wide-brimmed hat and a leather uniform, from which a heavy dagger or hunting knife dangled. When he saw that Simon had caught sight of him, he disappeared into the undergrowth.

Simon was so puzzled that he couldn't speak at first. For moment, he thought he'd seen a ghost. When he calmed down again, he leaned over as far as possible.

"Benedikta, look over there! There's a man hiding in the underbrush! We're being—"

At that moment, the branch Simon was standing on broke under him like a brittle bone. He could feel branches brushing past his face, and his heart started to pound. It took him a moment to realize he was really falling. He reached out in all directions in hopes of grabbing hold of a branch. The world around him was a blur of sky, earth, and branches that lashed him as he went by.

Suddenly there was a large ripping sound and Simon's fall was broken.

He dangled helplessly a full ten feet over the ground, swaying back and forth like a marionette on a string. Looking up, he could see that a sharp branch had slit his jacket open from his waist almost to his collar.

Down below, Benedikta stared up at him open-mouthed. "My God, Simon! What are you doing up there?"

"What do you think? I was falling to my death! Up there in the tree I saw a man with a crossbow observing us, and—"

"Simon, first calm down. Try to grab hold of something close by." Benedikta pointed to a branch that stood out at a right angle. It was about the thickness of an arm and looked solid. Simon tried to reach it but was just a few inches short. Carefully, he began to rock back and forth, coming closer to the branch each time. Above him, his jacket ripped a bit more. He was able to grab the bough just as the jacket finally tore into two halves with a loud rip. He felt a strong tug, he fell a bit more, and then he was able to get both arms around the bough. He hung there, his legs thrashing the air, and had no idea what to do next.

At this moment, he caught sight of the golden tablet right in front of him.

It was only about the size of a hand, and the bark of the tree had grown over it like a thick lip. It looked as if the tree had been eating away at the tablet, assimilating it bit by bit over the course of centuries. But the words in its center, inlaid in gold, had been unaffected by the wind, snow, rain, and hail and were quite legible.

Still suspended from the bough, Simon mumbled the engraved Latin lines as the crow came fluttering back and settled on the bough next to him, watching over his shoulder with curiosity.

IN GREMIO MARIAE ERIS PRIMUS ET

FELICIANUS. FRIDERICUS WILDERGRAUE

ANNO DOMINI MCCCX XVIII.

Despite the precarious position he was in, he couldn't help but laugh aloud.

"Ha! This damned Templar," he shouted so loudly it echoed all through the forest. "The sly, old devil! He did hide the message here—you were right!"

"What are you talking about?" Benedikta craned her neck to see better. "What's up there? Tell me!"

Simon stopped laughing. His arms had begun to ache as if he were attached to the torture rack with big, heavy rocks pulling him down by the legs.

"A golden plaque up here . . ." he groaned. "From Friedrich Wildgraf a year before his death. And a saying . . ."

"What kind of a saying?"

"Damn! First let me get down from here!"

Benedikta grinned. "How about just letting go?"

"Letting go? It's at least twelve feet down!"

"Oh, come now . . . ten, at most. Shall I catch you?"

Closing his eyes, Simon counted slowly to three, then let go.

With a loud shout, he fell kicking and floundering into a soft snowdrift at the foot of the tree. The landing was pleasantly soft. He lay there for a moment, checking that nothing was broken, but he seemed fine—something you could not say about his trousers.

"Damn, Benedikta!" he cursed as he thrashed about trying to free himself from the drift. "Who had the crazy idea of climbing up such a tall tree without a rope? I could have broken my neck!"

Benedikta shrugged. "At least it was worthwhile. Now tell me what it says up there on the plaque."

Simon was about to speak when he remembered the man in the fir tree. In one desperate leap, the medicus extricated himself from the snow. "We have to get out of here at once! The fellow in the tree was armed, and there are surely others here in the forest." He hobbled down the path as fast as he could, his tattered jacket fluttering behind him. "We've got to get back to the monastery! Follow me!"

Sighing, Benedikta ran after him.

Forty feet above, the stranger with the crossbow watched them leave. He raised his hands to his mouth and mimicked the caw of a jaybird.

• • •

Court Clerk Johann Lechner sat in his office, chewing on his quill pen and double-checking the city's ledgers. The result was disastrous. The constant attacks in recent days had brought traffic almost to a standstill. All commercial goods transported along the major highways from Augsburg over the Brenner Pass and the Fern Pass had to be stored temporarily in Schongau. While the city collected a nice tax on every single bale, the Ballenhaus, the storage warehouse, and the Zimmerstadel down on the Lech were practically empty now. And the recent snowstorm had delivered the final blow. Schongau was bleeding to death, and the clerk had no idea where to get the money to pay the city's long-overdue bills.

Johann Lechner sighed. The council had raked him over the coals that morning. The patricians respected him, but only as long as he was looking out for their interests, and Lechner had to wonder—and not for the first time—why he actually did so. The daily squabbles with these fat, pompous gas bags—who had nothing to think about but their next glass of wine, or their next shipment of salt or wool, or about how strenuous the trips to Munich and Augsburg were by coach—were the cause of all the miserable, unending paperwork. The city was a clock that had to be wound every day, and if it weren't for him, Lechner was sure Schongau would wither away and become just another small provincial town.

That made it all the more important for him to put his foot down, to do something to make it clear that nobody could just come along and spit in the town's face, and certainly not a band of filthy, ragged highwaymen and cutthroats.

There was a knock on the door. Lechner drew a line under the last entry and straightened his cap before calling out for his caller to enter.

Jakob Kuisl had to stoop to avoid bumping his head on the low doorway. His huge form completely filled the opening.

"You called for me, Your Excellency?"

"Ah, Kuisl!" Johann Lechner said, motioning for him to take a seat. "How strange . . . I was just thinking of you. Well, how was the excursion with Burgomaster Semer?"

"You know . . . ?"

"Of course I know. We talked about it in the council meeting. The other gentlemen are not exactly pleased that you are giving Semer special treatment. Now his business is booming, and the rest are sitting around twiddling their fingers. Or were you attacked?"

Kuisl shook his head. "No, there were no crooks or gangsters anywhere. But we also didn't tell anyone which route we were going to take."

The clerk frowned. "Do you really think someone on the city council is listening in on the others and sending thugs out to get them?" Johann Lechner smiled, toying with the goose quill. "Tell me frankly, who do you suspect? That ambitious fellow Schreevogl or one of the four burgomasters—or perhaps, me? Are you going to put me on the rack and make me confess?"

Kuisl didn't react to the clerk's scornful tone. "The city council is the place where town leaders discuss business," he replied simply. "If anyone wants to listen, that's the best place to do it. All the patricians are equally suspect."

Amused, the clerk shook his finger at the hangman. "The aldermen a group of murderers? Kuisl, Kuisl . . . It would be best to keep that idea to yourself. Executioners have been strung up on their own gallows for voicing suspicions far less serious than that. Besides, you're forgetting the merchant from Augsburg—this Weyer fellow. He wasn't at the council meeting, but he's dead and buried now just the same."

Jakob Kuisl shrugged. "We'll see how it all fits together. Semer, in any case, didn't talk to anyone and arrived safe and sound in Landsberg."

"I hear you asked the burgomaster a favor," Lechner said, abruptly changing the subject. "You wanted him to make some inquiries for you." The clerk looked up at the ceiling, feigning indignation. "The burgomaster is now the hangman's messenger boy, *o tempora, o mores!* What's the world coming to? Can you let me know what's so important you absolutely must know it, Kuisl?"

"No."

The clerk paused, stunned. "I beg your pardon?"

Kuisl shrugged. "That's my business. I'll let you know when I have news."

Lechner was silent for a moment; then he nodded. "As you will." He pushed the papers in front of him to one side and pulled a large notebook from a bookshelf alongside the desk. "Let's get to the reason I asked you to come." He leafed through the book as he continued. "Scheller and his gang had their trial today, and—"

"They had *what?*" Kuisl sat bolt upright in his chair.

"Don't interrupt me," Lechner said, giving the hangman a severe look. "As I said, we put the gang on trial this morning in the Ballenhaus. It lasted just a quarter hour. Your presence wasn't necessary."

"And Burgomaster Semer?"

"He was informed and agreed to the procedure. The execution is set for this coming Saturday; that's in three days." He cleared his throat. "Unfortunately, I was not successful in arranging the type of execution you requested. You'll have to torture Scheller on the wheel."

Kuisl could no longer stay seated. "But you gave me your word!" He jumped up so violently that his chair tipped backward and crashed to the floor. "I'm indebted to Scheller!"

The clerk shook his head as if he were speaking with a child. "Please, Kuisl! Indebted . . . to the head of a band of robbers?"

He pointed at the chair on the ground. "Now please pick it up. We still have some things to discuss."

Jakob Kuisl took a deep breath and stood there, his arms crossed.

"Believe me," Lechner continued, "it's the best thing for the city. We have to set an example. Every gang of robbers from here to Landsberg will hear Scheller scream. It will be a lesson to them. Besides"—he tapped his goose-quill pen on the document in front of him—"the execution will bring money back into the city coffers. We'll have a big celebration with dancing, music, mulled wine, and roasted chestnuts. People need a change of pace after these cold, anxious days." He leafed through the pages of the book. "You see, there are some things that have to be done. First, the execution site has to be cleaned. Also, I've checked and one of the beams is rotten. And down below, in the square, we'll need some gallows—at least three of them. And seats with canopies for the patricians so the fine gentlemen don't freeze their behinds off in the cold. I'm afraid the hunt for the other gangs of robbers will have to wait a bit."

The hangman, who had listened stoically to Lechner's words, stirred again. "And what about the children and the women?" he asked.

The clerk nodded. "They'll go free, as promised. We'll hang only the men and older boys. Scheller will be tortured on the wheel. Believe me, there were people on the council who wanted to hang the women and children, too." He smiled at Kuisl. "You see, I'm trying to meet you halfway. Now get started. By Saturday noon everything has to be ready."

With a nod, Lechner dismissed the hangman, who headed for the exit as if in a trance. After he closed the door behind him, the clerk groaned. He would never understand this pigheaded Kuisl! Torture on the wheel paid a full thirty guilders, yet Kuisl reacted as if he were being asked to string up his own daughter.

Lechner watched out the window as the large man walked away. A strange man, this hangman, he thought. Strong, bright, but a little too sentimental for his job.

And definitely too curious.

Once more, Lechner removed the letter from under the table. Written on the finest stationery, it had arrived that morning. He could see from the seal that the messenger who had been here a few days earlier had spoken the truth. Someone very powerful wanted to do everything possible to keep the hangman from asking too many questions in Altenstadt.

Johann Lechner cast a final glance at the seal, just to make sure it was genuine, then held the letter over a candle on his desk. Flickering, the fire ate its way through the thin paper until there was nothing left but ashes. The instructions in the letter had been clear. *No proof, no written documents, no evidence that would reveal the identity of the client.*

Johann Lechner counted out the freshly minted coins that had accompanied the letter. The money would help the city, as would the executions. Once again, the clerk was at peace with himself and the world.

Simon and Benedikta arrived in Schongau early in the evening. During the entire trip back, they'd been wondering about the strange words on the plaque, but also about the man who had watched them from the top of the fir. Was he part of the same gang that had been spying on them on the way to Wessobrunn? But why, then, hadn't the robbers attacked? Why were the two of them being observed and followed?

Simon escorted Benedikta to her quarters at Semer's inn, where she convinced him to remain a while for a glass of wine in the tavern.

"Is it possible these are the same men who were hanging around this area a few days ago?" Simon asked. "The same ones who ambushed the hangman in the crypt? Magdalena told her father about a few black-robed strangers in Strasser's Tavern in Altenstadt who were speaking Latin. Perhaps they've been following us the entire time, and—"

"Magdalena is a little girl who probably doesn't know a word of Latin," Benedikta interrupted. "Perhaps they were just itinerant Benedictines saying their prayers before they ate." She winked at him. "You're beginning to look at every stranger like a murderer." She put her hand around Simon's arm, but he quickly pulled away.

"Don't you sense that our every move is being watched?" he asked with alarm. "A highwayman who doesn't attack, the man in the fir . . . That can't all be a coincidence!"

"I think you're just imagining things!" Benedikta laughed. "Now I'll tell you what *I* think. The man you saw yesterday in the yew forest *was* a highway robber. We escaped. And the man in the fir tree was nothing but a figment of your imagination. You can't even give a good description of what he looked like."

"I know what I saw." There was a long pause. When Simon spoke again, he decided to put all his cards on the table. "You're right," he said. "Perhaps it's all just my imagination. Perhaps Andreas Koppmeyer was murdered for some completely different reason. Tell me, Benedikta, your brother surely must have left a will. What does it say?"

Benedikta stared back at him in astonishment and took a deep breath. "So that's what you think!" she finally blurted out. "You suspect *me* of having killed my brother! You have no doubt been harboring this suspicion for a long time, haven't you?"

"What does the will say?" Simon persisted.

Benedikta looked at him angrily, with her arms crossed. "I can tell you. I'm inheriting a leather-bound Bible from my brother, an old armchair, and a cookbook he wrote himself. And forty guilders that will hardly make up for the losses my wine business has incurred in the meanwhile." She leaned over to Simon. "Those are his personal bequests. Everything else goes to the church!"

Simon winced. He hadn't once stopped to think that the priest's possessions would, in fact, for the most part, revert back to the church after his death. In all likelihood, Benedikta had probably inherited no more than these few worthless things.

"And if that were the case," she continued, now in such a rage that other guests turned around to look at her, "why on earth would I want to hang around Altenstadt near the scene of the crime? Wouldn't I have just poisoned my brother, gone back to Landsberg without anyone noticing, and waited there for news of his death? Nobody would have suspected anything." She stood up quickly, knocking over her chair. "Simon Fronwieser, you're really out of line." Benedikta ran out, slamming the door behind her.

"Well, Fronwieser?" The brewer's journeyman, Konstantin Kreitmeyer, looked over at him and grinned. "Trouble with women again? Better stay with your hangman's daughter. She's crazy enough for you."

Some other brewer's journeymen at Kreitmeyer's table laughed and made a few obscene gestures.

Simon swallowed the rest of his wine and stood up. "Oh, shut your mouths!" He put a few coins on the table and left the tavern to a further chorus of lewd remarks.

Instead of turning into the Hennengasse and going home, Simon headed toward the Lech Gate. He couldn't possibly sleep the way he felt now. He had acted like such a fool with Benedikta! How could he even imagine she'd poison her own brother? Further, the journeyman's words had set him thinking of Magdalena again. Was she already on her way home from Augsburg? Perhaps her father had heard from her. Simon longed for a hot cup of coffee. The only thing awaiting him at home was work and a carping father who was fed up with his son's escapades.

The last time Simon visited the hangman, he brought Anna Maria a little bag of coffee beans, and he wondered now whether the hangman's wife would brew him a cup of his favorite drink. He decided to pay the Schongau executioner a visit.

Before long, he was down in the Tanners' Quarter, knocking on the front door of Kuisl's house. The moment Anna Maria Kuisl opened the door, he could see something was wrong. The face of the otherwise vivacious woman seemed pale and drawn.

"It's good you have come," she said, motioning for Simon to enter. "Maybe you can cheer him up a little. He's started to drink again."

"Why?" asked Simon, taking off his wet coat and torn jacket and hanging both up to dry alongside the stove.

Anna silently eyed the ruined clothing, then went to look for a needle and thread in a drawer. "Lechner says my husband has to break Sheller on the wheel," she said as she started sewing up the torn garment. "It's going to happen in three days, even though Jakob gave his word to the robber chief. It's a rotten group up there in the city council—they have money coming out their ears, but don't care a bit about honor and decency!"

The medicus nodded. He'd become accustomed to the hangman's excesses. Before executions, Kuisl would go on drinking binges, but amazingly, when the time came for the actual execution, he'd always completely sobered up again.

Simon let Anna Maria grumble on while he went over to the main room, where he found the hangman leaning glassy-eyed on the gallows ladder and brooding. The sweet odor of alcohol and sweat drifted through the room. On the table, a few opened books lay alongside an open bottle of brandy, and in a corner of the room, the pieces of a smashed beer stein flashed in the dim light. Kuisl's face shone in the light of the fire as he prepared to take another mighty swig.

"Drink with me or leave me alone," he said, slamming the bottle back down on the table. Simon put a fat-bellied clay cup to his mouth and sipped on its contents. It was something very strong that the hangman made from the fermented apples and pears from his orchard. Presumably, there were also a few herbs mixed in, which the medicus didn't even want to know about.

"We found a new riddle in Wessobrunn," Simon said abruptly. "Some words up in a linden tree. I thought you might be able to make some sense out of them."

Kuisl belched loudly and wiped the corner of his mouth. "Who gives a damn? But go ahead, spit it out. You can't just keep it to yourself."

Simon smiled. He knew how curious the hangman was, even when he was stoned. "It goes like this: *In gremio Mariae eris primus et felicianus.*"

Kuisl nodded, then translated aloud. "*You will be first at Mary's bosom, and a happy person.*" He broke into a laugh. "Just a pious sentiment, nothing more! That can't be the clue."

He picked up the bottle again with a vacant look, one that Simon had trouble reconciling with Kuisl's other, sensitive and educated side. People were always astonished that the executioner knew Latin so well, even when he was completely soused. They would be even more astonished if they looked around the hangman's library and saw all the books in German, Latin, and even Greek, written by scholars still completely unknown in most German universities.

"But it *must* be the next riddle," Simon objected. "He put his name at the bottom of it. Friedrich Wildgraf, anno domini 1328—a year before his death."

Kuisl rubbed his temples, trying to think clearly. "Well, it's not anything from the Bible that I can remember," he growled. "And I know most of those biblical aphorisms. You wouldn't believe how pious people become when it's time for them to die. I've heard it all, but never these words."

Simon swallowed before continuing. Jakob Kuisl's father had been the local hangman before him, and before that, his grandfather—a true dynasty of executioners now extending over a whole host of Bavarian cities and towns. The Kuisls had probably heard more whining and pious words than the Pope himself.

"If it's not from the Bible, maybe it's some secret message," Simon said, repeating the words. "*You will be first at Mary's bosom, and a happy person.* What does that mean?"

The hangman shrugged before picking up the bottle again. "Damned if I know. What's it to me, anyway?" He took such a long swig that Simon was afraid he might choke. Finally, he put the bottle down again. "For my part, I'm going to break Scheller on the wheel on Saturday, and there's nothing more I can do to help you. Till then, there's a lot to do. The people want a spectacle."

Simon could see from the hangman's bloodshot eyes that the bottle was almost empty. Jakob Kuisl was leaning farther and farther over on his stool. A whole bottle of brandy apparently was a little too much even for a big, broad-shouldered man six feet tall.

"You'll need some medicine," Simon sighed, "or you won't have a clear head tomorrow."

"Don't need no medicine from you goddamned quacks. I'll make my own."

Simon shook his head. "This medicine is something only I have." He stood up and walked over to the living room, where Anna Maria was still sitting at a table mending the rip in the Simon's jacket.

"Make a strong cup of coffee for your husband," Simon said. "But don't skimp on the beans. It'll only work if it's strong enough for the spoon to stand up in the cup without falling over."

Magdalena awoke to a monotonous humming sound that grew louder and louder until she thought her head would split. Her headache was even worse than the last time she woke up. Her lips were so rough and dry that when she passed the tip of her tongue over them, they felt like the bark of a tree. She opened her eyes, blinded at first by bursts of light, but after a while the flashing stopped, things came into focus—and what she saw was paradise!

Cherubs fluttered around the head of the Savior, who was wearing a crown and looking down at her compassionately from the cross. St. Luke and St. John were off to one side, keeping watch over the starry heavens, while down below, the serpent Lucifer writhed about, impaled by the lance of the Archangel Michael, and high above, the twelve apostles sat enthroned in glory on the clouds. All the figures were ablaze in gleaming gold, bright silver, and all the shimmering colors of the rainbow. Never before had Magdalena seen such splendor.

Was she in heaven?

At least I'm no longer lying in the coffin, she thought. *That's an improvement, in any case.*

As soon as she turned her head, she could see she was not in heaven, but in a sort of little chapel. She lay on her back on a stone altar surrounded by four burning candles. The walls of the whitewashed room were so densely covered with lavish oil paintings depicting various scenes from the Bible that there was hardly any space between them. Sunlight entered the room from the east through a tiny window, but the stone was so cold that her muscles felt like ice.

The murmuring came from one side. Turning her head a bit farther, Magdalena could see Brother Jakobus dressed in a simple black robe kneeling before a small altar to the Virgin Mary, his head bowed in quiet prayer. A golden cross with the two beams dangled at his chest.

"Ave Maria, the Lord be with you, blessed are you among women and blessed is the fruit of your body, Jesus Christ . . ."

Magdalena tried to sit up. Could she flee without the monk

noticing? Only a few steps behind her, she spotted a low wooden door with a golden handle. If she could only get to it . . .

When she tried to prop herself up, she found she was bound by her hands and feet like a lamb on its way to slaughter.

Christ, Lamb of God, who bears the sins of the world . . .

Magdalena panicked remembering the words from the Bible. What did this madman intend to do with her? Was he going to sacrifice her on the altar? Was this the reason for the lighted candles? Another Bible quotation came to mind.

God spoke to Abraham: Take your son Isaac, whom you love, and bring him to the mountain as a sacrifice . . .

The monk's monotonous chant grew louder and higher in pitch until he was almost screaming in a falsetto. Magdalena tried to fight the fear rising in her and forced herself to breathe calmly and evenly. Perhaps she could even manage to crawl through the door? Crawling, creeping, hopping—it didn't matter. She just had to get away from here. She rocked back and forth, managing to reach the left side of the altar. Just a few more inches and she would be there. She could already feel the edge underneath her when she tipped over and fell . . .

Her feet bumped against a large candlestick, which fell to the ground with a crash.

The singing stopped abruptly. She could hear footsteps, and a moment later, Brother Jakobus stood over her, his dagger drawn. Magdalena screamed as he pointed the dagger at her.

"Hold your tongue, stupid woman. Nobody is going to hurt you." The monk cut the cords tying her hands and stepped off to one side. "If you promise to hold still, I'll cut off the shackles on your feet as well. Do you promise?"

Magdalena nodded and was free a moment later. She stood up and tried to move her arms and legs but was still too weak even to remain standing. Breathing heavily, she sank down onto one of the pews and felt as if she were going to pass out.

"The poison does that to you," Brother Jakobus said, sitting down on the bench alongside her. "A mixture of opium poppies and a few rare plants from the nightshade family. You'll feel weak for a while; then it will pass."

"Where . . . where am I?" Magdalena rubbed her wrists, which tingled as if ants were crawling around inside them.

"That's of no concern to you," the monk said. "This is a place where no one will disturb us. The walls are thick, and not a sound can penetrate the windows. A wonderful place to find God."

He let his gaze wander over the splendid fresco on the ceiling. "Don't worry. For now, you are our guarantee that your father won't disturb us, and later . . ." He looked her directly in the face with what suddenly seemed like a soft, tender look. Again, the sweet scent of perfume wafted over to her.

"Magdalena . . ." he sighed. "The name brings many things to my mind." He paused for a long time. "You do know Mary Magdalene, don't you?" he asked suddenly. "The woman who was always at our Savior's side? The patron saint of whores and adulteresses, and unclean women like you . . ."

She nodded. "My father named me for her." Her voice sounded strange and grating after having remained silent for so long.

"Your father is a smart man, Magdalena. A . . . prophet, one might say." Brother Jakobus laughed, bending his haggard, hunched body down to her like a scarecrow in the wind and passing his long fingers gently over her dress—hands as slender and delicate as a woman's. "St. Mary Magdalene . . ." the monk whispered. "You really do resemble your namesake—beautiful and clever, but a pariah. A dirty hangman's daughter, the scum of the city. A pious whore who secretly devotes herself to the sins of the flesh."

"But—"

"Silence!" The monk's voice sounded shrill again. "I know women like you only too well! Haven't I seen you with your physician friend? So do not lie to me, Daughter of Eve!"

He closed his eyes, took a deep breath, and finally managed to calm down again. "But you are a believer, I can see that," he said, laying his hand on her forehead as if to bless her. "Deep inside you, there is a good heart. You women are not all bad. Even Mary Magdalene became a saint, and you, too, can be saved." His voice fell to a whisper now, and Magdalena struggled to hear what he was saying.

"Do you know the Bible, Hangman's Daughter?"

He was still holding his hand on her forehead. Magdalena decided to remain silent, and he kept on speaking without waiting for an answer.

"Luke, Chapter Eight, Verse One. Jesus was traveling with a few women he had healed and saved from evil spirits, among them Mary Magdalene, from whom he had driven out seven demons. Seven demons . . ." The monk's eyes flashed in the light of the candles. "You, too, are possessed by seven demons, Magdalena, and I will drive them out later, once your task here has been completed. Then you will be pure and good, a chaste maiden. Do not be troubled. We will find a place for you here in the monastery."

He walked toward the door, but then he stopped and turned around to her again.

"I will save you, Magdalena."

The monk smiled, then opened the door and disappeared. There was a grating sound as a key turned in the lock, then footsteps that became fainter until they finally faded away.

The hangman's daughter remained behind with the angels, the evangelists, and a savior. Two women knelt at the foot of his cross and wept.

Simon looked into the rigid eyes of the man laid out on the bed in front of him and put down his doctor's bag. The medicus didn't have to listen to his heart, feel his pulse, or put a mirror under his nostrils anymore. He knew the man was dead. Gently, he closed the old man's eyes, then turned to the deceased's wife, who stood alongside, whimpering.

"I've come too late," Simon said. "Your husband is already in a better place."

The farm woman nodded, looking intently at her husband as if her gaze alone could bring him back to life. Simon guessed she was in her mid-forties, but the hard work in the fields, the yearly births, and the bad food made her look older. Her hair was gray and unkempt, and deep wrinkles had formed in the corners of her mouth and eyes. A few rotting, yellow stumps of teeth could be seen behind her cracked lips. Simon wondered if Magdalena would look like this in twenty years.

Simon had been up all night thinking about the hangman's daughter. How was she doing in Augsburg? Her father had received no news from her yet, though he expected her return at any moment. But because of the blizzard, it was quite possible she'd be further delayed. No doubt she was waiting to join a group of merchants who awaited better weather—and an end to the attacks.

A child's cry startled Simon out of his thoughts. A girl about four years of age was fondling the face of her dead father, and at the back of the room, six more of the farmer's children were standing about with lowered heads. Two of them were coughing loudly; the medicus hoped they hadn't caught the fever, too.

In the last two weeks, over thirty people had died in Schongau from the mysterious illness, most of them the elderly or children. Along the city wall, St. Sebastian's Cemetery was filling up, and a number of the old graves holding victims of the plague were now being turned over to make room for the new arrivals. Simon and his father had tried everything. They had bled their patients, given them enemas, brewed them a drink of linden blossoms and wild marjoram. Bonifaz Fronwieser had even leafed through the pages of the so-called *Dreckapotheke,* or *Dirty Pharmacy,* in search of a magic potion for fever. When his father started mixing dried toads in vinegar and making powder from mouse droppings, Simon ran out of the treatment room, cursing.

"Faith, it's faith that helps," his father called after him.

"Faith! Is that the best we can do?"

The very thought of what his father was doing made Simon curse under his breath. Mouse droppings and dried toads! Next they'd be painting pentagrams and magic signs on the doors of the sick. If only he had some of that Jesuit's powder! The physician was sure this medicine, acquired from the bark of a tree in the West Indies, would quickly reduce the fever. Simon had long ago used his last bit of it, however, and the next Venetian merchant would not be heading their way until the mountain passes were open again.

Once more, he turned to the farm woman and her coughing children. "It's important now that you bury your husband as soon as possible," said Simon. "He could be carrying something that will infect you and the children as well."

"A . . . spirit?" the farm woman asked anxiously.

The physician shook his head in resignation. "No, not a spirit. Think of them as tiny creatures that—"

"Tiny creatures?" The woman's face became even paler. "In my Alois?"

Simon sighed. "Just forget about that and bury him."

"But the ground is frozen, and we'll have to wait until—"

There was a knock at the door. Simon turned around to see

a dirty little boy in the doorway, looking up at him with a mixture of fear and respect.

"Are you the Schongau physician?" he asked finally. Simon nodded. Secretly, he was happy to be addressed this way, because most residents still regarded him as nothing more than the coddled son of the local doctor, a dandy and a womanizer who had run out of money at the university in Ingolstadt.

"The . . . the Schreevogls have sent me," the boy said.

"I'm supposed to tell you that Clara is coughing up snot and mucus. And please, can you stop by as soon as possible?"

Simon closed his eyes in a silent prayer. "Not Clara," he murmured. "God, not Clara."

He grabbed his doctor's bag and, after exchanging a few more words with the farmer's family, rushed off after the boy. On the way to the marketplace where the Schreevogls lived, Simon couldn't help thinking of Clara. So much had happened in the last few days that he'd completely forgotten her! Usually, he stopped to pay a visit to his little friend several times a week. And now she was sick; perhaps she even had this terrible fever!

Maria Schreevogl was waiting for him by the front door. As so often, she appeared pale and agitated. Simon never understood what the patrician saw in the overly pious, sometimes hysterical woman. He assumed there were financial considerations involved in the marriage. Maria Schreevogl's maiden name was Püchner, and she came from an old influential family with political connections.

"She's in bed up in her room!" the woman lamented. "Please Mary, Mother of God and all saints, don't let it be this fever! Don't let this happen to my Clara!"

Simon hurried up the wide staircase and entered the room of the sick girl. Clara lay in her bed coughing, her pale face peeking out from a thick comforter.

Her stepfather, Jakob Schreevogl, sat anxiously at the edge of the bed. "Thank you for coming so quickly, Fronwieser," he said, standing up. "Would you like something to drink—perhaps some coffee?"

Simon shook his head, noticing with concern that the patrician peered back at him with vacant eyes. The councillor looked like he was in a trance. Just the evening before, he'd returned with the hangman from their trip with Karl Semer, and clearly, he was severely shaken by the news of his daughter's sickness.

Simon bent down to look at Clara. "Clara, it's me, Simon," he whispered, but Clara didn't react. Her eyes were closed and she was breathing fast. In her sleep her whole body shook from time to time with a coughing fit. The physician placed an ear to her chest and listened to her breathing.

"How long has she been this way?" Simon asked, trying to speak over the crying and wailing of Schreevogl's wife, who had followed him into the room, anxiously passing rosary beads through her fingers.

"Just since yesterday," Jakob Schreevogl replied. "The fever came on in the evening, very quickly. Since then we haven't been able to talk to her. Good Lord, woman, be quiet for a moment!"

The praying stopped. "Does she have the fever, Simon?" Maria Schreevogl asked through tears. "You can tell me! Oh, good Lord, does she have it?" She stared at the medicus wide-eyed.

Simon hesitated. The sudden onslaught of the illness, the rasping cough, the high fever—everything pointed to Clara's having been infected. Once more the medicus cursed himself for not having been able to ask Magdalena to pick up some medications for him in Augsburg. Perhaps the apothecaries there even had the Jesuit's powder! But now it was too late.

When Simon remained silent, that was sign enough for the patrician woman.

"St. Barbara, I will lose her!" she moaned. "St. Quirinus, help us!" She fell to her knees, fingering her rosary beads again.

Her husband tried to ignore her and turned to address Simon in a serious voice. "What can we do?"

Simon struggled to look him in the eye. "I'll be honest with you, Schreevogl," he said. "I can make a compress for her and a cup of tea, but that's about all. Beyond that all we can do is wait and pray."

"Saint Primus, Saint Felicianus, be with us in our hour of need and sickness!" Maria Schreevogl's voice turned shrill as she placed a chain of sacred amulets around Clara's neck.

"That will never cure her, woman," said Jakob. "Better to make her a cup of linden blossom tea. I think the cook still has some in the kitchen."

Maria hurried out the door wailing, and Simon bent down again over Clara.

"I'll put a salve on her chest," he said. "One of the hangman's recipes—calamint, rosemary, and goose fat. That will at least alleviate the cough."

He opened Clara's shirt and began applying the salve, leaving the chain with the saint's images in place—it couldn't hurt, in any case.

As he rubbed the salve on, his gaze fell on the individual figures pictured on the chain's silver coins, each engraved with a figure and a name, just as in the basilica in Altenstadt—St. Barbara, St. Quirinus, St. George, and of course, St. Walburga, patron saint of the sick and of women in labor.

But there were some here whom he had never heard of—St. Ignatius, who kept watch over children and difficult births; St. Primus again; and St. Felicianus, to whom Maria Schreevogl had prayed earlier.

Suddenly Simon stopped rubbing the child's chest and reached for two amulets on the chain in front of him, staring at the names.

St. Primus, St. Felicianus . . .

The two amulets felt like two clumps of ice in his hand. How could he have been so blind?

With a choked voice, he turned to Jakob Schreevogl and asked, "Can we withdraw for a moment to your library?"

The patrician raised his eyebrows. "Do you think you might be able to find a medicine for this sickness there? I'm afraid I'll have to disappoint you. My collection of medical books is limited."

Simon shook his head. "No, I'm looking for a book on the lives of the saints."

"On the lives of the saints?" Jakob Schreevogl looked back at him in astonishment. "I think my wife has something like that. But why—"

"Let's just go to the library. For the time being, there's nothing else we can do here, in any case. If my suspicions are right, I'll soon be able to buy Clara the best medicine in all of the Priests' Corner. And a Paracelsus bound in gold leaf for you. You have my word on that."

Jakob Kuisl set out on the painful mission. He almost felt like a condemned man on the way to the scaffold. The strong coffee the day before had helped him over the worst of his hangover, but his head still felt like a sack full of stones. But it wasn't the headache that troubled him the most; it was that he had broken his word.

When the bailiff Johannes saw the mood Kuisl was in, he quickly stepped aside to allow the hangman to enter the dungeon.

"A load of work, ain't it?" he called after him. "It will be a bloody show on Saturday when you break the prisoner on the wheel. I hope everyone has a ball. You'll break every bone, heh? I've bet two hellers that Scheller will still be screaming the next day."

Kuisl ignored him and trudged straight to the cell holding the robber chief and his gang. A quick glance assured him that this time, in contrast to the last, there were blankets, water, and fresh bread. The sick boy, too, seemed better. The medicine appeared to have helped.

Hans Scheller stood directly behind the bars, his arms folded. As the hangman approached, the robber chief spat in his face.

"The gallows, huh?" he growled. "A clean, quick matter? Bah! Damn liar! It's going to be slow, one blow after the other, and I trusted you, you goddamned hangman!"

Jakob Kuisl slowly wiped the spit from his face. "I'm sorry, whether you believe me or not," he said calmly. "I tried, but the authorities wanted to see screaming and wailing. So be it," he said, stepping right up to Scheller. "But we can still put one over on these fat cats," he whispered softly so that those standing around couldn't hear.

Hans Scheller looked at him in disbelief. "What are you thinking of?"

Jakob Kuisl looked around to see if anyone was listening, but the other robbers were too wrapped up in their own concerns, and the bailiff Johannes preferred to wait outside. Finally, the hangman took a little leather bag out of his coat. He opened it, and a little brown ball rolled into his wrinkled hand, a pill no larger than a marble.

"One bite and you'll be with our Lord," Kuisl said. He held it up like a valuable pearl. "I made it especially for you. You won't feel any pain. Just put it in your mouth, and when I strike, bite into it."

Taking the pill in his slender fingers, Scheller gave it a closer look. "No pain, you say?"

Kuisl nodded. "No pain, believe me, this is something I understand."

"And what about the big show?" Scheller whispered. "The people will be disappointed. I've heard they sometimes hang the hangman himself if things don't go as planned. They'll think you haven't done your job right."

"Let me worry about that, Scheller. Just don't take the poison now or the aldermen might decide to take out their anger on the others. Afterward, I'd have to break the boy on the wheel, too."

The robber chief was silent for a long while before turning back to the hangman. "Then it's right what they say about you, Kuisl."

"What do they say?"

"That you are a good hangman."

"I'm a hangman, but not a murderer. We'll see each other again on Saturday."

Jakob Kuisl turned and left the dungeon. For a long time, Hans Scheller rubbed the little ball between his fingers. He closed his eyes and tried to prepare himself for his long journey into darkness.

They found the book about saints at the far end of the shelf between the works of Plato and a dog-eared farmers' almanac that had made its way into Schreevogl's library unbeknownst to him. Presumably, his wife had acquired it from some itinerant merchant, along with the volume on the saints, the book of hymns and prayers, and the large eight-pound family Bible.

With the little book in hand, Simon summarized what he and the hangman had found in the crypt. He told Schreevogl about the riddles, of the feeling he was being constantly observed, and of his most recent find with Benedikta in the Tassilo Linden tree near Wessobrunn.

"We're firmly convinced that all these riddles will lead us to the Templars' treasure!" he concluded as he returned the other books to the shelves. "A treasure that the master of the German Templars, Friedrich Wildgraf, intentionally hid far away from the great cities. Not in Paris, nor in Rome, but right here in rural, provincial Bavaria, where he felt his treasure would be safe from the French king. The riddles are posed in such a way that only locals can solve them!"

Jakob Schreevogl was leaning against the edge of the table and listening with growing interest to what the medicus was telling him.

"It's possible that Friedrich Wildgraf passed along his knowledge to his sons and grandchildren here in Schongau," Simon continued, "and we assume that this line died out at some point and knowledge of the treasure and the riddles with it."

"And what does the most recent riddle say?" Jakob Schreevogl asked.

Simon looked warily out the window to see if anyone was watching. Only then did he continue in a soft voice. "It says, *In gremio Mariae eris primus et felicianus.* I thought for a long time it was just a pious saying from the Bible, something like, *You will be first at Mary's bosom, and a happy person.*"

"And what does it really say?"

"I'll tell you when I've found the right passage in this little book." Simon leafed through it, finally stopping to read a passage to himself. "I was right!" he exclaimed, then lowered his voice again to a whisper. "It's not a saying from the Bible, but simply a sentence that conceals two names—*Primus* and *Felicianus.* Translated, the names mean 'the first' and 'the happy,' but they are also the names of two saints from ancient Rome. Here!" He pointed to a page showing two fettered, naked men being tortured on the rack by a hangman's helpers. Nevertheless, the two saints smiled, knowing they would soon meet their Savior.

"Primus and Felicianus were two Christian Romans who were tortured and finally beheaded on the order of Emperor Diocletian," Simon continued excitedly. "But first they were able to convert thousands of Romans, according to this book, through pure steadfastness."

"But that was in Rome!" Schreevogl objected. "Didn't you

just say that this Templar intentionally chose our provincial area over the great cities? That can't be the riddle's solution."

The physician grinned and waved the little book around. "Don't come to any hasty conclusions, Your Honor. Primus and Felicianus were buried in Rome, indeed, but eventually their remains were moved to another place, where they're still revered today."

In the meantime, Jakob Schreevogl had gotten up out of his chair. "And where is that?" he asked. "Don't make all this sound so dramatic!"

Simon closed the book and placed it back on the shelf. "The Benedictine Monastery in Rottenbuch, just a few miles from here."

Schreevogl looked at him in disbelief. "Rottenbuch?"

Simon nodded. "A monastery, which, by the way, is devoted to worship of the Virgin Mary. *Primus and Felicianus at Mary's bosom.* That's the solution!" He slapped himself on the forehead. "I'm so stupid! As a child, I even went on a pilgrimage there to honor the two saints!"

Schreevogl smiled. "And if I know you, you're probably already planning another pilgrimage there."

Simon was already at the library door when he stopped to contemplate. "I won't go until Clara gets better," he said. "Your girl is worth more than any treasure in the world."

II

A DAY PASSED AND CLARA'S CONDITION DIDN'T change. The next morning she was feverish and coughing. Simon made her a drink of linden blossoms and rosemary mixed with the last honey he could find at home. Once more he cursed himself for not buying more of the Jesuit's powder the summer before. The Muslim merchant had demanded a high price, however, higher than a mere Schongau medicus could afford to buy in large quantities.

Simon paid Clara Schreevogl a visit both that morning and again in the afternoon, listening to her chest and speaking words of encouragement to the semiconscious child. He didn't once see Benedikta during this time, and he knew he was secretly trying to avoid her. The last time they were together, something had changed between them; her derogatory remarks about Magdalena had probably angered him most.

Magdalena is a little girl who probably doesn't know a word of Latin . . .

It was at that moment that he felt how much he missed Magdalena. What he once thought of as Magdalena's weaknesses —her quick temper, lack of education, her practicality, and shrewdness, things that were so far removed from Benedikta's French etiquette and finesse—all that now made Magdalena seem beyond compare, unique.

Once again Simon's thoughts were interrupted, as they were so often, by Clara's long, rattling coughing fits. The girl's chest rose and fell, and she spit up hard green mucus. Simon was glad to see that the phlegm was not red. Red phlegm, he knew, meant certain death in most cases.

As he sat holding Clara's hand, waiting for the next coughing fit, he wondered why he was so concerned about this one child when people were dying in their beds in Schongau almost every day. But with Clara it was different. A paternal love, nurtured in their adventures almost a year ago, bound him to this girl. He had freed this child from the hands of the devil, and he had saved her once before from a terrible fever. Could he sit by idly now as she died before his eyes? A few times she awoke, smiled at him, mumbled something unintelligible in her sleep, then drifted off again. Simon changed the cheese compress on her feet, wiped the sweat from her brow, and took turns with the Schreevogls in sitting at her bedside. All the while, Maria Schreevogl never stopped running rosary beads between her fingers and praying.

Ave Maria, the Lord be with you . . .

On the second day, Clara's condition seemed to improve. Simon knew from experience that the sickness entered its critical stage on about the second day. The fact that the fever was receding was a good sign.

It was Jakob Schreevogl who finally urged him to take a break.

"I don't think there's anything more you can do, Simon," he said, sitting on the edge of the bed with the physician. "My wife and I thank you for your concern, but you should leave for Rottenbuch as you had planned." He stood up and stretched. "But take the hangman along. According to everything you've told me, you're not alone out there."

Simon shook his head. "You forget that Scheller has his big day tomorrow. Kuisl has to break him on the wheel, and we certainly wouldn't be back in time for the execution." He stood up stiffly and looked out the window at a light snow that had been drifting down since early that morning, once again covering the city in a white, whirling shroud. "I'd actually be happy if I didn't have to be in Schongau on a day like tomorrow," he said. "We can only hope for bad weather. At least that would spoil Lechner's plans and his party would have to be canceled."

Jakob Schreevogl, too, was now looking out the window at the falling snow. "I want you to know that I spoke out in the city council meeting against breaking the prisoner on the wheel. It's . . . bestial, a throwback to a time I thought we had outgrown. But the war turned us into beasts again." He sighed. "As an alderman, I must unfortunately attend the execution. Perhaps I'm one of the few who takes no joy in the spectacle."

He motioned for Simon to accompany him out of the room, where Maria Schreevogl was still kneeling in prayer. As they descended the stairs, the alderman put his hand on Simon's shoulder again.

"I've been thinking about what you told me and about these words the men were whispering in the crypt—*Deus lo vult.* I've been wondering for a long time where I heard this expression."

"And?" Simon asked.

"Last night it came to me. It's the cry the Crusaders made as they rode off into battle against the unbelievers—*God wills it.* This is how they attempt to excuse all the massacres of the Arabs. God wills it . . ."

Simon shook his head. "The old Crusaders' battle cry on the

lips of murderers and bandits. Just who are these lunatics we're trying to track down?" He hesitated. "Do you know the bishop of Augsburg?" he finally asked.

"The bishop of Augsburg?" The alderman frowned. "Well, I've seen him once or twice in the Imperial City at large receptions—a young, ambitious man, people say. He's said to be very literal in his understanding of the Bible, very pious." Schreevogl smiled wanly. "The pope certainly has his reasons for sending one of his strictest shepherds to Augsburg, this den of iniquity, full of Protestants. But why do you ask?"

Simon shrugged. "Nothing in particular . . . a suspicion, that's all. No doubt complete nonsense."

Jakob Schreevogl shook his hand firmly. "In any case, keep alert. And there's something else . . ."

"Yes?"

"This Friedrich Wildgraf. I've seen his name somewhere before." The patrician bit his lip. "If only I knew where!"

Simon nodded. "I feel the same way. It's like a ghost that keeps coming back to haunt me, but when I try to grab hold of it, it slips away and dissolves into thin air. I think it has something to do with that little book about the Templars you gave me. Could you spare it for two more days?"

"Certainly," Schreevogl replied. "All I really want is for my Clara to get well again." They'd reached the front door now, and snowflakes were blowing over the doorsill into the house.

"I wish you much luck. Godspeed!" Jakob Schreevogl looked Simon firmly in the eye again, then closed the door.

The medicus turned to leave. And then he stopped short.

Benedikta was standing down below on the street. She had loaded her things onto her horse and bridled it, and she was waving good-bye.

Magdalena stared up at the benevolent Jesus on the ceiling, knowing he wouldn't be able to help her, either. Time slowed to a drag. She had been locked in this chapel for three days—three days of waiting, cursing, and sometimes crying. At first she thought of nothing except how to escape, but the only window, no more than a hand's breadth across and made of some sort of translucent stone, was located about fifteen feet above the altar.

Her cries for help had echoed from the walls of the chapel unanswered. The door was massive and furnished with a lock, an additional bolt, and a peephole at eye level that her jailer, the monk, used regularly to keep an eye on her.

Brother Jakobus was, in fact, the only person she'd been able to talk to during these three days. He brought her food and drink, provided her with blankets, and once a day took away the bucket she had to use to relieve herself under the watchful eyes of all the archangels and evangelists. Before entering the chapel, Brother Jakobus would open the peephole. Magdalena then had to sit on one of the prayer stools visible from the peephole, and only then would he push back the bolt and enter. This was intended to keep her from attacking him when he entered the chapel, and indeed, she soon gave up on the idea. The monk might have been haggard, but he was also very hardy and muscular and, besides that, always carried a dagger at his side, which Magdalena assumed to be poisoned.

At first she refused to say more than just a few words to him, even though Brother Jakobus tried several times to engage her in conversation. With time, however, she became more and more bored in the drafty chapel. By now she knew the ceiling frescos like the back of her hand, as well as how many paces it was from the altar to the door and from the shrine of the Virgin to the altar. The only book here was a dog-eared prayer and hymn book whose Catholic hymns she had practically memorized by now.

On the second day, she started paying more attention to the monk's diatribes—for the most part, endless, bigoted lectures full of quotes from the Bible. Brother Jakobus approached her with a mix of contempt, hatred, and even . . . adoration, something that increasingly confused her. Often, he passed his hands through her hair, only to break away a moment later and start pacing furiously among the pews again. More than once, she was afraid he would cut her throat in a sudden fit of madness.

"It was you women who brought evil into the world!" he lectured, waving his finger in the air. "You ate the apple, and since then, we have been living in sin!"

Magdalena couldn't resist an answer: "Aha, and Adam just stood there and watched?" A moment later, she regretted speaking up.

Brother Jakobus walked over to her and seized her head like a ripe pumpkin he wanted to crush between his hands. "She talked him into it, do you understand?" he mumbled. "Adam had a moment of weakness, but God does not tolerate weakness, not a moment. He punished us all—*all* of us!"

Once more, she could smell his sweet perfume, but now, for the first time, Magdalena detected another scent behind the fragrance of violets—a vile, overpowering breath. The monk's whole body stank like rotting flesh; his mouth smelled like a sewer, and his crooked black stubs of teeth jutted out from foul, festering gums. The white tunic he wore under his black hooded cowl was stained with wet spots, which she came to realize were caused by festering ulcers. Magdalena could see that his tonsure was not shaved by hand but, in fact, that his hair on top had fallen out.

Brother Jakobus seemed to be rotting from the inside out.

The hangman's daughter remembered she'd seen these symptoms before in a Genoese merchant who had come to see her father some years ago. The man had staggered into the hangman's house, evidently in great pain. Most of his hair had fallen off, like balls of wool flying from a spindle, and he was twitching oddly. Her father had spoken of a French disease and sent the merchant off with a phial of mercury and a drink of opium poppies to relieve the pain. When Magdalena asked her father whether the man could be cured, he'd shaken his head. "He's been sick for too long," he had said. "If he's lucky, he'll die before he's completely in the grip of madness."

Was Brother Jakobus in the grip of madness, too? Magdalena wondered what the monk intended to do with her.

At times, he'd gently stroke her head, almost lovingly passing his hand through her hair. Then his mind seemed far off, on some distant voyage. On one such occasion, Brother Jakobus had poured out his heart to her.

"When I was still young, I was in love with a girl like you," he whispered. "A . . . whore . . . And her name was Magdalena. She brought ruin upon herself—and me. I was lecherous, a drunken fool stumbling through Augsburg in search of gratification. But then God sent me a sign. He punished me with this disease, and I collapsed in front of the Dominican Church of Saint Magdalene!" He giggled softly. "St. Magdalene—what a divine irony!" His giggle gave way to a loud coughing fit, and it was a long time before he could continue speaking. "Since then, I have devoted my life completely to the service of the Order. And now God has given me the chance to make up for my past. Magdalena . . ." Lost in thought, he stroked her cheeks. "My Magdalena is dead, but *you* can be healed. I will drive the demons out of you like the smoke and stench from a stifling farmhouse parlor."

While he read verses from the Bible, Magdalena closed her eyes, thinking frantically about how she might escape.

The situation looked pretty bleak at first. The door was impregnable and the window too small. She had no idea how many guards were here assisting Brother Jakobus. Besides, she was unarmed. She estimated she'd been in the coffin for two days. At their last stop, the men had been speaking a Swabian dialect. Was she already beyond the Bavarian border or perhaps still somewhere in Augsburg? Had she been taken away on a ship?

All she knew was that she had to be near a large church. At regular intervals, she could hear big, heavy bells tolling—the kind only large congregations could afford.

For the hundredth time, she cursed her stupidity. Why didn't she tell anyone before she went down into the concealed vault under the cathedral? Capturing her had been an incredible stroke of luck for Jakobus and his accomplices. Clearly, she, along with her father and Simon, had been on the trail of a huge conspiracy with the Augsburg bishop at its head! With the hangman's daughter as their hostage, the conspirators could now be assured the mysterious Templars' treasure would not fall into the wrong hands. Magdalena was certain her father and Simon would do everything in their power to free her.

Simon . . .

She felt a tickle in her lower body just thinking of him. If they were together, they would certainly have figured out how to escape this prison. What she liked most about the physician was how clever he was. Simon was sly, funny, eager to learn things, and well, perhaps just a little bit too short.

Magdalena smiled, thinking of all the things they had been through together. As far as shrewdness was concerned, Simon was even a match for her father, and that said a lot. The medicus had solved the riddle in the crypt under the St. Lawrence Church on his own. But then along came that accursed Benedikta who put herself between them—that elegant, blasé woman from Landsberg! Even down here in her prison, the thought of Simon and Benedikta together made Magdalena flush with anger. Just let her get her hands on that woman!

Then it occurred to her that she had other problems at the moment.

To get her mind off these things, she thought back again on a conversation she'd had the day before with Brother Jakobus about the treasure. She'd asked the monk several times what the treasure was and if it really was something left behind by the Templars, but he avoided answering all her questions.

"It's a treasure that will determine the future of Christianity," he said, looking up to the Savior on the ceiling. "With it, we will finally destroy the armies of the Lutheran heretics! As soon as our master tells the Pope about it, the Pope will join forces with us in a holy war to drive the Protestant princes out of the German Empire. The master knows that the Great War is not yet over!"

"Who is your master?" Magdalena interrupted. "The bishop of Augsburg?"

Brother Jakobus smiled. "Our numbers are legion."

The nights were cold and damp. Even under the wool blankets and in the warm glow of the candles the monk brought each night, she froze. Her arms and legs were stiff and tingled from lack of movement. The only indication it was day or night was the narrow beam of light that came through the little shuttered window. She was in despair.

Then, on the third day, something happened.

It was around noon. She had gotten up from the cold stone floor and was dozing on one of the pews when, half asleep, she rolled off the narrow bench onto the floor again. Sitting there, with blankets around her shoulders, cursing, she noticed a small bundle hidden under a pew. She hesitated for a moment, then quickly picked it up.

It was the little bag of herbs she'd been carrying around with her for the last four or five days since her visit to the apothecary in Augsburg. It must have fallen off her waistband and wound up under the bench. She'd completely forgotten it.

Carefully, she untied the string and looked inside. There was a sharp aroma of herbs. Everything she'd hastily stuffed into the bag at Nepomuk Biermann's apothecary was still there—a little crumbled, perhaps, but still useable.

Magdalena rubbed the dried herbs between her fingers, thinking.

And in her mind a plan began to take shape.

From the top of the stairs leading to Schreevogl's front door, Simon looked down at Benedikta, who stood at the foot of the stairs in full riding costume. Her horse was saddled, and she was holding the reins in her hand. The sorrel pranced around nervously, and the saddlebags on both sides were filled to the brim.

"I've been looking for you," Benedikta said, patting her horse to calm it down. "I was told I might find you here. I'd like to say good-bye."

"You're leaving?" asked Simon, his mouth falling open.

The merchant woman swung up into the saddle. "After our last meeting, I had the feeling it would be best for me to go. And to be honest, I don't really put much faith in all this talk about treasures and murderers. It won't bring my brother back, so I wish you farewell!"

"Benedikta, wait!" Simon hurried down the stairway. "I didn't really mean what I said two days ago in the tavern. I was no doubt too harsh. It's just that . . ." He hesitated and eyed the refined lady from Landsberg again. With her fur coat, billowing skirt, and cape, she looked so different from all the Schongau women who were always chasing after him. She was a visitor from another world who would leave him now—alone in this filthy little provincial dump.

"What's the matter, physician?" She looked at him, waiting.

"I'm sorry, I was a fool. I . . . I would be really happy if you could stay and help with the rest of my search." The words simply tumbled out before he'd had a chance to think them through. "It's very possible that I'll urgently need your self-confident, refined demeanor once again! The superintendent in Rottenbuch probably won't want anything to do with a little field surgeon, but with you . . ."

"Rottenbuch?" Benedikta asked with curiosity. "The riddle points to Rottenbuch?"

Simon sighed. Without noticing, he'd already made a decision. "Let's go to one of the quiet side rooms at Semer's Tavern," he said. "I'll explain everything else to you there. We need to set out today."

Benedikta smiled and looked down at the medicus, who kept shifting around, trying to get out of the way of her nervous horse.

"All right," she said finally. "I'll stay. But this time, let's rent an obedient fast horse for you here at the post house. Do you think we might have to flee from robbers again?"

The monastery of Rottenbuch was only ten miles from Schongau, a journey of less than two hours.

Benedikta rode so fast and gracefully that Simon had trouble keeping up and not falling off his horse. As they raced past snow-covered trees, Simon often had to squint or close his eyes briefly in the light flurries and let the horse take its own pace—it seemed to know better than he where they were headed.

They had rented a young gray for a few silver coins in the post station at Semer's Tavern. Benedikta had paid, and Simon was embarrassed when she took out her purse and handed the coins to the postmaster. The medicus couldn't help grinning. This woman wouldn't let herself be bossed around by a man, and she didn't demand any favors, either. In these matters, Simon thought, she was just like Magdalena. Perhaps they weren't so different, after all, and perhaps under different circumstances, Magdalena could have become another Benedikta.

They arrived at their destination in less than two hours, leaving the forest and entering a snow-covered landscape dotted with houses, churches, walls, and archways. For a mile around, men had wrested open land from the surrounding wilderness, and at its center was the Rottenbuch Monastery. On a road entering the cleared land from the opposite side, Simon could see a group of silent monks giving alms to a wailing beggar. A farmer was pulling a calf on a rope across the paved main street of the town. Ladders and scaffolding lay against many of the as-of-yet unplastered buildings while workers rushed around with buckets, shovels, and trowels. Just as in Steingaden, people were obviously busy here removing the rubble of war and building a new, larger, and even more beautiful monastery.

Simon and Benedikta rode through a gate toward the wide square in front of the Augustinian Canon Monastery. A huge clock tower rose up in front of them. On their left was the church and, next to it, the monastery, which in contrast to the other buildings was already resplendent in a fresh coat of stucco. After they'd found a place to stay and a stable for the horses, they went in search of the superintendent.

Putting on a serious face, Simon addressed one of the monks entering the church. "Brother, may I have a word with you? We are looking for the venerable leader of this wonderful monastery. Could you direct us to him?"

"Do you mean our Right Reverend Brother, Superintendent Michael Piscator? You are in luck."

The monk pointed to a somewhat stout elderly man dressed in the typical white alb of the Augustinian canons. Standing nearby among some laborers, he seemed to be giving directions to the construction foreman. "You can see him engaged in his favorite pastime," the canon said, winking. "Building churches, for him, is the highest form of worship." With a grin, he disappeared through the portal to the monastery.

Simon couldn't help but think of the Steingaden abbot, Augustin Bonenmayr, who had devoted himself, just like the superintendent in Rottenbuch, to the construction of his monastery. Simon was certain that if the church authorities continued in this way, the most beautiful monasteries in Bavaria would soon be standing in the Priests' Corner.

"Your Excellency?" Benedikta walked toward the group and curtsied to the superintendent.

Like so many monks, Brother Michael had a weakness for the fair sex. He paused, then made a slight bow and offered Benedikta his hand, which was adorned with the signet ring of the monastery. "I'm honored, beautiful lady. How can I help you?"

The workmen and architects packed up their plans, disappointed, while Benedikta kissed his signet ring. Simon rushed to her side, doffed his hat, and went through the same routine that had been so successful in Wessobrunn.

"Allow me to introduce the lady. Before you stands none other than Madame de Bouillon, royal dressmaker to the mistress of the French king," the physician declared. "She has made the long trip from Paris in order to view the famous relics of Saints Primus and Felicianus here in Rottenbuch." Simon lowered his voice to a whisper as he leaned toward the superintendent. "She made a vow not to share her bed again with her husband until she'd kissed the bones of the martyrs."

Benedikta glanced at Simon in astonishment, but Simon maintained a serious face.

"The poor man," Brother Michael sighed. "What a waste! But may I ask how the lady came to choose these two particular saints for her long pilgrimage?"

"She gave her newborn twins the names Primus and Felicianus," Simon continued in a firm voice. "But they've fallen seriously ill, and now she hopes through her pilgrimage to be heard by our beloved Virgin Mary."

"Get a hold of yourself, damn it!" Benedikta whispered in his ear. "You're really going too far. Nobody will believe that stuff!"

But the superintendent nodded sympathetically. "What a misfortune! I'll guide you to the relics personally! Follow me."

Simon cast a surreptitious glance at Benedikta and grinned.

Then they followed Brother Michael's clipped steps to the church. Huffing and puffing, he pointed toward the scaffolding, where workmen were replacing old, broken church windows with stained glass.

"In a few years this monastery will be a jewel in Bavaria, believe me!" the superintendent said. "An incomparable pilgrimage site! We will house not just the relics of Saint Primus and Saint Felicianus here, but two teeth of Saint Binosa, some hair from the Virgin Mary, a knuckle belonging to Saint Blasius, the skull of Saint Lawrence, and the collarbone of Saint Brigida . . . to name only a few of the most important."

He opened the church door, and Simon cast his eyes on a splendor that had to look like heaven on earth to the simple people in the area. Bright paintings of angels and saints on the ceiling gave the impression of infinite heights, marble slabs memorialized the former superintendents of Rottenbuch, and a huge organ with pipes as big as a man was enthroned over the portal. On the east wall opposite them, an altar at least twenty feet high depicted the Ascension of Mary, flanked by the apostles Peter and Paul. At the sides, two skeletons stood upright in glass coffins, each with a sword in hand and a laurel wreath on its bare skull.

"Saints Primus and Felicianus . . ." Brother Michael whispered, pointing at the skeletons. "Aren't they beautiful? We placed them there during the dedication ceremonies for our new altar at this site. They look down on us protectively and benevolently." He turned away. "But now I shall leave you alone with the relics."

"Ah, excuse me," Simon whispered, "but Madame de Bouillon promised she would kiss the bones of the saint."

"Kiss?" The superintendent looked at Simon, bewildered.

"*Ah, oui,*" Benedikta interjected with her best French accent. "I must . . . how do we say it . . . *embrasser* . . . kiss the sacred bones with my lips. Only in that way can the vow be honored."

"I'm dreadfully sorry, madame, but that's not possible." The superintendent pointed up at the high altar. "As you can see yourself, the bones are up there, beyond our reach. Moreover, the coffins are sealed. Send a kiss with your hand, and I'm sure God will understand."

"*Mais non!*" Benedikta exclaimed. "I must kiss them. *Mes enfants* . . . my children . . ." She raised her hands to her neckline. "Otherwise, they will never regain their health!"

But Brother Michael couldn't be moved. "Believe me, it's impossible. But I'll include your children in my prayers of intercession at evening mass. Tell me their names, and I— "

"My dearest Brother Michael! The workmen told me I would find you here. What splendid windows you have installed here!"

The voice came from the church portal. When Simon turned around, his heart almost stopped. Approaching them with hasty steps, arms outraised in greeting, was none other than Augustin Bonenmayr, the abbot of Steingaden.

Now Michael Piscator also recognized his colleague from the Premonstratensian monastery. "Your Excellency, to what do I owe this honor?"

Bonenmayr gave the Rottenbuch superintendent a hearty handshake.

"I have some errands to run in Schongau and Peißenberg. The new chapel in the pasture near Aich is in dreadful condition! And whose job is it to care for it?" He sighed. "I thought that, on my way there, I might stop for a rest here. There's so much to discuss concerning the renovation of our monasteries. You must tell me the name of your glazier. Is he from Venice? Florence?"

Brother Michael smiled. "You'll never guess. Promise me you'll stay the night, and then perhaps I'll tell you the name of this artist."

"If you insist . . ." Only now did the Steingaden abbot notice

Simon and Benedikta, who were trying to slip away unnoticed behind the columns. "What a coincidence! The young widow from Landsberg!" he called to them. "And Simon Fronwieser! Well, have you made any progress in your investigations of the murder? Or are you applying for a position as physician here in Rottenbuch as well?"

Michael glanced from Bonenmayr to Benedikta and Simon, who came to a sudden stop between two columns as if they had been hit by a bolt of lightning. "Landsberg? Murder?" the superintendent asked, perplexed.

"Thank you. We . . . we . . . have figured everything out," Simon stuttered. "But we don't wish to disturb you gentlemen any further. Your Excellencies certainly have things to discuss." He pulled Benedikta along with him, leaving the two gentlemen alone in the church.

Outside, in the church courtyard, Simon began to curse so loudly that some monks turned around to look. "Damn! What bad luck! The Steingaden abbot will certainly tell Brother Michael who we really are, and then this whole masquerade is over!"

"A masquerade that began with you!" Benedikta snapped.

"Oh, come now, what should we have said in Wessobrunn, and now here in Rottenbuch—'Good day, we're looking for the treasure of the Templars? Can we desecrate some of your holy relics?'" Simon talked himself into a rage. More and more monks turned around to stare and whisper.

Benedikta finally softened a bit. "In any case, the superintendent won't let us open the coffins, and we can forget getting any help from him."

"So much the worse," Simon grumbled. "Then we'll never learn whether a message is concealed in the relics. What now?"

Benedikta looked up at the church's window frames, where workmen were just beginning to insert the new stained glass. The men were standing on a rickety scaffold, carefully raising the colorful windows on a pulley. Simon was certain that each window was worth a fortune.

"If the superintendent doesn't open these coffins for us, we'll just have to do it ourselves," Benedikta said. "Primus and Felicianus could certainly use a little fresh air."

"And just how do you intend to do that?"

Benedikta pointed again at the open windows. "We'll pay a visit to the two dusty old gents tonight," she said. "The glaziers certainly won't finish their work today, and I can't imagine that the church is guarded overnight. No doubt, the superintendent thinks that lightning will strike any grave robber and send him running."

"How are you so sure that lightning *won't* strike us?" Simon whispered. "Stealing religious relics is a sin that . . ." But Benedikta had already charged off.

Neither of them noticed the two figures hiding among the other monks. Like long shadows, they slipped away from the group and went back to following Simon and Benedikta's trail.

In his cell in the Schongau dungeon, the robber chief Scheller was turning the poison pill in his fingers, looking out at the snow falling in front of his barred window. Behind him, many of his companions were dozing in expectation of their imminent deaths. The women whimpered and fathers said their farewells to their children in whispered voices, telling them about a paradise that was also open to robbers and whores where they would all see one another again. They spoke of a better life in another world and made the sick ten-year-old boy swear to God and to the Virgin Mary that he would lead a respectable life. They had robbed and killed, but now most of them had become penitent sinners. Some of them prayed. The next morning, the local priest would come and take their last confessions.

Hans Scheller stared at the little pill and thought back on his life so far. How had it come to this? He'd been a carpenter in

Schwabmünchen with a wife and child. As a young boy, he'd witnessed the execution of the notorious murderer Benedikt Lanzl, who had screamed for two whole days while being beaten by the hangman. Tied to a wheel, the highway robber and arsonist had become the focal point of a spectacle unlike anything little Hans had ever seen before. At night, he could still hear Benedict Lanzl's scream in his sleep.

Sometimes Hans Scheller could even hear it today.

Never did he dream that one day he, too, would stand up there on the wooden platform. But God's ways were inscrutable.

Hans Scheller sighed, closed his eyes, and gave himself up to the memories that came flooding back. *A laughing boy, his face smeared with porridge . . . his wife bent over the washtub . . . a field of barley in the summer, a good glass of beer . . . the smell of freshly cut spruce . . .*

There was much that was wonderful about the world, and he could leave it behind without regrets. But he still owed the hangman something.

The night before, something occurred to him, a small matter he'd overlooked until then. But now, after everything Jakob Kuisl had told him, it suddenly seemed important.

He would tell the hangman the next day at the gallows.

Hans Scheller leaned against the ice-cold wall of the cell, fingering the pill, and whistled an old nursery tune. He was almost home.

He was called Brother Nathanael. This was the name the order had given him long ago—he'd long forgotten his real name. Where he came from, the sun burned brightly with a shimmering, unending heat, and thus the snow drifting down now in soft flakes seemed, to him, like a personal messenger from hell.

He was freezing under his thin tunic and black-hooded coat, clenching his teeth but not complaining. His former master had trained him to be tough. He was a guard dog of the Lord, and his command was to follow the woman and the man. And if they found the treasure, he was to kill them quickly and silently, retrieve the treasure, and report back to the brotherhood. That was his assignment.

Trembling with cold, he played with the dagger in his hand and pressed his back against the frost-covered wall of the monastery. Snowflakes melted as they fell on his brown, scarred face. He was from Castille, near the magnificent city of Salamanca, and his task at the moment seemed to him like a test from God. The Lord himself had sent him to this inhospitable, remote region and, as an additional punishment, had sent him Brother Avenarius.

The short, plump Swabian standing next to him and mumbling his prayers had been personally assigned to him and Brother Jakobus in Augsburg by the master. Brother Avenarius was second to none in his knowledge of the written word—he knew all about the treasure and was an expert in solving riddles—but as a comrade-in-arms, he was about as useful as an old woman. Once again, he started whining.

"Jesus, Mary, and Joseph! Why can't we go back to our quarters?" His thick Swabian accent sometimes drove Brother Nathanael crazy. "Who can say whether the two will really try to break into the church tonight?" the Swabian lamented. "And even if they do, we can catch up with them again in the morning! So what are we doing here?"

Nathanael ran the dagger along his fingers—from his index finger, to his middle finger, to his ring finger, and back, a little nervous routine he could repeat for hours. It calmed his mind.

"I keep telling you we can't let him out of our sight! The matter is too important. Besides, if you'd only solved the riddle before they did, we'd be back in Augsburg by now!"

Brother Avenarius looked to the ground with embarrassment. "I'll admit I underestimated the physician," he grumbled. "Who would have suspected that the words *primus* and *felicianus* referred to the two saints? At least I figured out before he did that the inscription referred to the Wessobrunn Prayer."

"And how was that of any help?" Nathanael was running the dagger through his fingers faster and faster. "We searched the entire damned monastery for the book, and it was in the *bell tower!*"

"But I had no way of knowing that," Brother Avenarius whined.

Brother Nathanael let loose with a curse to heaven and went back to playing with his dagger. Things had not gone as planned. Everything had looked so simple at first. It was just two weeks ago that the local master had summoned him and Jakobus, telling them that the greatest treasure in all of Christendom had been found, not in some far-distant place, but right nearby. It was a sign from God; he was one of the chosen!

Never would he have dared to hope God would choose him for this task! Cast into this world as a filthy little orphan, Nathanael had found a home among the Dominicans in Salamanca, where his special abilities were soon recognized. He was intelligent and well read, but he'd also retained much of the toughness and smarts he'd picked up from his days on the street—qualities the other monks lacked. Soon the Brotherhood had come to him. They had often recruited soldiers from the Dominicans, and they needed people like him. Nathanael was something special—a monk and warrior, like the Templars who had once been the greatest enemies of the Brotherhood. There were many unbelievers to battle in the Spanish provinces, and the church needed people now and then to do its dirty work. That was Nathanael's specialty.

A few years back, he'd been called to Augsburg, where the German Brotherhood had its headquarters. Much of the German Empire had fallen into the hands of the Lutherans, and many church treasures and relics were threatened by looting and desecration. Altars and shrines had been melted down, statues smashed, and in Konstanz, mobs of heretics had even cast the bones of St. Konrad and St. Pelagius into the Rhine! It was Brother Nathanael's job in the Brotherhood to return these threatened treasures to the bosom of the Holy Roman Church, a job that occasionally demanded not just his intuition, but his dagger.

A few years ago, he had met Brother Jakobus, the right-hand man of the master of the German provinces, in Augsburg. Jakobus was a vain but extremely devout man who, like himself, made no compromises and knew only one goal: the defense of the true faith. Together they'd been able to save many of the church's sacred objects from destruction—relics, pictures of saints, statues of Mary . . .

But never did Nathanael think that, after all these years of praying and waiting, they'd be the ones chosen to retrieve the greatest treasure in all of Christendom, a treasure the Templars had seized almost five hundred years ago, one believed to be forever lost. And then this damned hangman and his daughter got in the way, along with that smart-ass physician! Ever since then, everything had been going to hell.

Brother Avenarius was standing quietly beside him, mumbling his prayers and clutching a chain on his neck that held the cross with the double beams, the symbol of the Brotherhood. The tubby Swabian seemed to have resigned himself to standing a few more hours in the driving snow. With closed eyes, he recited the prayer for self-control from Holy Scripture.

"*Who shall set a watch before my mouth, and a seal of wisdom upon my lips? Who will set scourges over my thoughts, and the discipline of wisdom over my heart?*"

Nathanael sighed. At first, it seemed quite suitable for the Swabian monk to have been assigned to them. According to everything the master had learned from the letter of the pious Altenstadt priest, the Templars hadn't made it easy for them. Friedrich Wildgraf's heretical order was known for its secret codes and riddles, and Brother Avenarius was considered an excellent authority on the Bible, a bookworm who could put his finger on even the most obscure quotation and knew more about the history of the relics than anyone else. But up till now, he hadn't been of much help to the group, and after the completion of this assignment, Nathanael would speak to the master and recommend his removal.

But for now, he needed him.

Especially now that Brother Jakobus had headed back to Augsburg to report to the master and obtain some new poison. Again, Nathanael wondered why his brother monk had been so quick to set out on the long trip back. Did it, perhaps, have something to do with the festering rashes that had been tormenting him for weeks? Jakobus had changed a lot recently. These sudden, furious outbursts, these muffled cries of pain in the night, his hair falling out . . . It was sad when a once-brave companion let himself go. In the end, one was always alone.

Nathanael looked around in all directions. Had he heard something? For days he'd had the vague feeling they were being observed. But by whom? Was someone else interested in the treasure, someone they didn't even know about yet?

A short but unmistakable cry pulled him out of his thoughts. Two stooped figures approached the church. Snow lay ankle-deep over the church courtyard, muffling the sounds of their footsteps, but not the angry words of one of them. Nathanael grinned. This brash medicus would never learn to keep quiet.

So much the better.

The physician and his woman had approached the right-hand side of the church and were standing underneath the scaffolding. Nathanael gave Brother Avenarius a sign and set out after them. But suddenly, he hesitated. At first it was just a small movement he noticed out of the corner of his eye, but looking closer, he could see everything plainly.

On the other side of the church, where the memorial slabs

were set into the wall, three figures emerged from the shadows. Like ghosts, they glided along the side of the church toward the physician and his companion.

Nathanael pulled down his hood, stuck the dagger back in his belt, and hunkered down to hide in the snow. His intuitions in recent days hadn't deceived him.

It was time to find out who had been following them.

Simon glanced up at the icy scaffolding and gave Benedikta a skeptical look. "You want us to climb up there? We'll slip and . . ."

But Benedikta had already boosted herself up onto the first level of the scaffolding. Once again, the physician was astonished at how agile she was. He was about to tease her, but then he resigned himself to his fate, pulling himself up, groaning, then continuing on to the second and third levels. From up here, he had a view of the entire snowbound monastery. In some of the windows across the courtyard lights were burning, but otherwise it was completely dark. For a moment, Simon thought he saw something move in the courtyard, but his view wasn't good enough in the darkness and driving snow. Finally, he turned to the window frame through which Benedikta had already entered the church.

Her plan seemed to be working. The men hadn't been able to complete their work before the evening, and the glass was still not installed in some windows. Simon sat in the opening, his legs dangling down, watching Benedikta tie a rope around one of the crossbeams and climb down hand over hand into the church. The medicus crossed himself and followed. Soon enough, his feet touched the cold stone floor and he could look around.

Even though the church doors were closed at night, the monks had left some of the altar and votive candles burning, and their flickering light gave a ghostly appearance to the entire nave. From up on the high altar, the skeletons of Saints Primus and

Felicianus looked down at the intruders from inside their glass coffins, swords ever in hand and laurel wreaths on their bare skulls.

At this time of night, there was nothing sacred, soothing, or protective about the figures. In fact, Simon had the feeling that, at any moment, the skeletons would step down to throttle the two sinners with their thin, bony fingers. But they remained standing there, their bare teeth frozen in grins and their eye sockets dark and dead.

"Which of the two do you think it is?

"What?"

Simon was so wrapped up in the ghastly sight that he didn't hear Benedikta at first.

"I mean, which of the saints could be concealing the message?" Benedikta replied. "We probably won't have enough time to open both coffins."

"Which one . . . ?" Simon stopped to think. "Let's take Felicianus," he finally said. "*Felicianus* means 'happy' or 'lucky,' and the finder of the prize will be happy and lucky. And doesn't it say in Matthew that the first—that is, the *primi*—will be the last?"

Benedikta looked at him skeptically. "From your lips to God's ear."

They approached the high altar until they were standing directly beneath Felicianus's coffin.

"If you take me on your shoulders, maybe I can reach the coffin," Benedikta said. "Then I'll try to lift the lid."

"But it's much too heavy," Simon whispered. "You'll certainly drop it!"

"Oh, come now, it's just made of glass, after all. And the skeleton inside doesn't weigh any more than a few dusty old bones."

"And what happens if it falls, anyway?"

Benedikta grinned. "Then we'll just have to put old Felicianus back together again. You're a doctor, after all!"

Simon sighed and knelt down so that Benedikta could climb

onto his shoulders. Then, swaying slightly, he lifted her up. When the physician felt Benedikta's thigh brush against his cheek, a pleasant tingling coursed through his body.

Wonderful, he thought. *We're desecrating the bones of a saint while I'm dreaming of the thighs of a naked woman. Two mortal sins at the same time.*

Finally, Benedikta could reach the coffin. Reaching her arms around the lower part of the glass case, she whispered to Simon. "Now let me down—slowly!"

As Benedikta continued gripping the precious case, Simon knelt down slowly, bit by bit. The coffin swayed back and forth, scraped along the base of the altar, and finally touched the ground. Benedikta hopped nimbly down from Simon's aching shoulders.

"And now let's open it."

Benedikta laid the coffin down on the ground gingerly and examined the cover. The edges of the glass were soldered with a gold alloy. She pulled out her knife and began to make a clean cut through the seam.

"Benedikta," Simon whispered in a hoarse voice. "Are you sure we should be doing this? If we get caught, we'll be put on trial, and our punishment will make Scheller's torture on the wheel look like a walk in the park."

Benedikta looked up from her work for just a moment. "I didn't come all the way here to give up now. So come now and help me!"

Simon took out the medical stiletto he always carried with him, inserted it in the soldered crack, and pried open the seam, inch by inch. The alloy was soft and brittle, and it didn't take them long to remove the lid.

"St. Felicianus, forgive us!" Simon mumbled, though he didn't think his prayer would meet with much understanding in heaven. "We're doing it only for the good of the church!"

A musty odor rose up from the open coffin, and Simon stared

in disgust at the skeleton, which was covered in patches of green mold. The bones were tied to one another and to the glass coffin in back by thin wires. The dried laurel wreath atop the saint's head had slipped down over the forehead, and between the bony fingers of his right hand, St. Felicianus held a rusty sword.

"The sword and laurel wreath," Simon whispered, "are symbols of a martyr's death and victory."

Benedikta had already started examining the bones. She poked her fingers in the eye sockets and felt around the inside of the skull. "There has to be a message hidden here somewhere," she mumbled, "a piece of paper, a note. Damn, Simon, help me look! We don't have forever!"

Suddenly, something clattered behind them. Simon turned around but could make nothing out in the darkness. Shadows and light from the flickering candles at the foot of the Virgin Mary's altar floated back and forth between the columns.

"Did you hear that?" Simon asked.

Benedikta was now examining the slightly moldy chest cavity. "A rat, a gust of wind—what do I know? Now come over here and help me!"

Once again, Simon gazed out over the nave. The columns, the altar to the Virgin, the flickering candles . . .

The medicus jumped.

Flickering candles . . . ?

All along, the candles had been burning evenly. If they were flickering now, then—

"Simon, Simon! I've found it! I've found the message! Come and look!" Benedikta's shout tore him from his thoughts. She had scraped some of the rust from the sword blade, and her eyes glowed as she pointed to her discovery. "It was underneath the rust! You were right!"

Simon came closer, bending down over the sword. An inscription could be seen under the rust on the blade, though only a few words were legible.

Heredium in . . .

With his stiletto, he hurriedly set about scraping the rust from the rest of the inscription, letter for letter, word for word.

Heredium in baptistae . . .

As he continued scraping, he whispered a translation of the Latin verse.

"The heritage in the baptist . . ."

He got no further because at that very moment all hell broke loose around them.

Meanwhile, there was a quiet knock at Jakob Kuisl's front door. A messenger from Burgomaster Karl Semer, his personal scribe, was standing outside in the frigid night, pale, freezing, his knees shaking.

But it wasn't the cold that made his knees shake. He crossed himself as he entered the hangman's house, declining the cup of wine that Kuisl offered. Nervously, he noticed the execution sword hanging near a cross in the devotional area of the main room. It was bad luck to enter a hangman's house so soon before an execution, especially on a night when wolves were roaming around and it was so cold the snot froze in your nose. But what could he do? He had been ordered to deliver a message to the hangman that very night. Presiding Burgomaster Karl Semer had returned from his business trip and was now keeping his promise by delivering the information Jakob Kuisl was so eager to have.

"What did you find out?" Kuisl asked, sucking on the cold stem of his pipe. "You can look out the window as you tell me, or I'll put a mask over your eyes, if that will make it easier for you."

The messenger shook his head, ashamed.

"All right, then, out with it!"

Speaking quickly, with his head bowed, the scribe reported what Burgomaster Semer had learned on his trip. Jakob Kuisl kept stuffing his pipe, lighting it over the stove, and then blowing clouds of smoke toward the ceiling, terrifying the messenger. A contented smile passed over the hangman's face.

His suspicions had been confirmed.

Simon didn't know where to look first. With a loud crash that resounded through the entire church, the huge statue of Mary in the apse tipped to one side, fell, and broke into hundreds of pieces. Shouts came from the right. The medicus caught sight of a wiry monk in a black robe leaping through the air with a drawn dagger and kicking another man in the head, who fell with a loud thud among the pews. From somewhere else, he heard a loud cry, almost like that of a child. Panting, a second stout monk appeared from behind the altar of Mary, followed by two men, one of whom held a crossbow cocked and ready to fire. They wore the tattered trousers of the mercenary foot soldiers in the Thirty Years' War, long coats, and wide-brimmed hats with colorful feathers. The man with the crossbow paused, aimed, and pulled the trigger. With a gurgling sound, the fat monk fell forward into the baptismal font. Now the other monk turned around, dodged a candlestick aimed at him, then with a lightning-fast, almost imperceptible movement, thrust upward, plunging his scimitar deep into his opponent's chest. The soldier staggered for a moment, trying to pull the blade out again, then fell against a grave slab on the wall and slid down to the floor. A wide bloody streak reached from the slab down to the ground.

The two other soldiers drew their sabers now and ran toward the monk with the scimitar. The monk seemed to be considering for an instant whether to keep fighting, then changed his mind and raced toward the rope still dangling from one of the window frames. With a bloody scimitar between his teeth, he pulled himself up with amazing speed. His legs were visible for just a moment before he disappeared in the darkness above.

Everything had happened so fast that Simon was only able to

watch in astonishment. Finally, he pulled himself together. "Benedikta! Let's get out of here!"

"Simon, keep quiet!" she replied, trying to calm him down. "We have to . . ."

But the medicus was already running for the door. Suddenly, he stopped, stunned. He had forgotten something.

The sword!

There was no way they could leave the sword with the inscription in the church! Simon had recognized some of the men. The stranger with the crossbow was the same man he'd seen sitting up in a tree near the Wessobrunn Monastery. The other was the one who had been lying in wait for them in the yew forest. They were surely out to get the Templars' treasure as well. And the monks? Presumably, the Augustinian monks in Rottenbuch had seen the light in the church, come to check things out, and surprised the strangers there.

But didn't Augustinian monks wear cowls? And why had the monk stabbed the soldier to death like a dog?

Simon had no time to think this through. Turning, he ran back to rip the sword from St. Felicianus's bony hand.

There was a faint crunching sound as knucklebones fell to the ground like little dice. Simon grabbed the weapon, which was astonishingly heavy and reached up to his chest. Standing next to him, Benedikta still hadn't moved. She couldn't take her eyes from the two men staring back at them, still uncertain about what to do. Simon didn't want to give them any time to decide.

"Benedikta, follow me! Now!"

Swinging the sword through the air like a madman, the medicus headed for the exit, past the overturned statue of Mary and the dead monk, hanging down headfirst into the baptismal font. For a moment, Simon was entranced by the bloody cloud slowly spreading out in the holy water; then he continued directly toward the two remaining men, who jumped to one side when they saw the medicus approaching, screaming wildly and swinging the huge broadsword. He was just a few steps from the large church portal now. But when he finally reached it, it wouldn't open.

He shook it. Of course the door was locked.

Damn! This was the very reason they'd decided to enter the church through the window! In a state of panic, Simon looked in all directions. What next? He could never climb back up the rope with the sword in hand, and the two men were slowly drawing closer.

Suddenly, in one of the church's wings, he noticed a stained-glass window depicting Mary hovering in the air, surrounded by little angels as she ascended to heaven. In contrast with the other new windows, this one was only chest high. Without hesitation, Simon rushed toward it, smashing the lovingly painted glass with the broadsword. The window burst into a thousand pieces, and Simon dived through it headfirst, landing outside on the snowy pavement of the church courtyard. He felt his aching shoulder to see if anything was broken. Glass splinters were embedded in his clothes, his hair, even his face, and drops of his blood were falling onto the white snow.

He looked around. Had Benedikta followed him? At that moment, he caught sight of her head in the opening of the broken window. She jumped through it as nimble as a cat, rolled over, and stood up again. With a certain satisfaction, Simon saw that she, too, was showing some signs of fear.

"Quick, let's get back to our lodging," she said to him. "For the time being, we'll be safe there."

They hurried over the forecourt, past the icy spring, the clock tower, and the monastery garden, then through the open entry gate. Finally, they arrived at their quarters.

After they'd knocked three times, a sleepy innkeeper opened the door. "What in the world . . . ?" he asked in astonishment.

"A little brawl out in the street." With the huge broadsword,

Simon squeezed past the stout innkeeper. Blood trickled down his face, making him look like a somewhat small but very angry barroom brawler. "These days you're not even safe on the monastery grounds. It's good I always carry a weapon around with me."

Without another word, he hurried up to his room with Benedikta, leaving the astonished innkeeper standing there. Not until Simon had locked the door behind them and checked the street in front of the inn did he feel safe. Panting and puffing, he collapsed on the bed. "Who or what in the world was that all about?"

Benedikta sat down beside him. "I . . . I just don't know. But from now on, I'll be a little less cavalier in what I say about possible highway bandits, I promise."

Simon started to pick tiny splinters of glass from his face. Benedikta took out her white handkerchief and dabbed at the cuts.

"You look like—"

"Like some drunk who has fallen through a barroom window. Thanks, I know." Simon arose and reached for the broadsword leaning against the bed. "In any case, it's good we brought the sword along with us," he said. "I'm sure these men have been after us a long time. They're looking for the treasure, just as we are."

He ran his hand along the blade, then scratched away the remainder of the rust with his stiletto until the entire quotation was visible. Individual words were spread out in wide intervals along the blade.

Heredium in baptistae sepulcro . . .

"The heritage in the grave of the baptist," he translated aloud. "You can't say that the riddles are getting any easier."

"Well then, what do you make of it?" Benedikta asked.

Simon stopped to think. "The heritage could be the treasure.

The baptist is, perhaps, John the Baptist—that part is easy. But his grave . . . ?" He frowned. "I've never heard anything about John the Baptist's grave. I presume it's somewhere in the Holy Land."

"But we're in the Priests' Corner," Benedikta interrupted. "It *has* to mean something else. Think!"

Simon rubbed his temples. "Give me some time. Today was a little too much for me . . ." he said, closing his eyes. When he opened them again, he stared at the sword on the bed for a long time. "The coffin of Friedrich Wildgraf under the Saint Lawrence Church contained his bones, but no sword," he said, running his fingers over the blade again. Now, with the rust scraped away, it gleamed as if it had been forged just the day before. The pommel was set in silver and the cross guard decorated with a number of engravings. He examined them more closely, thinking.

They were Templar crosses.

"Perhaps this sword belonged to the master of the German Templars, Friedrich Wildgraf," Simon said. "His weapon is the riddle. That would be just like him, big enough."

"But that still doesn't solve our problem of what these accursed words mean! We've got to go first thing tomorrow—"

Benedikta was interrupted by a knock on the door.

"Who might that be?" Simon stood up and went to the door. "Perhaps the innkeeper . . . I'll tell him that everything's all right."

He opened the door, and there standing before him was not the innkeeper, but someone he would never have expected to see here.

Brother Nathanael cursed, and not for the first time in his life, but as always he asked God for forgiveness right away. He rubbed his left shoulder, which, for a moment, he thought might be dislocated. It hurt like hell but still seemed secure in its socket.

When he'd kicked the stranger in the face, Nathanael had fallen onto one of the pews. Climbing up the rope with only one arm had completely exhausted him. Despite the pain, he smiled. At least he'd sent one of those heretical dogs to hell. Now he was standing in a dark corner of the monastery courtyard murmuring the Confiteor.

Mea culpa, mea culpa, mea maxima culpa . . . Through my fault, through my fault, through my most grievous fault . . .

The murder, like so many he'd committed, was necessary. Committed in the name of the church. Nevertheless, it was a mortal sin. Tonight, Nathanael would flagellate himself for it.

From where he was located, the monk observed the activity in the courtyard. The noise in the church had quickly attracted some of the Augustinian monks who were already awake for prayers. Despite the late hour, a rather large number of workers, peasants, and the monastery superintendent himself had come running to the church, along with some other monks. Some were already shouting, "The devil, the devil is afoot in Rottenbuch!" A rumor started flying around that God himself wanted to signal his opposition to the superintendent's building mania.

When the group headed by Michael Piscator entered the church, shouting and wailing could be heard. Nathanael assumed the monks had just come upon the open coffin of St. Felicianus. Admittedly, that was not a very edifying sight. The martyr's skeleton had fallen to pieces, an act of desecration that probably not even the Pope could forgive. Perhaps, however, the monks' wailing had more to do with the destruction of the statue of Mary, the overturned church pews, the broken stained-glass window, or the soldier who had been stabbed to death.

And Brother Avenarius was also lying there.

Nathanael was sure he was dead. No man could survive an arrow in the back from a crossbow, especially if he was later found facedown in a baptismal font. Brother Nathanael felt a certain relief. Without the fat Avenarius, he could move faster and more discreetly. And the monk wasn't much help solving riddles. Now it would be simpler to just follow the medicus and his woman. They'd solve the riddle, and then he'd strike. The only problem was these strangers . . .

Nathanael's feelings hadn't deceived him. They were being watched, and it annoyed him to no end that he hadn't noticed it earlier. Of course, these men were good fighters, silent and unscrupulous. And like him, they were after the treasure. From now on, he'd have to watch out, even if only two of them remained.

Once more he tried to remember how the skirmish in the church had unfolded. When Nathanael observed the three men climbing into the church, he hurried in after them. But the fat monk had a hard time climbing the scaffolding, and they lost sight of the strangers in the dark nave. It was Brother Avenarius who finally found them again in his own way. He stepped on the foot of one of the men hiding behind a curtain!

After that everything happened very fast. Brother Avenarius wound up floating in the baptismal font with an arrow through his chest, and Rottenbuch experienced its darkest day since the Swedes' attack.

The monastery bells began sounding the alarm. Nathanael turned away from the excited crowd in the forecourt, which was now brightly lit with torches. For a moment, he considered returning to their quarters, which were not far from where Simon and Benedikta were staying. He and Avenarius had introduced themselves as itinerant Dominicans and been assigned two beds in the monastery by the Augustinians. But now that Avenarius lay dead in the church for all to see, a return to the monastery would probably be too risky. Thus, Nathanael found a barn nearby where he could await the coming day in a bed of warm straw.

As he was about to slip through a narrow barn door, he saw something outside that warmed his heart. Help was near! He sent a quick prayer to heaven and kissed the golden cross on his chest.

God hadn't forsaken him.

"You owe me an explanation," said Augustin Bonenmayr.

Like an angry schoolmaster, the abbot of Steingaden stared down through his pince-nez at Simon, whose mouth had dropped open. Without waiting for a reply, the abbot entered the room, closing the door behind him. Benedikta sat on the bed, mortified. Outside, the bells had started to ring.

"After your hasty departure, the superintendent told me about the poor Madame de Bouillon whose children were incurably ill. I was understandably quite surprised!" Bonenmayr said, starting to pace. "I asked myself why a woman from Landsberg, wife of a deceased wine merchant, whose brother had died in Altenstadt, had suddenly come up with such a story." He turned to Benedikta. "Or are you perhaps this Madame de Bouillon, after all, and you lied to *me,* then? Speak up!"

Benedikta could only shake her head silently.

"Your Excellency, let me explain—" Simon started to say, only to be interrupted by Bonenmayr.

"My astonishment changed to distrust when, half an hour ago, the remains of Saint Felicianus were desecrated in a manner more diabolical than anything the world has ever seen!" The abbot shook his head as if he had just looked down into the jaws of hell. "The desecration of the very remains that your loyal companion, Madame Bouillon, wanted to view this morning. What an astonishing coincidence!" Bonenmayr looked from one to the other. "So tell me now, what is going on here? Speak up before I forget that our dear Savior preached love and forgiveness!"

Simon swallowed. Frantically, he tried to think how to dig

himself out of this trap. Downstairs the Rottenbuch bailiffs were no doubt waiting to drag him off to the dungeon. He knew what would follow. It was as inevitable as the *amen* in church — namely, torture and an execution that would be the equal in every respect to what was in store for Hans Scheller. Desecration of relics! The hangman would probably rip open their stomachs, pull out their guts for all to see, and then burn them alive.

At the same moment, it occurred to Simon that the hangman would be none other than Jakob Kuisl! Ever since the death of the old Rottenbuch executioner, this district fell under his jurisdiction. Kuisl would look at them both with sad, empty eyes; shake his head, perhaps; then stuff them into an animal hide like slaughterhouse waste and drag them off to be burned.

And Magdalena would stand by and watch . . .

But perhaps there was a way out, after all. The medicus decided to lay all his cards on the table. He looked over at Benedikta, who was still sitting on the bed. She nodded almost imperceptibly.

"It's not what you think," he began. "This woman here is really the sister of Andreas Koppmeyer. Her brother discovered something that probably cost him his life . . ." Then Simon told the Steingaden abbot the entire story. He started with the death of the Altenstadt priest, then the crypt and the riddles, and his suspicion they were on the trail of the fabulous Templar treasure. He poured his heart out and put his future in the abbot's hands.

Bonenmayr sat down on the only stool in the room, listening attentively while Simon told his story. When Simon had finished, the abbot remained silent for a long time. Outside, the bells were still tolling.

Finally Bonenmayr turned to the medicus. "Riddles pointing to a treasure that people have been looking for centuries . . ." He shook his head. "Simon, either you are crazy or that is the greatest lie that a convicted heretic ever told."

"It's all true!" Simon cried. "So help me God!" As proof, he picked the sword up from the bed and handed it to Bonenmayr, who ran his finger across the blade, examining the inscription.

"*Heredium in baptistae sepulcro* . . ." he murmured. "*The heritage in the grave of the baptist* . . ."

He looked up. "That doesn't prove a thing. An epigraph on a sword, nothing more. Besides, who can prove this is, in fact, the sword of Saint Felicianus? It could be your own."

"Ask Michael Piscator!" Benedikta chimed in. "He'll verify that this is the sword from the coffin!"

"To do that, I'd have to hand you over to the Augustinian monks," he said. "Desecration of relics is one of the worst crimes again Christianity. They'll skin you alive— "

"I have a proposal," Simon interjected. "We'll work together to find this treasure! If we succeed, that will be the proof we're not lying. We'll donate all the money to the monastery in Steingaden, and nobody will ever find out who desecrated the bones of Saint Felicianus."

Augustin Bonenmayr frowned. "I'm supposed to make a pact with heretics and the defilers of holy relics?"

"For the good of the church!" Simon replied. "After all, you have nothing to lose. If we don't find the treasure, you can still turn us in."

The abbot thought it over a long time. Outside, they could hear church bells ringing and shouts from far off. Evidently, the people of Rottenbuch still believed the devil was afoot in the monastery.

I hope they don't look for him here in the inn, Simon thought anxiously.

Finally, Bonenmayr cleared his throat. "Very well, then. I'll take the gamble. Under one condition."

"Whatever you say," replied Simon.

"Beginning now, the two of you will be in my custody. Here in Rottenbuch, you're no longer safe, anyway. Brother Michael is not stupid. He'll soon have people out searching for a French lady and her companion. Therefore, we'll return to Steingaden at once." He took the sword and opened the door. Only now did Simon see two burly looking monks who had been waiting outside. Noticing the look on Simon's face, the abbot smiled. "Brother Johannes and Brother Lothar," he said, introducing the two. "Both are novitiates who haven't yet taken their vows and thus haven't yet foresworn violence. They have many . . . experiences from before." He started down the stairs. "Or did you think I would enter the room of two wanted defilers of the church without protection?"

Simon and Benedikta followed the abbot, with the two grim monks close behind.

Outside, four black horses hitched to a covered sleigh awaited them. Simon noticed that someone had already hitched Benedikta's horse and his own to the rear of the sleigh. They would disappear without a trace. They took their places on padded seats alongside the silent monks and the abbot. The two huge novitiates stared impassively into the night, but Simon was certain that the two thugs dressed in monk's habits would attack fast and decisively at the mere hint of an escape.

A whip sounded and the four-in-hand set out. Just before the wagon disappeared around the corner, a figure appeared and jumped up onto the back. Silently, the person climbed onto the roof and lay down flat so the cold wind would meet no resistance.

12

THE EXECUTION WAS SET FOR TWELVE O'CLOCK noon sharp on Saturday.

Since the early morning hours, people had streamed into the city from surrounding towns. At market stalls around the square, vendors sold sausages dripping with fat and piping-hot mulled wine that made everyone's cheeks red and their eyes sparkle. A scissors grinder strolled down the Münzgasse with his whetstone, loudly proclaiming his services, and in the wooden booths hastily set up the night before, copper pots, clay bowls, and withered apples were displayed for sale. The air smelled of coal, horse sweat, and cow dung, which had been trodden underfoot. People laughed and chatted, and only occasionally did anyone cast a furtive eye in the direction of the dungeon, where watchmen stood guard.

Finally, at around eleven thirty, the death knell began—a high-pitched, plaintive sound—and the crowd fell silent. Now all eyes turned to the dungeon door, which opened with a loud grating sound and spewed out a small band of ragged figures.

People laughed and hooted, pointing at the slowly approaching line of prisoners. Was this pathetic group really the notorious

Scheller gang? The night before, one of the robbers had died of cold and exhaustion. The five remaining men didn't walk so much as they staggered, looking straight ahead, their filthy faces black and blue, their hands roped together. The two measures of wine to which each condemned man was entitled on his execution day had all been emptied in a few gulps, and the men were clearly having trouble walking upright. Accordingly, the confessions the priest had taken from them earlier that morning were slurred and halting.

Behind them came the robbers' wives. One carried a screaming infant in a sling on her back, while the other pushed a crying boy forward. The boy kept reaching for the hand of his drunken father, but the bailiffs pushed him away each time.

The hangman walked in front. Despite the cold, he wore only a leather waistcoat over a linen shirt and gloves that would be burned immediately after the execution. He dispensed with the usual wide-brimmed hat that day so that his long black hair and shaggy beard blew in the wind. In his right hand, Jakob Kuisl swung a long, heavy iron rod like a walking stick. It was this rod he would use in a little more than half an hour to break the bones of Hans Scheller, the robber chief.

The crowd jeered and threw snowballs, bones they'd been gnawing on, and moldy bread at the robbers. In the midst of the group was Hans Scheller. He appeared composed and carried his head high. Despite his wounds and bruises, there was something almost sublime about his gaze. People could sense that and tried to say things to frighten him.

"Hey, Scheller," one called out. "Are your bones aching from loafing around so much? They'll hurt even more in just a while!"

"Start with the legs! Kuisl, start with the legs! Then he won't be able to run away!"

The Schongauers laughed, but Jakob Kuisl paid them no mind. At six feet tall, he towered over them. When the crowd got too close, he swung the iron rod through the air as if he were chasing away some barking dogs.

In the market square, they were joined by the aldermen and the court clerk, Lechner, who would preside over the execution as the representative of the elector. He gazed over the ragged crowd of robbers, nodded to Jakob Kuisl, then together they moved through the Hof Gate and down the Altenstadt Road, along a noisy line of people winding through the snowy countryside.

Accompanied by a fiddle, a street musician improvised on an ancient melody. "*Scheller, Hans, Scheller, Hans, Just wait to feel Kuisl's batons . . . !*"

Arriving at the gallows, Johann Lechner looked approvingly at the broad area that had been cleared of snow. The hangman had done a thorough job in the last few days. Alongside the ten-foot-high platform where the convict was to be placed on the wheel, Kuisl had sunk three posts into the frozen ground, each with a crossbar so as to form a triangle. This is where the other four robbers would be hanged. In the front row, benches had been set up for the aldermen. The rest of the crowd would have to be content standing.

The death knell was still ringing. When everyone had arrived at the site, the clerk climbed the narrow stairway up to the wooden platform and held up a thin black wooden stick. Despite the large crowd, absolute silence reigned for a moment. The only thing audible was the ringing of the bell and the breaking of the stick.

Then Johann Lechner called out, "In the name of the power vested in me and as representative of His Noble Majesty Ferdinand Maria, I herewith announce that the execution can begin!"

The moment of silence was past, and the crowd howled. The robbers' wives ducked as snowballs started to fly again. They withdrew with the children behind the gallows, protected from the angry crowd by two bailiffs. With the exception of Hans Scheller's wife, the council had given all the women permission to bury their husbands, a concession made at the request of the hangman. In fact, Jakob Kuisl had the first rights to the men's clothing and bodies and could have made a tidy sum through the sale of human fat, hides, and four pairs of the thieves' thumbs.

The crowd was getting more and more agitated, surging against the makeshift roped-off area around the execution site. Jakob Kuisl looked into their foaming mouths contorted with hatred and their predatory eyes glazed from the hot mulled wine.

I'm looking into an abyss, he thought.

Snowballs and pieces of ice were still flying. A clump struck one of the robbers in the face so that his skin split open and bright-red blood trickled into the snow. The robber seemed oblivious to the pain after two mugs of wine. He staggered a bit, but even the bawling of his little son wouldn't bring him back to reality.

Johann Lechner took his place next to the wooden platform. "Let's go," he whispered in the hangman's ear, "the people want to see blood. If you don't hurry up, it will be yours they see."

Kuisl nodded. It wasn't uncommon for a crowd to lynch a hangman if the execution didn't go according to plan. If the executioner slipped up, if his blow missed the target, or if, in the excitement, he simply slaughtered the condemned men, he could be quickly strung up on the nearest tree. Or even on the gallows.

Jakob Kuisl clenched his fists and cracked his knuckles — his ritual at the start of every execution. Then he put on his gloves, walked to the gallows, and went to work.

The hanging of the four condemned robbers went quickly and silently. The hangman went about his task as if he were just roofing a house or constructing a table. He climbed up the gallows ladder with each of the condemned men, placed the noose around his neck, tied the rope to the crossbeam, climbed back down again, and pulled the ladder away.

The men wriggled around briefly, wet spots appeared on their trousers, then they swayed back and forth like scarecrows in the wind. Only the fourth robber writhed a bit longer, much to the Schongauers' amusement, but soon enough it was all over for him as well.

None of this was new to the crowd. They saw something like this at least once a year. But this was only the prologue; the main attraction was yet to come.

The hangman looked at Hans Scheller, who clenched his fists and nodded imperceptibly. Then Scheller climbed up the stairs to the wooden platform.

A drawn-out, ecstatic cry went through the crowd as Hans Scheller reached the top and turned around to scan the surrounding countryside—the mountains, the forests, the gentle hills. He closed his eyes briefly and breathed in the cold January air.

There are worse places to die, the hangman thought. *A battlefield, for example.*

With the iron rod in hand, Kuisl now stepped onto the wooden platform and motioned for Scheller to lie down. In one corner lay a heavy wagon wheel encased in iron, which the robber chief would be bound to later. Wooden wedges were set on the floor of the platform at regular intervals so that Scheller's limbs wouldn't lie flat and would break more easily. The hangman would begin with the lower part of the legs, then slowly work his way up. The last blow to the cervical vertebra was the so-called coup de grâce. For especially abhorrent crimes, this blow was avoided and the condemned man left on the wheel to die out in the open.

"One moment, Kuisl," Hans Scheller said to Kuisl up on the platform. "I want to thank you for—"

The hangman waved him off. "Never mind. Take the poison and keep your mouth shut."

Scheller shook his head. "There's something else you ought to know. When we surprised those three other highwaymen, I didn't just find the perfume, but something else, too. I had forgotten, but it came to me again last night."

The executioner turned away from Scheller and looked down at the surging crowd. The people were getting impatient.

"Hey, Kuisl, what's wrong up there?" some of them shouted. "You're supposed to break his bones, not hear his confession!"

The first pieces of ice struck the hangman. Jakob Kuisl wiped the slush from his face and looked impatiently at the robber chief. "Spit it out, if it's bothering you, but make it quick."

Hans Scheller told the executioner what he'd found at the highwaymen's campfire. The hangman listened without batting an eye. For the people down below, it had to look like the robber chief was begging for mercy one last time. When he finished, Scheller bowed his head and whispered a short prayer.

"Thank you," Jakob Kuisl said softly. "If there is a just God, others will soon follow you. Now, put an end to it."

Hans Scheller opened his fist, put the little poison pill in his mouth, and bit down. There was a soft crunching sound, and he had just enough time to lie down before darkness raced upon him like a summer thunderstorm.

Magdalena pushed aside the silken altar cloth and shook out the contents of the leather bag—a colorful collection of black and red berries, little bouquets of herbs, and pressed blossoms. Even the bezoar had survived the long trip! Unfortunately, the little bag was damp and crushed from being transported under her skirt for so long, and the herbs inside didn't look very usable—some had even begun to take on a moldy sheen. Nevertheless, Magdalena hoped they would serve her purpose.

Basically, all she needed were two ingredients.

When she found the bag under the pew, she thought back on everything the Augsburg pharmacist Nepomuk Biermann had put together for her before Brother Jakobus appeared. Most of these ingredients she had been able to put in her pockets, along with some herbs lying out on the counter for another customer. Magdalena tried to remember which plants Biermann had already packed in the bag for her.

Ergot, artemisia, St. John's wort, daphne, belladona, and thorn apple . . .

Belladona and thorn apple.

A few moments later, she found the small dried berries between two little bunches of herbs. Small and deadly. She grinned. Both belladonna and thorn apple were known among midwives and hangmen as medicines, but also as poisons that could bring swift and certain death. Possession alone was a punishable offense, as they could allegedly be used to make a salve that Satan's playmates used to coat their brooms. Magdalena didn't know if that was true, but she did know that both plants triggered nightmares and hallucinations. Presumably, anyone ingesting these herbs would actually be able to fly, and unfortunately dosage was a problem, particularly for thorn apple. After taking it, not just a few people took their last flight.

Magdalena thought of something Paracelsus had said more than a hundred years before.

The dosage makes the poison.

She nodded grimly. Brother Jakobus would get a dose that would send him flying straight to hell.

Magdalena picked out the dried belladonna berries and the thorn apple seeds, which reminded her a bit of black mouse droppings. She kept checking the door to see if Brother Jakobus was paying her an unannounced visit, but all was quiet.

When Magdalena had gotten everything together, she looked around for something she could use as a pestle. Her eye fell on a small bronze statue of Jesus standing on the altar. She turned it over and, using the Savior's head, crushed the berries and seeds to a dark-brown powder. The hangman's daughter was certain God would pardon her this sacrilege.

But would he also forgive her for murder?

Perhaps Brother Jakobus would not die, after all, but fall into a sort of rigid trance. She doubted that, though, given the dose she had in mind.

Standing on the altar was the communion chalice. Jakobus had gotten into the habit of celebrating Holy Communion once a day with Magdalena. At first she'd refused, but she finally shrugged and resigned herself to her fate. At mealtime the monk brought her nothing but bread, water, and a thin, tasteless porridge. The wine brightened her spirits at least, and she didn't want to irritate Jakobus unnecessarily. By now Magdalena was certain the monk was insane. His behavior had to have something to do with his disease, but whatever the case, he was unpredictable.

Keeping an eye on the door, Magdalena poured the powder into the wine, stirred it with her index finger, then wiped her hand off on the altar cloth. The potion contained ten belladonna and just as many thorn apple seeds. She hadn't dared use any more for fear Brother Jakobus would be able to taste the poison.

Finally, she knelt down in one of the pews, folded her hands in prayer, and waited.

Just as the noon bells rang, the door opened.

"I see you are praying, Magdalena. That is good, very good," Brother Jakobus said. "If you make your confession to God, it will be easier to drive the demons out of you."

Magdalena lowered her eyes. "I can feel the presence of God. Tell me, Brother Jakobus, may I receive Holy Communion again today?"

Jakobus smiled. "You may. But first let us pray."

Magdalena let the mumbled Latin words wash over her like a warm summer rain, awaiting anxiously the moment they would approach the altar. Would Jakob taste the poison? And if he did, how would he react?

Would he force her to drink the wine herself?

Finally, the prayer was over. They knelt before the altar, and

Brother Jakobus began the celebration of Holy Communion. Holding up the host and chalice, he mumbled the words of consecration.

"This is the cup of the new covenant in my blood, which is poured out for you and for many for the remission of sins. Do this in remembrance of me."

Putting the chalice to his lips, he drank deeply. Magdalena stared at him as if in a trance, watching as little drops ran down from the corners of his mouth, over his unshaven, pimply chin, and dripped onto the altar. Jakobus wiped his mouth and handed the chalice to Magdalena.

He hadn't noticed a thing.

The hangman's daughter looked into the cup and froze—the powder hadn't dissolved properly! A dark silt remained at the bottom, and besides that, Jakobus had drunk only half of the wine! Would the dose be enough just the same?

Magdalena smiled at the monk, took the cup, and acted as if she was about to sip it.

"You are so hesitant today, Hangman's Daughter," Jakobus said. "What is wrong with you?"

"I . . . I have a headache," Magdalena stammered, placing the chalice back on the altar. "The wine makes me tired. I need a clear head today."

"How so?"

"I wish to make my confession."

The monk looked both astonished and delighted. "Right now?"

Magdalena nodded. The idea came to her out of nowhere, but it was just what she needed. She needed to detain Jakobus in the chapel for at least half an hour. What good would it do if he collapsed after leaving her in this prison? If her plan didn't work, she'd slowly die of thirst and hunger down here, unnoticed and unheard, while the monk's corpse lay rotting outside the door.

"We have no confessional here," Jakobus said, "but that's not really necessary. I'll simply take your confession here in the pew."

He sat down so close to her that his violet perfume couldn't cover up the stench of his festering wounds.

"May God, who illumines our hearts, give you the true realization of your sins and of His mercy . . ." Brother Jakobus began.

Magdalena closed her eyes and concentrated. She hoped that enough sins would come to mind to last until the poison took effect.

"You pulled a fast one on me, Kuisl!" Johann Lechner shouted, jabbing his finger into the hangman's broad chest. "And not only on me! You've been messing with every single citizen of this town! You haven't heard the end of this!"

Jakob Kuisl, almost two heads taller than the angry clerk, looked down at Lechner, his arms folded. Nevertheless, when it came to anger and assertiveness, Lechner was any man's match. The clerk had ordered Kuisl to report to his office in the palace right after the execution. He was still beside himself over the fiasco of Hans Scheller's execution.

The robber chief hadn't made a sound up on the wooden platform, not even a faint cry, even though the hangman had broken every single bone in his body! Lechner had heard the cracking and splintering, and it was only at the end that the hangman crushed the prisoner's cervical vertebra. The crowd was furious. They had expected a bloody spectacle, and all they got was a bored hangman thrashing away at a lifeless body.

The clerk had been sitting right up in front in the first row and had thus seen the smirk on the lips of the robber chief. Scheller's eyes were closed as if he were asleep, and his extremities limp, almost relaxed. The condemned man had escaped his just punishment, and Lechner was certain the hangman had something to do with it.

"I can't prove anything right now," the clerk snapped, walking back to his desk, "but you can be sure I'll find out, and then God help you! I'll get the Augsburg hangman to come and put *you* on the wheel, and this time it will be done right!"

"Your Excellency, I don't know what you're talking about." Jakob Kuisl remained calm. Only someone looking very closely would have noticed a faint smile on his lips, little dimples hidden behind his thick beard. "Often, condemned men faint out of fear and pain. There's nothing I can do to change that."

"Nonsense, you gave him a drug. Admit it!" Lechner took a seat again behind his desk and was busily scribbling notes in a document in front of him with his goose-quill pen. "It's about time for me to take away your damned crucibles, potions, and salves. I can do that, you know." His voice suddenly sounded threatening. "You have no right to give people medical care. Only the physician can do that. In other cities, they would have long ago revoked your permission."

"Then I will no longer be able to brew the drink Your Excellency has ordered from me. I'll just have to take the opium poppy I have at home and throw it in the Lech."

"Oh, just stop!" The clerk seemed to have calmed down a bit. "I didn't mean it that way. Turn your attention to this fever going around, and put a stop to it. If you can do that, I'll let you sell love potions, toad eggs, and hangman's nooses to your heart's content. Now, beat it. I've got a lot to do!"

Kuisl bowed and disappeared silently through the low doorway. Lechner stared after him for a long time. What a stubborn old fool! He just couldn't see what was good for the city and what was not. The clerk rubbed his temples and again studied the letter he was holding in his hands, which had arrived that morning. It demanded once more that he do whatever was necessary to make sure the hangman minded his own business.

Lechner cursed softly. What did the writer of this letter want him to do—watch over Jakob Kuisl like a nursemaid? And who the hell did he think he was, anyway, giving orders in *Lechner*'s city? Lechner took orders from Munich, from the elector personally, or from the elector's representative, not from some church dignitary!

He picked up the envelope and looked at the seal of the church. Then he examined the inside of the envelope again. There were no coins in it, nor a promissory note like the last time.

He ripped the letter up into small pieces and tossed it in the fire. Let the gentleman pamper the hangman himself. He had more important things to do.

A short time later, Jakob Kuisl entered his house in the Tanners' Quarter. Anna Maria was sitting at the kitchen table, rubbing her eyes.

"What's the matter, woman?" the hangman asked. "Is it on account of the twins?" He placed his hand on her shoulder to comfort her, but suddenly he felt the effects of the alcohol and lack of sleep. "Pull yourself together. It's probably not the fever."

Anna Maria sighed. She'd been awakened again and again by the coughing of her two youngest children the night before and hadn't been able to sleep. But she, too, thought it was just a simple cold. She was worried less about the children than about her husband, who, as so often before executions, had been drinking far into the night, mumbling and cursing about the evil in the world and the wickedness of the people of Schongau in particular. Anna Maria knew that, at such times, there was nothing she could do to help him, so she had lain awake thinking of Magdalena.

Magdalena, her eldest, the apple of her eye, stubborn and unrestrained like her father, and still not back from Augsburg.

Sitting at the dinner table, she was so burdened by grief she couldn't eat a thing. She didn't touch the bread, and even her husband couldn't console her. Worry about her daughter made her look older than her forty years. The first strands of gray were beginning to show in the long black hair she'd been so proud of as a child and that she'd passed on to her daughter.

"It's been a week, and Magdalena still isn't back," she lamented to Jakob, whose hand was still resting on her shoulder. "Something's wrong."

"Oh, come now," the hangman grumbled. "I think she's just having a good time in Augsburg. When she gets home, we'll give her a good spanking and then everything will be all right."

Anna Maria brushed her husband's hand away and stood up abruptly. "I'm sure something's happened to her. A mother can feel these things." She gave the stool a quick kick, and it tipped over, landing with a crash in a corner. "And Lechner has you out in the forest hunting for robbers instead of looking after your daughter! Doesn't he have bailiffs to do that?"

Jakob Kuisl remained silent. When his wife got wound up, there was no stopping her. The simplest thing to do then was not to fight it, but just to let the storm pass. The hangman's wife could rage and wail for hours, but this time she quickly ran out of steam.

"It's bad enough that you hang and break people on the wheel for Lechner and his fat burgomasters," she shouted. "What a dirty job! Let those big shots bloody their own hands!"

Jakob Kuisl grinned. He loved his wife, even when she lost her temper. "At least I screwed things up for him with the Scheller execution." He poured himself a mug of light beer and emptied it in one gulp. "And as for Magdalena, don't worry. She knows how to take care of herself." He brushed the dark foam from his lips with the back of his broad, hairy hand. "In contrast to Simon. He's in real danger, and he doesn't even know it."

The hangman's wife snorted. "Stop talking like a smart-ass. How do you know that?"

Jakob Kuisl picked up a loaf of bread from the table and turned to leave. "I know it, that's all." Without turning around, he marched out into the snow. "I've got to save Simon from doing something really stupid. I at least owe him that."

The hangman stomped down to the bridge over the Lech, leaving his nagging wife behind.

"Isn't that nice!" she shouted as he left. "Go and save the fine gentleman, but don't give a damn about your daughter! Go to hell, you old fool!"

But Jakob Kuisl, who had disappeared in the drifting snow, didn't hear a word of what she said, his hangover pounding in his head with every step he took.

Cursing under his breath, he hoped he wasn't too late for the physician.

As Simon leaned over the colorful illustrated Bible, he knocked over his cup of coffee, and a brown flood surged across the walnut table onto the polished parquet floor.

"Damn!" he shouted. "I'm sorry, I'm probably getting tired."

"Don't curse," Augustin Bonenmayr scolded, looking at the physician through his pince-nez. "God punishes every vice, even the smallest—even if there's a good reason to curse. The Bible in front of you is worth many hundreds of guilders, so please handle it with great care."

Simon nodded and carefully wiped the spilled coffee from the table with a parchment full of notes he'd taken. Since early that morning, he and Benedikta had been sitting in the Steingaden Monastery library, which they'd visited on their first trip. Together, they studied the Bible quotations and descriptions of landmarks in the Priests' Corner, looking for the solution to the riddle they'd found in Rottenbuch. All around them, books, folios, and parchments were piled high on the tables they'd pushed together. Simon had even been able to get a closer look at Friedrich Wildgraf's sales deed, but so far they hadn't found anything to help in their search.

Augustin Bonenmayr kept coming back to the library to check on their progress. The last time he'd even done Simon the favor of having the kitchen brew a cup of coffee from the physician's supply of beans. But whereas the black brew usually spurred Simon's thinking, it didn't work this time.

The physician was also having trouble concentrating because the two monks, Lothar and Johannes, who were sent to guard them, didn't even once leave their posts at the library door. The Steingaden abbot had made good on his threat and didn't let Simon and Benedikta out of his sight. They'd traveled to Steingaden in complete darkness in the horse-drawn sled, then spent the rest of the night in two monks' cells, which were locked from the outside. Simon knew he and Benedikta would be regarded as nothing but church desecrators by the abbot until they had convinced him otherwise.

He had to solve this damned riddle, or they'd be condemned to death and drawn and quartered!

He returned once again to the words scribbled on the parchment in front of him.

Heredium in baptistae sepulcro . . .

"*The heritage in the grave of the baptist . . .*" he mumbled. "That doesn't help us very much. I've never heard of a grave of John the Baptist, have you?"

He turned to Augustin Bonenmayr, who was standing next to him, leaning over his shoulder. The abbot frowned.

"There are supposedly such places in the Holy Land, but—"

"That wouldn't help us, either," Benedikta interrupted.

"The treasure must be here in the Priests' Corner, not in the Holy Land. Is there any place around here that you could call 'the grave of the baptist'?"

August Bonenmayr thought for a minute. "There's no grave, no, just a few chapels and baptismal fonts dedicated to Saint John—every parish church has such things. So that can't be it."

Reaching for the sword in one corner of the room, he passed his fingers over the rusty inscription again. "Maybe there's a second clue concealed somewhere on the sword."

Simon shook his head in resignation. "I've examined the sword three times already. There's nothing else there—no inscription, no hidden compartment, and the handle isn't hollow. The solution must lie in this one inscription!" He sighed and rubbed his eyes. "I'm at my wit's end."

"Then I'll have to hand you over to the authorities in Rottenbuch," Bonenmayr replied, turning to the door. "Enough of these antics! I have more important things to do."

"Just a moment!" Benedikta said. "May I have one more look at the sword?"

The abbot hesitated before turning around and handing it to her. Once more, Benedikta examined each word closely.

"There's something strange here," she said. "The words aren't inscribed in typical fashion—there are such wide gaps between them."

Simon shrugged. "No doubt the inscription was intended to cover the length of the entire sword, so whoever wrote it just left wide intervals between the words."

"Possible," Benedikta replied. "But the width of the intervals varies. Why? Perhaps . . ." she hesitated before continuing. "Perhaps because something belongs in these empty spaces . . . ?"

Simon jumped up so suddenly that the cup of coffee nearly fell over again.

"Words!" he cried. "That's it! There are words missing in between. That's the solution, of course!" He sat down again, staring at his page of notes. "We just have to figure out where these missing words are . . ."

"I think we both know," Benedikta said softly. "We just don't want to consider that possibility."

Simon exhaled softly and pushed the parchment away. There was a long pause before he replied. "On the second sword, the one belonging to Saint Primus—that's where the other words are engraved. The last clue pointed to *both* saints, so the next clue is to be found on *both* swords. How could I be so stupid?"

Augustin Bonenmayr took the sword back from Benedikta. "There's not much chance you can check your hypothesis now," he said with regret. "The relics in Rottenbuch are probably better guarded now than the bones of the Three Kings in Cologne."

"You're right," Simon sighed. "But perhaps we can figure this out anyway now that we know every other word is missing." He took a long gulp of coffee, reached for the parchment and a goose quill, and wrote down the words from the first sword, this time with the ordinary spacing.

Heredium in baptistae sepulcro . . .

"Let's assume that *heredium* is the first word. That would mean that the *treasure* of something is *in* something that belongs to the baptist and has something to do with a *grave.*"

"The first connection is easy," Benedikta said. "It would probably be *heredium templorum*—in other words, *the heritage of the Templars.*"

Simon nodded. "Perhaps. But what is the connection with the baptist—and above all, which grave could it be referring to?"

Benedikta leaned forward to look at the lines. "The most famous grave in Christendom is the grave of our Savior," she mused. "Judging from the spacing between the words, the word after *sepulcro* could be *Christi.* But that doesn't help us either, because that grave is certainly not in the Priests' Corner—unless I've overlooked some important lines in the Bible . . . Your Excellency?"

Benedikta looked over at Augustin Bonenmayr. His face had suddenly paled and little drops of sweat stood out on his brow. He began to polish his pince-nez excitedly.

"What are you thinking?" Simon asked. "Have you ever heard of such a grave?"

"Tell us!" Benedikta cried.

The abbot continued polishing his glasses without looking up. "It may be a coincidence," he said, "but here, in Steingaden, there actually is a very old chapel modeled after the Church of the Holy Sepulchre in Jerusalem."

Simon felt his mouth going dry, and his heart started to pound. "And the name . . . What's the name of this chapel?" he whispered.

The abbot placed his pince-nez back on the bridge of his nose and stared at him attentively. "That's the strange thing," he said, playing with the golden signet ring on his finger. "It's called Saint John's Chapel, and it's right next door to our church."

Simon groaned loudly. St. John's Chapel! They had walked right past it that morning, never dreaming that the small, unimposing chapel might conceal a treasure! Once more, he went over in his mind the words engraved on the sword. He could finally make a guess at how the inscription might fit together with the words on the other sword.

He whispered the sentence in Latin. "*Heredium templorum in domu baptistae in sepulcro Christi.*"

The heritage . . . of the Templars . . . in the . . . house . . . of the baptist . . . in the . . . grave . . . of Christ.

The passage had to read something like that! The Templars' treasure was secured in St. John's Chapel, which was modeled after the Church of the Holy Sepulchre in Jerusalem. If you knew that the two inscriptions belonged together, the riddle was easy. Simon couldn't suppress a grin. How carefully Friedrich Wildgraf had constructed his riddle! The Templars' seal at the ruined castle in Peiting also showed two knights in armor on horseback.

Two riders, two swords—everything had been grouped in twos.

Simon jumped out of his chair and rushed to the door. They were very close to solving the riddle! Soon the Templars' treasure would be in his hands! The Steingaden abbot would release them; perhaps he would even give them a little money, a valuable brooch, a golden chalice . . . After all, they'd helped him solve the riddle, and . . .

Only now did he notice that Augustin Bonenmayr had made it to the door before he did.

"My compliments! You really did excellent work," the abbot said, smiling. His bloodshot eyes sparkled behind his polished eyeglasses as if he had just enjoyed a good joke. In his right hand, he was carrying the Templar's sword. "It's time I introduce you to a true servant—perhaps you've met before," he said, opening the door.

Simon was stunned. In front of them was a monk in a long black robe, the same monk from the Rottenbuch Monastery who, just the day before, had slit open the soldier like a bag of wine. He was wearing a scimitar on his belt and around his neck, a heavy golden cross.

"*Deus lo vult,*" Brother Nathanael whispered. "God himself led you here."

As the Steingaden abbot held out his hand to the black monk, Simon noticed that Bonenmayr's signet ring bore the same cross as the monk's chain.

A cross with two beams.

13

I SINNED, TOO, WHEN I STARED AT THAT HANDSOME fellow, Peter, who works on the Huber farm, and just last week, I drank the cream from the top of the milk . . . and . . . And when I was a kid, I once threw a piece of horse dung at old Berchtholdt, and I never confessed to that . . ."

Magdalena was struggling for words. She was slowly running out of sins, and Brother Jakobus still showed no reaction to the poisons. Sitting alongside her in the pew, he bowed his head and only occasionally nodded or murmured his "*Ego te absolvo.*"

The monk sat completely still with closed eyes, lost in his narrow little world, soaking up her confession like a dry sponge and not reacting.

"Also, a week ago last Sunday, I was dreaming in church and made eyes at Simon, and during the hymns, I just mouthed the words . . ."

The hangman's daughter continued confessing . . . on and on . . . But inwardly, she was cursing. Were the thorn apple seeds and dried belladonna too old? Had they lost their effect? Or did this monk simply have the constitution of a horse?

This was her last plan, and if it failed, she had no idea what to do. The monk kept nodding and mumbling his pious prayers.

"Dominus noster Jesus Christus te absolvat,
et ego auctoritate ipsius te absolvo . . ."

Suddenly, something seemed to be happening to Brother Jakobus. Little beads of sweat were forming on his brow, and he licked his dry lips. Then he started rubbing his legs together as if he were trying to smother a raging fire between them. Finally, he cast a glance at Magdalena that made her blood run cold. His eyes were huge black holes, his pupils so dilated that he looked like an old woman slathered with makeup. Saliva drooled down from the corner of his mouth, and he reached out to grab her thigh.

"Oh, Magdalena, the sins!" he whispered. "The sins are overwhelming me again. Help me, Holy Virgin Mary, help me to be strong in the face of sin!"

Magdalena pushed his hand away, but moments later it was back, his fingers crawling up her thigh like a fat spider, toward her breasts, and his whole body beginning to quiver.

"Oh, Magdalena! Demons are coming to get me! There are too many of them! They are touching me in unclean places, licking me, kissing me with their clammy lips, fondling my naked skin. Holy Mother of God, help me. *Help me!*"

With a loud cry, the monk leaped up and threw himself at her. Only at the last second was Magdalena able to jump away. He knocked over the pew, fell to the ground with it, and like a bull in heat, rubbed his thighs against the polished wood. When he stood up, Magdalena could see how his robe bulged out from the huge erection underneath. His eyes gleamed like those of an animal.

Magdalena took a few cautious steps back.

Damn, I should have used less belladonna and more of the thorn apple seeds! She cursed under her breath at her error. She should have known better! Both her father and the midwife Martha Stechlin had often used belladonna as an aphrodisiac, but Magdalena hadn't been expecting such a strong reaction. By now Jakobus was bathed in sweat, breathing heavily, and his words came haltingly.

"Magdalena . . . Is it really you? Your breasts . . . your white skin . . . I will follow you wherever you go . . ."

The monk smiled as large drops of sweat rolled down his pale face. He seemed like a completely different person to Magdalena now.

"The brothel in Augsburg . . ." he whispered. "I'll pay fat Agnes a lot of money to let you go. We'll go . . . far away. To Rome . . . to the West Indies . . . From now on, your body must belong to no one else . . . no one but me!"

With a hoarse cry, he flung himself at her. She was so spellbound by his words that his sudden attack caught her by surprise. Flying through the air like a whirling dervish, the monk knocked her to the ground. His thin groping fingers seemed to be everywhere at once: between her thighs, inside her bodice, forcing her to the ground while his mouth searched for her lips. Screaming, Magdalena turned her head from side to side, nearly fainting from the stench of his putrid flesh. She could now clearly see the festering wound that stretched from his chest up to his chin, a wet, putrid wound pressing against her breasts.

"Magdalena . . ." Jakobus panted. "The sin . . . the two of us . . . can . . . be . . . one . . ."

Suddenly, his whole body began to convulse as if a crowd of devils were shaking him—all of them at the same time. But as fast as the convulsions came on, they stopped, and now he simply lay on her like a dripping sack, his arms outstretched.

It was eerily silent in the vault, the only sound being Magdalena's own panting.

She hesitated a moment, then pushed the limp body off her

in disgust. Jakobus rolled to one side, coming to rest on his back, eyes staring straight up, a final ecstatic smile playing around his lips. A damp spot spread from his robe.

"You pig! You filthy pig!"

Magdalena struck out wildly at the man on the floor. As bright blood began flowing from his nose and mouth, she suddenly realized that Jakobus was probably dead.

Frantically, she searched his robe for the key, rushed to the door, and then down a long dark corridor. On and on she ran, her only thought being to flee from this man.

In the underground chapel, Brother Jakobus stared with a frozen grin up at the ceiling, where a few fat, naked cherubs danced to heavenly music that played just for him.

The hangman hurried along the quickest route to Rottenbuch, his head pounding. He avoided the main highway—the danger was too great that he would come upon people there who didn't feel too kindly toward him after the execution that morning. Kuisl knew he'd ruined the big party for all of them. For far lesser shortcomings, other executioners had been strung up from the nearest tree.

As he moved quickly along, he only briefly thought about Hans Scheller and the four accomplices whom he'd hanged. The Schongau executioner felt no remorse. Hanging was his job, and he did it as quickly and painlessly as possible. He knew that all five condemned men had killed people, and probably in a far more bestial manner than he did. Now they were all in a better place, and Kuisl had seen to it that they hadn't had to suffer unnecessarily. Breaking a convict on the wheel had always repelled him, and he gloated over how he'd been able to spoil the celebration for Johann Lechner and the Schongau patricians.

He plodded through the snowy forest on narrow paths, his wide-brimmed hat pulled far down over his face and his ragged coat wrapped tightly to protect him from the cold and the wind.

He walked purposefully, like a beast of prey following a scent. He'd learned in Schongau that Simon and his companion had set out in the direction of Rottenbuch around noon the previous day. The fact that they hadn't yet returned didn't necessarily mean anything, but he was worried.

Kuisl's worry grew when he arrived at the Rottenbuch Monastery. He noticed at once that something was wrong. The church portal was sealed with a heavy bolt and guarded by two grim-faced guards with halberds. On the square in front of the church, monks and workers stood around in small groups, talking softly. Only then did the hangman notice that nobody was working. Nobody was on the scaffolding, and none of the men here was holding a bucket of mortar or even a trowel in his hand. Walking by a few wildly gesticulating monks, he overheard what they were saying.

"I tell you it was the devil himself . . ."

"No, it was the Protestants. The war is starting all over again, and they are robbing the last of our church's treasures . . ."

"The devil or the Protestants, it's all the same! In any case, Judgment Day is close at hand."

Jakob Kuisl paused for a moment. He guessed that Simon and Benedikta had found lodging in Rottenbuch; perhaps someone there would know where they were.

He had success at the very first tavern he stopped at, right by the gate opening onto the square. After he had knocked several times, the door opened on a thick-necked, sweaty barkeeper with a belly like a beer keg. When Kuisl described the medicus and his companion, the heavy-set man looked at him suspiciously.

"A little dandy and a refined-looking redheaded lady, huh? What business do you have with them?"

Jakob Kuisl answered cautiously; the tavern keeper seemed to be hiding something. "I'm just looking for them, that's all. So what do you know? Were they here?"

The tavern keeper hesitated, then broke out into a grin. "I

know you; you're the hangman from Schongau. I didn't think it would happen so fast. Well, everyone here is talking about the two people who desecrated the church." He looked the hangman up and down. "Where's your sword, your ropes, and the tongs, heh? What will you do with them? Will they burn in Rottenbuch or back in Schongau?"

It dawned on Jakob Kuisl that Simon had to be in far greater difficulty than he'd feared. He decided to play along. "Tell me, did the two run off on you?" he grumbled. "You didn't help them get away, did you?"

The innkeeper turned as white as a ghost. "Oh no! I didn't do anything. I swear by the Virgin Mary, it's just as I told our venerable superintendent. The two of them left last night on the sled belonging to the Steingaden Monastery, and the abbot was with them!"

"The abbot?"

The innkeeper nodded emphatically. "Augustin Bonenmayr himself. I watched His Excellency come down the stairs with the two. Ha!" Again he grinned, this time so widely that the black stumps of his teeth protruded. "He's probably taking them to the hangman in Steingaden, and you'll be left all by yourself with your ropes and tongs! You'll miss out on a nice heap of change." He started to count on his short, fat fingers: "The tongs, the rack—they'll probably be hanged, broken on the wheel, and then burned. Or maybe boiled alive in oil? Let's see, that adds up to . . ."

But the hangman had long since stopped listening. He was already on the way to Steingaden.

Across the street from the tavern, two figures emerged from the shadow of a shed and started out in pursuit of Jakob Kuisl. The two men, dressed like mercenary foot soldiers from the Thirty Years' War, were more than just worried; for the first time in a long while, they were slightly panicked. Somehow the physician and the redhead had eluded them and they'd lost one of their men in the fight with that damned monk in black. And now their cover was blown! This hulk of a hangman seemed their last hope.

With wide-brimmed hats pulled far down over their faces, they mingled with the workmen and the Augustinian monks still lamenting their loss, following Jakob Kuisl down the busy street full of horse-drawn sleds and hand carts, toward the forest.

Perhaps he would lead them to their goal.

Augustin Bonenmayr closed the door and motioned for Simon to take a seat. The physician plumped down dejectedly on a stool, so shaken that he couldn't say another word and so wide-eyed with fright he could only stare at the dark monk, who was still leaning against the doorjamb playing with his dagger. A faint smile played across Nathanael's lips. His golden cross swayed gently back and forth like a pendulum.

The abbot of Steingaden sat across the table from Simon and Benedikta and folded his hands as if in prayer. With his pince-nez, gray hair, and pinched lips, he looked like a compassionate schoolteacher preparing to give his students a stern lecture even though he didn't really enjoy doing so.

"I am dreadfully sorry it had to turn out this way," he began. "But apparently, God selected you for this role." He removed the pince-nez and started polishing the glasses again without looking at either Simon or Benedikta. "You have, indeed, led us to the Templars' treasure, and all of Christendom will be eternally grateful to you for that. But you must understand that allowing you to live is too risky. The word must not get out that the treasure was in the hands of heretics for centuries. Also, the fact that we had to spill blood to obtain it is"—he looked at Brother Nathanael reproachfully—"well, more than regrettable. It wouldn't be good if something like this became public knowledge. All in all—"

"You knew the whole time!" Simon interrupted, having regained his voice. "From the very beginning, we were no more than your stupid flunkies whose job it was to find the treasure for you. You deliberately showed us the sales deed here in the monastery so we could draw our own conclusions!"

The abbot shrugged apologetically. "I knew that you were smart and curious, Simon Fronwieser. You found the entrance to the crypt along with the hangman, and you've proved on a number of occasions that you think faster than most people—like a puppy sniffing for a bone, you poke your nose in every corner. I admire that." Bonenmayr smiled benevolently before continuing. "When you came to Steingaden, I considered hiding the document from you, but then I thought, why shouldn't I let him dig for his bone? You never noticed them, but my colleagues were always nearby. Only the hangman was too dangerous for me, so I saw to it that he had other things to keep him busy."

Simon groaned. "So you told Lechner to send Kuisl out to look for robbers!"

"Not directly. But the result leaves nothing to be desired, does it?" The abbot peered contentedly through the crystal-clear lenses of his pince-nez. "The robbers were hanged, we have the treasure, and the city has earned a little from it in the process."

By now, Benedikta had clearly recovered from her fright as well. "Your visit to my brother's funeral . . ." she said, looking angrily at the abbot. "You were only there to see how far along we were in solving the riddle. You didn't give a damn about my brother!"

The abbot looked almost a bit sad. "That's not quite correct. The death of your brother was regrettable, as I said. I wanted to pay him my final respects. He deserved it," he said with a smile. "Besides, I thought I could divert Simon from what we were up to by making Koppmeyer's sister a principal suspect."

Benedikta jumped up as if she were going to seize the abbot by the throat. "You goddamned . . . !"

Nathanael drew his dagger, but Simon pulled her back down onto the chair before the monk could intervene.

"Your plot almost worked," the medicus said after making sure Benedikta had calmed down again. "For a time, I did, in fact, suspect Benedikta of murdering her brother. How could I suspect that the abbot of Steingaden was behind it all?"

Augustin Bonenmayr shook his head sadly. "The order to kill the priest of the Saint Lawrence Church came from Augsburg—from high up, not from me. When Andreas Koppmeyer stumbled upon the crypt during the church renovations, he wrote a letter to the bishop. That's how we learned the treasure had reappeared. I would have perhaps chosen another way, but the bishop considered it best to make sure there was absolute silence about it. Koppmeyer was a good priest, but unfortunately also a gossiper who knew too much. The danger that others might pick up the trail was simply too great. After all, Koppmeyer had already confided in his sister. You must understand, we had to put an end to this!"

"Who's behind all this?" Simon asked in a hoarse voice. "The bishop? Or are there others?"

Bonenmayr laughed softly. His eyes sparkled like cold little diamonds behind his pince-nez. "There are many of us, in all Christian countries, from simple monks right up to the bishop. Not even the Pope knows our names, yet our members sit in the uppermost ranks of the Vatican. We fight against the spread of heresy and save the treasures of Christianity from destruction. For far too long we have stood by and watched as the Lutherans, Calvinists, Zwinglians, Hussites, and all the rest of them defame our sacred places and desecrate our holy relics!" He leapt up, pacing in front of the shelves full of books and parchment scrolls. "These vermin! They keep citing the First Commandment, but in truth, they're nothing but a gang of criminals! Disciples of Satan who melt down consecrated gold objects to make coins, who trample our altars and burn the bones of our saints!" His face had turned bright red, and his glasses started to steam up. Bonenmayr closed his eyes, took a deep breath, and a smile passed over his lips again.

"The fact that we learned so suddenly of Christendom's greatest treasure through a simple village priest's letter is a sign that God wants us to go forth and do battle in the greatest of all holy wars. The treasure is here! Right before our eyes!" Bonenmayr stopped and raised his arms to heaven. "It will adorn this church, and crowds of pilgrims will once again come flocking to Steingaden! Right here in the Priests' Corner we will have a pilgrimage site to rival Santiago de Compostela! The bishop has already promised that at least a part of the treasure will be kept here."

Smiling broadly, he approached Simon and Benedikta with his hand extended in benediction.

"You've helped us find it again and bring it back into the bosom of the Church," he whispered. "For that we owe you eternal thanks. I am certain that God has set aside a very special place for you in heaven."

"You can just go to hell for all I care; I'm not ready to go to heaven yet!" Benedikta shouted, running to the door. She tore it open and stormed out, bumping right into the two stocky novitiates, who were still standing guard. Brother Nathanael's muscular fingers dug into her shoulder and pulled her back into the library. He pressed his dagger against her throat and a thin trickle of blood ran down her neck.

"Shall I . . . ?" Nathanael asked, but Bonenmayr shook his head.

"Not yet. First I want to have the treasure in hand. We'll leave them here in the library. The windows are too small for an escape, and the door has a strong lock. We'll take care of them later."

Simon made one more desperate attempt. "Listen, Your Excellency! You're making a grave error. We will be missed. Surely the Schongau hangman is already looking for us and— "

"The Schongau hangman?" Bonenmayr interrupted him, laughing softly. "I don't think so. No one knows you are here, and even if someone did . . ." He seemed to be thinking it over. "Who knows, perhaps I should hand you over to the Augustinians in Rottenbuch, and then this Kuisl can draw and quarter you and break you on the wheel—a just punishment for the destruction of the relics of Saint Felicianus, don't you think?"

"We can keep quiet!" Benedikta pleaded. "And as for the Templars' treasure, you can keep the money! We don't want it, anyway. There's too much blood on it."

"Money?" The Steingaden abbot looked at them in surprise. "Do you really think all we care about is money?" He shook his head dolefully. "I thought you were smarter than that. You disappoint me."

Still shaking his head, Bonenmayr left the library with Brother Nathanael. The door closed with a crash, leaving Simon and Benedikta to stare at the tall shelves of dusty books, folios, and parchments.

My grave, Simon thought.

Then he stopped to think about the meaning of Bonenmayr's last words.

Do you really think all we care about is money . . . ?

Simon could feel things coming together. He was sure he was holding all the pieces of the puzzle in his hands now, and all he had to do was put them together.

A site to rival Santiago de Compostela . . . Crowds of pilgrims will once again come flocking to Steingaden . . . the treasures of Christendom . . .

"Of course! That must be the solution!"

The physician jumped up and started searching for a book in what seemed like endless rows of shelves.

If he had to die, then at least he wanted to know why.

Shortly after leaving Rottenbuch, Jakob Kuisl sensed he was being followed. He turned off the broad road into a forest and took a small path known only to a few of the locals. Nevertheless, he wasn't alone.

It was that familiar feeling between his shoulder blades, plus a soft, recurring rustling he could hear in the branches and the dull thud of snow falling in clumps from pine trees that he hadn't even brushed up against. His instincts were now on high alert. The men behind him were good, but they weren't good enough.

Suddenly, the hangman veered off the path, disappearing into a withered thicket of blackberry bushes weighed down by snow. Before him, a deer path appeared that had not been visible from the outside. Kuisl hunkered down amid the bushes and became completely silent. His years of hiking through the forest looking for herbs or hunting game had taught him how to blend in with his environment. If the wind was right, he could wait for a deer to pass, then break its neck with one well-placed blow with the side of his hand.

A crackling in the bushes told him the men were approaching. They communicated without speaking; only the faint sound of their steps in the snow revealed that one was entering the thicket, while the other walked around to the other side. He'd be able to knock them off one at a time. The hangman grinned.

An advantage for me . . .

Kuisl reached for the larch-wood club he always carried with him and waited for the first man to approach. He finally saw him crawling along the deer path, looking intently in all directions with a loaded pistol in his hand. He was wearing a slouch hat decorated with feathers and a colorful jacket beneath a ragged overcoat, showing him to be a former mercenary foot soldier—a bearded war veteran, hardened through innumerable battles, with the strength and skill of a man who had learned the art of killing at a very young age, a man just like the one Kuisl used to be.

Kuisl waited until the soldier crawled past him, then hit him hard on the hand with the club.

The man was quick.

At the last moment, he must have noticed movement out of the corner of his eye and rolled to one side, cursing and pointing his pistol toward the hangman. A shot rang out. Though Jakob Kuisl could feel a burning sensation on his cheek, he had no time to think about it. Howling furiously, he charged the man, who tossed the useless pistol to one side and drew his dagger. In the thick underbrush, the mercenary couldn't swing his arm back far enough, so he lunged at the hangman a few times, then made a headlong dive out of the bush. Jakob Kuisl was able to give the man one more light blow with the club between the shoulder blades before the man completely disappeared.

The hangman cursed. He'd lost the element of surprise. Now both soldiers were standing in front of the bush, while he himself crouched in his hiding place like a wild animal at bay. He could hear the men outside panting, and he could make out their shapes amid the branches. A snapping sound told him that one of them was loading his crossbow, while the other seemed to be refilling his pistol with powder.

I've got to beat them to it, or they'll shoot me down like a mad dog . . .

Without further hesitation, Jakob Kuisl stormed out of the bushes, howling. With a bloodied face and a torn coat splattered with mud, he now looked every bit a threatened animal at bay. His wild screams petrified the men for a moment, long enough to give Kuisl the advantage. The man with the pistol hastily threw his weapon aside and reached for his sword. The other was unable to load the crossbow in time and an arrow flew with a loud twang, nailing the hangman's boot to the forest floor. Now Jakob Kuisl screamed even louder. He tore himself free and rammed the club into the pit of the first man's stomach, and the man dropped to the ground like a felled tree. Then he took a wide swing and brought the cudgel down on the man's head. There was a loud crack like a walnut being shelled.

Next he turned to the second man, who tried to hold him off with a sword. The weapon whizzed through the air as the man danced back and forth, bobbing and weaving, lunging and retreating. He managed to hit the hangman's arm and slit open his coat, but the hangman retreated in time. When the man thrust at him again, Kuisl ducked down and suddenly came up face to face with his attacker.

"You filthy dog, I've got you now."

The hangman punched his opponent in the mouth so hard that he collapsed like a bundle of dry wood.

Soon thereafter, when the man regained consciousness, he found himself tied up and with a pounding headache. Jakob Kuisl was sitting next to a little fire nearby, his head glowing in the red light of the flickering flames. Blood streamed down his right cheek while he sewed up the gunshot wound with clenched teeth.

When the hangman noticed the man looking over at him, he grinned. "It'll be some scar," he said, "but nothing compared to the scars *you'll* have if you don't come clean with me right away." He nodded in the direction of the campfire. In the flames, the man saw a huge double-edged hunting knife, its blade glowing red.

Then he decided to talk.

Magdalena ran from the subterranean chapel, up through a dark tunnel, until she came to a junction. Corridors at about shoulder height branched off to the left and the right, illuminated by flickering torches spaced at wide intervals in the darkness.

Where was she? Which corridor should she take?

On an impulse, she decided to go left. The corridor curved around, ending after only a few steps in a stone grotto. In the middle of the almost cubical space stood two sarcophagi. Here, too, burning torches were attached to the walls. The grave markers each depicted a knight in full armor holding a sword. Carefully, Magdalena approached the huge stone coffins.

Was she imprisoned now in another Templar tomb?

She didn't notice the marble tablet embedded in the foot of the tomb until she stubbed her toe on it. Cursing softly, she hopped around a few times in a circle. When the pain finally subsided, she struggled to translate the ornate, slightly archaic Latin on the tablet in front of her.

> Beneath this marker lie the precious remains of the exalted and mighty Princes of Bavaria, the father Guelph VI and his son Guelph VII, equal in virtue to his father.

Magdalena held her breath. She was evidently in the crypt of the Guelphs, the mighty family of noblemen who ruled over Bavaria long ago. That much she knew. Her prison, the chapel, had to be their shrine! But she had no idea where their tomb was. In Munich? In Nuremberg?

Perhaps . . . in Augsburg?

Only now did she notice the soft humming, murmuring, singing sound, similar to what she'd heard below the cathedral in Augsburg. After her eyes grew accustomed to the dark, she could make out a slight glimmer along the ceiling of the room. Light fell through the cracks in a rectangle at the same place the sound was coming from. Magdalena's heart began to pound. Only a few meters above her were people who could come to her aid! Monks, perhaps, who were singing a chorale, or attendees at a mass, who were singing a last hymn. She was about to shout out for help, but then she stopped short.

What if the group above her was just another gathering of those maniacs—a secret meeting of the order of murderers and fanatics headed by the bishop of Augsburg?

Magdalena decided to remain silent until she'd first examined the other passages.

When she got back to where the passageways crossed, she heard a different sound for the first time: a barely audible scraping and shuffling coming from the direction of the chapel, as if something were being dragged along the ground. Magdalena was startled. Was Brother Jakobus not dead, after all? Was his spirit, an avenging angel, coming to get her? The hangman's daughter tried to shake this off, just as she would a night of bad dreams.

You're seeing ghosts, that's all . . .

This time she took the right corridor. After a few turns, it led to a steep spiral staircase. Again she heard the shuffling sound behind her. She decided to pay no more attention to it and hurried up the stairway, sometimes two steps at a time.

The top of the staircase ended in front of a dirty wooden wall.

Had she reached a dead end? She stood still, listening. There was that sound again; now she could hear it quite clearly. Down below, something was crawling slowly up the staircase, dragging itself, pulling itself, panting like a large, heavy beast. Desperately, she pushed against the wooden wall. Behind it, she heard muffled voices. Should she knock? Cry for help?

Never before in her life had Magdalena experienced such fear. In front of her these deranged people were probably waiting for her, and behind her something was panting and dragging itself up the staircase. In her despair she crouched down against the wall, trying to make herself as small as possible, as if this might allow her to vanish into the wall.

There was a click.

The wall creaked and tipped forward, and Magdalena fell into the room behind it with a loud crash. Wood splinters and bricks of plaster came raining down from the ceiling.

When the dust finally cleared and Magdalena raised her head, she didn't know whether to laugh or cry.

"What in the world are you doing?"

Benedikta stared open-mouthed at Simon, who was walking down the endless rows of shelves, examining the great number of books in the monastery library.

"I'm looking for a book."

"Well, isn't that nice! The Steingaden abbot gives us the choice of being stabbed to death by his hoodlums or broken on the wheel by the Schongau executioner, and my dear medicus friend is looking for a book!"

Simon paused for a moment. "I'm not looking for just any book, but a particular, special one. I suspect that when we finally know what this abbot is actually looking for, we'll at least have the possibility . . . Ah, here it is!"

He pulled a large leather-bound volume from a lower shelf. "I knew that a Premonstratensian monastery would have a work like this. Now let's see if I was right . . ."

Benedikta looked over his shoulder with curiosity. "May I ask what you're looking for?"

Simon leafed through the pages quickly as he spoke. "This is a standard work about the history of the Holy Cross—the *De Sancta Cruce* by the Jesuit Francisco de Borja. There's another copy in Jakob Schreevogl's library. I'm sure in this book we'll find that . . ."

He continued leafing through the book until he got to a

smudged page depicting various types of crosses. Benedikta recognized the Byzantine cross, the St. Andrew's cross with its diagonal cross beams, and the Maltese cross with the eight points. Even the Templars' cross was there. At the very bottom, there was another cross that caused Benedikta to hold her breath.

The cross had two crossbeams.

The upper crossbeam was shorter than the lower one. It was the exact same cross that Brother Nathanael was wearing on a chain around his neck and the abbot of Steingaden on his signet ring.

"The cross of Caravaca," Simon whispered. "Also called the Spanish cross or the Patriarchal cross. The crossbeam at the top stands for the INRI inscription on the cross of Jesus. Worn by archbishops, it is said to have been brought down to earth from heaven by two angels during the war against the Moors."

Benedikta nodded excitedly. "It's clearly the sign of this strange order. But why?"

A broad smile spread across Simon's face. "Ah, now comes the interesting part! The original cross of Caravaca supposedly contains a sliver of wood from the True Cross—the cross on which Jesus was crucified. I asked myself why the order chose this particular symbol, and I came to the conclusion that there is only one possible explanation . . ."

"They're looking for the True Cross," Benedikta gasped. "Of course! The abbot and his disciples are looking for the cross of Christ, the greatest treasure in Christendom! Not gold, silver, or jewels, just a goddamn rotten old wooden cross." The disappointment showed in her face. "If I'm not mistaken, there are hundreds of slivers of wood floating around that were allegedly once part of the True Cross. Every other village church has one—you could build a city out of them! This rotten old cross is just one of many." She sighed. "We could have saved ourselves this wild goose chase."

Simon shook his head as he continued leafing through the

Jesuit's book, looking for something else. "I don't think so. I've seen this book once before in Schreevogl's library, and there's a certain page that keeps coming back to me. Look at this . . ." He pointed to a section containing a number of illustrations and then started reading in a hoarse voice. "*Helen, the mother of Emperor Constantine, found the Holy Cross and had it set up for viewing in Jerusalem, but the cross was stolen by the Sassanids and returned only many years later to the Holy City. Since that time, the cross was carried into every battle waged against the infidels, and a group was charged with protecting this mighty relic from being stolen again.*"

"The Templars!" Benedikta exclaimed. "The cross is the Templars' treasure!" She paused for a moment. "But why do you think our cross is the real one? It could be just two more rotten beams of wood like all the other fake crosses."

Simon turned to the next page, which displayed a colorful image of two knights on horseback riding into battle, preceded by a person carrying a huge cross. The medicus pointed at the picture.

"The battle of Hattin," he whispered. "The cross was there as well. In that battle in the year 1187, the Saracen Prince Saladin vanquished the army of the Crusaders. Ten thousand Christians died, including hundreds of Templars. The prisoners were skinned alive—"

A pounding sounded from somewhere. Simon paused for a moment, but then the noise stopped. After a moment of hesitation, he continued.

"The battle of Hattin was the beginning of the end for the Crusaders. In the same year, Jerusalem fell to invaders. But worst of all, the True Cross was lost in this battle! It was believed that several Templars escaped with the cross and buried it in the sand so it could be retrieved later. But it was never found again."

"And do you believe it was the Templars who hid the cross at that time?" Benedikta asked.

"I don't just believe it; I know it." Simon grinned. "For days,

I've been trying to remember where I've seen the name of the German Temple Master Friedrich Wildgraf before. But while we were talking about the Holy Cross, it all came back to me."

"Well?" Benedikta asked. "Tell me!"

With a look of satisfaction, Simon closed the huge book and, from under his jacket, took out the little book about the Templars he'd borrowed from Jakob Schreevogl. "The battle of Hattin is also mentioned in this book by Wilhelm von Selling," he whispered, looking through the book until he found a soiled page full of scribbled notes. "There's a note in the margins mentioning several warriors from that battle that I didn't pay too much attention to at first. Just as in every army today there is a standard flag bearer, there was one person who carried the Holy Cross into battle for the Templars." He grinned and deliberately paused a moment before continuing.

"In the battle of Hattin that person was none other than a certain *Carolus Wildgraf.* I'll bet anything that Friedrich Wildgraf was a direct descendant of the person who carried the Holy Cross back then."

A brief moment later, the shelf above them gave way, sending a jumble of books cascading down on them. A particularly thick volume hit Simon on the forehead, and he fell to the ground. More books tumbled down until the whole world around them comprised nothing but ink and letters.

Magdalena stumbled through the hole that had opened up, rushing forward with outstretched arms, not knowing where she was headed. She could hear cracking, banging, and the muffled sound of falling objects. When she opened her eyes again, she saw a large roomful of books with shelves reaching almost to the ceiling. The wall behind the shelves had tipped forward along with the contents of the shelves, freeing up an opening behind it. Thick clouds of dust gradually settled on the floor, and behind them, a mountain of fallen books materialized in the middle of the room.

And then the mountain moved.

Ready for the worst, Magdalena picked up the heaviest volume she could find. Plato's *Symposium* would send whoever came creeping out of that pile of books to kingdom come.

Two heads pushed through the pile. Magdalena closed her eyes, then opened them again.

I'm dreaming. It's all a dream . . .

Before her, she saw Benedikta and an ashen-faced Simon trying to extricate themselves from the mountain of books. Blood trickled down the medicus's forehead. Covered in dust, plaster, and shreds of parchment, the two looked like revenants from the underworld.

The *Symposium* slipped from Magdalena's hands, her knees became weak, and she had to steady herself against one of the shelves. When Simon finally noticed her in the gaping hole, his jaw dropped.

For a long time no one said a word.

"You . . . ?" Simon finally managed to say.

Magdalena struggled to stand up straight, looked angrily at the two sitting in the mountain of books, then folded her arms.

"Yes, me. And just what are you doing here with this *woman*?"

Magdalena had survived imprisonment, poison, and a crazy monk; she had fled through dark passageways and been carted around in a coffin as a living corpse. Over the past few days, her life had come apart at the seams. But of all the things that had happened to her recently, seeing Simon in front of her, stumbling around and covered with scraps of parchment, had to be the limit. She forgot all the frightening things she had been through and directed all of her anger at the medicus and Benedikta.

"I just want to know what the two of you are doing here!"

she shouted. "Just *once* I leave town, and here you are cavorting behind my back with this hussy from Landsberg!"

"Magdalena," Simon said as softly and calmly as possible. "Benedikta is no hussy, and we're not cavorting around, either. Quite the opposite. We're locked up here in the Steingaden library for having defiled sacred relics, and we're about to be either stabbed to death or broken on the wheel by your father. So would you please tell me now what you're doing here?"

As Simon's voice got louder and louder, Magdalena stared at him wide-eyed, only slowly coming to a realization about what was going on.

"The . . . library in Steingaden, you say?"

Benedikta nodded. "We're being held hostage in the Steingaden Monastery. But now," she added, pointing to the opening behind Magdalena, "it appears we have at least one way out, and as fast as we can we ought to—"

"Just a moment," Simon interrupted. "Can't you see she needs some rest? Besides, she needs to tell us what's on the other side."

The medicus walked over to Magdalena and squeezed her hand. He could feel her pulse racing, her whole body shaking. Only slowly did the trembling subside.

The hangman's daughter dropped down on a pile of books and took a few deep breaths. Then she began her story.

14

JAKOB KUISL STRODE WITH GREAT HASTE TOWARD the monastery. The soldier had quickly confessed, so torturing him with the red-hot hunting knife hadn't been necessary. Instead, he branded his cheek with an image of the gallows, gave him a kick in the butt, and sent him packing. He left the soldier with the smashed skull behind as food for the animals.

Kuisl kept thinking about what the man had told him — his voice cracking and eyes wide open in fear — as the two sat around the fire. The hangman had had everything figured out anyway ever since he'd heard the report from Burgomaster Semer, plus what the head of the Scheller gang told him. Some details had been a bit hazy, but now it all formed a clear picture. He began to run. Simon was in danger; he'd have to warn that brash young medicus as fast as possible! He hoped it wasn't too late.

As he raced past some bundled-up travelers stranded on the narrow road with a cart stuck in the snow, he thought only of what might have transpired in Rottenbuch and what role Simon and Benedikta might have played in it. How had the abbot been able to take them along? Rottenbuch was not part of the Premonstratensian district. If the medicus and the Landsberg woman had been guilty of something there, they'd have to stay there until a trial took place. Apparently, this Bonenmayr had enough influence to do whatever he wanted.

When Kuisl finally emerged from the forest at the Steingaden Monastery, dusk was already descending and snow was falling in heavy, soft flakes from the darkening sky. Here, too, as in Rottenbuch, towering, icy scaffolding and pulleys were everywhere, as well as excavations blanketed in waist-deep snow. Deep-throated bells announced evening prayers, and here and there Premonstratensian monks hurried past on their way to vespers, almost invisible in their white tunics in the driving snow.

It seemed that construction work had been suspended several days ago due to the huge snowstorm. Kuisl glanced at the unfinished roof beams of the future inn and surmised that Simon and Benedikta had no doubt sought shelter in the monastery next door. He decided to knock on the main door in the hopes of learning something from the cellarer.

As Kuisl walked toward the multistoried, whitewashed building, a door opened in a wing just a few steps in front of him. A group of people came out, but it was hard to make out anyone in the heavy snowfall.

The hangman stopped at a distance to allow the procession to pass by. He strained and squinted in the fading light, but still had trouble seeing who they were. The person in front appeared to be Augustin Bonenmayr, recognizable as an abbot by his purple robe. Unlike the others, he wore a white hat, which he gripped tightly in the wind. The two broad-shouldered monks following him were also dressed in white, like all the Premonstratensians, but the third wore a black habit and hood. His strides were light and springy, and though he was a small man, his musculature was visible through the robe. The way he moved while constantly looking around reminded Jakob Kuisl of a ferret.

A very bad, dangerous ferret, he thought.

The hangman's experience as a soldier and warrior told him this man hadn't spent his life just praying and copying manuscripts.

Jakob Kuisl was just a few steps away from them when the dark monk turned abruptly to the abbot and said in a harsh voice, "We should have gotten rid of them. This medicus is a clever fellow who can always weasel his way out of every situation. And that hussy—"

"Silence!" Augustin Bonenmayr interrupted. "Make room in your heart for Christendom's greatest treasure. In mere moments, we will stand before it. Everything else can wait."

Kuisl was startled. He knew the voice of this monk! He had heard it only briefly back in the crypt at the St. Lawrence Church, but he couldn't forget the strange foreign accent and the hoarse panting. A few moments had been enough to burn the sound of that voice into his memory forever.

Kuisl tried to make himself as inconspicuous as possible. He ducked behind a small snowdrift, but he was a big man and his hat stuck out over the drift. Suddenly, the dark monk turned in his direction. He stopped in his tracks and stared intently through the falling snow straight ahead. Slowly, the hangman turned to one side, hoping it was as hard for the monk to see in the snowfall as it was for him. The sound of footsteps in the snow receded, and the murmur of voices became fainter until finally dying away. Kuisl waited a moment, then set out after the group. By now his overcoat was covered in a thin layer of snow, so the monks didn't notice the almost invisible colossus who followed them silently in the falling darkness.

After Magdalena had finished telling her story, they all grew quiet for a moment.

"The bishop of Augsburg is the leader of a secret order that will stop at nothing to steal the treasures of the church!" Simon shook his head. "And right at his side the abbot of Steingaden. No court of law in the world would ever believe this!" He gazed through the barred window; night was falling. "In any case, we don't have much time. We can assume that Bonenmayr is already in Saint John's Chapel to see the fruition of his life's dream. And after that, the dark monk won't waste any time getting rid of us." He quickly summarized for Magdalena what they'd learned, then pointed to the stone archway that had opened up when the wall of books collapsed.

"We can assume it's an old secret passageway leading from the monastery down into the Guelphs' tomb," he said. "It obviously hasn't been used for a long time. There must be another way in, or this monk wouldn't have been able to bring you something to eat every day." He looked at Magdalena and pointed at the entrance. "And do you think something is lurking around down there, lying in wait for us?"

Magdalena nodded, glancing again at the opening from which cold, moldy air streamed into the room. All that could be seen from the library were a few steps of a winding staircase and then nothing but darkness.

"Even if it's the devil himself prowling around down there," said Benedikta, "we still have to go. There's no other way out!" She pulled a little pistol out of her dress and began filling the weapon with powder. "At least the pious abbot did not search my skirt, so we still have one more shot." She grinned and pointed the loaded pistol toward Magdalena before placing it back inside her clothing.

Simon walked over to the top of the spiral staircase. "Aren't there any torches down there? I can't see a thing."

Magdalena walked over to join him. "It's strange," she murmured. "From here you should be able to see at least one torch. They're attached to the walls at regular intervals. Someone must have extinguished them . . ."

"Or the wind blew them out," Benedikta said, looking around. "In any case, we should take a few of these along," she said, reaching for a few especially large books nearby.

"What are you doing?" Simon cried. "Are you really going to—"

"These parchments are centuries old. They'll burn like the dickens," Benedikta interrupted. "If you grab them by the cover, they make wonderful torches."

Horrified, Simon pointed at the book in Benedikta's hand. "But those are the *Confessions of Saint Augustine!* The book includes commentaries! It's a sin to burn a book like that!"

Benedikta tossed the thick book to him and stuffed four others under her left arm. "That should be enough. Of course, if you want to, you can grope around in the dark and let someone creep up on you and slit your throat from behind." Heading for the entrance, she added, "Now, follow me. Before the abbot comes back."

She took one more step and disappeared in the darkness.

Augustin Bonenmayr's nerves were shot. Again and again, he removed the pince-nez from his nose and polished them frantically.

"It must be here! Keep looking!" He kept blinking, as if that might help him see in the darkness. "The cross lies somewhere here at our feet!"

Along with Brother Nathanael and the two novitiates, Johannes and Lothar, the abbot had hurried over from the library to St. John's Chapel in search of a clue, a secret chamber, anything that might lead them to the True Cross. For an hour they had been tapping on the walls, scanning for some kind of sign, but all they had seen so far were cold, bare walls. Augustin Bonenmayr looked around again, trying to figure out whether they had overlooked something.

The chapel was a small room built of sandstone blocks with

a small altar to Mary on the east side. Modeled after the Church of the Holy Sepulchre in Jerusalem, its circular form gave it the appearance of a stout, fortified tower from the outside. Above the portal hung a painting of Christ standing between Mary and John; a recumbent lion crouched on a stone slab on each side of the door.

Otherwise, the room was bare—and empty. Bonenmayr mumbled a soft curse.

Under his supervision, the monks had already tried to move the holy figures and pry up the large slabs beneath the lions. They had tapped along the walls searching for secret entrances and examined the flooring for trapdoors. They'd even checked underneath the vaulted chapel roof.

Now they were starting over again.

The abbot shouted and cursed, he kicked the altar, but all to no avail. St. John's Chapel was not divulging its secrets.

"The treasure of the Templars in the house of the baptist in the grave of Christ," Bonenmayr whispered, agitated. "The solution to the riddle is here! It must be here in the Chapel of Saint John! These accursed Templars . . ." He bit his lips and uttered a deep sigh. "We'll dig up the floor," he said finally.

Brother Johannes stopped tapping the walls and stared wide-eyed at the abbot. "But, Your Eminence!" he cried. "This is a holy place!"

"This is a hiding place for the damned Templars!" Bonenmayr shouted. "I won't let them trifle with me any longer, not on my own property! We're going to dig right here! Go and get the pickaxes—at once!"

Simon and Magdalena followed Benedikta down the steep winding staircase into the darkness. At the very next turn, Simon knew that Magdalena's suspicions had been right. He reached for the tip of one of the torches; it was still hot. Someone must have extinguished it just moments ago.

The opening in the wall above them was now no more than a faint glow, and even that disappeared after the next turn. Benedikta stopped, pulled out a box of matches, and soon they saw a flickering light in front of them—she'd set fire to one of the books. Simon felt a twinge in his heart; he didn't want to know which precious book had just met a fiery death. Aristotle? Thomas Aquinas? Descartes? He looked uneasily at the *Confessions of Saint Augustine* he held in his hands. He couldn't yet bring himself to set fire to the masterpiece.

Holding the burning book, Benedikta led the way. At the bottom of the staircase, the corridor extended to the intersection where, not even an hour ago, Magdalena had stood looking for a way out.

"Which way?" Benedikta whispered.

Magdalena looked around. "The chapel where I was held prisoner is to the left. The way straight ahead leads to the crypt of the Guelphs, but there's no way out there, so let's go right."

Now Magdalena, too, had set fire to a book and, along with Benedikta, entered a corridor even narrower than the others. In the flickering light, Simon imagined he was looking at two sisters—the older one wearing a finely woven fur overcoat, her red hair up in a bun, and the other, with shaggy black hair, wearing a dress tattered from her long imprisonment, her eyes fiery with youth. Both had the same determined look on their faces.

Magdalena seemed to have regained her old self-confidence now, casting a sideward glance at Benedikta. "In that black coat you're slower than a fat bear in hibernation," she whispered. "You'd better let me go first. I'm younger and quicker."

"*Petite garce!*" Benedikta hissed. "I hardly believe you could save us if we're ambushed in here. You forget I have our only weapon." She pulled out the pistol and stepped back a pace.

The hangman's daughter scoffed at the little handgun. "That's just a woman's toy. You couldn't shoot a chicken off the top of the manure pile with that little thing. You should see the weapons my father brought back from the war."

"But your father is unfortunately not here to protect his dear little girl!"

Simon lifted his hands, pleading. "Ladies, please! Let's just get out of here first, and then you'll have plenty of time to bash each other's heads in."

Benedikta cast Simon a scornful gaze. "For once, you're right. We've wasted enough time with this." Then she quietly stepped out in front of the little group.

Magdalena and Simon followed her down the narrow passageway. Extinguished torches hung in rusty sconces along the wall at regular intervals; in one corner they found an empty black pitch bucket no doubt used to prepare the torches. They passed a number of niches and small passages leading off on both sides, but they continued down the main corridor. At one point, Magdalena bumped into Benedikta, who had stopped suddenly at an intersection. Two corridors forked away from this spot, both the same size.

"And where now, Madame Smarty Pants?" the hangman's daughter whispered.

Benedikta held up her book, which had burned down about halfway. The flame guttered to the left with a thin trail of smoke.

"The passageway to the right seems to lead out," she said. "At least that's where the draft is coming from, so we should—"

She was interrupted by that shuffling, gasping sound. Now it was quite close, coming from a niche nearby. Or was it farther away? A clatter of little stones, then silence again.

Benedikta aimed her pistol into the darkness.

"Whoever or whatever you are, come out!" she cried. "I have a nice surprise for you here. Come and get it."

Someone giggled.

Simon and the two women held their breath. The giggling

echoed through the corridors, making it impossible to tell exactly where it was coming from.

Now came the sound of shoes shuffling over stone.

"Damn it, show your face!" Benedikta shouted. "You damn bastard, I'll cut your balls off! *Je te coupe les couilles, fils de pute!*"

Despite his fear, Simon was astonished that Benedikta could curse like a longshoreman. Where had she learned to talk that way? His thoughts were interrupted by a rasping, cracking voice coming from somewhere down the corridor.

"The demons, Magdalena. The demons. They have taken possession of me. They . . . are eating . . . consuming me . . . from inside . . . Can you see the demons, Magdalena?"

"Oh my God, it's Brother Jakobus!" Magdalena whispered. "He isn't dead yet!"

"Or perhaps he is," Benedikta replied. "This voice doesn't sound like it comes from . . . the living."

Simon could smell something now, at first just a faint odor, but then growing stronger and stronger. It was the pungent smell of burning tar, an acrid stench. It came from up ahead, riding on the draft of air. Now heavy, black, billowing clouds of smoke were drifting past them like thunderheads driven by a storm, and the voice was much louder, a rush of wind descending upon them.

"The demons, Magdalena. They . . . are consuming . . . me . . . Can you see them? *Can you see them?*"

As he spoke the last words, a small, flickering ball appeared on their right. It was rolling toward them, faster and faster, growing larger until it finally filled the entire passageway.

"Can you see them, Hangman's Daughter?"

Magdalena and the others were so terrified they couldn't move. Too late, they noticed that the fiery ball was the blazing monk's robe. The fire was consuming his habit, eating its way through to his body, a living torch racing toward them.

Then, like a fiery nightmare, Brother Jakobus threw himself upon them.

Like gravediggers, the monks pounded away with pickaxes on the chapel floor. Sweat poured down their faces as they hacked away at the floor slabs, smashing them to pieces, then digging them out with their shovels. Weathered memorial slabs, tiles decorated with crosses, inlaid mosaics—everything was pounded to rubble and tossed outside in a pile next to the church. Beneath the slabs they found nothing but dirt.

"Keep digging!" the abbot shouted. "Perhaps it's hidden somewhere in the ground! It *has* to be here!"

Breathing heavily, the monks went to work on the hard ground. The soil was full of little stones that made digging especially difficult. Despite the icy temperature, sweat stains formed on the monks' tunics, which were turning brown with dirt. The Premonstratensian monks groaned and moaned; they weren't accustomed to such hard work.

Brother Nathanael had assisted with the digging at first, but now he was standing alongside the abbot. The Dominican pointed to the pit in the ground, which got stonier as the monks continued to dig. "The medicus must have been mistaken. The cross isn't here!"

Frantically, Bonenmayr looked around the chapel, which appeared more and more like a pile of rubble. Where had they not yet dug? What had they forgotten? His gaze wandered to the only object not yet hacked to pieces.

The altar.

Brother Johannes noticed the abbot's gaze. "Your Eminence, not the altar!" he groaned. "It's sacred and—"

"Stop talking and give us a hand." Augustin Bonenmayr strode toward the large white block of stone, which was emblazoned with the relief of a simple cross. He yanked aside a dirty red velvet cloth covering the altar; then they all pushed against the stone block. The abbot gave orders in a loud voice. "One, two, three—now!"

With a loud grinding sound, the block tipped, then fell over. A cloud of dust formed, and after it settled, Bonenmayr looked down intently.

Bare earth.

So exhausted that they nearly fainted, the monks collapsed on the floor.

The abbot took a deep breath and sat down on the overturned altar. Sweat poured down over his eyeglasses so that he could only vaguely see. He removed the pince-nez and polished them.

He had forgotten something. What?

The solution to the riddle was correct—of that he was certain. If the solution was correct and he still couldn't find anything at the location, it could mean only one thing:

The place had changed.

His gaze wandered along the vaulted ceiling. All the way at the top, in the middle, he noticed the keystone had a number inscribed on it. Putting his glasses back on, he squinted to read what it said.

MDXI

Augustin Bonenmayr let out a little cry and clenched his fists. How could he be so stupid? The St. John's Chapel they were in was only built in 1511. This couldn't be the right place. The abbot knew from studying the centuries-old monastery records that there had been a St. John's Chapel in Steingaden before that.

But where . . .?

Bonenmayr closed his eyes and concentrated. After a while it all started coming back to him. Was it possible? Had the answer always been so close at hand?

A smile spread across his face.

"Put down the pickaxes!" he ordered. "We're going to look somewhere else!" He stomped out into the darkness. "And this time we'll find this damned cross, even if I have to burn this whole monastery to the ground!"

Immobilized with terror, Magdalena felt Brother Jakobus throw his whole weight against her and smelled the fire that had turned his robe into a gigantic torch. Desperately, she tried to push away his burning body, but his hands held her in a tight grip down on the ground. Out of the corner of her eye, she could see how long strings of a sticky, viscous substance were dripping down on her. Brother Jakobus must have taken pitch from the buckets in the corridor and rubbed it all over his body. The crackling heat from his tunic almost caused her to faint. The monk was looking directly into her face now. Fire had burned off his hair, eyebrows, and eyelashes, and all that was left were two deranged, glowing white eyes and a black hole that had once been his mouth from which a high-pitched, almost childlike cry emanated.

"Come back, Magdalena . . . !"

Frantically, Magdalena turned her head to one side and could see Benedikta waving her pistol toward the burning monk, trying to shoot without striking Magdalena, who was still pinned beneath him. The monk's robe had ripped apart and, in some places, was sticking to him, burning into his skin. Magdalena could feel the flames lick at her own clothing.

A shot echoed through the corridor. The bullet ricocheted off a rock right next to Magdalena, but Jakobus didn't let go and Magdalena could hear Benedikta cursing. The shot had missed.

The hangman's daughter was losing consciousness. The acrid smoke burned her lungs, and like an army of ants, a sharp pain ran down her leg where her dress had caught fire.

Once again the red hole in his scorched face opened up. "Maria Magdalena, do not leave me! Stay with— "

Augustine's *Confessions* struck Brother Jakobus on the side of the head like a brick. Simon delivered the heavy blow with both hands, then raised the heavy book again and again, pounding the charred body, flailing away even as the book caught fire.

A sooty, trembling hand reached up, seizing Simon's wrist and pulling him relentlessly to the ground. Simon stumbled, and in a flash, the burning monk had fallen upon him as well. With horror, Simon stared into the monk's face, which had congealed into a black lump, with only the whites of his eyes still ablaze. Charred fingers gripped Simon's neck, choking him.

My God, how can he still be alive?

The monk's face came closer and closer, his hands gripping him like glowing iron bars, cutting off his breath. His eyes bulged.

He's killing me . . . A dead man is killing me . . . Oh my—

Suddenly, a violent twitching ran through the monk's body, he stared off into space and, with a last soft hissing sound like a flame being extinguished, slowly tipped over, his mouth wide open in a muted cry. Then all went silent.

Behind the monk Magdalena stood holding in her right hand a shining silver object that dripped with blood. She looked at it with bewilderment, as if realizing only now she had stabbed the monk with it.

"A . . . letter opener," she said finally. "I took it from the library, thinking I might sometime be able to . . . use it." She threw it to the ground and ran her hands down her soot-stained dress.

Coughing, Simon stood up and eyed her. The hem of her skirt was torn, holes were burned into her bodice, and her thick black hair was singed in places. Her whole body trembled as she stared off into space. But then she seemed to pull herself together. Simon was proud to be in love with this girl.

She's a real Kuisl, he thought, *and nobody's ever going to intimidate her.*

Magdalena kicked aside the charred mass that had once been Brother Jakobus. "He had some illness that slowly made him lose his mind," she whispered. "What a horrible way to die . . ."

"Not any worse than what your father will do to me and the medicus when he burns us at the stake for desecration of holy relics," Benedikta said. "Now let's move along."

They were still standing at the intersection of the tunnels. Simon looked around in every direction. "Where shall we go?" he asked.

Benedikta looked to the right, thinking it over. "This monk brought Magdalena something to eat and drink from the monastery every day. Certainly, he was trying to flee there now as well, but changed his mind. So let's turn right."

They followed her through the narrow passageway. This led gradually upward, and they were soon standing before a huge wooden door.

Benedikta grinned and bowed slightly. "*Voilà,* the entrance to the monastery!" Then she pressed the door handle down.

It was locked.

She shook it a few times and finally pushed against it with all her weight. The door creaked and shook, but it wouldn't open.

"Are you crazy?" Simon hissed. "You'll wake up everyone in the monastery!"

Benedikta looked at him angrily. "Is that so? Do you have better idea of how to get out of here?"

"Let's first have a look at the other passageway," Magdalena interjected. "We can always come back here and try to beat the door down."

Benedikta nodded. "Not a bad suggestion, Little Hangman's Girl. Let's go!"

They ran back down the corridor to the intersection and

took the other tunnel. In contrast to the first, this one had a low ceiling and seemed to go on and on through the darkness. Simon still could not bring himself to set fire to any of these books. Destroying the *Confessions* was his limit. And so he followed the two women, who lit the way with the burning parchment pages. If he'd looked closer, he would have seen that Aristotle and St. Thomas Aquinas had just gone up in flames, but he really didn't want to know about that.

Finally, the corridor ended at a low door with rusty metal fittings. It looked much older than the door at the end of the other corridor. The door handle and lock were tarnished, and it seemed they hadn't been used in years.

"Well?" Benedikta asked, with a gesture inviting Simon to have a look for himself. "Would you like to try your luck this time?"

That was when they heard voices and the sound of someone approaching from the other side of the door.

The theater stood directly on the eastern wall surrounding the monastery complex. It was not yet complete, but it was easy to imagine how it would look some day. At the corners of the second story, gargoyles with demonic faces looked down from tower-like oriel windows. Above the main entrance was the monastery's coat of arms along with a relief of the comic and tragic masks.

Augustin Bonenmayr walked with such long, quick strides toward the building that the monks had difficulty keeping up. The theater was one of his most ambitious projects, one he had worked on a long time in order to gain the acceptance of his colleagues. Just like the Jesuits, the Steingaden abbot wanted to win converts to the true belief with light, music, and colorful scenery. The theater was a divine weapon in the struggle against the austere reformation, which was hostile to sensual feelings. It took a lot of imagination to realize Bonenmayr's dream of the divine theater.

Without slowing his pace, the abbot pushed open the double doors to the playhouse. The torches that the monks carried bathed the auditorium in a dim light; shadows danced over the bare walls and balconies. In front was a stage, almost ten feet high and constructed from spruce, and in front of that a deep orchestra pit opened up. In place of scenery, bundles of cloth and piles of boards lay around, and ropes and pulleys dangled from the unfinished ceiling.

Augustin Bonenmayr turned to his cohorts as he hurried up the narrow steps to the stage. "Faster! Good Lord, faster! We're almost there."

The abbot pushed aside a bundle of cloth and stepped to the middle of the stage, onto a wooden square in the floor, almost invisible from the auditorium. Then he pointed to one of the pulleys on the wall.

"The lever on the right!" he called out to Brother Johannes. "Pull it and lower the rope slowly."

As the others joined him on the square, Brother Johannes let out the rope, and the rattling, creaking platform moved downward.

"A trapdoor where the devil, the angels, or even the Savior himself can appear, or vanish," Bonenmayr explained to Brother Nathanael, who looked around approvingly. A dreamy look came over the abbot's face. "I've had pulleys installed everywhere. There will be scenery, curtains that can be rolled up and down, and even a cloud-making machine! Soon people will go out into the world after a performance here with the feeling they've met God! Paradise on earth, so to speak! *Ecce homo,* we are here . . ."

With a grinding sound, the platform came to rest on the stone floor of the cellar. The dark room they found themselves in seemed to encompass many niches and corners. Columns set at regular intervals supported the low ceiling, and weathered memorial slabs covered the walls and floor. The actual size of the vault was hard to estimate, as it was filled with moldy boxes, shelves, and trunks. A rotting statue of Mary leaned against the wall next to a pulley, and stone cherubs and gargoyles lay strewn around on the floor, worn by time, weather, and pigeon droppings. In the midst of all this were a few strange apparatuses whose functions were not immediately clear.

"We found this cellar during the construction on the playhouse," Bonenmayr said as Brother Lothar handed him a torch. "An old vaulted cellar that probably served as a hiding place during the Great War and was then forgotten. At first I thought about moving the graves to the cemetery and sealing the cellar up, but then I thought I could use it for the stage machinery and as a storeroom for the costumes. And now . . ." He stepped over to a grave marker. Running his hand over it, he whispered, "I feel we've almost reached our goal."

"And you think this is the old Saint John's Chapel?" Brother Nathanael asked skeptically. "How can you be so sure? The Steingaden Monastery is ancient, and this could just as well be any other forgotten crypt."

The abbot shook his head and pointed at the grave markers. "Just look at the inscriptions!" he whispered. "These are the graves of abbots and other religious dignitaries connected to the monastery. I've already taken a closer look at the dates of death, and the most recent entry is dated 1503. And the Saint John's Chapel alongside the church was not built until 1511—that's just eight years later. That can't be a coincidence! I'm certain we're standing in the crypt of the former Saint John's Chapel. In the years that war was raging in this country, it was simply forgotten." He started tapping on the grave slabs. "Now we must just find the entrance to the hiding place. I suggest—"

There was a soft creaking sound overhead, and the abbot stopped to listen. Then a thud followed, as if a heavy sack had fallen to the floor.

"Brother Johannes!" Bonenmayr cried out. "What in the world are you doing up there?"

The monk up above did not answer.

"Damn it, Johannes, I asked you a question!"

Again, silence.

The abbot turned to Brother Nathanael. "Please go up there and see what's going on. We have no time for such childish nonsense."

Nathanael nodded, clenching his dagger between his teeth, and climbed up the pulley rope to the stage.

Bonenmayr now inspected the plaques more closely. The reliefs depicted skulls, crossbones, occasionally a monk with his eyes closed and arms crossed, and Roman numerals indicating the year of death in each case.

Bonenmayr suddenly stopped in front of an especially weathered plaque.

"It's strange, but I've never seen this inscription before," he said, tapping his slender fingers against the plaque. "I have never heard of an abbot by this name." He bent down and examined the name again through his pince-nez. "And the dates can't be right, either."

He wiped the dust from the inscription so that the letters beneath the crossbones were easily legible.

H. Turris. CCXI.

"What does that mean?" Bonenmayr murmured. "Perhaps an honorable Horazio Turris, born 211 in the Year of Our Lord? A Roman officer who found his last resting place here?"

Brother Lothar nodded obsequiously. "It's just like you said, Your Eminence."

"You ass!" The abbot looked at the monk disdainfully. "This monastery is old, but not that old."

"Possibly the *M* for the number one thousand has simply been worn away," Brother Lothar quickly added, trying to correct his error. "Couldn't it be MCCXI—that is 1211 AD?"

The abbot thought about this for a bit and shook his head. "Then the other numbers would be worn as well. No, there's something behind all this. Quick! Give me your torch!"

The baffled monk watched as Bonenmayr took the torch and copied the letters of the inscription on the dust of the stone floor.

"*H. Turris. CCXI,*" the abbot mumbled, concentrating on the name and the year he'd scribbled beneath it. Suddenly an idea came to him. He started drawing the letters furiously in the dust, erasing them, writing them again.

Brother Lothar looked on, confused. "Your Excellency, what in the world—"

"Hold your tongue. Bring me some more light from the other torch over there," Bonenmayr grumbled. Silently the monk held up the torch Nathanael had left behind and watched as the abbot continued sketching and erasing the letters.

Finally Bonenmayr stopped. His face partly obscured in the shadows, his eyes narrowed to slits behind his pince-nez. He grinned like a schoolboy, pointing at the letters on the ground. Beneath the name and the year of death there were now two new words.

Two very familiar words.

Crux Christi . . .

"It's an anagram," Bonenmayr murmured. "*H. Turris. CCXI* is *Crux Christi,*" he said. "They have just moved the letters around . . . Those damned Templars and their riddles! But now, enough of this." He pointed at the memorial stone. "Now smash this plaque."

15

THE MUFFLED VOICES BEHIND THE DOOR BECAME louder and louder, then suddenly fell silent. Simon held his breath. He was sure he'd heard the Steingaden abbot. Had the secret passageway perhaps led them to St. John's Chapel? But they must have gone much farther than that . . . The medicus had lost all sense of direction. Placing his finger to his lips, he motioned to the two women to keep silent. After a while they could hear the sound of pickaxes. Someone on the other side of the door seemed to be pounding away at stone.

Carefully, Simon pressed down on the rusty door handle. The tarnished portal opened a crack, unexpectedly, and then jammed. Peering through the crack, Simon couldn't make out more than a few shapeless pieces of rubble that blocked his view. He pressed against the low wooden door with his shoulder, and it opened, squeaking, bit by bit. The pounding on the other side continued, and now Simon could clearly hear the abbot's voice.

"Faster, faster! There's an opening behind it, you asses! Hurry up!"

Suddenly, a loud crash sounded somewhere up above. Something big and heavy must have fallen over in the room above them. For a moment, Augustin Bonenmayr fell silent, but then he continued, even louder: "I don't care if the world is coming to an end up there! That must not stop us! Keep going!"

Finally, the crack was wide enough that Simon and the two women could slip through. Not far from the door, he spotted a tall, rotten shelf they could hide behind. But looking closer, he stopped short. The shelves were piled high with masks with crooked noses, dusty wigs, fake beards, and moth-eaten clothing. Beside the shelf, he saw a strange apparatus, something he'd never seen before: Standing upright on a small wagon was a barrel with a little handle sticking out of the side. The barrel itself was wrapped in a bolt of fabric. Simon rubbed his eyes. What place had they stumbled into? This couldn't possibly be St. John's Chapel, could it?

Carefully, the medicus peered out from beyond the shelving. He saw a huge subterranean dome. Through a tiny opening in the middle of the ceiling, a rope descended to a block of wood on the ground. In one corner Simon recognized one of the two monks from the library. He was hacking on a grave slab with a pickaxe, and next to him, Augustin Bonenmayr was frantically pushing rubble off to the side. When a large-enough hole opened up, the abbot pulled back his white robe and crept inside.

"Give me the torch—quickly!" The monk handed Bonenmayr the torch, and moments later, a shout came from behind the gravestone. "Holy Mother of Jesus, we've found it! We've really found it!"

The Steingaden abbot began to cackle hysterically, and Brother Lothar, curious, crawled in after him. Once the monk disappeared into the hole, Simon gave the women a sign and they all tiptoed over to the opening. One inch at a time, Simon moved closer to the edge.

Finally, he worked up the courage and looked inside.

• • •

Holding his dagger between his teeth, Brother Nathanael pulled himself out of the trapdoor and onto the stage, only to realize he had left his torch down below. The auditorium was as dark as a dungeon! Brother Johannes had a lantern with him, but it had disappeared along with the monk himself.

"Brother Johannes!" Nathanael called out. "Are you here somewhere?" His voice echoed through the drafty building, but there was no answer.

Nathanael remembered seeing candleholders earlier in niches along the stage. Blindly, he groped toward the niches, until his hand grasped a bronze candelabra. With frozen fingers, he reached under his robe for the little box of matches he always carried with him and lit the five candles. After a few moments, he could just make out the stage and the seats in the auditorium. Brother Johannes was nowhere to be seen.

With the candelabra in hand, Nathanael crossed the stage, stopping in front of a heap of crumpled curtain material. He was just about to go down the steps into the orchestra pit when something on the floor caught the light. Stooping down with the candelabra, he saw a little puddle spilling out from under the heap.

It was blood.

"What the devil . . . ?"

When Nathanael pushed the material aside, he saw Brother Johannes's badly beaten face peering out from under the heap like a discarded doll. He was moaning softly. Blood ran from his nose and from a wound at the back of his head, where a large lump had already formed. Nathanael glanced at the wound before giving the monk an angry kick in the side. Brother Johannes would have a headache for a few days, but he would survive. It was most important now to find out who was out to get them.

"Please stand up and tell me who—"

At this instant he heard a whooshing sound so soft that an untrained ear wouldn't have even noticed it. But Nathanael hadn't survived a half-dozen murderers' attacks in the Spanish provinces just to meet his end in a theater in the peaceful little Priests' Corner. He lunged forward just before the heavy stage curtain came tumbling down from the ceiling. It crashed onto the stage, burying the candles, candelabra, and the head of Brother Johannes, whose moans stopped abruptly.

Nathanael jumped up and scanned the ceiling. His eyes wandered along the balconies and up the stairs leading to the loft, while he played nervously with the dagger in his hand.

"Come out, whoever you are!" he called out. "You cowardly dog! Fight like a man!"

Out of the corner of his eye, the monk saw a little flame blaze up. Nathanael cursed. The candles he'd dropped had set fire to the curtain!

He was about to stamp out the flames when he heard the rattle of a winch unwinding. Turning around, he saw a giant of a man gliding calmly down from the ceiling. He held onto a rope with one hand and, in the other brandished a short but heavy wood cudgel.

"No one calls me a cowardly dog," the hangman growled. "Especially you. The three of you overpowered me in the dark once, but for you, I don't need the cover of darkness. I'll finish you off just like this, you shady, black-robed ruffian."

Jakob Kuisl jumped over the burning curtain. The flames cast a flickering light across the stage as the hangman raised his cudgel and approached the monk, ready for a fight.

Simon moved along the wall cautiously until he was able to peer into the opening behind the smashed gravestone. With low ceilings, the space behind it was only a few paces wide and deep and expelled a musty odor. In the torchlight, the abbot and his helper knelt before a simple stone altar with a wooden cross atop it. At about shoulder height, it looked very old and weathered; rusty nails just barely held the crooked and bent cross together, and in a few places, it appeared to have been charred. Nevertheless, Augustin Bonenmayr bowed his head as if the Holy Mother in person were standing before him. After a while he stopped praying, took the relic carefully from the wall, and kissed it.

"The Cross of Christ!" he whispered. "Our Savior once touched this wood. See for yourself . . ." He pointed to a place on one of the crossbeams.

Brother Lothar bowed down reverently to get a better look.

"Here, see the hole!" the abbot said. "His hand must have been nailed to this very spot!"

"Your Eminence . . ." Brother Lothar whispered so softly that Simon could barely understand him. "The cross . . . I always thought it was much larger . . ."

"You fool!" said Augustin Bonenmayr, slapping his helper on the head. "This is only part of the True Cross. The rest was destroyed! It was the Templars' duty to take the cross of Christ into every battle during the Crusades and to protect it. But at the Battle of Hattin, they failed. The cross fell into the hands of infidels and was almost completely destroyed. The cross bearer was an ancestor of this miserable fellow Friedrich Wildgraf." The abbot gripped the weathered relic. "He was able to rescue just part of it. Since then, the cross has been considered lost without a trace. But now it has come to light again, here in Steingaden. Who could have imagined!" Bonenmayr stroked the two rotten crossbeams like a long-lost lover.

Magdalena, eager to see something, too, nudged Simon. Her soft body pressed up close against him, and he could feel her warm, slightly sour breath on his neck.

"Simon, say something!" she whispered. "What's going on there?" She pressed even closer to him—too close, because he could feel himself losing his balance. He fell forward, crashing into the rubble of the gravestone.

Augustin Bonenmayr wheeled around, his face contorted with hatred. "Fronwieser!" he hissed. "I should have gotten rid of you right away! Well, it's not too late. Brother Lothar!" He pointed to the monk, who picked a heavy stone up from the floor and was walking toward the medicus. "Do it for God! *Deus lo vult!*"

"You'll do nothing of the sort!" Benedikta stepped into the opening, holding the little pistol she'd fired earlier at Brother Jakobus. Simon wasn't certain she'd reloaded the dainty little handgun in the meantime, but in any case, the pistol had the desired effect. Uncertain, Brother Lothar stopped and looked over to his abbot. Now Magdalena appeared in the opening as well. For a moment, Augustin Bonenmayr was clearly caught off guard, but then a smile spread across his face and he seemed to change his strategy.

"Ah, I see. The three lovers have found one another again. How delightful!" The Steingaden abbot advanced one step toward Simon. "Brother Jakobus told me your Magdalena seems to be something of a bitch. But what does a monk understand about women . . . ?" He grinned as if he'd just said something terribly amusing. "What divine providence, in any case, that he ran into her in Augsburg, of all places! We swear we wouldn't have harmed a hair on her head. She was just . . . collateral so her father would stay out of this in case things got too difficult. How is Brother Jakobus, by the way?"

"You could light up your whole damned monastery with him," Magdalena snapped. "He's burning, just as if my father himself had hauled him over the coals."

The abbot shook his head gently. "So much hatred! I have a proposal for you." Holding the cross in his right hand, he advanced another step toward the group.

Benedikta pointed the pistol at his head. "Stop right there! Not one more step!" she whispered. "Or blood will flow down this cross."

The abbot raised his hands in apology. "Let's not argue. If I remember correctly, you're still wanted in Rottenbuch for desecrating holy relics. I've already given your name to Brother Michael, the superintendent at Rottenbuch. Believe me, he'd rather see you burn today than tomorrow. But I could have been mistaken, and the real perpetrators could have been some highway robbers who just happened to come along. All it would take would be a word from me—"

"That's a filthy lie, *fils de pute!*" Benedikta growled.

The abbot shrugged. "Whether it's a lie or not, would you want to take the chance? Your future is in my hands. Kill me and you'll be chased through all of Bavaria as vagrants and outlaws. Let me leave with the cross and you're free."

"How can we be so sure you won't turn us in, anyway?" Simon asked.

Bonenmayr smiled and put his finger on the weathered piece of wood. "I swear on the True Cross of Christ. Is there any stronger oath?"

Benedikta looked at Simon and Magdalena, hesitating. For a while, silence filled the crypt.

Finally, Benedikta sighed. "For my part, I can live with this offer. I'd hoped for a real treasure, a gilded crucifix inlaid with rubies, perhaps, or a velvet-lined silver box—or whatever! But this rotten cross isn't worth any more than the thousands of other splinters of wood presumed to come from the genuine cross. I can't make any money from it . . . So you can keep it!"

"Benedikta is right," Simon said, turning to the abbot. "How are you going to convince your flock that this is the genuine cross?"

"This *is* the genuine cross!" Bonenmayr insisted. "At least part of it. The damned Templars never let the Church forget they had it, and for that reason the Holy See always protected those heretics, even when the Pope noticed that they were going their own way and becoming more arrogant and greedy. When the French king finally got rid of them, the Church hoped the cross would show up somewhere again. Many Templars were handed over to the Inquisition, but even under torture they all kept silent, and the cross remained lost. Our order has been looking for it for centuries! We were able to save many other relics from the heretics, who sprang up out of the ground like poisonous mushrooms, but the True Cross had disappeared from the face of the earth. Now it has returned to the bosom of the Holy Catholic Church, and everything has turned out for the best! The bishop of Augsburg will inform the Pope of what we've found, and His Holiness will confirm its authenticity."

"Do you really believe that?" Simon asked.

Augustin Bonenmayr nodded enthusiastically. "With the Pope's blessing, this cross will become Christianity's most important religious relic! People will make pilgrimages from all over the world to visit us. I already have plans for a magnificent pilgrimage church near Wies's farm—"

"Good Lord, there's blood on that cross!" Magdalena interrupted. She pointed at Benedikta. "The blood of your brother and of many others! I almost died because of that accursed cross!" She walked toward the abbot with a menacing look. "If you think you can simply go out and keep preaching your rubbish, then you've got another thing coming. I'll send my father after you; he'll break every bone in your body with that cross."

"Magdalena, calm down!" said Simon. "The abbot's suggestion is not so bad. What's dead is dead, and—"

"Just a moment!" Benedikta interrupted. "Do you smell that?"

Simon took a whiff and noticed the caustic smell of smoke coming from the larger room behind them. It was faint, but unmistakable.

"Fire!" Benedikta cried. "Everyone get out!"

They fled back to the domed vault where clouds of smoke were ascending through the hole in the stage floor. Just moments later, the entire ceiling looked like the sky on a gloomy November day, disappearing behind a billowing gray cloud of smoke. The abbot sat on the ruins of the gravestone, pressing the cross to his chest as if the relic could protect his scrawny body from the flames.

His lips moved in a quiet prayer.

On the stage above, flames were eating through the dry brocade as if it were straw. Fire climbed up the curtains to the ceiling and along the balconies, leaving a path of destruction in its wake. Soon the entire auditorium was bathed in a red glow, and despite the cold January day outside, an almost unbearable heat filled the theater.

The hangman and the monk circled each other like two wolves ready to attack, each waiting for the other to make the first move. Finally, Brother Nathanael struck. He feigned a move to the left, then attacked from the right with his dagger. The hangman dodged to the right and struck the monk with his elbow, knocking him down. Before he could fall onto the burning curtain, Nathanael rolled away, jumped up like a cat, and attacked again.

The hangman hadn't expected such a quick counterattack, and the dagger brushed his right arm in the same place the highwayman had cut him earlier that same day. Kuisl suppressed a groan and swung the cudgel but landed only a glancing blow on Nathanael's shoulder. The monk turned in a half circle, ducked, and thrust the dagger at the back of the hangman's knees. With a spirited leap to one side, Kuisl avoided this blow, but in the smoke-filled room, he was too late noticing the burning curtain at his feet. To avoid jumping straight into the flames, he changed direction in mid-jump, stumbled, fell over, and was just able to pull himself up on a painted backdrop of a sky full of white clouds from which the Lord looked down.

Just as the hangman was standing up, the heavy wall tipped forward, taking him with it, burying him with the Almighty. With a thundering rattle, additional backdrops fell over onto him.

For a moment silence prevailed, broken only by the crackling of the flames and the strange hissing voice of the monk. "I once met a man in Salamanca like you," he whispered. "Big and strong, but stupid. I slashed his throat as he was preparing to take a swing at me with his double-edged sword. He stared at me in disbelief before he fell forward."

Jakob Kuisl struggled to separate the heavy canvas-covered frames, but they were somehow stuck together. As hard as he pressed, they didn't move an inch. He heard steps approaching the fallen frame and the dagger scraping across the canvas. Nathanael was cutting the material lengthwise, and it wouldn't take him long to reach Kuisl's neck.

"The church is not a gentle flock of lambs waiting to be slaughtered," Nathanael said as his knife inched forward, cutting through the material. "The church has always needed people like me, and that's the only reason it's survived this long. It must punish and destroy, just as Saint John the Baptist prophesied about our Savior. Do you know the Bible verse, Kuisl? *He will thoroughly purge his floor, separating the wheat from the chaff and gathering the wheat into his garner. But the chaff he will burn up with unquenchable fire.*" The dagger had reached the hangman's neck now. "And now you are the chaff, Kuisl."

At that moment, the executioner's fist shot through the canvas—right at the spot depicting the kindly, smiling mouth of the Savior—and the hangman grabbed the hand holding the dagger, pulling Brother Nathanael down. Gasping, the monk lost his balance and fell onto the canvas as his dagger clattered onto the floor. Kuisl's other hand punched through the material and gripped Nathanael by the throat like a vise. Nathanael wriggled like a fish out of water and poked his fingers through the backdrop but couldn't get hold of the man underneath. The monk shook and waved his arms about, but his movements became weaker and weaker until his forehead finally fell into the canvas.

For a moment it looked as if he were kissing the painted Savior on the mouth. Then he rolled to one side and lay still on the stage floor with eyes wide open.

When Jakob Kuisl finally managed to extricate himself from under the backdrop, he cast a final, almost remorseful look at the dead Dominican. "Why did you always have to talk so much?" he said, wiping off his massive, soot-stained hands on his jacket. "If you want to kill someone, just shut up and do it."

Only now did Kuisl notice the inferno raging around him. The flames had reached the seats in the middle of the hall, and even the backdrops at Kuisl's feet had caught fire. The first heavy timbers from the balcony came crashing down.

Because of all the smoke, Kuisl could no longer see the trapdoor on the stage floor. He coughed, climbing down the stairs toward the main exit. One last time, he turned around and shook his head. Unless there was another exit, anyone still beneath the stage was doomed. At any rate, it would be insane to climb down there again.

He was already halfway to the back of the hall when he heard the squeak of a pulley.

In the meanwhile, the smoke down below in the crypt had become so dense that the upper third of the room was no longer visible. The ropes connected to the platform ended somewhere in a gray cloud. Simon stopped to think. The tunnel through which they'd entered was presumably already filled with smoke, so the only way out was, in fact, up. He ran to the platform, eyes peeled for the mechanism to set it in motion.

"There has to be a pulley here," he shouted to Benedikta and Magdalena. "A lever, a crank—something! Help me find it!"

Out of the corner of his eye, Simon could see Augustin Bonenmayr still standing in the opening to the crypt, clutching the cross. The Steingaden abbot stared at the flames eating through the floor of the stage above, the flickering light reflected in his pince-nez, which was perched at an odd angle atop his nose. Bonenmayr's murmuring grew louder, swelling to a long litany as the auditorium above him threatened to come crashing down. "And the first angel blew his trumpet," the abbot intoned, "and hailstones and fire mixed with blood fell over the land . . ."

"Where is the damned pulley?" Simon shouted into Brother Lothar's ear. The monk was staring, frozen with fear, at the cloud spreading across the ceiling. "If you want to get out of here alive, open your big mouth!"

Brother Lothar pointed silently to an inconspicuous crank on the wall next to a costume cabinet. Without another word, Simon ran to it and started turning the handle.

"Hurry!" he shouted to the two women. "Get onto the platform! I'll pull you up. Once you're there, let the lift back down again. Now hurry!"

Magdalena and Benedikta hesitated for a moment, then ran over to the platform. As Simon turned the handle, the lift squeaked to life. At the last second, the women jumped on.

"Watch out, Simon!" Magdalena suddenly shouted. "Behind you!"

A heavy blow struck the medicus on the back of the head, and as he fell, he saw the abbot standing over him with the cross.

"You set this fire, didn't you?" Bonenmayr whispered. "You wanted to make sure the cross would burn. But you won't succeed! Who are you, Simon Fronwieser? A Lutheran? A Calvinist? What connection do you have with this Templar gang?"

"Your Eminence, snap out of it!" Simon panted. "Why would we set this fire? We'll burn to death ourselves if we don't hurry. We have to, both of us—"

Bonenmayr swung the cross at him again. Simon had just enough time to put his hands in front of his face, but the blow was so hard that, for a moment, he thought he would pass out.

The sound of a pistol firing brought him back to his senses.

Apparently, Benedikta had reloaded her weapon. The abbot was still standing over him, the cross raised high for one last fatal blow. But then he put his hand down to his side where a red spot was slowly diffusing across his white tunic. Astonished, he looked at the fresh blood on his hand. "The same place the Roman soldier's lance pierced the body of our Savior," Bonenmayr murmured, looking up at the ceiling in ecstasy. "Now there is no more doubt that God has chosen me!"

Simon tried to get up, but his legs buckled under him. Lying on the floor, he had to watch as Augustin Bonenmayr, despite having been shot in the side, ran toward the two women, swinging the cross like a club.

"You accursed lot of heretics!" he shouted. "The cross has returned to the bosom of the Church! God has sanctified this place by delivering it to me! You will not stop me!"

As the abbot raised his hand to strike again, Benedikta ducked and managed to trip him. Bonenmayr stumbled, his glasses fell to the ground, and he staggered toward the wall on the other side, just managing to catch himself before he fell. He leaned on the cross, exhausted, as blood dripped down his robe. Still, he didn't seem to have lost much of his strength.

"Damn it, Brother Lothar!" he gasped.

His assistant's face filled with tears as his whole body started to shake like a little child's.

"Pull yourself together. Those before you are enemies of the Church. Heretics! Do what I have taught you to do! *Deus lo vult!*"

The final words awakened the monk from his panicked stiffness. He pulled himself together, the trembling stopped, and with a loud cry he charged at Magdalena, who was running to help Simon. The hangman's daughter was accustomed to giving an impudent workman a good slap in the face, but Brother Lothar was something else. He was almost six feet tall, with the muscular arms, broad shoulders, and the huge hands of an Augsburg raftsman. When he charged toward her, she ducked behind one of the shelves. She had no plan; she just knew she had to get away from the monk at all costs. Perhaps she would think of something as she ran from him.

Magdalena dodged again, but Brother Lothar was right at her heels. She dived under shelves, jumped over metal contraptions whose purpose she couldn't guess, and climbed over stone sarcophagi and piles of rubble.

Suddenly, she came to a huge cabinet of costumes. She slipped inside, hoping the clumsy monk would run past. The dusty garments inside had the mildewed smell of fabric stored in a damp place too long.

The hangman's daughter sensed she was not alone. She smelled the sweaty odor of a stranger breathing heavily beside her.

Pushing aside a silver angel costume, she saw Benedikta crouched in front of her. Benedikta put her finger to her lips, motioning for her to remain silent. Only a few inches separated the two women. Magdalena had never been so close to her rival. Benedikta, too, had a terrified expression on her face, and all the refined French mannerisms had vanished. Sweat poured down her face, her hair was in tangles, and the expensive lacework of her precious clothing was smudged and torn. But behind all that, Magdalena saw something else, something she had never seen until then—a wild fire burning in the eyes of the merchant woman from Landsberg, a readiness to fight, an unbending will, and an inner strength that would put many men to shame. Magdalena had seen eyes like that before.

In the mirror.

The two women stared at each other for a few seconds, until a grating sound pulled them out of their thoughts. Looking to one side, Magdalena was shocked to see that the closet was tipping over.

"Benedikta, watch out!"

Through the back of the closet, Magdalena could hear Brother Lothar panting as he pushed against the closet, finally toppling it and burying the women under it, along with the moldy costumes. Something was burning nearby; evidently, the costumes around them had caught fire.

Frantic, Magdalena pushed against the door of the wardrobe, but something was blocking it. The smoke was thickening, and alongside her, Benedikta was coughing. As Magdalena flailed her arms around wildly in all directions, she noticed light coming through a crack near the top of the cabinet. She pushed against the top and it popped off, crashing to the ground and letting in air and light. The two women crawled out, coughing, just in time to see the Steingaden abbot and the cross ascending on the lift toward the auditorium above. In the crypt, Brother Lothar was furiously turning the crank.

"The cross! I've saved it!" Bonenmayr screamed, staring up at the opening from the platform. "It's ascending into heaven while the heretics are burning in hell! It's such a pity that this play will never be performed. It really deserves an audience."

With these words, the abbot disappeared into a black cloud while the stage flooring began raining down on those trapped below.

Just before reaching the main portal, Jakob Kuisl turned around again to see a figure in a bloodstained white robe emerge onstage from below. The figure held a cross at about shoulder height and shouted something Kuisl couldn't quite make out over the ever-louder crackling of the flames. He thought he heard the words *heaven* and *hell.* Though the hangman was not an especially religious man, for a brief moment, he thought he was witnessing the Savior's return to earth to judge mankind with blood and fire.

Was Judgment Day at hand?

Jakob Kuisl blinked and only now realized that the white form staggering across the burning stage was the Steingaden abbot, who was evidently wounded. Bonenmayr was looking for a route down into the auditorium, but the stairway was already in flames. The hangman hesitated. What in the name of the Holy Trinity had happened down there under the stage? Just a moment ago, Kuisl had heard a shot; there must have been some sort of fight. But with whom?

In the meantime, Augustin Bonenmayr had recognized the hangman through the clouds of smoke. He screamed, pointing his clawlike fingers at Kuisl. "You will not stop me, either!" he shouted. "The devil sent you, Kuisl! But God is on my side!"

Holding the cross in one hand, Bonenmayr ran to the left side of the stage, where a narrow spiral staircase led to the upper balcony. The top third of the stairway was already a charred, glowing skeleton, but that didn't stop the abbot. Taking a huge leap, he managed to get one foot on the balustrade. With the cross still tucked under his right arm, he clung by one hand to the railing above the auditorium.

"For God's sake, just throw the damned cross away," Kuisl shouted. "Or you'll meet God face-to-face in a minute!"

In the inferno, though, the abbot couldn't hear him. He was trapped in a world of fire, hatred, madness. In vain, he tried to pull the wooden cross up with him over the balcony railing. Instead, he hung there like a huge pendulum, kicking in all directions, trying to get a foothold on the balcony. But then the burning railing gave way, breaking into pieces in a spray of sparks, and with a scream, Bonenmayr plunged headfirst into the flames that were eating through the rows of seats beneath him.

The cross seemed suspended in air for a moment before finally crashing down on the Steingaden abbot and shattering into pieces.

For a brief moment, Kuisl thought he saw a hand appear from beneath the seats, fingers desperately reaching for something, but then a mass of glowing debris showered down, and all that was left of Bonenmayr was a memory.

From the open doorway, the hangman watched the fire consume the theater. The entire auditorium had become one huge funeral pyre.

Glowing pieces of wood and burning scraps of curtain rained down on Simon and the two women. As the fire burned slowly through the stage floor and cellar ceiling, the air became so hot that it was harder and harder to breathe, and the smoke burned their eyes and lungs.

After he'd hauled the abbot up on the lift, Brother Lothar tried to crank the platform down into the cellar again, but the rope caught fire and the lift crashed to the floor, breaking into pieces. Now the monk looked around in panic. He was imprisoned with the same people he'd just tried to kill. Would they attack him? Why had the abbot abandoned him?

Simon struggled to his feet again. His head ached and blood spurted out of his nose and from a wound on his temple, but at least he could walk again. "We've got to leave through the underground passage," he croaked, "through the locked door in the monastery where we were before. Quick! Go before everything crashes down on us!"

Ignoring the monk, the three ducked and ran toward the low doorway as burning pieces of the ceiling continued to rain down around them. Brother Lothar stood in the middle of the room, petrified and undecided. Finally, he tore himself away from the spot and hurried after the others, but the smoke had now become so thick he couldn't see where they'd gone. The huge man groped through the smoke, coughing, bumping into shelves, and knocking over statues of saints.

"Wait for me!" he gasped. "Where are you? Where—"

At that moment, an especially large chunk of the ceiling directly above the monk broke loose and came crashing to the ground. Brother Lothar could only watch in horror as he was buried in burning timbers. After a few moments, his plaintive cries ceased.

In the meantime, Simon and the two women opened the door they'd used to enter the crypt. The medicus was relieved to see that the smoke in the tunnel behind the door was not as dense as he'd expected—the door had held it back, for the most part. They ran down the corridor, past the intersecting tunnel, until they finally arrived back at the entrance to the monastery. Benedikta leaned against the door, just as she had the last time, and pushed as hard as she could, but the wooden door would not budge this time, either. She cursed and rubbed her shoulder.

"Let me try," Simon said. He took a running start and hit the door as hard as he could. A sharp pain went through his leg, but still, the door didn't budge. Behind them, the corridor was already filling with smoke.

"You did close the door into the crypt, didn't you?" Simon asked uncertainly.

Benedikta shrugged and pointed to Magdalena. "I thought she had—"

"Aha, it gets even better," the hangman's daughter responded. "First your shot misses the abbot, and now you're blaming other people."

"You were the last, you silly little twit," Benedikta shouted.

"Cut it out!" Simon replied. "We don't have time for your petty quarrels! If a miracle doesn't happen, we'll suffocate here like a fox in its den. I've got to get this damn door open!"

Stepping even farther back, he took another run at the door, screaming loudly.

Too late, he noticed that the door had opened silently and an astonished monk was staring at him. "What in the world . . . ?"

Simon ran into him at full speed, knocking the monk down.

"Sorry to bother you," the medicus gasped, standing up quickly, "but this is an emergency. The monastery is on fire."

The monk's expression changed from astonishment to horror. "The monastery on fire? I'll have to let the abbot know at once."

The two women headed up a narrow stone stairway with Simon right behind them.

"I'm afraid that's not a very good idea," he called back to the monk. "His Eminence is very busy at the moment."

At the top of the stairway they came to another door, but unlike the last, this one opened easily. Stepping outside, Simon realized they were in the same cloister where he and Benedikta had first met Augustin Bonenmayr an eternity ago.

A group of white-robed Premonstratensian monks ran toward them excitedly, but to Simon's astonishment, they continued past them toward the rear exit of the cloister, paying the intruders no mind. In the distance, a shrill bell began to ring.

"Fire! Fire!" everyone was shouting. "The playhouse is on fire!"

Taking advantage of the chaos, the three followed the monks. As they rushed outside, they looked back at the monastery wall, where flames shot up into the night sky and people ran back and forth shouting.

"The playhouse!" Benedikta shouted. "Clearly, the cross was not in Saint John's Chapel, but in the theater! The underground corridor must lead from there to the cloister. What a labyrinth!"

Simon quickly realized that it was too late to save the burning building. All that remained of the two-story structure now was a glowing shell. When the roof collapsed, the physician could only shake his head. The theater! He had clearly overlooked something in the solution to the last riddle, but none of it mattered now. Simon wondered whether the abbot had managed to flee or had burned to death inside.

And with him, the cross of Christ!

He felt overcome by exhaustion now as the burden of the last few days' events came over him. Magdalena and Benedikta seemed weary and drained, too. Together, they dragged themselves to a small snow-covered cemetery nearby to watch the building consume itself like an enormous funeral pyre.

"Our search was for nothing!" Simon finally lamented, tossing a chunk of ice into the darkness. "Our dream of all that money came to naught! Now I'll no doubt end up as the poor town doctor of Schongau . . ."

Benedikta stood there silently, clutching a ball of snow so hard that water ran through her fingers.

"Do you think that crazy Bonenmayr got away?" Magdalena asked.

Simon stared into the fire. "I don't know. If he didn't, we're in big trouble. If the abbot was telling the truth, then the whole world knows that Benedikta and I defiled the holy relics in Rottenbuch. Bonenmayr is the only one who could have helped us."

Benedikta spit on the ground. She had clearly gotten her voice back. "Do you seriously believe he'd do that if he's still alive? I'll tell you what he'll do. He'll take the cross and watch with glee as the hangman breaks every one of our bones, one by one."

"I'm not going to break any bones," a voice boomed behind them. "At least not Simon's."

Surprised, the three wheeled around to see the Schongau hangman sitting astride an old gravestone. With his coat collar turned up to shield himself from the cold, he was blowing little puffs of smoke into the frigid January night.

Simon looked at Jakob Kuisl as if he'd seen a ghost. "How . . . how in the world did you get here . . . ?" he stuttered.

"That's just what I wanted to ask my daughter," the hangman said, turning to Magdalena. "Couldn't stand being away in Augsburg, hmm? Had to return to your sweetheart?" He grinned. "You women are all the same."

"It wasn't . . . exactly like that, Father," Magdalena replied. "I was—"

"You can tell me all about that later," Jakob Kuisl interrupted, hopping down from the gravestone. "But first tell me why the Steingaden abbot burned alive in there," he said, pointing to the roaring fire behind him, his face glowing red in the light from the flames. "I can feel in my bones that you had something to do with that. Am I right?"

"So Bonenmayr is really dead?" Simon asked.

The hangman nodded. "As dead as a witch at the stake. So tell me—out with it!"

"It was all about the cross," Simon began. "The Templar hid the True Cross underneath the playhouse. The riddles led us to this place . . ." He briefly told Kuisl everything that happened since they had last spoken.

Jakob Kuisl listened silently, and when Simon finished, he exhaled a huge cloud of smoke. "All that looking around just for a rotten old cross," he grumbled. "And now the accursed cross has fallen victim to the flames as well. I saw it all . . . ashes to ashes, dust to dust. Probably, it's best that way. That cross has brought nothing but death and misfortune."

"Let's get out of here," Benedikta said, standing up from the drift of snow she was sitting on, "before the monks notice we're here."

"You're not going anywhere, girl," the hangman replied suddenly, "except perhaps to the gallows."

"What are you saying?" Simon looked at Jakob Kuisl in astonishment. "This woman is a respectable lady from Landsberg. You don't talk that way—"

"She's nothing but scum." Kuisl knocked out his pipe on a gravestone. "She's not a respectable lady, and she doesn't come from Landsberg."

For a few moments, no one said a thing.

Finally, Magdalena spoke up hesitantly. "Not from Landsberg? I don't understand—"

Her father immediately cut her off. "Perhaps she'll tell us

herself what her real name is. In Augsburg, she was Isabelle de Cherbourg; in Munich, she was Charlotte Le Mans; and in Ingolstadt, Katharine God-knows-what . . . But I doubt any of those is her real name." Scowling, the hangman drew closer until he was only a step away from her. "Damn it, your name! I want to know—at once! Or I'll jam glowing embers under your pretty little fingernails until you beg for mercy!"

Simon and Magdalena both eyed Benedikta as she stood there clutching a gravestone with both hands. Her eyes flashed and she bit her lips as she lashed out at the hangman. "How dare you slander me like that! If my brother were still alive, then—"

"Silence, you brazen hussy!" Jakob Kuisl shouted at her. "You have sullied the good name of our priest long enough! I found the courier's letter pouch, and from there, I only had to do a little looking around. Your game is over! Do you hear? Finished!"

"Which letter pouch do you mean?" Simon asked.

The hangman took a drag on his cold pipe. Only after calming down a bit did he continue. "When we smoked out Scheller and his gang, I found a leather bag in the cave. It belonged to one of the couriers who deliver mail in our area. Scheller told me they'd taken the bag from another gang of robbers." Again, he paused long enough to stuff his pipe.

Just as Simon was about to say something, the hangman continued.

"I had a look at the letters, especially the dates on them. They were all written around the time the fat priest must have written to his beloved sister, Benedikta. Now, if all these letters were stolen . . ."

"Then Benedikta in Landsberg could not possibly have received a letter from her brother!" Simon groaned. "But how then did she—"

"This is all pure coincidence and nothing more," Benedikta said, smiling at Simon. "You don't really believe this, do you?"

"I'll tell you who this brazen hussy really is," Jakob Kuisl interrupted. "She passes herself off as a wine merchant in cities all over Bavaria. She spies on merchants' routes and passes the information on to her accomplices so they can rob the coaches."

"Where did you ever come up with this nonsense?" Benedikta replied angrily.

"One of your partners told me so himself."

"Rubbish!" Benedikta grumbled. "*C'est impossible!*"

"Believe me," the hangman said, lighting his pipe with a glowing sliver of tinder. "Sooner or later, I make everyone talk." He puffed until the pipe caught fire. "And after that, they don't talk to anyone ever again."

Horrified, Benedikta stared at him for a moment. Then she threw herself at him, beating her fists against his broad chest. "You killed them!" she shouted. "You monster, you killed them!"

Jakob Kuisl seized her hands and flung her away so hard that she bounced off a gravestone like a puppet. "They were robbers and murderers," he said. "Just like you."

The silence that followed was broken only by the distant crackling of fire and the cries of the monks desperately trying to save the adjoining buildings.

Incredulous, Magdalena eyed the self-declared wine merchant still crouching beside the gravestone, looking up at them with cold, scornful eyes. "Your gang robbed the courier and read the letter!" Magdalena shouted. "That must be what happened! They read that the fat priest Koppmeyer had found something valuable, and then you pretended to be his sister and spied on us."

"It wasn't only her, but her whole gang following us." Simon buried his face in his hands and groaned softly. "The people I saw in the Wessobrunn forest were *your* accomplices, weren't they? And it was *your* accomplices who started the fight with the monks in the Rottenbuch Monastery. How could I have been so stupid?"

The woman who just a minute ago had been Benedikta Koppmeyer smiled. It was a sad smile. She seemed to have lost all desire to fight and leaned against the gravestone like an empty shell. "They were there to protect us," she said softly, "not only me, but you as well, Simon. We knew earlier than you did that there were others trying to get their hands on the Templars' treasure. We knew they weren't people we could trifle with."

"Back there in the forest on the way to Steingaden, when we were attacked by robbers . . ." Simon murmured. "Those were your friends who helped me back onto my horse. Isn't that right? I thought it was a dream, but the men were really there."

The woman facing him nodded. "They always kept an eye on us."

"Nonsense!" the hangman exclaimed. "They were there so the loot wouldn't slip through their fingers. Wise up, Simon! If you'd found the treasure, her cronies would have slashed your throat without giving it a second thought, and she would have stood by and watched. That's the reason I came to Steingaden—to warn you about this hussy!"

Simon stared at the redheaded woman with delicate features whom he'd for so long viewed as a refined ideal of the fair sex. "So you're not from France at all?" he asked softly.

She chuckled, and for a moment, it seemed the old Benedikta had flared to life again. "Oh, but I am. I come, in fact, from an old Huguenot family, but even as a child I hung around on the streets. I wanted to be free—not wind up the dutiful wife of some fat, conceited merchant."

"Manslaughter, deception, and murder—that's the life you chose!" the hangman growled. "I asked the burgomaster to find out what this hussy had been up to. The trail of her gang leads through all of Bavaria—Munich, Augsburg, Ingolstadt . . . She always pretended to be a fiery, temperamental merchant woman and managed to wrangle information from old moneybags in the taverns about the routes they would be taking. Later, one of her accomplices would come to the tavern and get all the information from her. And if the madam was so inclined, she even went on the raids herself." Jakob Kuisl stepped up to the imposter. "How often did you have your hand in what went on in Schongau? Once? Twice? How many died because of you? Weyer from Augsburg? Holzhofer's servants?"

The woman fell silent and the hangman continued. "In Landsberg, there is, in fact, a Benedikta Koppmeyer. She lives a very quiet, modest life there and first learned of the death of her brother from Burgomaster Semer."

"So it was Karl Semer who gave you the final clue?" Simon asked.

"I should have known sooner," Jakob Kuisl said. "Scheller told me about the perfume he took from the other gang. Even then, I suspected the monk with the violet perfume had something to do with it. Only later, on the gallows, did Scheller remember having seen something else at the campsite."

"What was that?" Magdalena asked.

The hangman grinned. "A barrette. I've never heard of a man wearing anything like that."

Simon collapsed onto a snow pile. He still couldn't believe that he had been swindled. "What a fantastic plan," he groaned, not without a trace of admiration in his voice. "The worldly woman hangs around in the taverns to find out which routes the wagon drivers will be taking. She knows where they're going and how heavily they're guarded. Her accomplices need only stand at the right crossroads and hold out their hands. And then, more or less by accident, they hear something about a fabulous treasure . . ."

"We robbed the courier because we hoped to find something of value in his bag," the redhead whispered. "A bill of exchange, a few gold coins—but this time all we got were letters! I read a few of them out of pure curiosity and suddenly came across this incredible letter that mentioned a Templar's grave and a riddle.

In our family, the Templars were always the stuff of legend. When I was just a young child in France, my father told me about the legendary treasure. It could have been our last great exploit . . ." She stood up and brushed the snow from her charred dress. "Now what are you going to do with me?"

"First, you'll go to the dungeon in Schongau," Jakob Kuisl said. "After that, we'll see. It's possible they'll put you on trial in Munich."

The woman without a name bent down to wipe the snow off the hem of her dress. "Will you torture me in the dungeon?" she asked softly, as she continued brushing the snow from her boots. "Simon told me about the tongs and the brazier . . ."

"If you confess, I'll see that not a hair on your head will be harmed until the trial," Kuisl growled. "You have my word on that."

Suddenly, the dainty little woman sprang up and threw a handful of snow in the hangman's face. In the next second, she ran off between the gravestones.

"Stop, you bitch!" Jakob Kuisl shouted, wiping the snow out of his eyes. Then he looked at Simon and Magdalena standing alongside him, bewildered. "Why are you staring at me like two jackasses? Go after her! Her accomplices have killed people in Schongau!" The hangman ran after the fleeing woman as fast as he could.

Finally awakening from his paralysis, Simon set out after the hangman. He spotted a red shock of hair briefly above a gravestone, but then the woman disappeared again. The medicus turned left to run along the cemetery wall, hoping to cut her off if she tried to flee through the main gate. He reached the end of the wall, where he could see the hangman running through the crooked gravestones, but Magdalena was nowhere to be seen.

Arriving at the far end of the cemetery, Simon looked in all directions. The woman he knew as Benedikta had vanished from the face of the earth! He turned and started walking back slowly, checking behind the stones as he went. There was nothing there.

Perhaps it's really better this way, he thought.

At that moment he heard a soft, muted sound off to one side, someone gasping for breath. He tiptoed along a narrow, snowy path leading to a family burial vault through an archway whose columns were entwined with ice-encrusted ivy. Atop the archway was a statue of the Virgin Mary, smiling down benevolently and keeping watch over the dead. Behind a rusty gate, a few stone steps led down to a marble slab sealing off the entrance to the crypt.

Simon looked down in front of him at fresh tracks in the snow. Made by dainty feet.

Climbing over the gate, he saw her cowering at the foot of the steps—the woman who, for a week, had been the wealthy merchant's widow from Landsberg, Benedikta Koppmeyer. She had tucked her legs under her now and wrapped her arms around them. Trembling with cold, her tangled hair falling down over her face, her makeup smeared, she looked up uncertainly at Simon standing at the top of the steps. Her eyes seemed to be begging for mercy, and her narrow lips formed a thin smile, like a child asking for forgiveness.

Simon looked at her for a long time. Behind the genteel exterior, the vanity, the ruthlessness, and the greed, he saw her now as a human being and believed he grasped who she really was.

"Well?" a voice asked from far off. It was the hangman. "Did you find her?"

Simon looked the redheaded woman in the face again, then turned around. "No, she's not here!" he called out. "Let's have a look over there."

After searching another half-hour, the three finally met again at the main cemetery gate. Not only Benedikta, but also her horse was gone as well; the swindler had clearly managed to flee.

Magdalena, who hadn't joined in the chase, was leaning

against a gravestone waiting for the two men to return. "I don't want to take part in a chase like that," she said. "Even if I couldn't stand her, she didn't deserve that."

"You fool!" Jakob Kuisl scolded. "That woman is responsible for the cold-blooded killing of at least a dozen men! She's a murderer! Can't you get that into your head?"

"She didn't act like a murderer with us," Simon said. "On the contrary. Back in the forest, on the other side of Peiting, she even saved my life."

The hangman gave him a long, piercing gaze. "Are you certain you didn't see her somewhere here in the cemetery?" he finally asked.

"I thought I saw her," Simon said, "but I was mistaken." Then he stomped away in the snow toward the dark monastery.

16

THEY SPENT THE REST OF THE NIGHT WITH A farmer near Steingaden. Old Hans crossed himself three times when the Schongau hangman materialized in front of him, but he didn't dare turn away the surly colossus with stitches in his face and a bloody bandage around his upper arm. So they remained till dawn in the warm farmhouse living room.

The entire night, Simon sat hunched over next to Magdalena on a narrow bench by the fire. He couldn't fall asleep, not just because of the trumpet-like snoring of the hangman at their feet, but also because of all the thoughts racing around in his head. How had his judgment of Benedikta been so wrong? She'd used him, and he'd run after her like a trusting little puppy. But at the end, when he saw Benedikta cowering at the bottom of the stairs to the crypt, her eyes told a different story. Did she have any feelings for him, after all? At any rate, both of them would be sought now as fugitives, defilers of holy relics. Simon had no idea how he would ever get his head out of this noose. Worst of all, for the fleeting dream of fortune and happiness, he'd put his relationship with Magdalena at risk. The hangman's daughter lay alongside him now as stiff as a corpse. He touched her once, tentatively, and she turned away, giving him the cold shoulder. But he could sense she wasn't sleeping, either.

Shortly before daybreak, Magdalena sat bolt upright and glared at him, her eyes flashing furiously. Straw clung to her matted hair and a deep frown ran across her forehead. "So tell me the truth," she hissed. "Did you sleep with her? Out with it, you shameless good-for-nothing!"

Pinching his lips together tightly, Simon shook his head. He was certain that, had he nodded, she would have taken a blazing log from the fireplace and killed him with it.

"There was nothing between us," he whispered. "Believe me."

"Swear to it, by all the saints!"

Simon smiled. "Let's keep the saints out of this. I'm not on especially good terms with them right now. I swear by our love—will that do?"

Magdalena hesitated, then nodded earnestly. "By our love, then. But you must ask my forgiveness. Right now."

Humbly, Simon closed his eyes. "I ask your forgiveness. I was a stubborn fool, and you knew better from the very beginning."

She smiled and settled down next to him on a straw-filled pillow. Simon could feel her body had relaxed a bit, and he passed his hand gently through her hair. For a long while, they said nothing; the only sound was the hangman's rattling snore.

"I could have had Philipp Hartmann," Magdalena finally said softly, "the rich Augsburg hangman and his life of luxury. And what do I do instead? I fall in love with a skinny quack who flirts with other girls and whom I can't marry in any case . . ." She sighed. "It doesn't get stupider than that."

"I promise you, we'll get married someday," Simon whispered. "Even without this treasure. We'll move to another town where nobody knows you are the daughter of the Schongau hangman, and I'll become a famous doctor, and you'll help me with herbs and medicines, and— "

At this moment, she seized his hand and squeezed it so hard he almost let out a cry.

"What's the matter?" he asked.

"Nothing," she said. "Keep talking. Talk until I drift off into my dreams."

He held her in his arms and continued telling her about their new life together. After a while, he could feel that his hand was wet with her tears.

They set out early the next morning. The sun was shining brightly in a clear blue sky, and even though it was still mid-January, everything had begun to thaw. Water dripped from farmhouse roofs along the way, and they could hear finches and robins chirping in the forests. Simon knew that this taste of spring would probably last only a day, but for that reason he enjoyed holding his face up to the warm sunshine all the more.

In Schongau people were just coming from Sunday morning mass. They looked suspiciously at the three figures strolling through the market square and whispered among themselves. The son of the town physician together with the Kuisls! The old village women were certain the hangman's daughter would be the downfall of young Fronwieser. Such a handsome fellow, but the Kuisls had cast their spell on him—that much was clear.

The three paid no attention to the piercing glances but continued up the Münzgasse to the castle. Jakob Kuisl had insisted that Simon come along with him to pay a visit to the clerk, but he didn't say why.

"Don't always ask. You'll send me to an early grave with all your questions" was all he said. Then he winked and left Simon to ponder on his own.

In the clerk's office on the top floor of the castle, Johann Lechner was sitting, as usual, at his worn, massive, wood table, leafing through some old papers. He looked up in surprise as the three entered the room.

"If you're coming to excuse yourself for the botched execution, Kuisl, I'll have to disappoint you." He turned back to his documents. "There will be consequences. I've heard that the Memming executioner's second son is looking for a job. Just because your family has been here for generations doesn't mean that will always be the case."

Ignoring the threat, Jakob Kuisl settled comfortably into the easy chair opposite the desk. "There's no longer a second gang of robbers."

"What?" The clerk looked up again.

"I said there's no longer a second gang of robbers. I got rid of them all in Steingaden. Only the leader could flee, but I'm sure she won't show her face around here anytime soon."

"But you were alone," the clerk replied.

Jakob Kuisl shrugged. "There were only four of them—trained mercenaries, to be sure—but I dispatched them one after the other. The merchants can get back on the road again. There's no one spying on their routes anymore."

"Kuisl, Kuisl . . ." Johann Lechner grinned and shook his head. "You always have some surprise up your sleeve. Now don't torment me any longer! What happened? How did the gang go about it?"

The hangman told him about the woman posing as Benedikta Koppmeyer and how she'd spied on the merchants and wagon drivers. He recounted his fight with the robbers in the Steingaden forest but avoided saying exactly how many robbers there were or what had happened in the playhouse. The clerk listened, spellbound.

"Indeed," Lechner said finally. "This woman often sat together with the merchants over there in Semer's tavern and would sometimes ask about the best routes to take. Who would have believed she was working with the robbers?"

"And that's not all," Jakob Kuisl continued. "That shameless woman and her gang were also trying to steal the sacred remains of two saints in Rottenbuch. First they snooped around the monastery and then started a fight with the monks. One of the bandits almost looked like our young Fronwieser . . ."

Simon looked at the hangman in astonishment. What was Jakob Kuisl doing?

"Like young Fronwieser?" Lechner asked, bewildered.

"I can swear to it," Kuisl said. "I almost thought it was Simon myself. The problem is that the Rottenbuchers believe our medicus had something to do with it, and they want to draw, quarter, and burn him—the sooner, the better."

Johann Lechner laughed. "Simon Fronwieser a defiler of holy relics? The only thing he defiles are the young maidens in town." He laughed and shook his head. "What a crazy idea. I'll send the Rottenbuch superintendent a letter telling him there must be some mistake. That should take care of the matter."

Reaching for some parchment and his quill, he began to write a short note. Simon smiled furtively at the hangman. Once more, Jakob Kuisl had gotten him out of a jam.

"Thank you, Your Excellency," Simon said, bowing slightly in the clerk's direction. "Such a regrettable misunderstanding. I don't know myself how—"

"All right, all right," the clerk interrupted. "Express your thanks in deeds. We need our physician, after all, to take care of this dreadful fever, don't we? Since you left, three more people have died. You're not on very good terms with your father, to put it mildly."

Simon blushed, remembering that he'd visited neither his father nor little Clara since his arrival.

"You're right," he replied in a subdued tone. "I really ought to get right back to work." He said a hasty good-bye and rushed back to the Schreevogl house on the market square. In this miserable search for the Templars' treasure, he had completely forgotten about the terrible illness still raging in Schongau. So many people had died while he was out chasing a fantasy. For a while, he'd even forgotten Clara!

After he had knocked a few times at the patrician's house, Maria Schreevogl opened the door. Her face was pale and she held a rosary in her scrawny fingers. "It's good you're here again," she whispered. "Our Clara is worse again. She hasn't awakened since yesterday, drinks nothing, and is coughing up red mucus. May God have mercy on her! My husband is upstairs with her now. Ave Maria, the Lord is with you. Blessed are you among women . . ."

Without paying any further heed to her prayers, Simon hurried up the stairs and knelt alongside the bed, where Jakob Schreevogl was holding the feverish hand of his stepdaughter. The alderman looked up briefly, then continued wiping the perspiration from Clara's forehead. The girl's breathing was shallow and irregular, like a little bird's, and interrupted occasionally by a dry rattling sound from her mouth.

The physician realized at once that Clara didn't have long to live if her condition didn't quickly improve. In recent days, he'd seen the same symptoms in Schongau over and over. Once the patient started spitting blood, it wasn't long till the trumpets of heaven would be sounding.

"I hope your trip was successful," Jakob Schreevogl said softly, without turning his eyes from Clara, "even though all the gold in the world means nothing to me now. Clara is so precious to us, and if she dies, a part of me goes with her . . ."

Simon shook his head. "Our search was a failure. But that's of no importance anymore. The only important thing is that your daughter gets better. No Templars' treasure can restore her health, and it appears that I can't, either. Only God can do that."

"God!" The patrician closed his eyes. "You sound like my wife! We always depend on God, and then God abandons us! Is there no medicine—perhaps something that hasn't been tried yet—that can save my Clara?"

"I don't know of any." Simon stood up. "Jesuit's powder might help, but I don't have any left, and it will be April before the merchant makes his way over the mountain passes from Venice. Perhaps there's something in Augsburg . . ." Suddenly, a thought came to him, and he hesitated.

Jesuit's powder.

Didn't the hangman say that Magdalena had gone to Augsburg to get herbs and medicine? How could he have forgotten? Perhaps some of the medicines she brought back could help him now!

"Excuse me," Simon said, standing up from Clara's bedside. "But I have to check. Perhaps there's something that can help your daughter, after all."

Jakob Schreevogl looked at him hopefully. "Then run! Every moment is precious."

Simon ran back to the market square, where he bumped into Magdalena, who had paid the blacksmith a visit after the meeting with Johann Lechner. Their grumpy old Walli urgently needed new horseshoes after Simon's escapades.

"Magdalena," he gasped. "The medicine you were supposed to pick up in Augsburg . . . Do you still have it?"

The hangman's daughter looked surprised. "Of course, I even have it with me, but—"

"Then let's hurry back to my house," he cried, turning to leave. "I want to have a look and see if there's anything there for a fever."

"Simon, wait, I . . ."

But the physician had already run off down the Weingasse to his father's house. Clara needed help—at once! Any delay could mean her death. His inability to heal his patients from the fever, plus his guilty conscience at not having been there to help in recent days, came into focus on this one little person. It seemed to him that if he failed Clara, he would never become a doctor worthy of the name. He would be like . . .

His father?

Bonifaz Fronwieser tore open the front door even before Simon reached it.

"Aha, my noble son back from the country?" he snarled. "People are dying on me like flies while you've been away, touring the local monasteries with beautiful ladies."

Simon opened his mouth to speak, but his father wouldn't be interrupted.

"Don't lie to me! This sort of thing gets around fast in a little place like Schongau. First, there was that dissolute hangman's girl, and then some flighty tramp from Landsberg. You are bringing shame to me and the Fronwieser name!"

Suddenly, Magdalena appeared behind Simon, gasping for air. "Simon, I must tell you something—" she whispered.

But Bonifaz Fronwieser launched right back into his tirade. "And here she is! Speak of the devil! Stop following my son around, do you hear? Right away! We are decent people and want nothing to do with you hangman riffraff."

"Oh, come on, Father, just shut your goddamned mouth!" Simon blurted out. "I can't stand your yammering anymore, you old quack!"

Even as he spoke, Simon was startled by his own words. He'd gone too far this time. Bonifaz Fronwieser was stunned as well. Blanching, his mouth fell open. In the houses nearby, people were peering out from behind their shutters. Finally, the gaunt old man pulled himself together, buttoned his coat in silence, then made his way out toward the market square.

Simon knew that his father was no doubt heading to one of the taverns to wash down his anger with a mug of beer. The young physician shook his head as he entered the house. He would never be able to make his father happy, not as a son, and certainly not as a doctor! But that was of no importance now. He had to help Clara—that was all that mattered.

"Quick, Magdalena! Show me what you brought!" Simon hurried toward the living room window, where a big worn table covered with all sorts of mortars and pestles doubled as a pharmacist's workbench. "Maybe there's something here we can use. Do you have Jesuit's powder? Tell me you have it."

Without saying a word, Magdalena pulled the little linen bag from her jacket and emptied the contents on the table.

Simon studied the damp, whitish-green clump tied together with a string. In addition to the aromas the various herbs gave off, they smelled of decay.

"What . . . is this?" Simon asked, horrified.

"The herbs I brought with me from Augsburg," Magdalena replied. "Ergot, artemisia, daphne . . . I also took a few other herbs, but I don't know what they are, except that they're all moldy! I've been carrying them under my jacket far too long. I kept trying to tell you, but you wouldn't listen!"

Simon stared mutely at the moldy pile on the table in front of him. The herbs from Augsburg had been his last hope. "It's . . . all right, Magdalena," he finally said. "At least we tried."

He was about to sweep the damp herbs off the table and onto the floor, when he stopped. He couldn't disappoint Jakob Schreevogl! Simon had seen the spark of hope in the patrician's eyes when Simon spoke of a possible cure. If he went back empty-handed now, the Schreevogls would die of grief even before their stepchild. Experience had taught Simon how important it was for sick people and their families to *believe* in a cure. Faith was sometimes the best medicine.

Often the only one, Simon thought.

And so the physician tossed the moldy seeds into a mortar and ground them into a fine powder.

"What in the world are you doing?" Magdalena asked. "The herbs are spoiled! They can't do anyone any good now!"

"Clara needs medicine," the physician murmured, laboriously grinding the seeds with the pestle. "The rest is out of my hands."

After a while, Simon added honey and yeast to the ground herbs and rolled the mix into little pills that he dried in a small pan over the fire as Magdalena watched, frowning. Finally, the physician placed the medicine in a box of polished cherrywood embossed with an alchemist's symbol. He closed the little box and said a quiet prayer as he passed his finger over it.

"After all, our medicine has to look impressive, too," Simon said with a sad smile, as if he'd already been caught in this little deception. "Otherwise, it won't work."

Magdalena shook her head. "Medicine from moldy herbs! Who ever heard of anything like that? Just don't let my father hear of it." Then she suddenly kissed him on the cheek. "And don't let *your* father know about this, either."

A warm feeling passed through him from deep inside, extending right out to the roots of his hair. He would love this woman forever, no matter what their two fathers and all the people in Schongau thought of it! Tenderly, he passed his hand through her hair and pulled her to him. She smelled of sweat and ash.

But Magdalena pushed him away. "I don't believe our beloved physician has time for that sort of thing now." She broke into a broad smile. "But he can come to my window and visit me tonight . . ."

Simon sighed and nodded with resignation. One last time, he passed his hand through Magdalena's hair, then stuffed the cherrywood box in his coat pocket and headed straight for the Schreevogls, who were anxiously awaiting his return.

"My husband already told me about your miracle drug!" exclaimed Maria Schreevogl, standing at the door with the rosary still in her hand. "Praise be to God! Perhaps there is hope, after all!"

"I can't promise you it will work," Simon protested. "It's a . . . new, very costly medicine from China. The doctors there are very knowledgeable. They call it . . . uh . . . mold that grows on herbs."

"Mold that grows on herbs?" The patrician woman looked at him, confused.

"I myself prefer the term *fungus herbarum,*" Simon quickly added.

Maria Schreevogl nodded. "I like that better. It sounds more like medicine."

Taking several steps at a time, the physician hurried to the top floor. In Clara's room, Jakob Schreevogl was still kneeling by the bed, just as Simon had left him, his face almost as gray and haggard as his stepdaughter's.

"Do you have the medicine?" the alderman asked softly.

Simon nodded, carefully opening the little box and placing three little pills in Clara's mouth. Her lips were narrow and hard as leather, and her mouth was dry. Then he gave her something to drink from a cup and tenderly passed his hand over her sweaty brow.

"There's nothing more I can do," he whispered.

Jakob Schreevogl nodded humbly and closed his eyes. It seemed to Simon that the alderman had aged years in the last few hours. Fine gray strands appeared in his otherwise blond hair and wrinkles framed his narrow lips.

Suddenly the physician fell to his knees alongside the patrician and folded his hands. "Let us pray," he said softly.

First haltingly, then in firmer voices as the words came back to them, they murmured the words of consolation they had both learned as children.

"The Lord is my shepherd. I shall not want. He maketh me to lie down in green pastures, he leadeth me beside the still waters . . ."

It was the first time Simon had prayed in a long time. He'd never been an especially devout person, but he was suddenly seized by a longing—something in him *wanted* to believe. God had allowed so many terrible things to happen, and the horror had to end sometime!

> O, God, if you really exist, help this poor little girl . . . If you let her live, I will make a pilgrimage to the black madonna in Altötting, barefoot, in the winter!

After a while, when the physician looked up at Clara again, he thought he saw a slight smile on her lips. Her breathing seemed easier and regular, and her eyelids were no longer fluttering. He stopped praying, leaned over the bed, and felt her pulse.

It was quiet and slow, just like that of a healthy sleeping girl.

This isn't possible . . . is it?

Only now did Simon notice an object on the bare wall in front of him—an object so ordinary it hadn't attracted his attention until now, almost as if it hadn't been there before.

Over Clara's bed hung a plain, small wooden cross.

EPILOGUE

IT WAS THE SECOND OF FEBRUARY IN THE YEAR 1660. The bells of the Altenstadt basilica resounded through the countryside around Schongau as people streamed into the large church to celebrate Candlemas. In the Schongau market square, booths had already been set up with fat sausages frying over charcoal fires, roasting chestnuts, and long white candles awaiting consecration. Even a group of acrobats from Munich was on hand.

According to tradition, Candlemas signaled the end of winter, and people came from miles around to celebrate mass in the largest church in the area. Even though it was bitter cold in the basilica, the people in their Sunday best—clean, colorful clothes—looked happier and more lighthearted than they were just a few days ago.

This was, to a large extent, because the dreaded fever that had been plaguing the town for so long finally seemed to have passed. On every street corner, people were talking about the young Schongau physician and his miracle drug, *fungus herbarum*—or as some said in an undertone, the China Mold. The physician gave all his patients the little round pills from that distant land, and in a short time they'd all recovered! Since then, people doffed their hats and greeted Fronwieser's son with respect on the street. Only a few still grumbled about his love affair with the hangman's daughter down in the Tanners' Quarter. Indeed, some aldermen even wondered whether Fronwieser might be a good match for their young daughters, now that he seemed prepared to follow in the footsteps of his father and would surely become a rich and respected doctor. He looked impressive in his tailored jackets from Augsburg and with his perfectly trimmed Vandyke beard. One could learn to overlook his small stature and lower-class origins . . .

Simon sat in one of the rear pews of the Altenstadt basilica, glancing over the shoulders of the aldermen and their families, who had taken their seats in front. Among them were the Schreevogls, including Clara, who had now completely recovered. Not far from them, a great wooden cross hung over the altar. For hundreds of years, the Great God of Altenstadt had looked down benevolently on churchgoers. The physician enjoyed listening as his voice merged with those of all the others in the congregation, swelling into a single mighty voice reciting the Lord's Prayer.

Since his experience at Clara's house two weeks before, Simon's attitude toward God had changed. Had he witnessed a miracle? Had the pills actually cured Clara completely—and the others as well? He still hadn't figured out why the moldy herbs had worked. The hangman told him mold could prevent infections. For this reason, Kuisl occasionally placed moldy rags on the wounds of his patients, but the assertion that the white strands were effective against fever and coughing was something new, even to the hangman.

By now he'd used up all the miracle pills and took to pestering Magdalena with questions about exactly which herbs were in the bag she had taken from the Augsburg pharmacy. But she couldn't remember for the life of her.

Simon sighed. He probably would never be able to recreate those pills. Well, at least they helped improve his standing in

Schongau and with his father. Bonifaz Fronwieser was seated beside him, reciting the Lord's Prayer in a croaking voice. He still smelled of last night's brandy, but he'd come to church with Simon, something they hadn't done for a very long time.

Simon looked out of the corner of his eye to see Magdalena kneeling with the women in the last row of pews. Her hands were folded and her eyes closed, but as if sensing his gaze, she suddenly turned to wink at him. The physician felt a tingle course through his body. Perhaps they'd have a chance to be alone for a while this evening at the Candlemas celebration . . .

"Don't fall asleep during the doxology," a dark voice grumbled next to him. "And if I catch you with Magdalena tonight, the Lord's Prayer itself won't be enough to save you." With a grin, the hangman nudged him and sat down next to him in the pew. Usually, the hangman's place was at the rear of the church, but at the Candlemas service, the priest didn't pay much attention to ceremony.

"When do you set out on your pilgrimage?" the hangman asked loudly enough that some of the parishioners turned around. "If you wait until summer, going barefoot won't be a problem, but I think God wants to see you suffer a bit."

Simon cursed himself again for having told the hangman about his promise at Clara's bedside. "There's still too much to do here," he whispered. "My patients — "

"Your father can take care of them," the hangman interrupted. "I've already told Lechner you'll be traveling the next few weeks."

"You did *what?*" Simon's voice was loud enough now that even the priest up at the altar cleared his throat. "But . . ."

"Magdalena also didn't think that was a good idea," Kuisl sighed, lowering his voice again. "She still doesn't trust letting you out of her sight, so I made her promise to go along with you to Altötting. You'll go through Munich and pick up a few herbs for me, and some books. A fellow named Athanasius Kircher has written a new book about the plague and how to cure it . . ." The hangman's face broke out in a broad grin. "If you don't behave yourself in the next few days, I'll think it over and perhaps come along, too."

Simon could hardly believe his good fortune. He'd have a few weeks together with Magdalena, far from this place where she was the ostracized hangman's daughter. Nobody would know her!

"Kuisl, how can I thank you . . . ?" he whispered.

"Don't thank me; thank the one up there," he replied, pointing up at the Great God of Altenstadt. "He convinced me to do it. Now I've done him two favors."

"Two favors?" Simon asked, baffled.

Jakob Kuisl drew on his cold pipe as if he were at home and not in the church. "The larch wood in his back was rotten," he began. "The day before yesterday, the carpenter Balthasar Hemerle had to repair the Savior for Candlemas, and he couldn't find a good piece of wood for it . . . old, solid wood that had already survived sixteen hundred years . . ."

Slowly, it dawned on Simon what he was talking about. "The True Cross of Christ in Steingaden . . ." he started to say.

The hangman knocked out his pipe on the pew. "I was able to save a small piece from the fire as a keepsake. It fit exactly into the back of the Savior."

When Simon looked up at the Great God of Altenstadt, he thought he detected a smile cross the chiseled wood of Jesus's face.

But, of course, that was just an illusion.

A FEW WORDS IN CONCLUSION

Some time ago, I was in Hohenschäftlarn visiting my grandmother, who is now eighty-five years old. She lives in what was once a farmhouse that encompasses over twenty rooms filled with old furniture, paintings, and all sorts of knickknacks she's collected in the last few decades at flea markets all over Bavaria. On the property there's an enchanted garden, a deep, dark cellar, and a drafty attic, where my cousin and I used to sleep under thick down comforters. Every room, every object in this house, has a story to tell.

In the large kitchen — at the same table I often hid under reading comic books as a boy — my grandmother used to sit with me all evening long, telling me stories about our ancestors, the Kuisls: my stubborn great-great-grandfather, Max Kuisl, who emigrated to Brazil during the 1920s with his entire family; my great-great-uncle, Eduard, who wrote fairy tales and who reminded her so much of me; my great-great-aunt, Lina, who studied at the Munich Academy of Arts, then fell head over heels in love with a French painter — all these ancestors whom I had known until then only through faded photographs and paintings. My grandmother could go on and on with stories and anecdotes about all these people until my head started to spin.

Since the appearance of my first book, *The Hangman's Daughter,* it's strange to see how huge my family has become. Again and again, I receive calls or letters from people who are part of the large Kuisl family, too. They ask about a distant great-great-uncle or a long-lost aunt; they've traced their ancestry back many centuries, until we eventually encounter our common ancestor, the hangman Jakob Kuisl.

We'll never know what sort of man Jakob Kuisl was. All I can say with any certainty is that he was a hangman in Schongau during the seventeenth century and one of the first in a long line of Kuisls who were hangmen in Bavaria. All together I've counted fourteen executioners so far in our family.

The Schongau town archives have little to say about Jakob Kuisl. We know he once killed a wolf. The documents also mention a daughter named Magdalena; his wife, Anna Maria; and the twins, Georg and Barbara. (There were two other children whom I've left out of the story for dramaturgical reasons.)

Jakob Kuisl assumed the position of Schongau executioner at the age of thirty-six—a position also held by his father and grandfather—and lived a full eighty-two years. What he did before that time is unknown. It's quite possible my ancestor served as a mercenary during the chaos of the cruelest of all German wars. His wife died just two years after he did. I can imagine they had a long and happy marriage, but this is where the realm of imagination takes over.

Every book finds its own theme. Unintentionally, my second novel became a book about religion—all the madness, the insanity it can cause, but also the consolation and refuge it offered at a time when people could easily have doubted God. The natural setting for a book like this is a region like the Priests' Corner, with its many monasteries and churches, its pious people, and heavenly countryside. And sometimes reality is stranger than fiction.

Many things I didn't have to invent, like the innumerable macabre relics in the Rottenbuch Monastery—they were just waiting for someone to write about them. The history of my family was also there long before I came along. I just embellished it a bit and put it down on paper.

That evening at my grandmother's house in Hohenschäftlarn, my son, daughter, and I visited the Kuisl gravesite on a hill directly above the entrance to the village church. I pointed to the names overgrown with ivy, and we stood there silently as darkness fell. I've always tried to create an awareness in my children that a family is more than just a father and mother, that it can be a large community, a place of refuge—and an endless treasure trove of stories.

Later I sat in the kitchen correcting the first draft of this book far into the night. It was a strange feeling sitting in the same house, the same room, where so many of my ancestors had lived, worked, laughed, and brooded before me. It almost seemed as if their shadows were leaning over my shoulder to see what their descendant had to say about their large, old family. I hope they're happy.

The story you can read in these pages developed during the course of long hikes and bike tours and was inspired by the ideas and information from many people.

Unfortunately, I can't list them all here, but I'd like to give special thanks to the local Schongau historian, Helmut Schmidbauer, who told me about the Altenstadt Templars and without whose extensive knowledge the first novel, and also this second one, never could have been written. Many thanks likewise to Wiebke Schreier, who showed me around Augsburg and gave me enough ideas for three books. Professor Manfred Heim has, I hope, been able to correct most of my errors that concern the history of Bavarian churches. In addition, he's an excellent Latin teacher!

Dr. Claudia Friemberger of the University of Munich filled in the gaps in my knowledge of the Bavarian Templars, and Matthias Mederle from the German Rafting Society knows how fast a raft moves and at what times of the year it would have been used on rivers. Eva Bayer corrected my miserable French and knew the proper Parisian expletives. The pharmacist Rainer Wieshammer, who's an expert on ancient medicines, prepares herbal medicines in his facility in Rottal and has a magnificent collection of *Breverln*—little cloth and paper talismans adorned with images of saints and prayers, which as late as the twentieth century were thought to have healing and protective properties. (Incidentally, Magdalena's charm necklace looks just like the one Rainer Wieshammer donated to the Müllner-Peter-Museum in Sachrang. Perhaps someday you'll have the chance to stop there for a look.)

Everything I know about executions comes from the enormous collection of notes by my deceased relative Fritz Kuisl—a wealth of information I draw upon even to this day.

Thanks also to my editor, Uta Rupprecht, who came up with the idea of the *fungus herbarum* antibiotic, and to my agent, Gerd Rumler, for a first-class Italian meal over which a few new ideas for the novel were born.

And last but not least, thanks to my entire extended family: my wife, my children, my parents, brothers, grandmother, and all the aunts, uncles, and cousins who surround me and support one another. Without you—your patience, your pride, and support—this book would never have been possible.

A TRAVEL GUIDE THROUGH THE PRIESTS' CORNER

If, like me, you're one of those people who like to read a book's epilogue first, you should stop now. This book is a journey that will take you from one riddle to the next and to some of the most beautiful places in Bavaria. What pleasure is there in solving riddles when you already know the solutions? So stop reading!

STOP!

If, on the other hand, you have finished reading the novel, then sit back and enjoy this section. The following pages will help you plan your next vacation to the Priests' Corner, absolutely my favorite area in the Alpine foothills. If I had to explain to an extraterrestrial what Bavaria is—what it smells and feels like—I would just set him down on the mountain Hoher Peißenberg and tell him to look around for himself at a countryside as colorful as a robust painting from the Bavarian baroque period: monasteries, chapels, lakes, gentle hills, and the distant Alpine peaks that, when the warm, dry foehn is blowing down from the mountains, appear as close as the nearest cow pasture.

The people who live here are all a little bit like my ancestor

Jakob Kuisl: stubborn, grumpy, and reserved. But if you approach them with humility, respectfully doffing your hat politely in church, they won't bite. Be brave!

You can find all the places mentioned in this novel on a map today. After a trip through your imagination, what makes more sense than actually traveling to this area to check out all the riddles and the history behind them? To best appreciate Kuisl's time, of course, you should travel on foot or at least by bicycle. Back then, things were not as fast or hectic as they are today. In researching this book, I walked everywhere and got lost several times in the Ammer Gorge. Why should you get off any easier?

Enough said! Pack this book in your backpack with a pair of good hiking boots, a water bottle, and a local map, and come along with me to . . .

THE LITTLE CHURCH OF ST. LAWRENCE IN ALTENSTADT

To find the place where my story begins, I had to search an awfully long time. The former Church of St. Lawrence lies on the outskirts of Altenstadt, at the far end of St. Lawrence Street (Sankt-Lorenz-Straße). Though it dates back to the twelfth century, it was renovated and converted into a farmhouse in 1812. For this reason, I walked right past it twice on my first trip, winding up in the parking lot of a nearby company before I finally realized that the old ivy-covered building at the edge of town actually had once been a church. Only its massive blocks of igneous rock and the navelike structure suggested a time and place when fat priests like Andreas Koppmeyer preached to their flock. The babbling of the Schönach next to the house, the reed-covered river valley, and the roadway lined with mountain ash, however, conjured up that ancient locale in my mind's eye. I'm sure they will for you as well.

In Roman times and also later, in the Middle Ages, Altenstadt must have been an important trading center. Here, the Via Claudia Augusta, the greatest Roman highway this side of the Alps, intersected with the medieval Salt Route, which stretched from the Berchtesgaden area to the Allgäu. But the many merchants and travelers in that area also attracted robbers and hostile armies, and in the thirteenth century, citizens decided, therefore, to move to a protected hill a few miles away. That marked the birth of the town of Schongau, while Altenstadt—the "old city"—became a sleepy town and remained so until modern times, like Sleeping Beauty in the fairy tale.

When the St. Lawrence Church was remodeled in the nineteenth century, they say a crypt was found containing some unusually large human bones. We don't know whether this was the crypt of a Templar knight, but it's an established fact that the order of knights was active here. Near the former little church, there is to this day a Templar Street (Templerstraße). Also, the bill of sale, dated 1289, an agreement between the Premonstratensians and a certain Fridericus Wildergraue, "Supreme Master of the Templars in Alemania and Sclavis," still exists. When I first saw a copy of this document, I knew at once that this was the start of a new novel.

Please follow me now to the center of town and . . .

THE BASILICA OF ST. MICHAEL IN ALTENSTADT

Within sight of the property formerly belonging to the Templars is my favorite church in the Priests' Corner. Amid all the baroque splendor of the region, the Basilica of St. Michael, with its simplicity and large dimensions—its huge towers, massive outer walls, and rounded arches—looks more like a Romanesque castle than a sacral building.

Over the main portal, a relief depicts a battle between two

knights and a dragon, which gave me material for my second riddle. In the opinion of the local historian Helmut Schmidbauer, the two warriors are Enoch, the son of Cain, and the prophet Elijah—and I certainly accepted his opinion without question. His words, by God, are sacred! Anyone who wants to convince him of the contrary is welcome to try, but be prepared for the same Bavarian Priests' Corner stubbornness you see in Jakob Kuisl.

The "Great God of Altenstadt," the huge crucifix inside, dates from 1200 and is famous throughout Bavaria and beyond. Whenever I stand before it, looking into the rough-cut, sad, kindly face of the Savior, I always feel like Simon, an enlightened man suddenly infused with the Holy Spirit. And I like to imagine a piece of the actual True Cross secured inside this simple crucifix, even though, unfortunately, not a shred of evidence supports this.

All that remains of the fourteen auxiliary saints in the north aisle is a fragment, so no one can prove that a holy St. Fridericus wasn't among them at one time. As for the memorial plaque on the exterior church wall, I'll freely confess that's my own invention.

Now let us set out on the way to . . .

SCHONGAU

Even though no riddle is hidden here, Schongau is the centerpiece of my first novel, as it is of this one. Schongau is a quiet little town with a medieval walkway along the battlements and many of the historical buildings that also appear in Jakob Kuisl's adventures.

Here's my suggestion for walking through town in the footsteps of my ancestor:

Start your trip out, just as the coffee-lover Simon might

have, with a cup of black espresso in the Marienplatz; then enter the Ballenhaus, which is easy to recognize by its stepped gable. Here, in the former town hall, you can visit the second-floor meeting room where the clerk Johann Lechner and the Schongau patricians sealed the fate of the Scheller Gang. The beautiful carved wood ceiling dates from the sixteenth century, and the green tile stove plays a small, but not inconsequential role in my first novel.

At one time the Golden Star (Goldener Stern) Inn stood next to the Ballenhaus. It belonged to the Semer family, and in this novel it's where Benedikta lodges when she visits Schongau. Today it's home to a music school. The rich plasterwork and the former private chapel inside will remind you that, at one time, only the upper classes visited the Stern. Simon and Jakob Kuisl probably patronized the shabbier establishments in the tavern quarter behind the Ballenhaus.

From there, take the Old Gate (Alten Einlass) through the city wall and turn right, where you'll see the Witches' Tower (Hexenturm), where more than sixty women awaited execution in the famous Schongau witch trials.

Turning left at the Old Gate will take you to the Lech Gate (Lechtor) and along the unfortunately rather busy Lechberg Street (Lechbergstraße). The former Tanners' Quarter is located near the raft landing where a bridge now crosses the river toward Peiting. Here, outside the city, where tanners plied their foul-smelling trade, was the house of the executioner Jakob Kuisl. Although nothing remains of that house, the Lech flows by just as slowly and lazily as it did when Magdalena set out on the ferry to Augsburg.

Go back up to town and take the walk along the battlements in the direction of the St. Sebastian Cemetery. If you've read *The Hangman's Daughter,* you'll remember this cemetery as the sinister backdrop against which Jakob Kuisl and Simon Fronwieser exhume children's corpses. In those days the dungeon was located next to the cemetery, along with the Schongau executioner's torture chamber. Until modern times, justice was meted out here; now, fortunately, it's under the jurisdiction of the police. A bit farther down the road, you'll come across the office of the district administrator. It was at this location that the ducal castle used to stand, the same spot where the clerk Johann Lechner planned the hunt for the robbers with Jakob Kuisl.

I highly recommend walking past the medieval Max Gate (Maxtor) to visit the Schongau City Museum, which is housed in a former church hospice. Look for the executioner's sword, the portrait of Johann Lechner's father, and the Kuisls' cupboard, which served my ancestors as a medicine cabinet.

Finished?

Then you've earned a good supper. Tomorrow we'll head to . . .

THE CASTLE RUINS IN PEITING

Peiting is the village on the other side of the Lech. Don't be disappointed here: All that remains of the Guelph Castle on the hill is some rubble. Nevertheless, a short walk up the hill is worthwhile, as you will be able to see the Hoher Peißenberg from up there. A meadow of waist-high grass covers the foundation of what was once the rulers' castle complex, but in the woods, you can still see the oaks that lined the former entryway to the castle.

In the year 1155, Emperor Barbarossa himself visited the Guelph ruler in this castle. Later the castle became the property of the Staufers and then the Wittelsbachs. After an earthquake in 1384 partially damaged the structure, the fortress began losing its importance. In 1632 it was dismantled and hauled away, and by the time Simon and Benedikta visited there in the winter of 1660, all that really remained was a ruin. What that looked like is just a matter of conjecture—yours and mine.

Hold on tight because just on the other side of Peiting is the Ammer Gorge. There you will find . . .

SCHLEYER FALLS

When I headed out to find Schleyer Falls the first time, I had to turn around when I realized I'd started out from the wrong place. The second time, I turned off before (instead of after) the Ammer Bridge and trudged along the wrong side of the river, deeper and deeper into the woods, until I finally arrived at the edge of a steep gorge. If I'd taken one more step, I might have landed in the raging torrent of the Ammer almost a hundred feet below me—and this book would never have been written! Sweating and suffering low blood sugar, I didn't want to believe I'd gotten lost. I kept trudging on aimlessly until coming to an idyllic meadow full of flowers. Unfortunately, I have hay fever. Nowhere was a waterfall to be seen, but I did encounter a few helpful bicyclists, and while they had no idea how to get to Schleyer Falls, they were able to direct me back to where I came from.

Schleyer Falls became an obsession over the course of my research. So when I finally found it, I was a bit disappointed. Perhaps, after all my hardships, I expected something at least as impressive as Niagara Falls. But Schleyer Falls is rather small; the water flows over moss-covered limestone, forming a fine silver curtain of mist. If you are lucky and go in the off-season, you'll have it all to yourself and feel as if you're in one of Caspar David Friedrich's paintings.

The entire area is a honeycomb of caves large enough to hide entire armies of bandits and was thus exactly right for the robbers' smoke-filled lair in my novel.

For all those who don't wish to get as hopelessly lost as I did, here is a description of the most scenic route: Coming from

Saulgrub, walk down to the Ammer. After the bridge, the route climbs again and turns sharply to the right after the power plant. After a good twenty minutes, the path winds down again into the valley. There you'll find yourself face to face with Schleyer Falls.

Pause with me for a few moments of reflection, then follow me to . . .

THE WESSOBRUNN MONASTERY

Wessobrunn is a bit far from the other riddle locations. It would be best to take a car or make a special bicycle trip there, either from Schongau or from Ammer Lake (Ammersee). If you approach it by bicycle from Dießen, as I did, it's a long, uphill climb. It might have even been faster on foot, but I made it all the way without dismounting—so try to follow my example!

If you do, you'll enjoy the rest stop all the more at the three springs by the former Benedictine monastery, which stands in solitary splendor on a hill south of Ammer Lake. Some of the best stucco workers in all of Europe once lived in this area, but nowadays the monastery and the village are sleepy. Don't be surprised if the locals glare at you from behind the safety of their garden fences. When I stopped to ask an elderly man if I could rent a room for the night, he eyed me suspiciously, but by breakfast the next morning, he'd poured out his entire life story and told me about the best bike route back to Schongau. People in the Priests' Corner just need time to warm up to you.

Many of the front doors in town bear the names of once-famous families of artists. If it interests you, go to the Post Tavern (Gasthof zur Post) and ask to see the dance hall, whose ceiling brings the storied past back to life. East of the village, you'll find the yew forest that Simon and Benedikta passed through, where they met the presumed highwaymen.

Some of the sisters offer tourists an interesting tour of the monastery interior. When you see the magnificent stuccowork on the ceilings, you'll understand why Wessobrunn craftsmen were known as far away as Venice. The halls and rooms here, by the way, served as models for the Steingaden library in the book.

The old Romanesque tower where Simon and Benedikta found the collection of precious books is at the far end of the building. I don't know whether it was ever used as a library, but the massive defensive tower could have offered valuable protection during the Thirty Years' War.

At the time of Simon and Benedikta's travels, the so-called Wessobrunn Prayer, one of the oldest prayers in the German language, was, in fact, safeguarded here in this monastery. Now you'll find it housed in the Bavarian State Library (Bayerische Staatsbibliothek).

Leaving the monastery, if you turn right and follow the outer wall for about ten minutes, you'll come to the famous Tassilo Linden, where Simon almost broke his neck. Anyone who wants to check that there is, in fact, a plaque with a riddle up in the tree should be warned. There's a hornet nest up there!

So it might be best to move along to . . .

THE ROTTENBUCH MONASTERY

Yes, the holy relics of Primus and Felicianus really do exist! Though not—as during the Thirty Years' War—standing upright with swords in hand and crowns of laurels on their skulls. Instead, you'll find they're almost invisible among the richly carved reliquaries up front in the chancel. Try to find them amid all the cherubs, stuccowork, and statues! It took me a while—with the help of a kind nun.

The other relics that the superintendent, Michael Piscator, mentions were also in the monastery's possession at that time: St.

Binosa's teeth, St. Mary's hair and fragments from her robe, as well as relics of Pancratius, Blasius, Valerius, Virgilius, Johannes, Philippus, Bartholomew, Thekla, and Brigida . . . And those are only a small fraction of the treasures.

For anyone overwhelmed by all the Baroque splendor — the gold and stuccowork of the former Augustine monastery church — I recommend leaving the church through the little gate at the rear of the property. From there it is a beautiful walk down to the Ammer Gorge — past trees, cows, and little chapels. God can be found everywhere in the Priests' Corner.

Then follow me along to . . .

THE STEINGADEN PREMONSTRATENSIAN MONASTERY

The grand finale! At first I wanted the novel's final scenes to unfold at Schleyer Falls, but then I happened on an old monastery floor plan dating from 1803 that showed a playhouse. A theater in a monastery! After that I couldn't resist devoting a final scene here to my antagonist, in the truest sense of the word.

The playhouse is now in private hands and no longer has much in common with my concept of a monastery playhouse. The library, the secret subterranean passageways, and Magdalena's prison in the chapel are all inventions. I'm sorry. I recommend you just sit down with a glass of *Weißbier* (a type of German wheat beer) in the little tavern nearby, close your eyes, and just imagine the rest. What I can show you, however, is the Romanesque cloister connected to the church where Simon met Abbot Augustin Bonenmayr for the first time. (That is the actual name of the abbot at that time. The correct spelling of his last name has pursued me like a curse.) There is also a St. John's Chapel that, in fact, stood at another location originally. And naturally, there is a Guelph crypt directly beneath the church, its entrance decorated with a gravestone whose inscription I quoted in the book. I didn't dare try to raise it up. Who knows? Perhaps there are secret tunnels down below!

If you're looking for the Steingaden Wies Church (Wieskirche), the pearl of Bavaria's Baroque period, you will search my book in vain. It wasn't constructed until the eighteenth century, but you ought to visit this magnificent place just the same.

One final tip: A wonderful bike route runs some distance off the main road through Peiting, Rottenbuch, and Steingaden—a day trip I recommend to everyone. There is no better way to get to know the Priests' Corner. On my trips by bicycle, car, and on foot, gathering material for this book, I discovered many other places that didn't make it into this novel—crooked wayside crosses, chapel ruins, impenetrable forests, deep gorges, and magnificent churches, as well as cairns, crossings, and secluded ponds. Each place has its own story to tell.

And who knows, maybe they'll appear in another novel.

Enjoy your reading and bon voyage!

—Oliver Pötzsch

TURN THE PAGE FOR A PREVIEW OF

THE BEGGAR KING: A HANGMAN'S DAUGHTER TALE

THE OPPRESSIVE SUMMER AIR LAY OVER SCHONGAU like a musty blanket.

Magdalena Kuisl ran down the narrow overgrown path from the Tanners' Quarter to the Lech, her skirt fluttering behind her. Her mother had given her the day off and her strict father was far away, so she raced through the cool, shady land along the river, happy to escape the stuffiness and stench in town.

Magdalena looked forward to a swim in the river, as the odor of manure, feces, and mold clung to her matted black hair. She and her mother had been busy in town all morning collecting garbage and shoveling it into their cart. Even the nine-year-old twins, Georg and Barbara, had to help. The work seemed harder than usual because Magdalena's father had left for Regensburg a few days ago. As the family of the hangman, it was the Kuisls' job to clear the streets in Schongau of garbage and animal carcasses. Every week mountains of trash piled up at the corners and intersections in town, rotting in the hot sun. Rats with long, smooth tails scampered about on top of the piles and glared at passersby with evil little eyes. At least Magdalena had the afternoon to herself.

After just a few minutes, the hangman's daughter arrived at the riverbank. She turned to the left, away from the raft landing where there were already a half-dozen rafts tied up. She could hear the shouts and laughter of the raftsmen as they unloaded the barrels, crates, and bales and took them off to the newly rebuilt storage building, the Zimmerstadel, on the pier. She turned off the narrow towpath and made her way through the green underbrush, which now, in midsummer, was shoulder-high. The ground was swampy and slippery, and with each step, her bare feet sank in with a slurping sound.

Finally Magdalena reached her favorite spot, a small, shallow cove invisible behind the surrounding willow trees. She climbed down over a large dead root and removed her soiled clothes. Then she scrubbed the dress, apron, and bodice thoroughly, rubbing them over the sharp, wet pebbles. She laid them out to dry on a rock in the warm afternoon sun.

As Magdalena stepped into the water, the gentle tug of the current flowed past her ankles and she sank gradually into the swampy ground. A few more steps and she slipped into the river. Here in the cove, hollowed out of the river ages ago, the current wasn't quite so strong. The hangman's daughter swam out, taking care not to get too close to the whirlpool in the middle of the Lech. The water washed the dirt from her skin and hair, and after a few minutes, she felt fresh and rested again. The foul-smelling city was far, far away.

As she swam back to the shore, she noticed her clothes had disappeared.

Magdalena looked around, unsure of what to do. She'd laid her wet clothing out on the rock right there, and now all that remained was a damp spot gradually vanishing in the hot sun.

Had someone followed her here?

She looked up and down the shoreline but couldn't see her clothes anywhere. She tried to calm down. No doubt some children were just playing a joke on her—nothing more. She sat down on the tree root to dry off in the sun. Lying back with her eyes closed, she waited for the pranksters to start giggling and give themselves away.

Suddenly she heard a rustling behind her in the bushes.

Before she could jump up, someone wrapped a hairy, sinewy arm around her neck and placed a hand over her mouth. She tried to scream, but not a sound came out.

"Not a word, or I'll kiss you till your neck is red all over and your father gives you a good spanking."

Magdalena couldn't help giggling as she sputtered through the hand held over her mouth.

"Simon! My God, you nearly scared me to death! I thought robbers or murderers . . ."

Simon kissed her gently on her neck. "Who knows, maybe I am one . . ." he said, giving her a conspiratorial wink.

"You're a flake, a runt, and a quack, and nothing more. Before you even touch a hair on my head, I'll wring your neck. God knows why I love you so much."

She extricated herself from his grip and threw herself at him. In a tight embrace they rolled across the wet pebbles in the cove. Before long, she had pinned Simon to the ground with her knees. The physician was slender and wiry rather than muscular. At just five feet tall, he was one of the smallest men Magdalena had ever known. He had fine features with bright, alert eyes that always seemed to sparkle mischievously, and a well-trimmed black Vandyke beard. His dark hair was lightly oiled and shoulder length in accord with the latest fashion. In other respects as well, Simon was well groomed, though at the moment his appearance was somewhat in disarray.

"I—I give up," he groaned.

"Oh, no you don't! First you're going to swear to me there's no other woman in your life."

Simon shook his head. "No—nobody else."

Magdalena rapped him on the head and rolled down next to

him. She'd never quite forgiven him for flirting with the red-headed merchant woman more than two years ago, even though Simon had sworn a dozen times that there really hadn't been anything between them. But the day was just too beautiful to waste quarreling. Together they looked up into the branches of the willows swaying back and forth above their heads in the gentle breeze. For a long time they were silent, listening to the wind rustling in the branches.

After a while Magdalena spoke up. "My father will probably be away for a while."

The medicus nodded and gazed out at two ducks flapping their wings as they rose from the water. Magdalena had already told him about her father's trip to visit his ill sister. "What did Lechner have to say about that?" he finally asked. "As the court clerk, he could have simply ordered your father not to leave town—now of all times, in summer when the garbage stinks to high heaven."

Magdalena laughed. "What was he to do? Father just got up and left. Lechner cursed and swore he'd have him hanged when he came back. It was only then that it occurred to him that my father would have trouble hanging himself." She sighed. "There will probably be a big fine to pay, and until he comes back, mother and I will just have to work twice as hard."

Her eyes took on a dreamy look. "How far away is Regensburg, anyway?" she asked.

"Very far." Simon grinned as he playfully passed his finger around her belly button. Magdalena was still naked, and droplets of water sparkled on her skin, tanned from her daily trips into the forest to collect herbs.

"Far enough in any case that he can't torment us with his lectures," the physician said finally, with a big yawn.

Magdalena flared up. "If there's a problem, it's your old man, who's always hounding us. Anyway, the purpose for my father's trip was serious—so stop your silly grinning."

The hangman's daughter was thinking about the letter from Regensburg that had troubled her father so much. She knew her father had a younger sister in Regensburg, but she never realized how close the two of them had been. Magdalena was only two years old when her aunt fled to Regensburg with a bathhouse owner. They left because of the Great Plague but also because of the daily taunts and hostilities in town. Magdalena had always admired her for her courage.

Silently she threw some pebbles, which skipped a few times before finally being swallowed by the rippling water.

"It's a mystery to me who's going to clean up all the garbage in town for the next few weeks in all this hot weather," she said more to herself than to Simon. "If the aldermen think I'm going to do it, they have another thing coming. I'd rather spend the rest of the summer in a hole in the ground."

Simon clapped his hands. "What a great idea! Or we can just stay here in this cove!" He started kissing her cheeks, and Magdalena resisted, though only halfheartedly.

"Stop, Simon! If anyone sees us . . ."

"Who's going to see us?" he replied, passing his hand through her wet black hair. "The willows certainly won't tell on us."

Magdalena laughed. These few hours spent down at the river or in nearby barns were all they had to show for their love. They'd always dreamt of getting married, but strict town statutes wouldn't permit that. They'd been courting for years, and their relationship was like a desperate game of hide and seek. As the daughter of the hangman, Magdalena wasn't allowed to associate with the higher classes. Executioners were dishonorable, just like gravediggers, bathhouse owners, barbers, and magicians. Accordingly, marriage to a physician was out of the question, but that didn't keep the couple from clandestine meetings in the fields and barns around town. In the springtime two years ago, they'd even made a pilgrimage together to Altötting, basically the only longer time they'd been together. In the meantime, the affair between the physician and the hangman's daughter had become a hot topic of conversation in the Schongau marketplace and taverns. Moreover, Simon's father, old Bonifaz Fronwieser, was urging his son with increasing insistence to finally settle down with a middle-class girl. That was actually essential in advancing Simon's career as a doctor, but he kept putting his father off—and meeting secretly with Magdalena.

"Maybe we should go to Regensburg, too," Simon whispered between kisses. "A serf gains his freedom after living a year and a day in the city. We could start a new life . . ."

"Oh, come now, Simon." Magdalena pushed him away. "How often you've promised me that! What will become of me then? Don't forget I'm dishonorable. I'll just end up picking up the garbage again, no matter where I am."

"Nobody knows me there!"

Magdalena shrugged. "And what will I do for work? The cities are full of hungry day laborers and—"

Simon held his finger to her lips. "Just don't say anything now—let's forget it for just a while." His eyes closed, he bent down and covered her body with kisses.

"Simon . . . no . . ." Magdalena whispered, but her resistance was already broken.

At that moment, they heard a crackling sound in the willow tree above them.

Magdalena looked up. Something seemed to be moving there in the branches. Suddenly she felt something warm and slimy hit her and run slowly down her forehead. She put up her hand to feel it and realized it was spit.

She heard giggling and then saw two boys, about twelve years old, quickly climb down the tree. One of them was the youngest son of the alderman and master baker Michael Berchtholdt, with whom Magdalena had often exchanged strong words.

"The doctor is kissing the hangman's daughter!" the second

boy shouted as he ran away. Disgusted, Magdalena wiped the rest of the spit from her forehead. Simon jumped up and shook his fist at the smirking boy.

"You impertinent little brats!" he shouted. "I'm going to break every bone in your bodies!"

"The hangman's daughter can do that better than you!" cackled the second boy, disappearing into the bush. "Do it on the rack, you scum!"

Then little Berchtholdt stopped short. He turned and looked at Simon defiantly, with clenched teeth, trembling slightly as the physician charged after him like a madman, his shirt open and his jacket undone.

"It wasn't me," he squealed as Simon raised his hand to strike. "It was Benedikt! I swear! Actually, we were just looking for you because—uh—"

Simon had raised his hand to strike the boy when he noticed that young Berchtholdt was staring open-mouthed at the half-naked hangman's daughter, who was trying to hide as best she could behind a rock while she buttoned up her bodice. The physician gave the boy a gentle poke on the nose strong enough to send the boy reeling backward into the mud.

"Didn't the priest teach you any sense of decency?" Simon growled. "If you keep staring like that, God will strike you blind. So what are you up to here?"

"My father sent me," the boy mumbled. "He wants to see the Kuisl girl."

"Old Berchtholdt?" asked Magdalena stepping out from behind the rock now fully dressed. "What could he possibly want from me? Or is he sitting up there somewhere in the tree staring at me, too?"

The Schongau master baker was known around town as a lecherous old philanderer. He'd made a pass at Magdalena some years back and been rebuffed. Since then he'd been spreading gossip that the hangman's daughter was in league with the devil and had cast a spell on the young physician. Three years ago, the superstitious baker almost succeeded in having the midwife Martha Stechlin burned at the stake for alleged witchcraft—something Magdalena's father had just barely been able to prevent. Since then Berchtholdt harbored a deep hatred for the Kuisls and, whenever he could, tried to make life miserable for them.

"It's on account of his maid, Resl," the boy said as he continued to stare at Magdalena's low neckline. "She has a fat stomach and is screaming like a stuck pig."

"Does she have a child on the way?" Magdalena asked.

Puzzled, the boy just stood there picking his nose. "No idea. People think the devil has gotten into her. You should have a look, my father says."

"Aha, so now I'm good enough for him." She looked at the boy suspiciously. "Doesn't he want to go see Stechlin?"

"Berchtholdt would rather cut his guts out himself than send for the midwife," interjected Simon, who'd dressed himself in the meantime. "You know, he still thinks Stechlin is a witch and would love to see her burn. Anyway, many people in town think you're just as good a midwife as she is, maybe even better."

"Enough of your nonsense!" Magdalena tied her wet hair up into a bun as she continued talking. "I only hope there's nothing seriously wrong with Berchtholdt's maid. Now come along, let's go!"

The hangman's daughter hurried down the narrow towpath to the Lech Gate, turning around to Simon once more as she ran. "Perhaps we'll need a professional physician, even if it's just to go and fetch water."

As soon as they arrived at the narrow Zänkgasse, Magdalena was sure this was no ordinary birth. Through the thin bolted windows of the baker's house, the screams sounded more like a cow awaiting slaughter than a woman giving birth. Farmers and workers had come running to the door of the bakery and were whispering anxiously to one another. When Simon and Magdalena approached, the group stepped back reluctantly.

"Here comes the hangman's daughter to drive the devil out of the baker's maid," somebody snarled.

"I say they're both witches," an old woman whispered. "Just wait, and we'll see them fly out through the chimney."

Magdalena pushed her way past the gossiping women and tried not to take what they were saying too seriously. As the hangman's daughter, she was accustomed to people thinking of her as the spawn of Satan, and ever since she started working for the midwife, her reputation had grown even worse. Mostly it was the men who were convinced the hangman's daughter prepared magic elixirs and love potions, and in fact, a few of the aldermen had already obtained such preparations from her father. Up to now, however, Magdalena had always refused to swindle people with such nonsense, primarily to avoid arousing even more suspicions about her being the devil's consort. But to no avail, she had to admit to herself with a sigh.

As the crowd continued whispering and gossiping, she entered the bakery with Simon, where they were received by Michael Berchtholdt, who looked as white as a sheet. As so often, the scrawny little man smelled of brandy, and his eyes were ringed in red circles as if he'd passed a sleepless night. He was rubbing a dry bouquet of mugwort between his fingers to ward off evil spirits. His wife, who was just as skinny, knelt before a crucifix in a corner of the room, murmuring prayers which were, however, drowned out by the screams of the maid.

Resl Kirchlechner lay by the fire on a bench covered with dirty straw. She writhed in pain as if a fire were burning inside. Her face, hands, and legs were covered with red pustules, and the tips of her fingers had turned a shiny black. Her belly was distended into a little round ball and almost looked like a foreign object on her otherwise spindly body. Magdalena presumed that, until now, the maid had wrapped her dress tightly around her to conceal the pregnancy.

At just that moment, the young woman sat up suddenly as if someone had rammed a broomstick up her back. Her eyes were vacant and her dry lips opened as she let out a long drawn-out scream.

"He's in me!" she gasped. "My God, he's eating through my body and tearing out my soul!" A loud moan followed. "Oh . . . I can feel his teeth. I can hear the smacking of his lips as he gnaws through my belly! I want to spit him out like a rotten piece of fruit!" She made a retching sound as if preparing to regurgitate something large and undigested.

"My God, what is that?" Simon asked in horror as he stood in the doorway.

"Can't you see? The devil is in her!" Maria Berchtholdt moaned from the corner of the room, rocking back and forth on her knees and tearing at her hair. "He's eating her alive from the inside out. Holy Mary, Mother of God, pray for us sinners . . ."

Her prayers turned into a wailing monotone as Michael Berchtholdt stared silently at his maid thrashing around in spasms.

"It looks like Resl took something to abort the child," Magdalena whispered to Simon so the others couldn't hear. "Perhaps castoreum, or rue." Suddenly she frowned. "Wait—she didn't . . ."

Magdalena cautiously approached Resl Kirchlechner and felt the pustules on her arm. When the maid started thrashing around again, the hangman's daughter jumped back. "I think I know what it is now," she whispered. "It must be St. Anthony's Fire. Resl probably took ergot to abort the child."

Simon nodded. "I don't know much about it, but I think you're right. The pustules . . . the black fingertips . . . and then the feverish dreams. Everything points to that. My God, the poor girl . . ."

Magdalena squeezed his hand and then uttered a curse under her breath. As a midwife she knew about ergot, a fungus that grew on rye and other kinds of grain and was used now and then to abort a pregnancy. But the ergot could be taken only in small doses or it would cause cramps and horrible visions in which the victims encountered witches, devils, and demons. Their fingers and toes turned black and finally fell off, and because they felt like they were being burned by fire inside, the sickness was called St. Anthony's Fire.

Simon turned to Michael Berchtholdt. "This girl isn't possessed by the devil," he snarled, pointing to the girl's swollen belly. "Resl took ergot, and I wonder who might have given it to her."

"I—I have no idea what you're talking about," the master baker stuttered. "It may be that Resl has been fooling around with some young fellow and— "

"No, with Satan!" his wife interrupted. "She's been carrying on with Satan!"

"Nonsense!" Magdalena whispered softly enough so Berchtholdt couldn't hear it. She dabbed the face of the screaming maid with a damp cloth and tried to comfort her. But suddenly Magdalena couldn't control herself any longer. Her eyes flashed as she turned around and glared furiously at the baker.

"Like hell it's Satan!" she snarled. "Everybody in town knows that you've been running after Resl! Everybody!"

"What are you trying to say?" Michael Berchtholdt asked softly. His facial features looked even sharper than usual. "Are you saying that maybe I— "

"You knocked up your maid!" Magdalena blurted out. "And so that nobody would find out, you gave her the ergot. That's what happened, isn't it?"

Berchtholdt's face turned beet-red. "How dare you talk about me like that, you fresh little hangman's girl?" he gasped finally. "You're forgetting that I sit on the city council and all I have to do is to give the word and you Kuisls can pack your things and leave. All it takes is one word from me!"

"Ha! And who will give your wife her little sleeping potion then?" Magdalena jumped up and pointed at the praying Maria Berchtholdt. "How often has she come to my father for a little potion to calm down her husband at home so he will nod off after drinking his wine?"

The baker glared in disbelief at his wife, who looked down at the ground, embarrassed, her hands folded. "Maria, is that right?"

"Quiet!" Simon said. "It's disgraceful to quarrel like this while the poor girl is probably dying. If we are to help, we at least have to know how much ergot it was and who gave it to her." He looked at Michael Berchtholdt in desperation. "For God's sake, say something! Did you give the medication to the girl?"

The master baker remained defiantly silent, but suddenly his wife spoke up in a soft voice. "It's true," she whispered. "It would be a lie to say anything else. God help you, Michael! You, and all of us!"

The baker struggled for words but gave in at last. He slumped over, sighing, and ran his hand through his hair, which was thinning and matted with flour. "Well yes, then, I—I gave it to her," he stammered. "I—I told her to take it all at once just to make sure it worked."

"All at once?" Magdalena looked at him in horror. "And how much was that?"

Berchtholdt shrugged. "A little bag, perhaps as large as my fist."

Simon gripped his forehead, groaning. "Then there's no way we can save her. All we can do is try to relieve her pain." With clenched fists he advanced toward Michael Berchtholdt. "Who in God's name gave you so much ergot?" he snarled. "Who, damn it! What quack?"

The baker retreated toward the doorway and finally murmured something so softly that Simon couldn't understand him at first. "It was your father."

The young medicus stood there dumbfounded. "My father?"

Berchtholdt nodded. "The stuff cost me two guilders, but your father said it was the surest way."

Simon had trouble speaking. "Did my father at least tell you how much to give her?"

"Actually, he didn't." The baker shrugged. "He just said it would be better to take too much than too little, just to make sure it worked. So I just gave her all of it."

Simon was tempted to seize the baker by the throat, but at that moment the maid began to scream again—this time longer and higher-pitched than before. Resl Kirchlechner reared up so far it seemed her spine would break. Her pale thighs were spread far apart, and the white sheets between them were stained with blood. Suddenly the maid slumped down, and a bloody little body the size of a cat fell from the bench onto the floor.

It was a stillbirth.

Simon rushed over to the maid and felt her neck for a pulse. Her face was now relaxed and peaceful, and her dead eyes appeared to stare down at the bloody straw spread out on the floor.

The physician closed her eyes and laid her out gently on the bench. "She's in a better place now," he mumbled, making the sign of the cross. "with no more pain, or demons, or people who would do her harm."

For a moment all was silent, except for the whimpering of the baker's wife. Finally Michael Berchtholdt came to his senses. He walked over to the fetus still lying on the floor next to the stove, picked it up gingerly, and walked out through the back door into the garden. When he returned a while later, he wiped his muddy hands on his trousers and attempted a slight smile that froze midway into a grimace.

"Resl is dead, and that's a shame," he said in a soft voice. "I'll see to it that she gets a decent burial in St. Sebastian's Cemetery with a priest, funeral meal, and all the trappings. I'll also see that her parents are taken care of financially. As for everything else"—he gave an embarrassed smile—"we don't want word to get around that the devil had possessed our maid. That could end badly. And as the young physician here can certainly attest, Resl had a high fever—that can lead to bad dreams, can't it?" The baker looked at Simon expectantly.

"You don't seriously believe that—" the physician started to say, but Berchtholdt raised his hand, interrupting him.

"I know your house calls are expensive. How much? Tell me—five guilders? Ten? How much do you ask?" He pulled a trunk out from behind the table and began to rummage through it.

"Just keep your money and choke on it!" Magdalena shouted, slamming the lid closed on Berchtholdt's fingers. He pulled them out, whining and clenching his teeth. His wife looked back and forth from one to the other as if they were ghosts. Simon assumed the shock was too much for her. Maria Berchtholdt had decided to withdraw into her own world.

"I'm going to tell everyone—everyone!—that you jumped on your maid like a randy old goat and let her die of ergot poisoning," the hangman's daughter whispered. "It's always we women who are expected to pay for men's lechery. Well, not this time!"

The baker's little weasel eyes took on a glassy sheen. "Aha, and who is going to believe you?" he snarled. "A hangman's daughter and the horny son of an army doctor. What a pair! Go on, go and tell the people, and I promise I'll make your life hell!"

"My life is hell already." Magdalena turned to go and beckoned Simon to follow.

With a facetious bow, the physician took leave of the alderman and master baker Michael Berchtholdt. "If the hemorrhoids in your ass itch or your bowels get plugged up," Simon said in a cloying tone, "you know where you can find me."

They walked out together and were met by a group of curious onlookers. Behind them they could still hear Michael Berchtholdt's muffled cries and shrill curses. Magdalena stopped for a moment and looked into the faces of the bystanders, who were staring at them with expressions of disapproval and disgust.

A hangman's daughter and the horny son of an army doctor. What a pair . . .

Magdalena was no longer certain anyone would believe them. The farmers and workers moved aside to make way for them, as if they had some infectious disease.

As Magdalena and Simon headed down toward the Lech Gate, they could feel the looks directed at their backs for a long time.

A few hours later Magdalena's anger had subsided a bit. She and her mother were busy getting the twins ready for bed, a job that always occupied her so completely she had no time left for gloomy thoughts.

"Just one more story, Magda," little Barbara pleaded. "Just one more! Tell us the one about the queen and the house in the forest! You haven't told us that one for a long time!"

Magdalena laughed and carried her nine-year-old sister up the narrow stairs to the bedroom. Her back ached under the weight of the squirming child. The twins had grown an astonishing amount in the last year, and soon she wouldn't be able to lift Barbara any more. Clearly they took after their father.

"Oh, no, it's time to go to bed," Magdalena said with feigned severity as she put her little sister in bed, covered her up, and blew out a smoking pine chip standing on a stool in the corner. "Look, your brother's eyes are already closed."

She pointed at Georg, Barbara's twin brother, who in fact seemed to be asleep in his narrow little bed.

"Then at least sing something for me," Barbara pleaded, trying hard not to yawn.

With a sigh, Magdalena began to sing a soft lullaby. Her little sister closed her eyes, and soon her breathing was regular and calm and she seemed to drift off to sleep.

The hangman's daughter looked down at Barbara, stroking her cheek tenderly. She loved her younger brother and sister, even if they sometimes got on her nerves. For Georg and Barbara, their father was a growling bear who fought off bad men but was loving and tender with them, his own children. It almost made Magdalena a bit jealous that the hangman seemed to develop a kindlier attitude as he grew older. When she had misbehaved as a little girl, she had received a good spanking, but with the twins, her father usually just growled his displeasure—which didn't necessarily achieve the desired effect.

Magdalena was thinking about her father in faraway Regensburg when she suddenly heard footsteps behind her. Her mother smiled as she entered the room.

Anna-Maria Kuisl had the same long black locks as her daughter, the same bushy eyebrows, and the same temper, as well. Jakob Kuisl had often complained he was married to two women, both of whom had a tendency to flare up. When they both were angry with him, he would often withdraw to his room and brood over the medical books that he kept in his pharmaceutical closet.

"Well?" Anna-Maria asked softly. "Are the children finally asleep?"

Magdalena nodded and stood up from the bed, groaning. "A

dozen stories and certainly a hundred rounds of bouncing up and down on my knees playing horsie! That should be enough."

"You spoil them too much." The hangman's wife shook her head. "Just like your father. He was like that with his little sister."

"Lisbeth?" Magdalena asked. "Did you know her well?"

Anna-Maria bit her lip, and Magdalena sensed that her mother really didn't want to talk about Magdalena's aunt, certainly not on such a beautiful summer evening. Just the same, she persisted with her question until her mother was finally persuaded to tell the story.

"After Lisbeth and Jakob's parents died, she lived here in the house with us," Anna-Maria said. "She was so young—almost a child—but then this owner of a bathhouse came along and took her back to Regensburg with him. Your father cursed and scolded, but what could he do? She didn't care a whit what her big brother thought—she was just as stubborn as he was. She just packed up her things and left. For Regensburg, of course . . ."

She stared blankly into space for a while, as if some macabre image had arisen from the past like a monster emerging from a dark abyss. She remained silent for a long while.

"Why?" Magdalena finally asked, breaking the silence.

Anna-Maria merely shrugged. "Love, perhaps? But to tell you the truth, I think she just couldn't stand it here anymore. The constant whispering, the evil glances, how people would make the sign of the cross whenever she passed by." She sighed. "You know yourself it takes a thick hide to be a hangman's daughter and stay in a place like this."

"Or maybe just stupidity," Magdalena murmured softly.

"What did you say?"

Magdalena shook her head. "Nothing, Mama." She sat down on a stool in the corner and looked at her mother in the moonlight that fell through the open shutters.

"You never told me how you met Papa for the first time," she said finally. "I know so little about you. Where did you grow up? Who are my grandparents? You must have had a life before father came along."

In fact, her mother had always kept silent about her past. Father, too, never spoke about his time as a mercenary. Magdalena could vaguely remember mother crying a lot, and in her mind's eye, Magdalena could still see her father rocking her mother gently in his arms to console her. But this was a very distant memory, and in listening to her parents speak, it almost seemed as if their life hadn't begun until Magdalena was born. Everything before that was darkness.

Anna-Maria turned away and glanced out the window and across the river. Suddenly she looked very old.

"Much has happened since I was a child," she said. "Much that I don't want to be reminded of."

"But why?"

"Let's leave it at that, child. We'll save the rest for another day, perhaps when your father returns from Regensburg. I don't have a good feeling about this trip." She shook her head. "I dreamt of him just last night, and it wasn't a nice dream, but a bloody one."

Anna-Maria stopped speaking and laughed. But it sounded like a tormented laugh.

"I'm already behaving like a silly old woman," she said finally. "It must have something to do with that accursed Regensburg. Believe me, a curse lies over this region, a bloody curse . . ."

"A curse?" Magdalena frowned. "What do you mean by that?"

Her mother sighed. "As a child I went to Regensburg often. I went to the market there with your grandmother, as we lived not far from the city. Whenever we passed by the city hall, Grandma said that the noblemen inside were plotting wars." She closed her eyes briefly, then continued in a soft voice. "It made no difference whether it was against the Turks or the Swedes; it was always the little people on the anvil who had to suffer the blows. Why did father have to go to Regensburg, of all places?"

"But the war ended long ago," Magdalena interrupted with a laugh. "You're seeing ghosts!"

"The war may be over, but the scars remain."

Magdalena didn't get to ask her mother what she meant, because at that moment they heard footsteps and whispers in front of the house.

And in the next moment, chaos broke out.